LINDISFARNE

FURY OF THE NORTHMEN

Also by Owen Trevor Smith

Seven Roads To Travel

The Day Bonny Blue Raced For The Cup

LINDISFARNE

FURY OF THE NORTHMEN

OWEN TREVOR SMITH

Swa cwæð eardstapa

Old English: 'So spoke the wanderer' (lit. earthstepper)

OWEN TREVOR SMITH

First published in New Zealand by
WordsmithNZ 2018

ISBN: 978-0-473-42346-9

Cover Image: Steven Novak

Novakillustration.com

CONTENTS

DEDICATION

To my Father

who instilled in me a love of reading

and taught me that the freedom of imagination

found between the pages of a book

is unmatched by any other media.

ACKNOWLEDGMENTS

Thanks to Aidan Smith for a keen editing eye, and for enthusiastically joining the journey from the very beginning.

Thanks to Trevor Watkin for unfailing support and for always being there to discuss and encourage.

England, Scandinavia and North-Western Europe (793-794CE)

OWEN TREVOR SMITH

A furore Normannorum libera nos, Domine

"From the fury of the Northmen, deliver us, O Lord."

Allegedly a common Latin prayer in medieval churches
conveying the despair invoked by the Viking raids in Europe.

PROLOGUE

June 8, 793CE

St. Cuthbert's Monastery, Holy Island of Lindisfarne, Northumbria

'Raiders on the beach!'

Fenn lifted the neck of the feeding bag to stop the flow of oats into the goat trough and looked up to see Master Nerian running through the gate, his cassock held high, red-faced and breathing hard. The monk cried out again, his voice cracking with urgency.

'Bishop Higbald! Quickly! Men with weapons have landed on the beach. They're coming this way!'

For a moment Fenn stood still, wondering what he should do. He heard someone calling for the monastery gates to be closed. The two men closest to the gates grasped one each and started to swing them closed. They were designed to keep livestock in, not raiders out, but they may buy some time.

Then, with clarity, Fenn knew exactly what needed to be done. He must save the Book of Gospels from these raiders; for he had no doubt that the monastery's treasures were in danger. To Fenn, the treasure that stood above all of the fine objects of gold and silver contained within the monastery walls – was the great book.

He could still hear Master Nerian calling for the Bishop, the pitch of his voice rising with every word. People around Fenn were shouting the warning to others, calling out names, moving in all directions. Fenn dropped the feeding bag and pushed through the goats. He vaulted over the side of the enclosure, crossed the courtyard and ran up the narrow lane to the church.

He met Master Oswald as he entered the church.

'What's happening?' asked the Master, curious but unperturbed. 'I heard shouting.'

'Raiders have landed on the beach! They will be after the treasures of the monastery.'

'Men on the beach? Perhaps they just want to trade.'

'Master Nerian has seen them. He says they're armed.'

'That's probably a mistake. Nobody would dare steal from the monastery.'

Master Oswald looked toward the gates and said: 'I will talk with them.'

He strode away down the lane toward the courtyard.

'Master! No! Please. We must save the Gospels.'

Master Oswald either did not hear or ignored Fenn. He continued walking purposefully down the church lane.

Fenn paused. Master Nerian would not mistake armed raiders for people wanting to trade. He should stop Master Oswald but he had no time. To reach the monastery from any of the sandy beaches on the island would not take long. He could hear screams now from the direction of the courtyard, maybe the raiders were already there. He turned and ran into the church.

He opened the doors of the enclosure behind the altar and eased out the wooden box containing the precious book. The box was a work of art in itself, beautifully inlaid, and Fenn tried to think whether to keep the book in the box or remove it. He decided the extra weight would be a burden so he opened the lid and reverently lifted out the book, muttering a prayer as he did so to St. Cuthbert, asking his blessing for these hasty actions.

He searched in the alcove for a sack or a cloth to cover the book but found nothing. He looked frantically around but still could not see anything suitable. Clutching the book tightly to his chest, he stood up – and froze.

Standing in the doorway, framed by the outside sunlight, stood a huge man, his head only an inch or two shorter than the top of the door. He was covered to his knees in a dark garment that looked like a bear skin and wore a studded metal helmet on his head with a wide nose-guard extending down the front of his face. He carried a circular wooden shield on one arm and held a long sword raised and ready in the other.

The weapon was stained with the red of fresh blood.

The man scanned the church. Fenn stood still, hidden behind the altar, and held his breath as the man's gaze passed by. Satisfied, the raider lowered his shield to the floor, leaning it against the church door.

Fenn backed slowly away from the altar but the movement alerted the bear-like man who shouted and charged down the aisle. Fenn turned to run but had only taken a few stumbling steps before a strong hand grabbed the neck of his tunic and twisted him around.

The huge man's eyes widened when he saw that the object Fenn was holding was covered in a plate of gold and silver metalwork and set with precious gemstones. He seized the prize and roughly pushed Fenn away using the back of his sword hand, easily pulling the book from Fenn's grasp. He opened it and flicked impatiently at the pages. Then he turned it over and shook it as if to dislodge anything hidden inside.

'No! You can't *do* that!' cried Fenn and heedless of his own safety, he reached out for the book.

The man used the blunt pommel of his sword to knock Fenn to the ground. He shouted a string of meaningless words and extended the weapon, the bloody tip wavering a foot from Fenn's throat. Fenn lay rigid, aware that any movement might provoke a fatal thrust.

After an agonising pause, the raider backed away from Fenn. Keeping a careful watch, he laid his sword on top of the altar. Then he grunted and using both hands, to Fenn's intense horror, the man tore the jewel-encrusted cover from the book, tossed the remaining pages contemptuously to the ground and pushed the cover into a bag at his waist.

A cry of anguish erupted from Fenn's throat as he scrambled forward on his knees and reached for the discarded book. In one movement, the man took up his sword from the altar and raised it above his shoulder to strike at Fenn – a blow that would surely take off his head. He raised his arms in a futile gesture.

'Olaf!'

The commanding voice came from a few feet away. Another man, equally tall and broad, used the end of his sword to check the killing stroke. The raiders exchanged some heated words. The newcomer pointed urgently at the chalices and gold crosses standing on the altar, then at Fenn while he moved one hand around the other to mime tying with rope. The bear man growled angrily. He spread his arms wide and let loose a guttural roar that could have been frustration or pleasure, Fenn couldn't tell which. The loud cry echoed around the church interior. The second man laughed and cuffed the raider called Olaf heartily on the shoulder. Fenn watched him then move to the side wall, reach up and grasp a hanging tapestry and with one powerful tug, bring the fine artwork crashing to the floor.

He turned his gaze back to see Olaf taking a step towards him. Before he could move, Olaf cracked the pommel of his sword hard against Fenn's temple.

CHAPTER ONE

Two days before the raid…

On Saturn's day Fenn had a free half-day.

He laid his goose quill pen to rest at the sound of Sext, the midday bells and, if the tide allowed, he would cross the Pilgrim's Way to the mainland and roam the forested hills. At low tide, a wide sandy causeway joined the island of Lindisfarne to Northumbria and the Pilgrim's Way was a mile-long path marked by stakes across the exposed sea-bed that provided pilgrims and other travellers access to Lindisfarne and the monastery. As the tide came in, the Pilgrim's Way was covered and Lindisfarne became an island.

If the sea blocked his path on his free afternoons, Fenn would wander the island coastline of white sand beaches and rocky coves or walk its rolling lowland instead.

He searched for life.

Any new beetles, bugs and other insects that he found would be placed in the small wooden containers that his friend Olgood had crafted, with tiny holes to allow in the air, and the lids would be tied tightly with twine. Later in the evening he would carefully produce a detailed likeness of each of his captives on scraps of parchment which he secreted in his dormitory room, continually keeping watch through his half-open door and listening for the heavy tread of Master Nerian who would not look kindly on Fenn's use of ink and parchment for such purposes.

15

Once he was satisfied with the drawings, he allowed the creatures to escape outside the walls of the monastery.

The monks were called Masters, a reference to their being Master of their life as well as Master of their craft; a title of respect. Master Oswald said Fenn's ability with the pen was a 'true gift'. He proclaimed Fenn's talent to be the greatest he had seen since Bishop Eadfrith – and as he said this he always turned reverently towards the place where the great Book of Gospels, created by Eadfrith more than eighty years ago, was housed behind the altar in the main hall of the church. Fenn had seen the book several times, and at each viewing it filled him with wonder. It was formally displayed on special occasions; the most recent being when Aethelred, who was again king of Northumbria after an absence, and his new wife Elflaed had visited the monastery the previous autumn to view the great work that was the pride of St. Cuthbert's Monastery.

The interior of the Book of Gospels held marvels enough. Eadfrith's unsurpassed multi-coloured illuminations with intricately interlaced designs were accompanied by a flowing and perfectly formed script. But it was the front cover that Fenn considered the masterpiece. The leather was overlaid with a finely-crafted plate of gold and silver. Small square and oblong shapes wrought in the precious metals decorated the edge with a circular design in the centre. Most marvellous of all, each bordered area was beautifully set with a large gemstone.

The Lindisfarne Book of Gospels was a priceless treasure revered not only on the island but throughout the whole country.

*   *   *

Fenn was tall and had the air of confidence that often characterised youth. With tight wavy black hair cut midway down his neck and a tan complexion that had been further darkened by the sun, his colour was distinctive among the mostly paler skins of the monastery community. The hue of his face made his deep blue eyes seem startling. They displayed a keen intelligence and missed little.

Academically, he absorbed knowledge without difficulty because he enjoyed the experience, and this had brought him to the early attention of his teachers. Outside of the school, he sought instruction from everyone – the tradesmen, farmers, gardeners, the miller – and in particular Master Egbert, the physician in the monastery infirmary.

Although, strictly speaking, he was still an apprentice with two years yet to serve in that capacity – over recent months his skill had resulted in the tasks assigned to him in the scriptorium becoming increasingly more important. He was now often working on originals and final copies, and he was encouraged to create illuminations from his own designs.

Fenn also worked occasionally with the goats, pigs and sheep and helped in the garden, but his formal apprenticeship saw the majority of his time spent in the monastery scriptorium.

He enjoyed the life of a scribe. He liked the precision of the lettering and the detailed process of drawing the illuminations, and the care required to achieve good work in both areas. He enjoyed creating objects of beauty and he felt deep satisfaction when a project was finally finished and it could be bound in leather and placed in its proper position in the library. Even when he was producing copies of other works, he still felt proud when he could hold the completed book or text in his hands.

Once he had been chosen to serve as a scribe, he had eagerly learned the skills of his craft – the use of the pen from Master Oswald, the manufacture of parchment from Master Wilfrid and the production of inks from Master Nerian.

It was the ink that most interested Fenn, because its production was a fascinating and complicated process and because it required exact measurement and care. The basic ink came from oak trees grown around the monastery – from a gall formed by the tree to protect itself around the place where a wasp had gnawed into the bark and laid its eggs. The oak galls were crushed in vinegar, mixed with mineral salts to impart colour and thickened with acacia tree sap which was called 'gum arabic'. Master Nerian stressed that the minerals and the inks were poisonous and must be handled carefully.

Fenn experimented by mixing small amounts of ink with extractions from insects and plants from field and garden, to change and enhance the colours. He had recently produced a golden colour with flecks of white that seemed to provide a shine to the ink. Master Nerian was excited by this new ink, but unfortunately the beetle that had secreted the drop of serum which kept the colours mixed but not merged, was rare. Fenn had only ever found one, and that one had surprised him in the middle of his drawing, when it had lifted part of what had seemed to be a hard and smooth surface to reveal wings and had flown from his room.

He had enough of the new ink to produce only a small illuminated letter 'L'. Master Nerian kept this sample locked in a box in his room and asked Fenn every week if he had found any more of the 'magic' beetles.

*   *   *

'What's so important that you need to be in such a hurry?'

The voice from behind startled Fenn. He had been walking swiftly across the courtyard, head down, deep in thought. He turned guiltily, expecting to see a Master chiding him for running within the monastery walls. Instead it was Olgood who stood with his large hands on his hips, smiling his broad smile.

Olgood worked in the community as both blacksmith and carpenter. He was a striking young man, fair-complexioned with blond sun-bleached hair worn long to his shoulders, a broad handsome face to match his solid build, and muscular arms and shoulders earned from his hard physical work with both wood and iron. He was two or three years older and, although Fenn was tall, Olgood stood a half head taller. The two had been friends since young boys. Olgood was always in good humour with a smile on his face. That, and the fact that he spoke so little, made some think him slow-witted, but Fenn knew that Olgood seemed calm and quiet simply because nothing troubled him, and he considered talking just for the sake of it a waste of time.

Fenn smiled back with relief. 'I was looking for you, Olgood.'

'Off to hunt for insects?'

'I'm going to get some rabbit kittens if I can,' said Fenn. 'I saw a rabbit hole as I was returning to the monastery at dusk last week, by the copse of elms in the Brightwood Valley. There were young kits alone outside the hole which is unusual. They may have been abandoned. If they're still alive I'll bring them here.'

'If you can catch them.'

'I can catch them.'

Olgood laughed. 'I like the way you have your own names for the places you visit.' He laid an approving hand on Fenn's shoulder. 'Brightwood Valley – that's a good name.'

'The elms shine in the sun,' explained Fenn.

'I know the place. I think I'll call it Brightwood Valley too.'

Olgood leaned back suspiciously as a thought occurred to him.

'Where will you keep your kits?'

'I was going to ask if you could build me a box with slits – look, I have a drawing here…' Fenn pulled a piece of parchment from inside his tunic, '…and perhaps there would be a space behind your benches?'

'And what am I to say if a Master asks why I'm keeping rabbits amongst my wood?'

'You'll tell him that I asked you to, and I will explain,' said Fenn.

Olgood sighed. 'Let me see your drawing.'

Fenn handed him the drawing and Olgood studied it. 'Yes, I can make this. Your drawings are good. They make the building easy.'

'Thank you, Olgood. Now I must hurry.'

'If you're caught running, you know what will…'

'I know!' said Fenn, with a wink. 'I won't run – I'll just walk quickly.'

He backed away from Olgood and collided with a young girl passing behind him. She was carrying a pail of milk with both hands and as Fenn's shoulder hit her she shrieked, stumbled back a few steps and sat down in the dirt. Her entire concentration was on the milk pail and she managed to place it upright on the ground as she fell. It somehow did not topple and only a small amount of milk spilled over the edge.

'Fenn! Look what you've done! I've spilt some milk.' The young girl stared accusingly at him.

'Yseld, I'm sorry. I didn't see you. You didn't lose much.' Fenn reached out to help her up. He looked at her, trying to determine if her anger was an act – a chance to tease him.

'I can get up myself, thank you!' Yseld waved his hand away, got to her feet and waved a finger at him. 'If *you* watched where you were going you wouldn't knock people over.'

She bent down and lifted her pail. 'Mistress Miriam will think I didn't fill it.'

Yseld was a girl on the verge of becoming a woman, in body as well as mind. Her fine straight blond hair was pulled back from a lightly freckled face and tied by a cord to form a tail. Tall and slender with the quickness of mind to match his own, she seemed to Fenn to have changed in a matter of weeks from a gawky and skinny child that was fun to be with and often made him laugh; to someone with innate grace and an unusual beauty – from a good friend during their shared school time to someone whose every action Fenn found interesting.

If opportunity and politeness allowed, he could have watched her all day.

'Mistress Miriam is as blind as a baby ferret.' Fenn smiled at her. 'Just keep the pail more than two feet away and she'll never notice.' He reached out. 'Let me carry that for you to make amends.'

Yseld gripped the handle firmly, then relented and held the pail out to Fenn.

'Thank you, good sir,' she said, unable to maintain an angry frown in the face of his warm smile.

Fenn took the pail and together they walked back the way Fenn had come, Yseld brushing at her clothes.

'Oh, that's fine,' said Olgood loudly, just before they were out of hearing. 'In too much of a hurry to talk to his best friend, but a pretty girl arrives and all the plans are changed!'

Fenn waved at Olgood over his shoulder.

* * *

Fenn was a monastery orphan, left as a baby at the gates. Master Oswald had christened him 'Feran' which meant 'wanderer' in the old language, a name suggested from a dream the night before Fenn was found. As Master

Oswald told the story; he had dreamed that night of a man who had undertaken a long journey for an important reason. Unfortunately, now, many years later, he no longer remembered the traveller's purpose.

The stone mason, Lenglan, and his wife Aerlene had taken him in as Aerlene was due to give birth within days. Lenglan was as solid as his stone, short in stature and gruff by nature but with a kind and generous heart. Aerlene had strict ideas about who should do what about the household which she managed with an iron hand but like her husband, the iron was often encased in a velvet glove. Aerlene was a skilled seamstress and worked in the craft room where she ruled the crafters as effectively as her own house.

The two babies grew up together. When they were old enough to talk, his brother Mikhael had called him 'Fenn' and the name had stuck. Now he was most often called Feran only when he was in trouble.

Mikhael had caught a fever when he was five years old, and had tragically died two days later. Fenn missed his brother but only had such fleeting memories of him that he wondered if they were real. When he tried to talk with Aerlene about Mikhael, he could see the hurt in her eyes so he didn't press her.

As far as Fenn was concerned, Lenglan and Aerlene were his parents and he knew they loved him as their own. Lenglan had wanted Fenn to learn to be a mason like him, but Master Oswald who taught the early classes at the school, had noticed Fenn's ability with the pen and insisted that he become a scribe as soon as he was old enough.

*   *   *

'Would you like to come with me across the Pilgrim's Way to get some rabbits?' asked Fenn as they entered the hallway to the kitchen. 'The tide is out.' He hoped he didn't sound too eager.

'Rabbits? They'd be welcome in the larder I'm sure. Our stores have become a little sparse lately,' replied Yseld. She sighed. 'I like to come with you but I can't.' She ticked off the items on her fingers. 'First, Mistress Miriam wants me to wash the kitchen steps and then collect honey for the mead and then gather the goose and chicken eggs.'

21

Fenn laughed. 'No, the rabbits aren't for eating. I've seen some young kits and I want to catch them, draw them and watch them grow. We'll be back before the mid-afternoon bells so I'll be able to help you afterward with the steps and the honey and eggs. I know where there are quail's eggs too just inside the southern forest. You'll be back before anyone knows you're gone.'

'Fenn, you'll get me into trouble for sure.'

'Then you'll come?'

'Back before the bells?'

'Maybe long before.' He grinned.

She smiled back at him. 'Then, yes – I'd like to. I'll just put the milk into the cool store.'

* * *

Fenn led the way to the edge of the copse of trees at the eastern end of Brightwood Valley. He paused at the last tree and crouched down resting his hand on the slender trunk, holding up his other hand to keep Yseld behind him.

'The kits I saw were just below the crest up ahead,' he whispered. 'Can you see the rabbit hole?'

Yseld moved up close to Fenn and crouched behind him as she searched the hillside. To steady herself she placed a hand on his arm below his shoulder. Her touch felt warm through his shirt. She had let her hair down from the tied-up tail she normally wore while working in the kitchen and he could feel that too brushing against his shoulder.

'Yes I see it,' she said softly in his ear, and pointed at the hole.

Fenn drew in a breath and nodded. 'That's it.'

They waited, watching the rabbit hole. There was no sign of life.

Across the whole hillside the long grass waved slowly, following the directions of the occasional gusts of gentle breezes. The only sound was a soft swishing from the grass and the leaves rustling in the trees around them. The fresh smell of the grass combined with the musty damp odour from the dead leaves beneath their feet.

It was one of those perfect peaceful moments that Fenn loved. He breathed deeply.

Fenn turned in his crouch to look behind them into the western sky. Their knees met and as Fenn looked down to her, Yseld kissed him on the mouth. Just a light brush of her lips held firm for an instant and then it was gone. Fenn reached out slowly to touch her face but at the same moment Yseld moved back to look at him, a half smile on her lips and a tinge of pink on her cheeks. Fenn turned his movement into a gesture at the heavens. He cleared his throat.

'In a few moments, the sun will appear from behind that cloud and the hillside will be sunny and warm. If they're still alive, that's when they'll come out.'

He turned back to watch the hillside, his mind a turmoil. He would very much like to repeat the kiss but he couldn't think of a way to make that happen without the risk of destroying the moment. The last thing he wanted was for her to be any further away than she was now. To ignore the kiss was probably the wrong thing to do. To mention it was also probably wrong. To do anything was wrong, to do nothing was wrong.

He would never find the correct path by reasoning.

Yseld was looking at him and she met his eyes.

'Yseld...'

She smiled and her smile was wonderful. Fenn was fascinated by her mouth, her skin, her sparkling green eyes and the contrast of her hair. In every way he could think of, Yseld was a beautiful young woman, and that simple fact rendered him momentarily speechless. Her eyes, especially her eyes, were somehow fascinating. He reached out and took her hand.

'You are so... beautiful,' he said.

Yseld rested her other hand on top of his. 'I didn't think you would ever notice me,' she breathed. Her eyes flicked up. 'Oh, look! There are your kits.'

Fenn would have thought nothing could have torn his gaze away at that moment, but without thinking he followed her eyes and saw four rabbit kittens emerging cautiously from the hole. He smiled and reached down to untie the soft sack he had knotted at his waist.

'Wait here,' he said to Yseld. 'I won't be long.'

*   *   *

'How did you get so close? Why didn't they just run away?' asked Yseld, with wonder in her voice, as soon as Fenn's easy loping downhill stride brought him back within hearing distance.

'I talked to them, well… no, I just made some noises,' Fenn tried to explain. 'I don't really know how it works exactly. The animals just seem to know what I want.' He shrugged, unable to explain further.

'I never seen anything like that before. From here they just seemed curious, certainly not frightened. Are they alright in that sack?'

'They'll be fine. It's just like being in their nest.'

Fenn opened the top of the sack so Yseld could see in. Four small creatures lay quietly in the bottom of the sack. They looked contented, huddled together with only their noses and whiskers moving, as if they were about to settle down after a good meal, though from what Fenn had told her they were more likely to be half starved.

'Come on,' said Fenn. 'There are quail nests on the edge of the forest over the hill and with luck we can get enough eggs to make Mistress Miriam give you the evening off in gratitude.' His smile was mischievous. 'We'd better hurry because there's a storm coming.'

Yseld looked up at the sky and turned in a circle. It was clear and blue in every direction. She could see some dotted white fluffy clouds lazily floating in small groups to the west and north.

'I don't see any storm,' she said.

'Tonight. But it may get here quicker than that.' He pointed to the north. 'There it is. See the high strips of cloud on the horizon just above the sea? They're just wispy now but they'll grow. Those are the scouts moving ahead of the storm and marking its path.'

Yseld giggled; a delightful sound to Fenn's ears.

'Scouts for the storm? Huh! We'll see.'

She ran ahead of him towards the forest.

*   *   *

The storm announced its arrival with a fierce lightning display out to sea. Dark rain-filled clouds covering half of the sky hovered menacingly a few miles to the north of Lindisfarne as if gathering strength for the assault. The dimmed light from the setting sun cast an eerie yellow glow over the island as the lightning forked down from the heavens and repeatedly struck at the sea while great peals of thunder rang across the waves after each mighty blow.

The gathering storm-clouds soon obscured the sun and brought an early twilight. The thunder grew louder with the storm's approach until it was so loud it seemed to cause the buildings to rattle. The inhabitants flinched and covered their ears with each crashing rumble and the bright lightning flashes penetrated even tightly closed eyes. A strong driving rain hit the monastery, pounding against the roof with deafening fury. Fenn felt helpless beneath the onslaught.

'*Take heed, mortals,*' the awesome force seemed to be saying. '*Witness the power of your God in Heaven. Ignore my wrath at your peril!*'

He endured in the darkness, the violence numbing his senses and rendering him unable to do any of the drawing or other work he would normally enjoy at this time of day.

The storm passed slowly over the island, so slowly that Fenn thought they must have been under full attack for half of the night. He hadn't heard the midnight bell but he may have missed it with the noise. Gradually, almost imperceptibly, the rain eased and the thunder became muted by distance.

As soon as he thought it safe to venture out into the elements, Fenn stole from his room and hurried outside. The wind was swirling forcefully around the monastery walls with a moaning wail and it was still raining, but much lighter. Fenn ignored the discomfort and he made his way quickly to Olgood's wood-store. He ducked inside the opening and went to the box placed out of sight behind one of Olgood's work benches under the open window. There was only minimal moonlight from the window and he waited until his eyes were adjusted then opened the lid and checked that the rabbit kittens were alive and warm and dry. They seemed calm although the storm must have terrified them, and he saw with satisfaction that they had finished the food he had left. He replenished a small amount and checked they had access to water before gently closing the lid and returning to his room.

He was so unsettled by the experience of the storm it took a long time to find sleep.

CHAPTER TWO

The day before the raid…

The storm was the main topic of discussion. Nobody could remember a storm of such ferocity. The day had dawned surprisingly clear and sunny with no hint remaining of the dark foreboding clouds of the previous evening. The morning air smelt and tasted clean and fresh as if newly made, somehow lacking its usual saltiness, and Fenn found himself breathing deeply just for the feel of it. On his way to the refectory, he heard the same opinion offered several times. When he was stopped, he nodded and agreed that he had never experienced a storm like it.

He collected his meal of poached fish and oats and had just seated himself when he overheard the voices of Bishop Higbald and Master Nerian behind him.

'We have all become too lazy, your Grace. We have let bad habits into our lives. We must become more devout; more strict. The message was obvious!' Master Nerian said.

'But was the message 'I am displeased' or was it *'if* I were displeased this is what I could do' – merely a demonstration?' argued Bishop Higbald. 'Do we not obey our Lord in all we do as best we know how?'

'We have become lax and lazy,' repeated Master Nerian. 'If I were in charge of educating the children, I would have them spend twice the time at prayer that Oswald requires. He pampers them.'

'They are children. They need a little freedom.'

'All children, the young ones especially, need discipline. The soul is more important than the body. As your Grace well knows, one endures while the other perishes. If we fail the child we will fail the adult.'

'I'm aware of your views, Master Nerian; I share them…,' the Bishop paused, evidently chewing, '…in the main, but Master Oswald is a good teacher and I am very happy with the discharge of his educational duties.'

'It was a sign – mark my words,' persisted Master Nerian. 'We must change our ways or worse will befall us.'

There was a pause. Master Nerian obviously thought he had made his point for there was the scrape of a stool as he stood up.

'Please excuse me, your Grace, I have much to attend to.'

He picked up his plate with a clatter and Fenn heard him moving toward the kitchen. Bishop Higbald sighed loudly and returned to his eating.

Yseld passed by the doorway to the kitchen, obviously on some errand, and he rose at the same time as Olgood entered the refectory from the cloisters. Fenn waved to catch Olgood's attention and pointed to his half-eaten meal sitting on the table as an invitation for Olgood to join him. He walked swiftly toward the kitchen, his haste drawing disapproving glances from some of the seated Masters and looks of interest from a group of farm hands and gardeners.

'Yseld!' he called, hopefully loud enough for her to hear but not so loud that it might be considered a disturbance. Yseld's head reappeared in the kitchen doorway.

Without thinking, Fenn reached for and held Yseld's hand, then quickly dropped it as he remembered where they were. Yseld reddened then crossed her arms and smiled at him.

'Did you want me for something, Master Feran?' she asked.

Fenn laughed. 'I cannot teach. I'm not a Master.' Then, becoming serious, he leaned toward her and whispered, 'Can you get away after Vespers this evening and meet me at the top of the hill?'

Yseld thought then nodded. She bent her head to escape the stares from the refectory and hurried away in the direction she was headed when Fenn had stopped her. Fenn returned to finish his meal.

'So, my friend,' he said to Olgood, oblivious of those still looking his way. 'Tell me about my kits. Are they well?'

*   *   *

The island of Lindisfarne had a few areas of elevated land but only one promontory that could properly be called a hill. Situated a short distance along the southern coast from the monastery, the rocky outcrop rose abruptly from the low-lying surrounding land. The top provided little shelter and was exposed in wild weather. It was almost always windy there but it was not unpleasant if the wind was from the prevailing west or south-west. However, even on sunny days, if the wind came fast across the sea from the north it could chill to the bone.

For Fenn, the isolation and solitude of the hilltop made it a favourite place. In the spare moments he was able to spend there, he would huddle under a small ledge which afforded fair protection from the wind. From there he could look out to sea and imagine the lands across the water and the people who lived there.

Several of St. Cuthbert's monks had travelled on pilgrimages to other lands and many foreign pilgrims came to the monastery to study and learn about the Gospels and about the monastery's founders, St. Aidan and St. Cuthbert. They told Fenn of people called Muslims, Franks, Saxons, Danes and Jutes and, from the far east, the Avars, the Slavs, and the mysterious Byzantines. He found the names and the stories fascinating.

There was one other source of information to whet Fenn's appetite for news from the lands across the sea. Bishop Higbald talked often of a friend named Alcuin, a monk whom the Bishop called a very learned scholar. Fenn had never met Alcuin but he knew of him from the Bishop's stories and from the letters the Bishop received every few months. Alcuin was an advisor to the court of the King of the Franks, Charles the Great. The letters contained discourses on many subjects such as mathematics, languages, and education, but also included commentaries on his travels and the people he met who ranged from high nobility such as kings and lords to interesting ordinary folk.

With the Bishop's permission, when a letter was delivered from the pack of a travelling pilgrim, Fenn eagerly read every word that Alcuin wrote. To

Fenn's appreciative eye, the letters had been carefully penned by a skilled and cultured hand, each word perfectly uniform, but the script also contained beautiful flourishes which Fenn had added to his own penmanship. It was the contents though, especially the names of the places and the descriptions of people, that filled him with wonder and he would bring each of them to mind as he gazed over the sea from the bleak hilltop.

* * *

In the scriptorium, Fenn did not stop for Sext, the midday bells.

He had been working on one task for days – copying the seventy-three chapters of the Rule of Benedict. The work of Benedict, a monk from Nursia in Italy, the manuscript had been prepared more than two hundred years ago and outlined his rules and laws for monastic life. A volume had recently been delivered to the monastery at the request of Charles the Great, who was encouraging all monasteries both within his domain and beyond, to follow the Rule of Benedict. Master Oswald said the Rule contained 'admirable balance and moderation' and was under consideration by the Bishop. He had given Fenn the original 'with minor modifications' to copy.

Today Fenn had only the last three short chapters to complete. He tried to form his script quickly, but without sacrificing his usual care, so he could finish as early as possible. He was feeling a tightening in his pen hand and the last chapter was a struggle. He had to put down his pen and shake his hand to free the muscles at the end of each line. Then he would meticulously compare the line he had just completed to the original Latin text.

When he was satisfied that the copy was accurate and the inks were dry and stable, Fenn took up the sheets he had completed today along with the original chapters, carefully inserted the parchments into a leather holder and left the scriptorium to seek out Master Oswald. He looked first in the church and in the cloisters, but then chanced on him in the lane outside the library. Master Oswald was pleased that Fenn had finished so quickly and took Fenn's offering eagerly to hand.

After a few moments he said: 'So these are the final chapters?'

When Fenn nodded, he continued: 'Good. Yes. Excellent work as usual.' Master Oswald glanced back and forth between the originals and Fenn's copies. 'Consistently better indeed than the Franks can produce.' He beamed. 'You are already a master of your craft by my judgement, and we're lucky to have you at St. Cuthbert's.'

Master Oswald paused for thought and looked upward as if for inspiration. 'I think we should consider if it is time for you to join the order.'

'Join the order?' said Fenn, astonished. 'But… I thought…'

'Oh yes. Just a matter of time. I'll speak to the Bishop.' Master Oswald dismissed the subject and turned his attention back to the chapters.

Fenn forced himself to concentrate and remember the reason he had sought the Master. When he saw that he was again fully engrossed in studying the text, Fenn asked if he could finish early as he had things he would like to do.

As he hoped, Master Oswald waved him away, muttering 'Of course, of course.'

With his nose close to the parchment, Master Oswald continued walking blindly down the lane towards the courtyard. Fenn watched to make sure he descended the two steps at the end of the lane without mishap.

He checked the sun and decided he had time to draw one of the rabbit kits before Vespers and his meeting with Yseld. He would think about what the Master had said later.

Olgood was bent over his bench when Fenn entered his workshop. When he noticed who his visitor was, he finished shaping one of the feet of a wooden stool in two quick movements, then put his tools aside and took up a cloth to wipe his hands.

'Can you stop those kits from squeaking? People think I have mice,' he said. His smile took the sting from his pretence of annoyance.

'They're probably hungry,' said Fenn. 'They love the carrot tops I brought them.' He indicated the sack containing vegetable offcuts from the kitchen. 'Just drop some in the box when they squeak.'

'Yes, Master.' Olgood bowed.

'That's the second time I've been called Master today. Still, if that's what it takes to get you to obey me, so be it. Observe!'

He reached into the sack, felt for some carrot tops and placed them in the box, his hand emerging with a small rabbit kitten sitting on his palm. Fenn transferred the kitten to his other hand and Olgood could only shake his head in wonder as it seemed to not mind the handling.

'Can you tack this to a block please, my good servant?'

Fenn withdrew a small circular piece of parchment from his tunic. Olgood took it with a murmur, choosing a block of wood from his scrap pile and selecting a hammer from his bench. Meanwhile, Fenn produced another object wrapped in linen from his tunic. With one hand he unwrapped the linen and Olgood saw there was a thin black stick inside.

'What's that?' he asked. 'Some of the charcoal you wanted from my kiln?'

'Yes, I've pressed it into this stick. Last week, a crafter from Mercia showed me how to crush the charcoal then bind the pieces with a little honey and press them together. With careful use, it's very good for drawing, but it sticks to everything.'

Fenn smiled at his play with the word 'stick' but Olgood was concentrating on tacking the parchment and didn't respond.

When Olgood handed him the parchment piece now attached to a thin block of wood, Fenn knelt down on the floor and set the block on top of a bigger piece of wood. He raised his left hand and turned it back and forth studying the rabbit kitten sitting quietly in his palm with only its nose and whiskers twitching. He began to draw.

Fenn's ability to draw anything he saw amazed Olgood. Olgood was good with his hands. He could mend broken equipment and shape wood and metal to any purpose, but with a pen in his hand he was a child. He watched as an ear and the top of a head appeared. He moved to get a closer look as Fenn detailed the tiny whiskers with delicate strokes. The small nose on the drawing looked wet just like on the kit. Precisely and without need of retouching, the entire form of a crouching rabbit kitten took shape on the parchment, until Fenn leaned back on his heels and stood up just as the bells sounded for Vespers. He placed the kit back in the box and it scampered happily into the nest with its fellows as Fenn closed the lid. He wandered to the door and took note of the sun while he picked out the tacks, then he gently covered the drawing with a piece of linen, rolled it up and tucked the parchment into his tunic.

'Yseld will want to see the first drawing,' he explained, then said with exaggerated formality: 'Thank you, kind sir. I am, of course, *your* eternal servant. But for now I must take my leave.'

Fenn headed through the doorway and across the courtyard. Olgood shook his head with amusement. He took a step back to admire the stool he had completed.

Fenn turned east out of the gate and headed for the hill at an easy walk. A trio of farmhands were herding a dozen cows towards the gate so Fenn stepped off the path to let them go by, his nostrils taking in the heavy odour of the beasts passing close enough for him to touch. He nodded to the men. He knew their names but they were older and he did not associate often with them. He watched as one whispered something to the other two behind a concealing hand. They all smiled broadly at what had been said, then in unison they doffed their hats and bowed to him. Fenn could not understand their actions until one said: 'Please say hello from us to the pretty Yseld.' The three laughed heartily and ran to catch up with their herd. It took a moment for Fenn to decide whether he was pleased or not. He decided he was, and his step contained more bounce as he continued toward the hill. He was in no hurry. He expected it may be a while before Yseld would be free – if she was able to get away at all. He hoped she would catch up with him on the way.

When he was able, he moved off the path and down onto the stony shore. In contrast to most of the island, there were no long sandy beaches on this southern part of the coast. The shoreline stretching from the monastery to the hill was studded with rocks of varying size punching through the sand like oversized cobblestones with tidal mud flats beyond. There were also small seawater pools and areas of rounded sea-worn stones and pebbles. He would normally have examined these pools for fish and shellfish, but today he bypassed them, his gaze sweeping the ground and roving left and right. Every few moments he reached down to pick up a stone, which he held up and studied before either discarding it with a flick or dropping it into a small bag tied to his belt.

When the bag was full, he stopped and unwound a length of braided cord from his belt. He slipped his middle finger through the loop at one end and grasped the other end between thumb and forefinger, climbing up a shallow bank to return to the path. On level ground, he placed a rounded stone in the oval-shaped pouch of leather that now hung at the bottom of the looped cord, took quick note of the wind direction and strength and looked about for a target.

With practised ease, Fenn whirled the sling over his head three times and released the free end of the cord as the pouch completed the third circle. The stone was flung from the sling and whistled as fast as an arrow toward a dried tree stump twenty yards away. There was a cracked piece of bark that had unfolded from the trunk as the stump dried and shrank. The target Fenn had chosen was no more than a few inches wide but the stone and the two that followed combined to tear the bark strip from the trunk.

His father, Lenglan, had tried to teach Fenn to use the sling with a more vertical circle made at his side. He said that was how the slingers in the Frankish army were taught.

'It allows for better accuracy,' he had said. 'Depending on the direction of the swing, you can release the stone either from the bottom or the top of the swing.'

But to Fenn, that action felt constricted and risked hitting the ground, so he had developed his overhead throw instead which felt more natural, and he had persisted until accuracy came. His arm and eye now combined to deliver the stone exactly where he wished it to be.

*   *   *

He sat on the flat rock beneath the ledge, leaning forward with his elbows on his knees and his chin resting on his hands. There was a slight wind occasionally buffeting his face but the summer sun still held some heat and the air wasn't cold. The rhythmic wash of the sea against the rocks below created a sense of calm, allowing him to shut out his surroundings. He was staring out to sea but with half-closed unfocussed eyes, the scene before him serving only as a background to his thoughts.

Master Oswald's announcement that he expected Fenn to join the monastery's order of monks had come as a complete surprise. Fenn had never considered that possibility in his future.

St. Cuthbert's Monastery functioned as a collaboration between the church and the monks on the one hand, and the artisans and workers needed to support the monks and maintain the community on the other. Although he attended prayer services three times a day, the minimum expected of him, he considered that he would always be part of the latter group.

His thoughts were interrupted by a small movement in the hair at the back of his head. Absentmindedly, he brushed away the wind-blown stick or insect that had landed there.

Fenn admired the monks. He admired their learning, their inner peace and especially their dedication and service. He aspired to become an expert at his craft and eventually become a Master, a teacher, or an equivalent role, but had not thought of the direction his life would take beyond that point. Master Oswald had probably intended this path for him from the beginning. Typically, he just hadn't mentioned it to Fenn. Fenn's recent exposure to the Rules of Benedict meant he was well aware of the requirements and consequences of the life of a monk. The idea needed serious consideration without delay but initially he felt ambivalent. Something worried him, but he couldn't quite lay his finger on what it was. He needed time to think it through. He knew this could be a turning point in his life with far-reaching implications.

Again there was a small tug at his hair – he had obviously failed to dislodge the problem with his previous attempt. He felt a slight annoyance that his important thinking was being interrupted, so with both hands he rubbed vigorously at the hair on the back of his head and heard a delighted giggle from behind.

His problem was instantly forgotten. He whirled and caught Yseld's hand outstretched in the act of reaching again for his hair. He pulled her to him and she cried out in mock alarm as they fell together on the rock platform. She seemed to soften and mould to him, laying her head on his shoulder and resting one hand across his chest. He had an arm under her head and he allowed his hand to rest on her neck brushing her chin and cheek with his thumb.

'You were very deep in thought,' she said. 'You didn't hear me coming.'

'You surprised me,' he acknowledged. He lifted his head to look at her and smiled. 'I have a gift for you.'

'Oh?' She raised herself on one elbow. 'What is it?'

He studied her face, enjoying the excitement in her eyes.

'This…'

He pulled out his drawing, unrolled it and removed the linen covering, and handed it to her.

Yseld took it and sat up to better hold the parchment in two hands. She looked at the drawing in silence.

'It's perfect,' she said. 'It looks real.'

She bent down and kissed him.

'Thank you, Fenn. I'll treasure this.' She replaced the cover on the drawing and carefully rolled it.

'And I will treasure that,' he replied, touching his lips. 'But I've some news too, quite unexpected news.'

'What news?'

'Master Oswald told me he wanted me to become a monk.'

'Oh, how marvellous,' she exclaimed, and then looked worried. 'But… but that would mean…'

He knew what she was about to say and he also knew what had been at the root of his troubled thoughts. The monks were celibate and did not marry.

He made up his mind. 'I cannot accept.'

He saw that she had tears in her eyes.

'I want to be with you Yseld.'

To his surprise, the tears spilled down her cheeks and her breath caught in a sob.

'I'm sorry. Was it wrong to…? I hoped you would be happy.'

'I am, Fenn. I want to be with you too. It's all I want. Right now I'm very happy, really I am.'

'Then we must plan…'

She laughed and wiped her eyes with the back of her hand. 'No, not now. Please. Can't we just lie here as long as possible and enjoy this moment?'

Fenn lay back and Yseld nestled to him. He held her close. Her hair smelled of fresh flowers. The wind had died and a calm settled on the hill. The sea and the cries of gulls were the only sounds, both quiet enough to be pleasant. The warmth of the setting sun provided a perfect ending to a day that had just become very beautiful.

*   *   *

'Fenn, look at the sky! What *is* that?' Yseld pointed behind him, past the ledge.

Fenn roused from his doze and rolled over to see what she was indicating. The sun had just set but there was still faint light in the sky and some shadows of thin clouds were visible in the west. To the north, in the clear sky above the horizon, a fiery red streak was painted across the whole width of the heavens. To the left, toward the west, the colour was darkest and it was twisted and jumbled to resemble a huge dragon's head breathing fire. The body and tail of the dragon extended like a ribbon to the east, fading in intensity with the distance from the head.

The painted dragon shimmered and writhed as if alive.

Fenn could only stare.

37

CHAPTER THREE

The day of the raid…

Fenn's head hurt and he was sure if he opened his eyes it would be worse.

'Who *are* these people?' Fenn recognised Olgood's voice from nearby.

Someone called: 'Bastards!' and there was a groan of pain from the same direction.

He forced his eyes open and found his right eye would only open to a slit. His hands felt constricted and he looked down to see they were tied together, with a length of rope extending to the similarly bound hands of Master Nerian sitting at his left. There were about fifteen or twenty people, young men and women, tied in a line, all seated along the side of the barn facing the courtyard. Master Nerian was the only monk he could see in the group. Olgood was sitting on his right.

'Northmen,' replied the Master to Olgood's question. 'I've heard of them before.'

'Why have they tied us?' asked Olgood. 'Why don't they just take what they want and go?'

The Master sighed. 'We will become slaves,' he said. 'To work on their farms or be sold to the highest bidder – if we survive. We are property now just like the gold and silver they are looting. Although…' he grunted, '…I don't know why they want me; I'm too old to fetch a good price. God help us all.'

While Master Nerian was talking, Fenn scanned the courtyard and gasped with horror when he saw Master Oswald by the gates, crumpled on the ground, lying on his back, his head and chest covered in blood. Beside him, two of the farmhands he had met yesterday with the cow herd lay in a similar manner, one with a bloody gash at his throat and a pool of blood around his head, the other without visible harm; but all three lay with the stillness of death. He saw another monk lying face-down on the far side of the courtyard but he couldn't tell who it was. A fifth body lay further up the path by the blacksmith.

Two of the raiders that Master Nerian had named 'Northmen' stood in the middle of the courtyard, casually talking to each other and ignoring the prisoners. Fenn saw with astonishment that the one facing him was a woman, and possibly the other as well. They were both dressed in the same manner as the others he had already seen, with helmets, swords by their sides and shields slung on their backs. Those two were the only raiders visible and he wondered where the others were and how many had attacked the monastery. Fenn looked at Olgood. His face was bruised and dirty with bloody grazes on his forehead. The sleeve of his left arm was torn and bloody.

'Are you alright, Olgood?' he croaked.

Olgood looked at him. 'So, the babe awakes,' he said with a grin. He nodded towards Fenn's face. 'You don't look very pretty.'

'Nor you.'

'You had me worried,' said Olgood. He glanced down at his left arm. 'They cut my shoulder with a sword but I think the bleeding has stopped.' Then his face looked fierce as he said: 'But, even with one arm, it took two of the monsters to hold me!'

Fenn nodded. 'I can believe it.' He looked around. 'Have you seen Yseld?'

'Sorry, no I haven't,' replied Olgood. He paused wondering if he should say more, then added: 'I heard screams from the kitchen area, but they would have no reason to kill the women.'

'Lenglan and Aerlene?'

'Sorry, they aren't here.'

The Northmen may have no need to kill the women, but they had no reason to kill anyone as far as he could see, and Fenn knew Lenglan would not submit easily. He would fight to protect what he thought should be protected. Fenn groaned as he remembered his own feeble attempt to protect the most important of the monastery's treasures. He tried to move himself into a more comfortable position and found his ribs ached from some blow.

He turned to Master Nerian. 'You said you've heard of these Northmen before, Master? What do you know about them?'

'Four years ago,' said Master Nerian, 'the year that Beorhtric, King of Wessex, married Eadburg, the daughter of King Offa of Mercia – do you remember...?' He looked meaningfully at Fenn whose first thought was that this was hardly the time for a history lesson, but he nodded and the Master continued: 'Three ships containing Northmen like these arrived on the coast to the south, in Beorhtric's land I believe. The King's Reeve rode to meet them thinking they were traders and he was slain.'

Just like Master Oswald, thought Fenn.

Two more of the Northmen entered the courtyard from the church lane, each carrying a large sack over their shoulder just as two others came through the gate. The two groups conferred, then the two with sacks continued towards the gate and the other two headed in the direction of the prisoners.

One of the pair headed their way was Olaf and Fenn thought they must be coming for him, but instead they stopped in front of Master Nerian. Fenn looked for the bag tied at Olaf's waist containing the cover of the precious book. It was bulging, with the top of a gold cross visible. The other man he had not seen before. He was a small man, much shorter than Olaf. He wore a bulky tunic in the manner of the Northmen but had no sword or shield and wore a round cap on his head instead of a helmet. He also had a leather collar around his neck.

'Please you tell where more gold,' the short man said in a thick accent. Fenn thought he sounded Saxon or Frisian.

Master Nerian regarded the man silently.

'Please or he will hurt.'

Master Nerian set his mouth firmly and did not reply.

Olaf snorted and drew his long sword.

'Olaf!' called Fenn sharply.

Both Northmen looked at Fenn together. The short man was wide-eyed with astonishment. Then Olaf recognised him. He laughed, pointed at Fenn's face and said something to the short man.

'Olaf say he make you look better,' said the man. He shrugged. 'Is a joke.'

A loud shout from the entrance to the church lane drew everyone's attention. Fenn recognised the man who had stopped Olaf from killing him in the church. He looked to be their leader. A group of a dozen or more Northmen could be seen behind him. He called some commands and pointed towards the gates. Olaf called back to him, using a name that sounded like 'Ragnall', and waved a finger at Master Nerian. Fenn imagined he was saying that Master Nerian had refused to say if there was more gold.

Ragnall shook his head and pointed again – in the direction, Fenn realised, of the beach. He was saying it was time to go.

Maybe he was worried that men may arrive from the mainland. King Aethelred was residing at Bebbanburgh Castle which could be seen from the island, just five miles along the coast. There could be a chance of rescue.

Olaf muttered what sounded like an oath then bent to pick up the lead part of the rope that tied them all together.

'He say you lucky man,' whispered the short man to Master Nerian and walked away along the line, looking intently at each of the tied prisoners, checking their bonds, and calling out: 'Stand. Get on feet! We walk now.'

'Thank you for distracting that man, Fenn,' said Master Nerian. 'I think you may have saved my life, but I was certainly not going to help them plunder the monastery.'

'It was all I could think of to do. I don't know what he would have done but they don't seem to value our lives very highly,' replied Fenn.

He had a sudden thought, glanced at his waist and saw with relief that the cord of his sling was still wrapped around his belt. He felt around to the back and made sure the leather pouch was tucked behind the belt and out of sight. The cord could be interpreted as decoration but not the pouch. He tucked the small bag he used to carry his stones inside his trousers.

With a chorus of grumbles and groans, the prisoners got to their feet. The group from the church lane came forward into the courtyard, and Fenn saw that these men were carrying long-handled axes in their belts rather than swords. There were two women from the monastery in their midst. He strained to see, but neither was Yseld or Aerlene – he recognised the two as women who assisted Master Egbert in the infirmary. He wondered about the fate of Master Egbert, the physician, and hoped to be able to ask one of the women when he got a chance.

A man from the other end of their roped line whom Fenn recognised as Nameth, one of the cooks, moved forward out of the line as far as the rope would allow, and called out to the women, asking about his wife, who worked in the gardens and was the herbalist for the infirmary. One of the woman raiders took two swift steps toward him and struck him in the face with her fist. He fell backwards, dragging the two tied to him to their knees. The woman shouted at him and pointed to where he should stand. He scrambled to his feet, a trickle of blood showing at his nose. The other woman raider pushed the two infirmary women forward and joined them onto the end of the line. Fenn saw one of the women look at Nameth and shake her head. He hoped that meant Nameth's wife hadn't been seen rather than anything worse.

Olaf pulled on the rope to start them walking. Some of the Northmen arranged themselves to walk alongside the prisoners with Ragnall in the lead and the two women who had been guarding them earlier moved to the end of the line.

They were pulled through the gates and towards the northern beach. Fenn deliberately did not look at the bodies of Master Oswald and the herdsmen, but just outside the gates he could not help seeing Master Wilfrid lying as if asleep except that the top of his head was covered in blood. Fenn could not imagine the circumstances in which these people had been killed. They could not possibly have been any threat to the Northmen. Further along the path was another body, a man, with an arrow protruding from his back. He did not want to know who it was, so looked away until they had passed.

'Bishop Higbald? Did you see His Grace?' he asked Master Nerian.

'Everything happened so fast. I didn't reach him. I wasn't even able to warn him.' He gazed at the ground and shook his head as he shuffled forward. 'I don't know what happened to him. I can only trust in God.'

The walking was difficult as Fenn could not use his hands and arms for balance and could only see properly from one eye. The length of rope between each person was short and Fenn could not help treading on the heels of Master Nerian and was kicked in turn by Olgood. If somebody fell, a nearby Northman would deliver a heavy blow from a kick or the back of an axe. After several examples, anyone who fell was quickly helped back to their feet by the person behind.

They climbed a small sand dune before the beach and Fenn looked back at the monastery as he reached the top.

'Oh no!' he cried. 'They've set it afire!'

The people who heard him looked around and gave cries of dismay.

Several columns of thick black, white and grey smoke rose from the monastery. Fenn stared at the only home he had known and watched its destruction. It would soon have neither buildings nor inhabitants and the thriving community that existed only yesterday would be gone.

'Our God has abandoned us. We have fallen from Grace,' intoned Master Nerian.

'But why?' Olgood asked, his voice choking. 'Why burn the monastery? They are barbarians. I don't understand.'

Fenn also could not comprehend this desire for destruction. It was both needless and foolish. If the presence of the Northmen at the monastery was not known on the mainland before – it would be now. Maybe that was the very reason.

This time Master Nerian could not answer Olgood's question. Instead he murmured: 'It was foretold.'

Fenn thought of his rabbit kittens in the wood-store and their helplessness in the face of fire, but he knew there was nothing he could do. He thought of Yseld and hoped she had escaped. She had the wits and the courage to do so if it were at all possible. She would have been afraid and it hurt him that he had not been with her when she needed him most. Lenglan and Aerlene may have evaded the raiders too of course but, in Lenglan's case, his belligerence might make his chances of survival slim.

Slim chance also that the library would survive a fire. All those years of hard painstaking work were probably disappearing in the smoke, together with all his drawings. For the first time in his life Fenn felt real despair. He didn't realise he was crying until he saw around him that the faces of the men and women alike were streaked with tears. Only then did he feel the wetness of his own cheeks.

His dark thoughts were interrupted by a tug on the rope. Fenn turned away from the monastery and was pulled down onto the beach.

Then he saw the ships.

As with everything associated with the savage Northmen, Fenn had never seen ships like these. There were two, standing in the shallow water just off the beach. They were larger than he expected. The broad deck narrowed at bow and stern to produce a double-ended vessel with each end-piece extending high above the deck. The huge prow and prominent keel towered above the beach and tapered to become the neck and carved head of a serpent or dragon. The sides of the vessel and the visible part of the keel were also richly carved. There was a single broad rectangular sail fixed to a centre mast and rows of oars protruded through holes along the entire length of each side.

These were not trading ships; they were ships of war.

Fenn could see from the receding water marks that the tide was going out, and realised it was more likely to have been considerations of tide that prompted Ragnall to order the withdrawal, rather than any worry about retaliation from the local militia.

He counted the Northmen on the beach and in the ships and estimated the raiding party was between fifty and sixty strong. Those he could see clearly were well-armed with most carrying axes rather than swords, but some had both weapons. Several carried a bow. These were as large as Northumbrian bows and looked of similar design except they were distinctly curved at each end.

He looked out to the horizon. There was heavy cloud to the north that promised rain and a freshening wind from that direction. The sea was disturbed but not rough. It should pose no problem to these solid ships.

There was a sharp tug on his hands. Fenn tripped and fell to his knees, but the strong arm of Olgood lifted him easily. He smiled his thanks. Olgood's shirt was showing signs of fresh blood.

'Let me look at your wound as soon as we can,' he said.

CHAPTER FOUR

A journey by sea…

Fenn had sometimes accompanied Lindisfarne fishermen to sea in a small boat, and had enjoyed the experience. He liked to think of himself as a fair sailor but, after only a short time away from the shore, the irregular lurching of the huge ship of the Northmen made him feel nauseous. Only by lying flat on his back and closing his eyes was he able to gain some control over the dizziness. He felt no better, but he also felt no worse. In particular, the urge to void his stomach was held in check.

Master Nerian succumbed to seasickness immediately. To Fenn's knowledge, the closest the Master had ever been to the sea was ankle deep on the shore. He vomited and some of the bile splashed onto a rower's leg. The Northman bellowed an oath, stood up from his oar and delivered a hefty kick that just missed Master Nerian's head and landed on his shoulder. Before he could repeat the action, Ragnall stepped forward and pushed the Northman back to his oar. The acrid stench of the vomit put a further strain on Fenn's condition, and he had to concentrate hard to maintain his equilibrium.

After a while, he managed to open his good eye enough to glance at Olgood to see how he was faring. Olgood caught the glance and gave a half smile in reply. He did not seem to be affected by the movement of the ship, sitting with his hands loosely resting on his knees and looking about with interest. Fenn closed his eyes again. He wouldn't be able to check Olgood's arm or bind it until he felt better – he hoped that would happen before the end of the voyage.

The prisoners had been separated on the beach into two groups and half had been taken on board each ship. There was a small raised deck at each end of the vessel and Fenn's group was again split in two and made to sit on these decks at opposite ends. There were four others with Fenn in the bow of the ship. Apart from Master Nerian and Olgood, there was Audrey, who sat next to Olgood – a small slender woman with a pleasant pixie-like face and light-brown curly hair that made her look like a child although she was a few years older than Olgood. She was a weaver and tapestry worker, whom Fenn had often seen in the craft room with Aerlene. Eldric was on the end of the line. He was a farmer, very knowledgeable about all animals but especially cows and horses, with thick forearms and a sway to his walk.

Audrey cried continuously and muttered to herself, sometimes praying and sometimes repeating phrases such as 'God help us', 'We are lost' and the word 'Ames.' Ames was her son, a boy of seven or eight years. There had been no young children among the prisoners. Audrey's husband had died some years before after being thrown from a horse and she had not remarried. Fenn worried about her state of mind, as she seemed not to notice what was happening around her, although that may have been a blessing. He wanted to ask her about Aerlene but that would have to wait.

Eldric was showing the opposite reaction to Audrey – stoic and silent, staring straight ahead past the mast and into the sky, his only movement an occasional blink. He may have been feeling seasick, it was hard to tell. His reply was just a grunt when Fenn tried to talk to him. He did not persist because the Northmen discouraged talking among the prisoners and their method of discouragement was always violent.

Ragnall had timed the launch of his small fleet well. The Northmen dragged their ships backwards away from the shore with powerful coordinated pulls on the long oars. They reversed well out to sea until Fenn wondered if they intended to continue to their destination in that manner, but the rowers stopped at an order from Ragnall and each one moved to the other side of their oar to change the direction of the row. It was obviously a familiar manoeuvre. They turned the ship about and continued rowing while the sail was hoisted. The brisk wind filled the cloth and the ship immediately gathered speed. Each oar was pulled on board, the blades fitting through a wide slit cut high on one side of the oar-hole, and placed lengthways on the deck, then a round disk of wood attached at the side was moved to cover the hole.

The raiding ships of the Northmen, together with their crew and the captives from St. Cuthbert's Monastery, confidently turned their dragon-headed bows to the north-east leaving the island of Lindisfarne to recede in the distance.

It began to rain. It was a warm rain but Fenn knew that at sea the wind could be fierce and once they were wet they could quickly get very cold. He shuffled closer to Olgood and, without attempting to open his eyes, whispered: 'Can you open your wound to the rain? It will clean it.' He lifted his hands towards Olgood as far as the rope allowed so Olgood could move more freely. He heard fabric tearing.

'That's the best I can do.'

Fenn risked opening his eye and saw Olgood had torn his shirt, exposing a long sword cut across the top of his left arm just below the shoulder. Around the wound there were streaks of dried blood, wetted but not yet washed by the rain, and the skin was discoloured in shades of yellow, brown and purple.

The ship lurched and Fenn was forced to take a deep breath, close his eye and lie his head back down on the wooden deck.

He remained as still as possible for a long time until at last he felt his head clearing. The ship was still rolling but they were now among wide deep-water swells so it was a regular movement that he could anticipate and his body had adjusted. He tried sitting up and found he could, but again felt the ache from his ribs – bruised, he thought, but not broken.

The rain was now more like a mist in the air, keeping everything damp and obstructing his vision as if they were in the clouds. From his sitting position Fenn could not see the surface of the sea, but he could hear the constant noise of the ship moving through the water; the rhythmic wash of the sea passing beneath the keel punctuated by a loud thump each time the bow encountered a wave. Despite the high prow, the collisions regularly caused seawater to splash over the side and flow across the deck.

He could see that most of the Northmen were fully occupied with sailing the ship. A small group were gathered around the mast and talking together. He couldn't see anyone watching them.

He took the opportunity to wave encouragement to the other group of captives in the stern. One, he thought it was Nameth, started to wave back but his face registered alarm. A booted foot connected painfully with Fenn's shoulder, knocking him to the deck and he automatically curled his legs and protected his ribs with his arm in case there should be a second kick. When none came, he looked up to see one of the women raiders mimicking his wave and making it clear that there was to be no communication between the groups. He hadn't seen her standing on the side of his closed eye. Fenn nodded that he understood and struggled to sit up again, rubbing at his shoulder.

Master Nerian was lying on his side, knees drawn up and his hands clasped in front of him as if in prayer, moaning. As the ship rolled, enough seawater was now on the deck to cause a small wave to flow from side to side. It had been uncomfortable but bearable for Fenn when he was lying on his back, but because the Master was on his side, each wave washed into his face and left him coughing and spluttering. He didn't have the strength to avoid the surge. Fenn feared he would drown and tried to get him to change position onto his back, but Master Nerian resisted him, returning to his side. Fenn then attempted to coil the free part of the rope attached to the Master's hands underneath his head to raise it out of the water. It was a laborious and tiring task. He was hampered by his own bonds even with Olgood trying to help by extending his hands in Fenn's direction. That action must have pained his shoulder, but Fenn persisted until he saw the Master's head was safely out of the water.

Audrey had thankfully ceased her constant muttering. Fenn rested until he had regained some strength then leaned forward to look at her past Olgood. She had her eyes closed but he could see she was breathing shallowly, not the breath of sleep.

'Audrey,' he whispered. 'Can you hear me?'

Watching to ensure he was not being overheard by the Northmen, he repeated his soft call twice before Audrey opened her eyes. She looked his way and her eyes were clear.

'Did you see Ames?' she asked, looking at both Fenn and Olgood. 'Do you think he's safe?'

'I haven't seen him,' said Fenn. Olgood shook his head. Audrey's lips pressed together and her eyes filled with tears.

'But he's probably safe – he's a smart boy,' said Fenn, quickly adding: 'Audrey, I need your help.'

'Yes, he's a smart boy,' Audrey agreed. 'Oh, dear God...' she murmured. It took a moment for his other words to register.

'What do you mean? Help with what?'

'Do you have a needle?'

Aerlene had always carried her needles and pins with her in a box and he hoped Audrey did the same.

'Of course.'

'Mistress Aerlene had a curved needle for corner work. Do you have one like that?'

'Yes, I do.'

Fenn was quiet a moment, wondering if this was a good time – so soon after Audrey's question about her son.

'Audrey, was Mistress Aerlene with you when you were captured?'

Audrey didn't reply at once. She stared at Fenn, then slowly shook her head.

'I wasn't in the craft room. I was alone – on the path by the orchard. A large, dirty man...' she gestured at the Northmen. 'One of these... these... I don't know what they are – came running up the path. He caught me by the hair... I asked him what... He dragged me...' She put her hand to her mouth and sobbed.

'Audrey, please. Speak quietly.' He glanced anxiously at the group by the mast. They were still talking amongst themselves.

He said: 'Can I please have your curved needle?'

'Yes... Yes, I'm sorry. Of course we don't know what has happened to the others. They may be...' She drew in a sharp breath. 'Well, we trust in God. What do you want a needle for?'

'I'm going to sew up Olgood's wound.'

Audrey stared at him and shook her head as if she didn't believe him.

From her dress, she pulled out a cloth bag that hung around her neck. She took a small box out of the bag. The ship crested a large swell and lurched forward. The three of them had to place their hands on the deck to steady themselves, but Audrey kept a good grip on the box.

Fenn turned to Olgood who had heard the exchange and was looking wary.

'I need to mend your arm. I'm going to sew the skin together.'

'Have you done this before?'

Fenn nodded.

He needed more freedom to use his hands. He reached over and shook Master Nerian firmly but received only a groan in response. Fenn got to his knees and tugged on the rope. There was another groan but no further objection as Fenn leaned back and dragged Master Nerian's hunched body a short distance across the deck so the monk was lying with his head by Olgood's feet. As Fenn started to regather the coil of rope he had used for a pillow, Eldric's hand reached out and gently lifted the Master's head. Fenn nodded his thanks and Olgood also helped to tuck the coil into place.

He could now reach Olgood's arm without restriction.

Carefully, he ripped the sleeve of the woollen shirt where Olgood had originally exposed his wound and eased the torn sleeve off his arm. He tore off the cuff and handed the rest to Audrey.

'Can you please pull threads from this, and twist them?'

The wound was three or four inches long and an inch deep. He rolled up the cuff of Olgood's discarded sleeve into a tight tube and told him to bite down on it. Olgood's eyes were wide but he said nothing and took the cloth between his teeth.

The wind had risen and the seawater coming on board when the ship hit a wave was augmented by continuous wind-blown spray. In his cupped hands Fenn gathered some water that looked clean and washed the wound several times as best he could. Olgood gave an intake of breath at each bite of the salt. Fenn shook the water from his hands, took the threaded needle from Audrey and looked at Olgood, who inhaled another deep breath, held it, and nodded.

He had to time his actions to the movement of the ship. The deck would roll to one side and pause, then roll the other way and pause again. During the rolls, he had to stop whatever he was doing and wait for the ship to be momentarily still.

Fenn inserted the curved needle into the skin beside the beginning of the wound, pushing it in smoothly at an angle so it emerged at the bottom of the cut, then continued to push the needle trailing its tail of wool into the other side and upward to emerge from the skin opposite where the needle had first entered. Olgood let out his breath in a rush and panted several times but he made no sound. His brow was beaded with sweat and his big right hand had clenched the front of his trousers into a ball. Fenn pulled the needle from the thread leaving the two exposed ends lying loose. He handed the needle back to Audrey who inserted another twisted thread pulled from the torn shirt sleeve.

Having his hands tied together was not the problem Fenn thought it might be. In fact, by holding Olgood's arm with one hand, he found the other was nicely anchored to apply the necessary pressure to do the stitching. However, he dared not let go and, being unable to wipe his eyes, found he had to shake his head often to clear the rain and salt water from his face.

They waited until the ship had completed a roll, then Olgood nodded again and Fenn repeated his actions at the other end of the wound. Three more times, at Olgood's nod, Fenn inserted the needle and pulled the woollen thread through the flesh, moving alternately from each end of the wound and finishing at the centre.

'That's the worst of it.' He said to Olgood, who smiled weakly.

Audrey gave a sharp gasp. 'Fenn…'

Fenn ignored her, concentrating on the next delicate task. He tied each of the threads as quickly as the ship movement permitted, carefully and gently pulling the skin together and making two fisherman's knots to hold the thread tight.

When he had finished he reached up and took the cloth from Olgood's mouth. Olgood was looking away from Fenn, over his shoulder, probably not wanting to show the pain from the tying in his eyes.

'We have no chance of keeping it dry with the rain and the spray, but it should be dried as soon as you can and then covered.'

Olgood looked down and inspected his arm. 'Thank you,' he said.

Fenn turned to check on the Northmen around the mast, and saw two legs standing beside the inert form of Master Nerian.

Fenn looked up at Ragnall who was watching him closely, the large man swaying easily on his feet in accord with the ship. Behind him several other Northmen were also gathered. They were looking at both Fenn and Olgood with curiosity – interested, Fenn reasoned, in what he had been doing but possibly also in Olgood's ability to handle the pain.

Fenn realised Olgood had seen them approaching and Audrey had tried to warn him.

Ragnall called a command and the short man who had accompanied Olaf earlier came to his side. Ragnall uttered a few words.

'He ask – where you learn that?'

'From the physician at the monastery. I've done it once before – on the leg of a goat.'

The man relayed this to Ragnall, who gave an explosive grunt, turned to the men behind him and said something in a loud voice. There were nods and murmurs of agreement.

'He say that funny – on goat,' the small man said with a grin.

Ragnall stepped over Master Nerian and lifted Olgood's elbow for a closer look at the sealed wound. The others also crowded around forcing Fenn and Audrey out of the way. Their faces expressed surprise and interest, and possibly a little respect.

One by one several Northmen stepped up and inspected Fenn's stitching. One of the women took a long look, holding Olgood's elbow and slowly raising his arm to check the stitches under movement.

A lanky man with long straight black hair pushed forward. Fenn caught a glimpse of his eyes. They looked wild, like an animal's. He had a loosely strung bow across his back and a bunch of arrows in a soft holder at his side. He stared closely then poked at the stitches to test their strength. Olgood gave an annoyed grunt and moved his arm away using his other hand to shield the area of the wound. The lanky man grabbed Olgood's left arm roughly and pulled it towards him. Olgood started to stand up and the man pushed down on his shoulder to keep him on the deck. Olgood remained unmoved in his crouch, the push instead forcing the man backwards. He lost his hold on the arm and stumbled over Master Nerian, cursed angrily, and transferred his attention to the unfortunate monk. He kicked at the back of the Master's legs then moved toward his head, shouting down at him, spittle or spray dripping from his mouth. He drew a short knife from his belt. Fenn and Olgood both stood up together, Eldric a moment later. They were still bound but they instinctively raised their hands, Fenn's only moving as far as his tie to Master Nerian would allow. The Northmen standing around stiffened and moved apart to give themselves room for action, their hands readying on weapons.

There were more shouts, some heated and some trying to calm but Fenn couldn't tell whether they were directed at the prisoners or the lanky archer. He glanced about hoping to see Ragnall ready to step in and cool the tempers as he had done before, but he couldn't see past the surrounding crowd. From the corner of his eye he saw the knife raised. He reached forward to put his arms in the path of the blow.

A hand grabbed the archer by the shoulder and pulled him off balance. Fenn was surprised to see it wasn't Ragnall, but Olaf, who smothered the knife hand with his own then smoothly shifted his grip from the shoulder to the front of the archer's tunic, screwing it tight with a twisting motion so it was constricted around the man's throat. He held him easily in that position while the shouting quieted and the tensions in the crowd relaxed.

Pushing his face right up to that of the squirming archer, Olaf talked to him in a tone that offered no room for argument.

'Olaf say holy man lucky for him. He want him alive.' The small man with the collar was standing behind Fenn.

'He was going to kill this holy man at the monastery,' said Fenn without thinking.

'No, just hurt to make tell where gold. Olaf say he bring back first person he see in your land. Fat priest is first. Olaf think this man good luck.'

'Who is the archer?' asked Olgood at Fenn's shoulder.

'Torston. He think this christian will try steal power from gods. He crazy man.'

'I will remember him,' said Olgood and turned away.

Fenn looked at the small man. 'And you... Who are you?'

The man narrowed his eyes and looked directly at Fenn without speaking. Around him Fenn could hear people moving away, losing interest. He shifted his feet to better compensate for the movement of the deck, realising as he did so that he was finding it easier to stand on the swaying surface than he had thought he would. A tug on his wrist told him Olgood had sat down again. The wet rope was chafing at his skin making it red and uncomfortable. He looked back at Master Nerian whose condition was unchanged; the monk blissfully unaware that he had just been at the centre of a possibly deadly confrontation. He wanted to check on the Master, but he didn't want to miss the opportunity to talk with this man who spoke the language of the Northmen. Olgood would attend to the monk's health.

He saw that Olaf had dragged the man called Torston back to the foot of the mast. He saw Ragnall then, through the mist, holding the steering oar at the stern of the ship. He turned back to the translator.

The small man made up his mind. 'I am Hakon. You?'

'Fenn.'

Hakon studied him for a moment. He spread an arm to encompass the ship.

'This your new life, Fenn,' he said.

Then he added with a wry smile. 'You like?'

*   *   *

The nights were the worst. The constant need to brace against the pitching deck was exhausting and although Fenn felt tired enough to be able to sleep despite the circumstances, he managed only short fitful periods of rest broken by frequent interruptions.

Their clothes were completely unsuitable for the conditions and they felt the cold keenly as soon as the sun had set. They huddled in the lee of the side of the ship as far from the touch of the wind as possible and moved close together to share whatever warmth they could.

Just as the rhythm of the ship became familiar enough to ignore, a rogue wave from an unexpected angle would hit the hull with a loud thump and cause the vessel to quiver.

If one person was disturbed it affected them all.

After the first night, the prisoner's hands were untied, but they were still confined to their original positions. Twice daily they were fed small pieces of salted fish and dried meat and sometimes a hard biscuit. The meat was tough and needed extended chewing to become soft enough to swallow. Fenn learned to take the salt fish sparingly or endure a good thirst until water was provided from tied bags made from animal skins. The water was warm and tasted stale but it gave relief from the heat of the sun and did slake his thirst. They were sometimes given apples, probably taken from the monastery, but whatever their source they were a welcome addition to the meat and fish.

Several barrels of ale that had definitely been plundered from the monastery stood in the centre of the ship near the mast. The Northmen gathered there at sunset and filled drinking horns presumably as a reward for the day's work, but the captives were not offered any. Olgood grumbled that those barrels had been made by his hand and he wished he had not made them so strong.

At dusk, Olaf would re-tie the Master's hands, attach the free end to his own wrist, and sleep beside the monk, which Fenn understood was to prevent Master Nerian from deliberately falling over the side and escaping his torment by sliding mercifully into the deep. Fenn doubted the Master had the strength to get to his knees let alone stand. One of the few voluntary movements Fenn saw from him happened when his hands were freed in the morning. At that time, he would tuck one of his arms under his head and remain motionless in that position all day.

The days and nights drifted into each other and the lives of the prisoners of the Northmen developed a sameness. They floated in an inhospitable world with wild and angry water as far as the eye could see, buffeted by a cold impartial wind and surrounded by the noises of the creaking of wood and rigging and the flap of the sail, punctuated by the guttural calls of the Northmen as they moved about the deck adjusting ropes.

During the fourth night at sea, the wind that had scarcely slackened since leaving Lindisfarne eased to an irregular breeze. The sail flapped and did not fill, and the forward rush of the ship slowed, leaving it sometimes still in the water accompanied by only a gurgling sound from the sea instead of the normal hiss. There was a conference among the Northmen and, at Ragnall's order, the sail was brought down.

Since then the ship had been making its way by use of the oars.

Both groups of prisoners were herded like cows to the rowing seats, stumbling across the deck in the pale cloudless light of the moon and stars. Fenn quickly checked that the pouch of his sling was still tucked behind his belt as he rose to his feet. Although the two groups from the monastery were close together for the first time since leaving the beach at Lindisfarne, they avoided calling or talking to each other, wary of the unpredictable reaction of the Northmen. They silently sat where they were placed and bent to their task. One of the Northmen wandered among them carrying a short whip to ensure their effort was honest, and correction was swift for any perceived lack.

Fenn hauled on his oar and grimaced as he felt the protest of knotted muscles across the top of his back. He tried to ease the tightness by hunching his shoulders on the forward stroke as he lifted the oar. Audrey was seated in front of him. He was surprised that the women were also forced to row, but the only person spared was Master Nerian – the women raiders and even Hakon, who now sat behind Fenn, were all required to take their turn. After a while Audrey complained that her hands hurt and she couldn't pull. He whispered to her to pull lightly but that she must make it seem as though she was working. He prayed for wind to end their ordeal, but the night passed without respite.

They had been rested well before dawn with fresh rowers taking their places. Fenn lay on his back to gather his strength and looked at the stars, wondering if his fate was written there, requiring just some secret knowledge to understand the message; but the language of the stars was as foreign to him as that of the Northmen.

'I suppose it's good to be able to see again with both eyes,' observed Olgood, lying beside him on the deck.

The swelling around Fenn's right eye had reduced and he was able to open it normally, although, according to Olgood, a wide purple bruise still covered his face above and below the eye.

Fenn agreed with a murmur.

'How's your wound? Is it bleeding?' he whispered. Fenn knew Olgood was strong enough to row using only one arm but hoped his needle-work had not been damaged by the constant movement.

'No, it's holding well and not bleeding.' Then he added: 'And it doesn't smell.'

His arm was bandaged by a piece of cloth torn from Audrey's under-garment, tied in place with some double-twisted threads from Olgood's shirt sleeve.

'Good. It should be scarring now. I'll look at it again in the morning.'

They lay sprawled on the deck without talking, each thinking their own thoughts – accompanied once more by the creaking of the timbers, the sounds of the sea and the added rhythmic splash of the oars combining with the low hum of distant conversation.

Olgood said: 'Fenn, do you have a plan?'

'A plan? What do you mean? A plan for what?'

'Escape. A plan to escape from these barbarians and get back home. Shall we take the first opportunity we get when we land? Or maybe as soon as we get close enough to land we could jump overboard and swim. That might be the best chance.'

Until now, Fenn had not thought about anything beyond the next moment.

'We need to concentrate first on surviving,' he said. 'We need to learn about these people and this land and find out where we are. The chance will come.'

Olgood was silent. Fenn wondered if he expected more.

'Once we know what we need to know, Olgood, we *will* find a way.' He paused, then, stressing each word, he said: 'We... will... go... home.'

For a moment Olgood still did not reply, but then he turned his head and looked at Fenn with a steady gaze.

'Yes, you're right,' he said. 'Thank you. That's what I wanted to hear.'

CHAPTER FIVE

A foreign land…

The crest of the sun breaching the eastern horizon coloured the sea a deep rich yellow. Back on the oars, Fenn stared fascinated at the painted sea and it seemed to him they were moving through a huge pool of liquid gold.

He was roused from his daydream by a shout, followed by a general commotion. He looked east and realised the shout had announced the sighting of land, which appeared as a dark line on the horizon. There was an immediate raucous celebration by the Northmen with wild yells and the raising of arms to the sky, no doubt thanking their gods. Fenn heard the names 'Ran' and 'Thor' repeated. Two burly men linked arms and danced a heavy-footed jig to cheers and claps. There was a general sigh of relief, tensions on board eased noticeably and the faces became more relaxed.

A short while later there was another shout. Fenn followed the pointing arm and, through the haze, saw the second ship, behind them but easily visible. There were more cheers. Somehow, throughout the voyage, even during the thick darkness of cloudy nights where you could not see more than a few yards in any direction, the two ships had kept together. Fenn could not imagine how these Northmen managed to achieve that feat on the endlessly wide expanse of the sea. He could see Ragnall standing easily at the steering oar, smiling and sharing a story or a joke with a small group, and had to admit that in spite of their obvious faults, these Northmen were extremely competent deep water sailors.

Fenn leaned his body so he could look past the line of rowers to see if Master Nerian had been roused by the sighting of land. There was enough light for him to see that the monk lay where he had been for the whole voyage, curled against the side of the ship, his face a deathly white, looking as usual more dead than alive. He had refused any food but swallowed when water was poured into his mouth. Hopefully with land in sight, his suffering would soon end.

Fenn scanned the deck for the archer, Torsten. During the daytime, Torsten would often pause in what he was doing to glower at Master Nerian, muttering to himself and to whoever was in hearing. His intense stare and incantations reminded Fenn of a witch casting a spell. Olaf was alert to his activity, however, and made sure Torsten knew it. Torsten stopped and looked away when he saw Olaf was watching.

Fenn located the archer, and was glad to see him engaged in talking with one of the women raiders rather than attempting to make life more miserable for Master Nerian.

Although the rising sun had revealed a sea that was calm on the surface, the long powerful swells still moved through the depths and it was alternately easy and then difficult to row as the swells passed beneath the keel. Audrey was barely moving her oar, making only minimal movements in time with the other rowers. He looked over her shoulder and could now see that her oar was bloodied with red streaks wherever her hands had touched. Some of her nails were split and torn.

There was a crack and Audrey shrieked. Fenn caught a blur of movement in his eye and a red line appeared on Audrey's cheek together with beads of blood. He turned to his side to see a Northman coiling his whip as he walked around to stand in front of Audrey. He spat on the deck in derision and yelled at her in a scornful tone.

'He say she lazy and no use.' Hakon said from the seat behind Fenn.

The Northman pointed at Audrey and made a flicking motion as if tossing a stone into the sea.

'Tell him he's wrong, she's not lazy,' Fenn twisted to look at Hakon. 'She has tried as hard as she can.'

Hakon stared at Fenn with a startled expression, and mouthed 'No!' – but the man questioned Hakon, obviously asking what Fenn had said.

Hakon stiffened and spoke to the Northman.

'Tell him her hands are injured, she cannot row,' Fenn added.

Hakon hesitated, and Fenn repeated: 'Tell him. Tell him exactly what I said.'

Hakon shrugged and spoke again to the Northman.

Fenn did not dare to stop rowing during the exchange. The foremost rule was that oars had to keep moving together. He said to Audrey: 'Show him your hands.'

She tried to lift her hands from the oar but they were stuck to the wood. She cried out as she painfully pulled her hands free and turned them over to reveal palms and fingers that were covered with raw and weeping blisters. The Northman was unimpressed. He snorted and pulled Audrey's oar half on board and out of the water, then walked to the stern and took up a wooden bucket which he dragged over the side. He walked back with the bucket of sea water swinging at the end of a rope. He motioned Audrey from her seat and took her hands as if to wash them. Instead, he forcefully thrust her hands into the salty water. Audrey screamed and the Northman's laughter was joined by that of others.

'They enjoy inflicting pain.' Olgood's voice came from behind Fenn. Under his breath Fenn heard him say: 'They're no more than savages!'

Hakon said: 'Salt water good for blisters.'

The Northman called out a question and received a reply from Ragnall. He spat out a derogatory name, took hold of Audrey's hair at the back of her neck and dragged her back to their normal position next to Master Nerian, then he roughly pushed her down onto the deck. She fell to her knees and sat weeping with her head down, hugging her hands.

'What did he call her?' asked Fenn.

'She is woman dog ready for…' Hakon waved one hand, searching for the word. 'Have pup.'

'Ready for mating?'

'Yes – ready for mate.'

Another call from Ragnall made the Northman look up. Fenn could see Ragnall was pointing at him and his heart jumped. Was he about to be punished for speaking out?

'Ragnall say Haldor take her place,' Hakon explained. 'Haldor not like he told to take place of thrall.'

The Northman clenched his fists, swore an oath, then shook his head violently. He strode purposefully to the side of the ship and stood there, staring forward, away from Ragnall, towards the land across the sea. He was a big man, heavy in the shoulders with thick arms. His face bore the marks of violence, a twisted nose and scars on his forehead and cheek, with a long puckered red line extending from his ear down the side of his neck.

Ragnall took a deep breath then slapped one of the men standing with him on the back and indicated the steering oar. They changed places, and Ragnall walked slowly down the ship until he stood three paces from Haldor. He said nothing, just stood there with folded arms, waiting. Fenn could see that, although Haldor was a big, dangerous, battle-hardened raider, Ragnall stood half a head taller and was broader in the body. His stance was confident and ready.

Haldor didn't move. In a calm voice, Ragnall repeated the words he had spoken earlier.

Still Haldor stared out to sea. Ragnall waited.

Just as Fenn thought Ragnall was about to act, Haldor turned about and brushed past Ragnall, deliberately making a slight contact, then walked slowly back toward Audrey's seat. He continued walking past Fenn, struck Hakon on the shoulder with enough force to knock him from his seat and spoke to him angrily. Hakon scrambled back onto his seat and managed to grab his swinging oar.

'Haldor say tell you this your fault and he not forget.'

Haldor gave a low growl, kneed Fenn in the back as he pushed past and sat down heavily on Audrey's seat. He pushed the oar through the hole, bunched his shoulders and immediately pulled powerfully, leaning back so far that Fenn had to move to one side to avoid him. He managed to keep his rhythm and adjusted quickly to Haldor's powerful strokes. The Northman turned his head to glare at Fenn, his face twisted into a savage scowl. He had been forced to back down in front of the crew, no doubt a serious insult in their culture, and that outcome had filled him with resentment and anger.

Another Northman approached and held out his hand toward Haldor.

Haldor looked up at the man and asked a gruff question. The Northman's only reply was to withdraw his hand slightly and present it again. Haldor snarled like a dog then pulled his whip from his belt and threw it on the deck at the man's feet. The Northman grinned broadly as if it was a joke, then picked up the whip and cracked it.

After a short while Fenn had another reason to wish for a fresh breeze. Haldor stank with the thick odour of sweat mixed with rancid fat.

Fenn closed his mind, ignored his nose, and rowed.

*   *   *

'What land is this?'

There was a hum of conversation about the ship, which had increased in volume as they neared the land. Fenn thought it would be safe to risk talking.

The thin line on the horizon had resolved into hills and then mountains. When Fenn looked over his shoulder, towards the bow, he saw a towering mass of land rising from the sea. He could hear a dull roar of surf although they were still a long way from shore. While he was looking back, the ship seemed stationary with their efforts to move forward making not the slightest difference, but over time he could see that they were making progress, and the mountains grew steadily higher. It was mid-morning and he felt the stinging heat of the sun on his shoulders, on the back of his neck, and on his hands grasping the oar.

Hakon answered him: 'They call this land 'Nordwegr'. It means way to North. This part Viken. All you see.' He paused, then added: 'But we go further north from here. We go Ranriki.'

'What is Ranriki? Is Ranriki the name of a town?'

'No, Viken big part, Ranriki small part, town name Lognavik.'

So Viken was the county, Ranriki the shire, and Lognavik the town.

He was thirsty and looked about for the man who brought the water skin to the rowers.

When they were still a good distance from the shore – it looked to be about a mile but Fenn found it difficult to judge the distance – Ragnall gave the order to ship the oars. It looked like a normal change of rowers but when Fenn, Olgood and Eldric had been taken to join Audrey sitting beside Master Nerian, they were again roped together by their wrists. This time though, Fenn and Olgood were roped to Master Nerian and Audrey and Eldric were roped together. Olgood looked at Fenn and gave a knowing smile. One of the opportunities for escape that he had mentioned, had just come and gone.

Having the rope about his wrists again brought the full realisation of their predicament back to Fenn. They would soon be landing in a foreign land where, if Master Nerian was correct, they would be slaves, with no rights, and no opportunity for change, probably treated no better than a farm animal, able to be sold for profit like property. He could live or die at the whim of his owner. He had no idea, in fact, who his owner was. Was it Olaf, who had captured him? Or Ragnall, as the leader – could he choose? Or were slaves shared like communal property by these Northmen? Would he be given as a prize to someone who had performed well on the raid? His eyes widened. Haldor? Fenn uttered a short prayer against that possibility, then he deliberately stopped his useless speculation – he would know the answer soon enough.

Yseld came to mind. Would she fear the worst for him or hope for the best? His throat constricted as he thought of the bright flame of their future that had been brutally smothered by their forced parting – or at least put on hold – if she was alive…

'If you live, I will see you again, Yseld, I promise you that,' he thought, his hands clenching to give weight to the promise.

True to Hakon's prediction, once the new rowers were in position, they turned to the north and moved parallel to the coastline. Previously, the ship had rocked from stern to bow but with the turn, it now rocked from side to side with a twisting motion and Fenn fought the beginnings of dizziness. He put his head down and swallowed.

He heard Hakon whisper to him: 'Look where water meet sky, not at ship.'

When he followed the suggestion, he felt instant relief as his head made sense of the movement. He gave Hakon's advice to the others. Olgood looked puzzled, but Eldric and Audrey nodded their thanks.

Fenn had expected to land on a beach somewhere on the coast. Instead, at midday, after rowing in shifts all morning, they turned from their path along the coastline and steered into a wide bay. As far as Fenn could see, the terrain was as mountainous and rocky on both sides of the bay as it had been since they first sighted land. It did not look like an area that invited settlement and he wondered where the town of Lognavik could be located within this harsh environment.

In the calmer water of the bay there was another change of rowers. Fenn used the increased movement on the deck to take a searching look at their fellow captives sitting at the stern; to assess how they had fared now that their sea journey was nearing an end. They were all alert and did not seem to have suffered from seasickness. He held up a hand and clenched his fist in what he hoped would be interpreted as a sign to 'endure', or 'be strong'. He saw that Nameth was watching him and was heartened when he nodded and returned the gesture. Fenn discreetly glanced around but this time the exchange had not been noticed.

The two ships, now only separated by three or four boat-lengths and travelling one behind the other, crossed to the southern side and proceeded into the bay rowing only a few hundred yards from the shore. Fenn could see the details of individual trees and plants clearly, but there was no sign of human habitation. The bird life was plentiful and varied and he noted with interest many birds he did not recognise. On prominent rocks, large grey birds resembling herons watched solemnly as the procession passed by. Apart from the fact that their heads slowly moved, they could have been statues carved from the stone on which they stood.

They rowed past a large tree-topped island followed by several smaller barren islands, some little more than large rocks. One interesting feature in the otherwise desolate landscape was a spectacular waterfall whose outflow tumbled from such a height that it reached the rocky shore as only a fine spray.

The sun was midway to the horizon when they departed the relatively wide expanse of the bay and entered a long narrow inlet bordered by sheer rock walls that emerged directly out of the sea and then became thickly wooded as they soared precipitously to majestic heights. After the relative lowlands of Northumbria, the immense height of the walls, now that they were so close, was breath-taking.

It became quiet. The water was still, barely moving against the smooth moss-covered stone walls, and the wind died completely. The only sounds were the occasional cry of a soaring bird and the rhythmic splashing of the oars and even those were muted in the confined space.

As they progressed up the inlet, it narrowed further and the imposing size and steepness of the mountains pressed in from both sides and threatened to crush the two small insignificant vessels intruding on the sanctity of this god-like domain.

CHAPTER SIX

Welcome to Lognavik...

The short wooden pier that jutted from the land was filled with cheering people. Three small fishing boats had been pulled up onto the stony beach a short distance away. On both sides of the pier and around the boats, more people were gathered on the beach. Children were standing on the seats of the boats and the other people crowded right to the water's edge. Behind them, up a slight rise from the beach, Fenn could see a scattering of thatched-roof buildings with smoke rising in the still air from fires. There were even more figures moving in the village. It looked to be a well-established, thriving settlement situated on a flat area on the side of the inlet and extending up a small valley. The valley terminated beneath the same tall and rugged mountains that had bordered the inlet leading to this place.

Beyond the settlement, where the inlet ended, the mouth of a large river curved out of sight around a bluff.

He could see children and women, some carrying babies, and older men and women amongst the people on the shore, but only a few young or middle-aged men. At the head of the crowd on the pier though, stood a group of blond men with axes and swords at their sides. Some men would need to be left behind to guard the village, thought Fenn, but obviously most of the fighting men from the settlement were on the ships.

In front of the armed men stood an older man with long white hair, leaning on a thick staff. Beside him was a woman who looked to be of similar age. Her hands were extended toward the ships, and she was calling out in a shrill voice that could be heard clearly above the shouts and cheers of the townspeople.

When they were a few hundred yards from the pier, a young Northman leapt onto the side of the ship and, while the men on the oars continued rowing, he balanced himself there and then stepped on to an oar outside the ship. Displaying a skill and daring that brought Fenn to his feet, the youth ran along the full length of the moving oars, his feet lightly touching each oar. He leapt from the last oar, grasped the edge of the raised bow and pulled himself back on board. A huge cheer sounded from the shore, echoed by the men on the ship and several crowded around the youth thumping his back and shoulders.

Another man attempted to repeat the feat, but had only just begun his journey along the oars when he missed his footing and fell into the water with a cry and a loud splash. This time the crowd responded with howls and hoots and there was laughter from the ship. The man had been fully clothed and wearing a chain mail vest and a sword so Fenn expected the ship to slow so he could be rescued, but the oars did not miss a beat and the man in the water was ignored. Fenn craned his head to search for the man, expecting to see him in the process of drowning. Instead, he appeared in the wake of the ship, moving strongly through the water toward the shore, unencumbered by the weight of his heavy clothing and his weapon.

Under Ragnall's guidance, using the steering oar and calling for strokes from alternate sides, his ship was manoeuvred up to the pier and the oars on that side were brought smartly on board just as they pulled alongside. A slight jolt told Fenn the keel had grounded on the beach. Ropes were thrown and the ship was made fast to the pier which extended halfway down the vessel. The captives remained seated while the crew jumped onto the pier and carried out a series of noisy and sometimes violent greetings. Some, impatient to get ashore, leapt overboard, landed waist height in the water and made their way to the beach where the same hugs and vigorous slapping of backs took place. The noise was deafening, with several excited dogs adding their barks to the din.

The second ship was turned around and approached the other side of the pier backwards. With identical precision it nudged the beach and came to a gentle rest against the pier. The crew from that ship eagerly joined the celebration. Once again, in spite of his situation, Fenn marvelled at the display of control the Northmen had over their large sea-going ships.

The captives were momentarily forgotten and, above the noise from the shore, Fenn heard a call from one of the infirmary workers, a young girl named Briony, from the other end of their ship.

'How is the Master?'

Fenn knelt beside Master Nerian, gently turned him onto his back and tried to help him sit up. The Master groaned but seemed to sense that the motion of the ship had ceased, so made an effort to sit and opened his eyes. He looked inquiringly at Fenn.

'The journey is over, Master, I think we'll soon be going ashore.'

Master Nerian smiled weakly. He tried to speak but no sound emerged. From his lips Fenn read: 'Thank you.'

Fenn waved to the other group and called: 'The Master is alive but very weak.'

Briony waved back and Fenn called again: 'Briony, was Master Egbert hurt?'

She shook her head. 'He was called to the castle. He wasn't at the monastery.'

Fenn was relieved. That was the first good news he'd had in a long while.

He took a moment to check Audrey's hands. The blisters were still raw but no longer weeping and they looked clean. He nodded at her in encouragement.

'If you get a chance, show these to Briony.' He pointed toward the stern.

He turned away and she stopped him with a hand on his arm. 'Thank you for standing up for me.'

Fenn smiled at her and touched her shoulder, showing a confidence he did not really feel.

'I think we must stand together,' he said.

The reunion on the beach continued for a long time until some people, individually and in groups, began moving up the rise into the village. The light in the inlet was dimming, with the sun touching the mountains in the west when Olaf came striding along the pier with Hakon behind him. Ragnall followed them – he had his arm around one of the women raiders and they were talking closely as they walked. Two other Northmen followed them, one of whom was Torston.

They all came on board and stopped in front of Fenn's group. Ragnall said something to Hakon.

Hakon pointed at Fenn, Olgood and Master Nerian. 'Ragnall say you, big one, christian, go Olaf. Woman, this man, go Birgitta.'

Fenn kept an eye on Torston, who was sneering with obvious disdain at Master Nerian. The archer made some derogatory comment about the Master's condition, then took some staggering steps about the deck miming someone unable to walk. Ragnall pushed him away, pointing at the other group of captives. Torston reluctantly turned and Ragnall, Hakon and the remaining Northman followed him towards the stern. More Northmen from the pier were boarding the second ship.

Olaf gestured for his captives to get to their feet.

'May God be with you both,' Fenn said to Audrey and Eldric as they stood.

'And you,' replied Eldric. He reached out and Fenn clasped his hand. Eldric repeated the gesture with Olgood. As best they could with their tied hands, they gathered briefly together. Fenn gave Audrey a hug.

Master Nerian wasn't able to stand, but Olgood and Fenn got him up with Olgood taking most of his weight. He tried to say something but just coughed. Eldric and Audrey both touched his arm, and he smiled and nodded at them.

The woman called Birgitta took hold of the rope attached to Audrey. She was the one who had hit Nameth in the monastery courtyard. She looked formidable. A strong face and steady blue eyes, not pretty but with attractive features, her hair was a light fawn, pulled back and tied just like Yseld's but where Yseld's hung straight and fine in a small tail, this woman's was twisted together and reached the small of her back. She carried her chin high and had a powerful stance which displayed confidence and possibly high status.

Without speaking, Birgitta guided Audrey and Eldric onto the pier, with Eldric taking Audrey's arm and helping her to step off the vessel. Audrey gave Fenn a dismayed look over her shoulder but Fenn could do no more than give her a final encouragement with the clenched fist gesture he'd used earlier. Olaf helped Olgood to lift Master Nerian onto the pier and Fenn struggled behind them, hampered again by the fact that his hands were tied. The pier wasn't wide enough for three abreast so they moved slowly and awkwardly, with Olaf and Olgood supporting the Master. Fenn looked behind to see the other captives climbing onto the pier and they were joined by the prisoners from the second ship.

When they reached the beach, Master Nerian could stand but was not steady. Olaf left Olgood to support the monk and led them towards the buildings. He obviously enjoyed the stares of the children and the other people who had waited on the beach. Olaf took the bulging bag from his belt and held it in triumph above his head, displaying the golden cross to the appreciative crowd. The cover of the Book of Gospels was in that bag and Fenn vowed to one day retrieve it and take it back home to be reunited with the Book.

In a moment of reflection, he recalled that he had made several vows lately – to Olgood, to Yseld, and now to himself – to return home, but he had no idea how that could be achieved or indeed if it were physically possible.

He reminded himself of his words to Olgood – 'First survive, then learn, then plan.'

Most of the eyes of the crowd were focussed on Master Nerian in his monk's cassock or on Olgood because of his height which was equal to that of Olaf. Walking behind Olgood, Fenn found he was able to observe without being noticed.

Some younger children ran up close and poked at the captives with sticks then ran away squealing, which Olaf found amusing. The dogs were more menacing. A few stood back and barked at the strangers from a distance but three hairy brutes as large as wolves circled them, drawing their lips back from their teeth and snarling fiercely. From time to time one would lunge at the captives then retreat. One came close to Fenn, snarling, but when he rested his gaze on the animal the snarl faded. It sniffed at him curiously from a short distance and then withdrew. Olaf laughed at the dogs and ignored them at first but when one persistently threatened

Master Nerian, he tired of their behaviour and drove off the beasts with curses and hefty kicks.

As they approached the first buildings they were struck by a foul smell – the odour of death.

At the top of the beach stood a row of poles and hanging from each was the remains of a decaying animal carcase. Fenn expected Olaf to steer well clear of the stinking remains but instead he walked right up to them and deliberately rubbed the back of his hand against one of the poles before moving on. The stench was terrible. Olaf gave no sign that anything was amiss, but Fenn saw Olgood's nose wrinkle in disgust and he himself almost gagged as they passed by, even though he held his breath as long as he could.

Among the first rows of houses, the fading light of day was augmented by more poles, each topped with a burning flame like giant candles that had been placed in the ground at regular intervals. Fenn peered into the open doors of buildings that they passed but was unable to see any detail in the interior gloom.

Only children still accompanied them now and they had resorted to dancing and chanting and clapping their hands as they followed a few steps behind Fenn. He got the impression they were being paraded through the village as they changed direction often and encountered several groups of people who pointed and fell into animated discussion as they passed.

They eventually came to a large open space on the edge of the village where there were several animal pens, two holding pigs and the rest standing empty. Beside these were larger fenced areas for cattle, with open pasture beyond. Ahead was a large building and through the open doors Fenn could see that this was a barn with a dirt floor and stacked bales of feed. He could hear the noise of chickens and more cattle inside.

Olaf waved the children away and led them inside the large house that stood on a small rise next to the barn.

They walked down a short covered entranceway which opened into a wide circular room with a fire burning on stones in the centre. In the flickering firelight, Fenn could see that the floor was wooden, except around the fire which was set on packed earth. Two short poles had been driven into the ground on each side of the fire as cooking supports, and a heavy iron chain hanging from beams in the roof suspended a cooking pot over the fire. The smoke curled lazily up to a small hole in the thatched beehive-shaped roof. Around the sides of the room were enclosures with solid walls that only extended half-way to the roof making them look more like barn stalls than rooms. Some of these could be closed by drawing a curtain across the opening. The curtains and some cloaks that Fenn could see hanging on the wall were all coloured blood red. On one wall, just inside the entrance, two red-handled crossed axes were on display between a pair of round wooden shields.

In one of the open enclosures stood a solid table containing some stacked bowls and a basket of herbs. There were no other people visible but some of the curtains were drawn.

Apart from the entrance and the hole in the roof, there was no other view of the outside.

Adjacent to the entrance, an annex had been built with a low roof. Olaf led them into the annex where there were several low benches covered with woven rugs that were obviously used as beds. The benches were arranged against the walls, leaving a clear space in the middle. Fenn was surprised to see Hakon resting on one and on another was a boy about his own age. Fenn's first impression of the boy was that he looked filthy. His face and arms were covered in grime and on his head a dirty woollen hat was pulled down to cover his hair and his ears. Like Hakon, he wore a collar.

Olgood lowered Master Nerian onto a bench while Olaf untied the rope from the Master's hands and then Olgood's. He motioned for Olgood to untie Fenn, and left the room. A few moments later he returned with three leather collars in his hand. He tossed these to Hakon and then he was gone. Hakon looked at Fenn and shrugged. Fenn understood. The collar was the mark of a slave. Hakon was a captive, a slave, just like himself, brought on the raid because he could speak English.

He bent his head so Hakon could reach his neck.

They rested in silence, each absorbed in their own thoughts. Hakon was subdued and morose, sitting with his head down. Perhaps he was reflecting on his change of status. He had been an important member of the raiding party, needed for talking to the captives. Now he was again just a slave.

After a while Fenn rose and asked Olgood if he could check his wound. Olgood thanked him and they removed the crude bandage. In spite of the often damp conditions on board the ship, the cut was healing well and Fenn was able to see, even in the poor light, that the scab looked healthy. He indicated that he thought the bandage was no longer necessary. Olgood gently felt his scab and nodded agreement.

Fenn returned to his seat.

'Hakon, are we now slaves of Olaf?'

Hakon roused, and gazed at Fenn through lowered eyes. He took a slow breath, then shrugged.

'You thrall of Olaf and Ragnall,' he said.

Fenn didn't understand. 'Thrall? Is that a slave?' Hakon shrugged without answering.

Fenn recalled what Hakon had said. 'Olaf *and* Ragnall? Both of them?'

'Olaf little brother of Ragnall. This house of Ragnall. Olaf live here.'

Fenn considered this information. That explained their similar size and build. He smiled at the ridiculous thought of describing Olaf as a 'little' brother. Also, they did both seem to be in charge during the voyage.

'Does Birgitta live here too?' he asked, remembering Ragnall and Birgitta had been close on the pier.

'Sometimes, not always. She has own house.'

At Fenn's querying expression, Hakon added: 'Birgitta has house in the hills. She like it there. Husband leave her after she have baby who die. Ragnall has long time...' he searched for the right word, '...strong like for this Shield Maiden.'

'Shield Maiden? What is that?'

'Woman who fight with men.'

Fenn nodded and sat back, thoughtfully. He was beginning to realise how completely different this society was from his own.

'What will be expected of us?' he asked.

Hakon laughed. 'You work. You work whatever they say.'

The boy lying on the bed alongside was following their conversation looking from one to another as they spoke.

'Who is this?' Fenn asked Hakon while smiling at the youth.

'This Kael.'

Fenn nodded to Kael who stared back at him with large brown eyes and did not return the nod.

'Also a thrall of Ragnall and Olaf?'

'Thrall of Askari, mother of Ragnall, Olaf.'

At Fenn's puzzled frown he added: 'Askari was on pier. Medicine Woman.'

Fenn remembered the old woman at the end of the pier who seemed to be calling a formal welcome to the ships.

He took a moment to digest what Hakon had told him and said: 'Please tell Kael my name is Fenn. This is Olgood and, over there, Master Nerian.'

Hakon repeated the names to Kael, whose stare flicked to each person as their name was said, but he made no reply, his gaze coming back to Fenn.

'Does he talk?' asked Fenn.

Hakon simply said: 'No.'

Bemused, Fenn looked at Olgood with raised eyebrows.

Olgood leaned forward. 'Why were the dead animals hung on the poles at the beach?'

Hakon shook his head and sighed. 'Offers to Gods. Some offer to Ran, some offer to Thor.'

'Sacrifices? What ignorant peasants these people are. Offering sacrifices to their pagan gods.' Olgood shook his head in disbelief. He blew a long breath from his mouth and leaned back on his bed.

Hakon held up his hand. 'Take care what say about gods, even if nobody understand words,' he warned.

Olgood just grunted.

'I've heard of Thor but who is Ran?' asked Fenn.

'Ran goddess of sea. If she catch men in net, they drown. Thor god of storm. Offer animal to keep us safe on sea.'

74

At that point a young woman who looked to also be of a similar age to Fenn and Olgood, walked into the room. Her hair, which was the colour of wheat, framed her face and was drawn back at her neck and, like Birgitta's, was then woven neatly together, extending down her back to her waist. She also wore a leather collar around her neck. Her slightly hunched shoulders and downward gaze gave her a shy look but there was also defiance and confidence in the bold way she had entered the room. She had a beautiful wide smile with full lips. Her dress was tight and displayed what Aerlene had always called 'a womanly shape'. She carried a wooden platter containing a round loaf of bread and a slab of cheese, which she placed on the floor in the centre of the room. Fenn and Olgood reached together for the bread, but Hakon said sharply: 'No! Wait.'

They withdrew their hands like scolded children. Fenn was hungry, not having eaten since mid-morning and then only some hard dried meat and an apple, but he sat back and waited, thinking there might be some ceremony that had to be observed.

The woman withdrew and soon returned, this time carrying another platter holding six small wooden bowls. The steam and sweet smell of honey revealed that the bowls contained warmed mead. Fenn heard Hakon gasp in surprise. She lifted each bowl and placed them carefully in a circle around the bread platter.

Once again she left the room. Olgood stood and made to follow her, but Hakon was quickly off his bed and caught him by the arm.

'Not go to big room unless asked. Not go to entrance. Not be seen from big room.'

'She has a lot to carry. I could help,' explained Olgood.

'Not be seen,' Hakon repeated. 'Only her go big room.'

Olgood sighed and sat down.

Fenn caught his attention and indicated the food in front of them. He raised his eyebrows and smiled. After the sparse fare they had been offered on the ship, what was already laid before them was a feast.

The next time the woman entered, there were again six bowls slightly larger than before on the platter. As soon as she came through the entrance, the room filled with the tantalizing aroma of hot cooked meat. Fenn felt his mouth fill with saliva. She went first to Hakon.

These bowls had two small wooden extensions one on each side, so they could be held. Hakon took a bowl, held it out in front of him and uttered a few words, carefully watching the annex entrance as he did so. Fenn was looking at the woman, waiting for her to offer him a bowl, and saw her eyes widen. She glanced at Kael and bent her head but not quick enough to hide a smirk of amusement. Fenn got the impression that Hakon had not said exactly what he was supposed to.

She held the platter out to Fenn. The bowls contained a stew of meat and some vegetables, cabbage and maybe turnip or something similar. He chose one. Kael reached past Fenn's shoulder and took a bowl.

'*Skause*,' said the woman.

'*Skause* name of food. You call stew, I think,' explained Hakon.

She gave a bowl to Olgood, who thanked her as he took it. He put it to his lips and started slurping the stew, at the same time reaching for one of the bowls of mead. She placed a bowl in Master Nerian's hands and sat on the bed next to his taking the last bowl for herself. She looked around at the newcomers one by one, then settled to eating.

The stew was delicious. The meat had been boiled and was firm but compared to the rock-hard meat and salty fish of the previous days, it was both tasty and edible. It was not pork; it could be goat but there was something about the taste he couldn't place and Fenn hadn't seen any goats. As he suspected, there were also turnips and cabbage. The sauce was thick with meat juices. No wonder that these people grow so big if they eat like this.

When he had finished the stew, he leaned back to let it settle, and had to resist an urge to burp.

'Are you always fed this well?' he asked, his eyes travelling from his bowl to the food on the floor.

Beside Fenn, Kael gave a snort. Fenn glanced at him, but Kael was concentrating on his bowl.

'No. This get you strong after ship,' said Hakon. He shook a finger. 'Mead never. Only when men come home. Sometime maybe ale. At night we eat only after big room finished.'

'So…' said Fenn, '…we should enjoy it while we can.'

A thought occurred to him and he asked Hakon: 'Are there any more thralls in this household?'

Hakon shook his head. 'This all now.' He pointed at the serving woman. 'This Gisele. Two others given so men from other village join raid.'

Fenn thought about what Hakon had said, and looked at Olgood for support.

'I think he's saying that two slaves were sold so that Ragnall and Olaf could pay some men to sail with them,' said Olgood.

'Not sold – not pay men – thralls given to *Yarl*. He give ship and men for raid.'

Olgood asked: 'The thralls were given? – do you mean like hostages?'

Hakon thought for a moment. 'Yes, hostage. If raid no good, Harald keep thralls. If good, give thralls back to Ragnall. But now Ragnall get two more thralls.'

'Who is Yarl?' asked Fenn.

'Yarl is title, not man. Like your king but more small.' Hakon held his hands apart then brought them together leaving a small gap between.

'Yarl Harald is Yarl of Ranriki. Ragnall ask him for ship and men.' He smiled. 'Haldor is Yarl Harald man. Yarl's ship need work – three or four days, then Haldor and other men go back to Borg, Yarl Harald village. Best you hide from Haldor till he go.'

Fenn felt some relief that Haldor would not be staying in Lognavik. The fact that Haldor was not from Ragnall's village explained some of the antagonism that existed between him and Ragnall. He decided not to pursue Yarl Harald for now and waved to include himself, Olgood and the Master.

'The brothers have gained three men, not two,' he said.

Hakon laughed and shook his head. 'No, christian not thrall. For now, he…' Hakon paused, searching for a word.

Olgood was alarmed. 'What is he?' he demanded, half rising.

Hakon laughed louder and waved his hand in a negative gesture.

'Not for offer like animals.' He paused, thinking and smiling broadly – the idea obviously amused him. 'He is treasure – no, he is…' Again he stopped and muttered to himself. Then he grinned. 'He is prize.'

'Prize? What do you mean – prize? Prize for what?' Olgood spread his hands with palms up, trying to grasp the meaning.

'I think…' began Master Nerian, and all eyes turned to him. 'I think he means I am a trophy.'

With that announcement, he lifted up his bowl and began to eat slowly and deliberately. Olgood subsided onto his bed, his brow still wrinkled in thought.

They finished the *skause* in silence. Master Nerian's status would soon become clear no doubt. Once again Fenn reasoned that as he could do nothing about it, it was useless to worry.

He shifted to the edge of his bed and looked across at Gisele. He pointed to himself, Olgood and Master Nerian in turn and said their names. She nodded at each name, repeating it aloud. She had trouble with 'Master Nerian' but achieved a resemblance. She smiled at Fenn to thank him. Her attractive smile reminded him of Yseld.

Gisele pointed at the platter on the floor and said something to Hakon.

'She say eat now, drink mead when warm.'

Olgood looked thoughtfully at Gisele, and asked Hakon: 'Did Gisele cook this food?'

Hakon repeated Olgood's question to Gisele. She nodded.

Olgood said: 'Please thank her from us.'

Hakon frowned, but talked to Gisele again. Gisele seemed startled by Olgood's comment, as if it were not what she expected, but then she smiled at him and he responded automatically with a broad smile of his own. The first time since Lindisfarne that anyone had cause to smile like *that*, thought Fenn.

Still looking at Olgood, Gisele shrugged and spoke a sentence to him.

'She say it is what she do,' Hakon said, spreading his hands in agreement.

Olgood nodded to her then took up the bread loaf and broke it in half giving one half to Fenn. He did the same with the cheese. Fenn broke his parts into three and gave a handful of bread and cheese to Hakon. He turned to give another to Kael. The youth accepted the bread and cheese with slow movements, all the while studying Fenn with an almost insolent stare, before dropping the bread and cheese into his lap and holding out his hand for a bowl of mead.

Fenn handed him a bowl then picked up his own. He leaned towards Olgood, raised the bowl and offered him a salute.

'We have a lot to learn, my friend, and I think we need to learn fast.'

CHAPTER SEVEN

Once a thrall, always a thrall…

On the morning after the 'feast', Olaf attached a rope to Master Nerian's collar and led him around the village like a dog. The Master described later how he had been dragged into several houses and displayed like a prize bull. People turned him around, felt his arms and legs, poked him in the stomach and stroked his hair. In one house he had been stripped to his underwear for the examination. Master Nerian withstood the treatment philosophically, saying he thanked God for every day he was still alive.

Later on that first morning, Fenn was sitting on the pier. The second ship, which must be Yarl Harald's ship, had been pushed up onto the beach a hundred yards from where he was sitting. The mast had been taken down and some men were working on the base. The steering oar had also been dismantled and was undergoing some repair.

It was a fine summer morning. A fresh breeze ruffled the surface of the inlet, but it was pleasantly warm. The air carried across the water had a fresh and salty smell that invited Fenn to breathe deeply and reminded him of times spent walking the beaches and coastline of Lindisfarne.

He and Hakon were waiting for Olaf to finish talking with some fishermen. Nets and fishing lines had been placed on board the three fishing boats and they were about to be launched.

Where the second ship had been tied to the pier yesterday, stood an unusual small boat Fenn hadn't seen before. It looked like a copy of the ship that had carried them to Lognavik – the same design but less than one-quarter the size. The ends were high-pointed and carved just like the larger vessels, but it was only wide enough for two people to sit in the centre and one at bow and stern.

When Hakon nudged him, he turned to see Askari and the man who had stood beside her on the pier when they had arrived, walking slowly down the beach toward the pier, the man was using his staff but walking steadily. Kael was following a short distance behind them and they were being observed by a small group of onlookers gathered in front of the buildings.

Suddenly Kael ducked and raised his hand to his head. Fenn saw that he had been hit by a stone, thrown by one of a pack of taunting boys standing behind him at the top of the beach. Kael inserted two fingers under his hat to feel his scalp and when he withdrew them Fenn could see they were bloody. With surprising speed, Kael ran directly at the group, singled out a stout lad much taller and broader than himself and, without pausing his stride, struck the boy on the nose with his fist, the impetus of his run adding weight to the blow. The startled boy fell onto his back and before he could recover Kael struck with his heel into the boy's groin. The boy let out an 'oof' sound then started a keen wailing like a hurt dog. Kael turned immediately and without looking back walked calmly down the beach to resume his position behind Askari, who had watched the incident unfold with a startled look that had soon turned to one of amusement.

Fenn had stood up when Kael had been hit, worried that the situation might get worse, but after Kael's swift resolution he resumed his seat. As Kael passed by, he looked at Fenn with an expression that was a mixture of satisfaction and a readiness to deal with whatever came next. Fenn couldn't be sure because it was so fast, but Kael may have winked at him. In any case, Fenn was impressed and nodded his support.

Kael, Askari and the man boarded the miniature ship. Kael sat in the stern with Askari on the centre seat and the man in the bow. When they were settled, Kael untied the mooring ropes and pushed the boat from the pier. Fenn and Hakon stood up to watch them go. The boat was rowed with paddles instead of oars and it headed upriver around the bluff.

'Boy foolish,' observed Hakon. 'Kael fight like demon when angry. I have seen before.' He snorted. 'That one not even like people to touch him.'

'It's not cold; does he always wear a hat?'

'Always.'

Hakon told him that Askari, the man, whom he named Thorvald, and Kael were returning to Askari's hut up the river where she prepared her medicines, potions and powders, but he didn't know where the hut was located as he had never been there.

'Ah. So Thorvald is the father of Ragnall and Olaf?'

Hakon answered: 'No, he not father – but like father,' and did not elaborate further.

Fenn would have liked to know more about the mysterious woman, Askari, but Hakon said she was very 'closed'. Fenn gathered he meant secretive. She only appeared in the village when needed or, like yesterday, to give thanks to the gods for the safe return of her sons.

Fenn commented dryly that Kael was also very 'closed', adding: '…and he needs to wash.'

Hakon laughed. 'I see your nose think Kael smell,' he said. 'Kael not wash here in Lognavik – when I ask he say water not good. Say only wash in clean water – a spring in hills. In Lognavik he always dirty. I not see him clean.' Hakon shook his head from side to side. 'He very strange. He think lot, say little.'

Fenn gave a grunt of amusement. He studied Hakon.

'Hakon, where are *you* from?'

Hakon sat down on the edge of the pier.

'I am born in Hedeby, in land of Danes,' Hakon said, swinging his legs under the pier. 'Hedeby large market town to south.' He waved his hand vaguely in that direction. 'My father trader in spices. We travel many places. He teach me your language.'

He looked at Fenn with an eager expression. 'I go your land before – to Northum-ba.' He stumbled over the pronunciation.

Fenn corrected him. 'Northumbria.'

'Yes, Northum-bria. Not to island – but we go Bebbanburgh Castle. You know castle I think. I see your island from castle.'

With sudden insight, Fenn wondered how much Hakon had told Ragnall about his experiences and travels in Northumbria, and how much they had influenced Ragnall's decision to attack Lindisfarne.

'How long have you been in Lognavik?' he asked.

'This my second Lognavik summer.' Hakon shrugged. 'But I am thrall for three summers.'

Fenn decided he could ask about the previous 'summers' later.

'And Gisele – and Kael?'

'Gisele from more south than me and I think east. She remember warm place. She say her family all killed in battle. She here many summers. Only small girl when taken.'

He stopped talking and stared up the river. Fenn was about to prompt him when he said: 'Kael here…' he paused, '…I think he say four summers. Ragnall buy or capture Kael and give to Askari, or Askari ask – I not know. I not see him much in Lognavik – only when Askari come from hills.'

'Where is he from?'

'I not know. He not say to me.'

Fenn thought for a moment and looked about to ensure they could not be overheard – and immediately felt foolish. Secrecy was unnecessary – nobody could understand him.

He asked Hakon: 'Have you thought of escape?'

Hakon snorted derisively. 'Over mountains? This country all mountains. Even Northmen not cross mountains, they sail around. They call mountains 'the keel', like upside-down ship. Whole country is keel. Very high, very steep. Which way you go? You not cross without ropes, boots, good clothes. They catch you.'

He pointed down the inlet toward the bay. 'And steal boat? Sail to home in small boat? That funny. You not get far by sea. You have seen them – they live on sea. They catch you.'

He paused. 'You escape – they catch – they kill – and…,' he shook his finger for emphasis, '…make sure you not die quick. Very bad try escape.'

Fenn leaned back against a post. He was sobered but not disheartened. It may be much more difficult than he first thought. He repeated to himself: 'Survive, learn, plan.'

Hakon said: 'If you like, I teach you Northmen language.'

'Thank you,' said Fenn, 'but I don't intend to be here long.'

Hakon stared at him then shook his head in bewilderment.

They relaxed and enjoyed resting in the morning sun until disturbed by Olaf's deep voice calling Hakon's name. Fenn opened his eyes to see Olaf beckoning them to follow him.

*   *   *

In the evening of the first day, when they had finished eating their meal, Ragnall appeared in the annex entrance, spoke a sentence to Hakon and left.

'Ragnall want talk with you, Fenn. Come,' said Hakon.

Fenn followed Hakon into the big room. He had heard people coming and going throughout the mealtime, but he was surprised at the size of the crowd in the room, sitting on several rows of benches that had been brought up to the fire. Ragnall and Olaf sat on one side and Fenn recognised Birgitta sitting next to Ragnall. Ragnall said something to her and she laughed and laid her hand on his cheek with affection.

Gisele was working at the table in the area Fenn thought of as the kitchen. There were broken loaves of bread, scattered pieces of cheese and platters with scraps of meat covering the table – the remnants of their meal. She looked up as they walked into the room and smiled but then she glanced anxiously at the assembled people, wondering what was about to happen.

Twenty or more men and women occupied the other benches circling the fire. Fenn saw that both Torsten and Haldor were among them. He recognised some Northmen that had been on his ship but there were many others he didn't know.

Fenn and Hakon were directed to a bench situated apart from the others.

When they were seated, Ragnall stood up and addressed the assembled crowd. When Hakon started to translate he was quieted with a sharp rebuke from Ragnall, who then continued to speak for some time. Finally, he turned to Fenn and talked to him directly. Hakon looked at Ragnall and at his nod, said: 'Ragnall talk about raid. He say good raid – all return. Much treasure, many thralls. Now ask if you can speak for other thralls from your land.'

Fenn considered this. 'That depends on what he wants to know,' he replied. Hakon translated.

When Ragnall spoke again, Hakon said: 'He want know about your country. He think you know things.'

Fenn did not see any point in lying to the Northmen. He did not know anything that would be useful if the Northmen wanted to attack his country in force, and they could easily check what he said with the other captives.

He said: 'I will tell him what I know.'

Ragnall asked questions about the climate and the land – especially it's suitability for farming – what types of farming did the land support? He asked about the people and their readiness, willingness and ability to fight. Here Fenn stressed he had no experience with fighting. Ragnall asked about the kingdoms that Fenn knew, Northumbria, Mercia and Wessex; about their kings – he had heard they were weak, was that true? How many people did they rule? Did they fight each other? What rivers did Fenn know and how deep were they? The questions continued and when Ragnall paused, someone would call out a question from the crowd.

Haldor said something loudly and derisively. Hakon didn't translate his words until Fenn looked at him with raised eyebrows.

Hakon shrugged. 'Haldor say he believe only half what you say.'

Fenn smiled and slowly nodded his head, hoping that would confuse Haldor still more.

When there was only low conversation and there had been no questions for a while, Fenn enquired: 'Can I ask a question?'

Hakon hesitated, but Ragnall tilted his head and Hakon repeated what Fenn had asked. There was a roar of laughter and loud comments. Ragnall smiled and pointing at Fenn, called out something to the room.

'He say you pup who barks at big dog,' said Hakon.

There was a crack of a whip as someone at the back of the room demonstrated what he thought should happen to the impertinent 'pup'. Ragnall quieted the noise and looked at Fenn. He rested his chin on his hand and stared at him, thinking, for several heartbeats. Then he nodded to Hakon. There was a murmur of protest but it died when Ragnall glanced sternly around the room.

Fenn said to Hakon: 'I want you to translate exactly what I say – not what you think I *should* say.'

Hakon licked his lips, drew in a breath and nodded.

Fenn directed his question to Ragnall. 'The people at the monastery were unarmed and no threat to you. Why did you kill them?'

When Hakon did not speak, Fenn turned to him. Hakon looked alarmed and shook his head firmly. 'They not like this question – may hurt…'

He was interrupted by Ragnall who spoke a command to him.

'Say it exactly,' reminded Fenn. 'Every word.'

He turned back to look at Ragnall while Hakon asked his question. He wanted to watch the big man's reaction. In a low voice Hakon translated Fenn's words. He extended his arms toward Fenn to reinforce that it was not himself speaking.

If the response before was loud, this one was deafening. Everyone in the room wanted to speak at once, and most were on their feet and waving their arms.

Ragnall had not risen. He met Fenn's gaze. The noise continued but eventually subsided as the people waited to see what Ragnall would do. Ragnall got to his feet. He pointed at Hakon who translated as he spoke.

'This pup think he has teeth. Think he can growl. Maybe he needs whip so he know who he is. But…' he paused to allow Hakon to catch up, '…I answer his question.'

Ragnall walked over to stand in front of Fenn. He towered over Fenn looking down at him from a huge height and blocking the firelight. He turned sideways so he could be heard by the others. Hakon translated in Fenn's ear as Ragnall talked.

'Some here think thrall should not ask questions. Thrall work *without* question. I say you ask because you not understand. You answer my questions, so I answer you.'

Ragnall took two paces so he crossed in front of Fenn. He paused in thought then again addressed the room. Hakon translated but Fenn watched Ragnall and converted Hakon's words into the speech Ragnall was giving.

'This land is at war,' Ragnall said. 'But this war is being fought not just by men but by the gods. We hear that the christian god is approaching our borders on every side. We know he is in your land and has taken your people. We know he says 'have mercy – let our enemies strike us and then forgive and be at peace'. Ha! This is the talk of a weak god who wants to run away and not fight. Our gods say *fight* if attacked, *kill* or be killed, take revenge if someone hurts your family or village – be *strong*!'

There were murmurs of agreement and Ragnall paused again. Fenn could see he was talking as much to the crowd as to him.

'We know our gods are strong,' Ragnall continued. 'They show us every day. When we decide to raid your land for gold and thralls – we also *prove* whose gods are stronger. We see that the christian god could not protect his priests and could not stop us from killing them. Our gods protected all of us...' he swept his arm around the room, '...and guided us home safely across the sea. This is how we know we have the favour of our gods.'

This was accompanied by shouts of agreement and thumps of feet on the floor. Torsten stood up, threw back his head and howled like a wolf. Ragnall waited for him to finish.

'There were some who tried to prevent us killing the priests. They were brave and I hope their god will welcome them to the great hall.'

Ragnall placed his hands on his hips and looked down at Fenn. He seemed to be saying – does that answer your question?

Fenn thought of Master Oswald and Master Wilfred. He looked directly at Ragnall.

'You killed many good men who were unarmed, had no quarrel with you and did you no harm. These are the actions of cowards and I am sure you will not profit from those deaths in this life or the next,' he said, as forcefully as he could.

He turned to stare hard at Hakon, whose face was pale but he set his chin and started to speak. Fenn turned back to Ragnall.

Hakon's last words were drowned by a furious roar from the crowd. Ragnall's eyes blazed. Olaf stepped forward, his hands raised in anger. Haldor leapt from his seat and rushed at Fenn, who stood up to defend himself, but Ragnall stepped into Haldor's path. Haldor tried to push around him and was met by Olaf. In the face of both brothers, he resorted to shouting and waving his arms threateningly with clenched fists. Many others were obviously agreeing with what he was saying.

'Haldor say you a problem,' said Hakon, close to Fenn's ear so he could be heard above the noise. 'Never be good thrall, always be problem. Others say you talk too much, insult them. Ragnall should get rid of you. Some say kill.'

Ragnall spoke forcefully to Haldor.

Hakon whispered: 'Ragnall say if you problem, you *his* problem and that is end of it.'

Ragnall waved dismissively at Hakon and Fenn who withdrew to the annex. The crowd remained noisy and angry with heated loud discussions.

Olgood and Master Nerian were waiting anxiously, concerned about the uproar and the angry shouting. Fenn first turned to Hakon, took him by the arm and asked: 'Did you tell them exactly what I said?'

Hakon smiled broadly and nodded with enthusiasm. 'Yes, I say true what you say. I enjoy to say your words. See their faces.'

Fenn explained what Ragnall had wanted to know. Then he told them the question he had asked and Ragnall's reply. Hearing the reason why the Northmen had slain the monks brought a cry of anguish from Master Nerian and Olgood opened his mouth in astonishment. Finally, Fenn repeated his statement condemning the killings and calling the Northmen cowards, and described the reaction from Ragnall and Haldor.

'Not wise, perhaps, but… well said,' said Olgood, and Master Nerian nodded and reached over to pat Fenn's shoulder.

The Master's eyes moistened and he said: 'My friends are gone. Brutally murdered.' He drew in a long breath and made the sign of the cross. 'Be with God in peace. I believe I shall not be long in joining them. So is my life written.'

His words sobered the mood in the annex, but they reminded Fenn of a comment the Master had made on the day of the raid. He gave the Master a moment and then asked:

'When we saw that the monastery had been set on fire, Master, you said it was foretold. What did you mean?'

Master Nerian hunched his shoulders. 'Ohh… I don't want to remember any more of that horrible day.'

He put his hands to his head and closed his eyes as if to shut out the thoughts. Fenn waited for his pain to ease. The Master breathed heavily in and out through his nose for a while.

When he was calm, he said quietly: 'I said those words because it was true.' He held out his hands. 'The raid on Lindisfarne – and all this…' he spread his hands wide, '…was foretold in the heavens – it's even more obvious now. We were given two clear signs immediately before these heathens attacked us. A mighty storm and the fiery dragon in the sky – both came from the north, warning us specifically of danger from that direction. We took no heed. We deserve what now befalls us.'

The next day, Hakon came into the annex late in the evening after helping Gisele who was still working in the big room. Fenn and Olgood were sitting together eating a soup of vegetables, trying to make it last. There may have been some meat in the soup but none had yet been found. Master Nerian had finished his soup and was sitting on an adjacent bed, murmuring his prayers.

Hakon crossed the room and crouched in front of Fenn and Olgood.

'Ragnall and Olaf talk. I learn about thralls from island,' he said. 'You want hear?'

Fenn and Olgood eagerly nodded, and Master Nerian came to join them.

'Most will soon be sold in thrall market – probably Hedeby.' Hakon glanced at Fenn who remembered that Hedeby was Hakon's home town.

Hakon continued: 'Ragnall and Olaf argue over this. Ragnall want sell thralls and gold soon, before winter. Olaf want keep his treasure to show people. He say he sell in spring. Ragnall say that is two voyages, need stock more than gold and jewels, but Olaf not change mind.'

Fenn drew in a breath. That meant the cover of the Lindisfarne Gospels would remain in Lognavik – at least until spring.

He said to Hakon: 'I'd like to know where Olaf keeps the items he stole from the monastery.'

Hakon was puzzled: 'I not know. I can ask Gisele if she know.'

Fenn nodded: 'Please.' He indicated Hakon should continue.

'Four thralls go with Haldor to Borg in two days. Woman who come with you – stay with Birgitta, but Birgitta sell man. Life can be bad for woman thrall but Birgitta will protect against men who... want her – if you have worry. Two or three others stay Lognavik. You two...' he waved his finger between Fenn and Olgood, '...stay here, Ragnall house, but priest...' he looked at Master Nerian, then shrugged and said: '...not sure.'

The three looked silently at each other, digesting what Hakon had told them. There was sadness that friends they knew well were to be sold like cattle, and frustration that they were powerless to do anything about it.

Master Nerian gave them a resigned look, made the sign of the cross and returned to his bed.

In the morning, Ragnall banged his fist on the annex entrance and beckoned them all outside. He led them past the pens and into the meadow where a large crowd was assembled. To Fenn, it looked like the whole town was here. He was suddenly apprehensive. Were the new thralls going to be subject to some sort of trial? He shared a glance with Olgood whose face showed he was thinking the same thing.

He moved close to Hakon. 'Do you know what's happening here?'

Hakon shook his head. 'I not know, but I think it is court.'

'Court? What do you mean?'

'Someone has done wrong. Court decide how to punish.'

Ragnall pushed through the crowd, clearing a way for his following thralls. When the last of the crowd parted, Fenn could see that the people were formed into a large circle and in the centre lay a man and a woman spread-eagled on the ground and staked at their feet and hands. The man was lying quietly but the woman was squirming against her bindings, her wild eyes searching the crowd.

Ragnall pointed to a place beside Olaf who stood with his arms folded. Birgitta stood beside him. She looked distastefully at the newcomers, but as Ragnall obviously wanted them here, she dismissed them and turned her attention to the two victims. Everyone wore a solemn expression.

It seemed to Fenn that if this was a trial, the verdict had already been given. Maybe the trial, if there had been one, had taken place elsewhere.

Ragnall spoke to the crowd. Hakon translated in Fenn's ear.

'These two guilty of…' Hakon shrugged and turned up his hands. He didn't know the English word. 'They found together, but each belong to other. Law say punishment for man is death, for woman nose cut off.'

Ragnall stopped and let his gaze roam slowly around the circle.

'I say both have committed same crime. Both are equal. Both should be punished equal.'

There were murmurings of dissent in the crowd – the beginnings of a protest. Ragnall silenced it by looking hard in the direction of any voice.

'I say both shall die. Anyone who disagrees – let him stand forward now.'

Olaf stepped forward to stand beside Ragnall. Fenn moved back, thinking Olaf was about to challenge Ragnall, but then realised Olaf was giving his brother support. The two brothers presented a formidable pair. If a challenge came it would need several men to have any chance of prevailing. Many men looked about but nobody moved.

Ragnall waited a moment more, then waved at the people to move back from the two lying on the ground. The circle parted and formed two lines. Fenn looked out into the open meadow and saw three men on horseback.

The woman screamed. She cried out, pleading and sobbing. The man was also talking but to himself or to his gods.

It took a moment for Fenn to realise what was about to happen. The men started their horses moving forward and gathered together until they were riding three abreast, heading down the channel formed by the witnesses. They increased their pace in unison until the horses were galloping but only at about half-speed. The woman was screaming continuously. The man had fallen silent.

The horses tried to avoid the obstacles on the ground but the men held them steady. Once they had passed over the bodies, the horses were wheeled about. The woman's screams of fear had changed to shrieks of pain. The man was still silent; he may have been already dead. Fenn wanted to block his ears but would not give the Northmen that satisfaction.

Three times more the horses galloped across the mangled remains until the features that stayed in Fenn's mind were the startling white of the bones and the brilliant red of the blood. Some blood flicked up by the horses' hooves had stained his tunic.

The crowd began to move away. Olgood had his arm around Gisele. She had averted her eyes by pushing her face into Olgood's side. When they started to walk back to the house, Fenn saw her face was streaked with tears.

'There are easier ways to deliver a sentence of death,' observed Fenn.

Hakon looked up at him. 'They are a cruel people.'

* * *

Yarl Harald's ship was made ready for sailing the next morning.

Fenn did not observe the departure but Hakon told him that there had been an argument between Haldor and Ragnall on the beach regarding the disposition of the plunder from the monastery. Hakon had a knack for gathering gossip and useful information – he said he just listened to conversations happening around him but Fenn suspected he was one of those people who was not noticed and could get close to open doors and gatherings by pretending to be occupied with some small task nearby.

'Haldor want bigger share but Ragnall say each man keep what he find,' related Hakon. In a confiding tone, he added with a smile: 'When we enter gates of monastery, Ragnall send Haldor to mill and workshop while he and Olaf go to church.'

The mention of the church made Fenn wince at the memory of his first meeting with Olaf and Ragnall. His hand reached up to touch his face.

Hakon told him that Ragnall and about a dozen Lognavik men had sailed with Haldor to attend a 'Thing' where they would discuss the raid with Yarl Harald, and bring back Ragnall's two thralls.

'A Thing? Is that what you said?' Hakon nodded. 'What's a Thing?' asked Fenn.

'Thing is Northman meeting where all can talk about anything and Yarl say who right when two people not agree,' explained Hakon. 'However, I think this Thing not end well.'

Fenn was intrigued. 'Why not?'

'I hear Harald greedy man. He not like Ragnall have more than him. He give one ship and some men. He will want half gold and half thralls, maybe more – you see. I think this is trouble. Ragnall go on raid, Harald stay home. Ragnall not want give half.'

Fenn would have liked to have been present at the Thing.

*   *   *

Some of Hakon's other predictions proved to be correct – about both the mead and the food. They had not been offered mead again but they were occasionally given ale. Unfortunately, it was a poor relation to the monastery ale – being overly sweet and watery.

Their subsequent food was also much plainer than the 'feast' of the first night. What food they received often depended on what remained after the Northmen in the big room had finished their meal, which meant it could be of dubious quality – the meat fatty and grisly, the fish smelly and the fruit bruised and rotten. Some relief from the poor quality was provided by Gisele who occasionally managed to smuggle good meat, fruit and eggs into the annex. This usually occurred when Ragnall and Olaf had drunk their fill of ale and were not as vigilant as usual. After the first time, Olgood asked Hakon what would happen if Gisele was discovered bringing the extra food to them.

'They punish. I not think Ragnall hit or use whip. Maybe no food for week.'

'She should not take the risk,' said Olgood. 'Tell her that. We can manage.'

'I already tell her is big risk,' Hakon answered. 'She just smile and say she do what she can.'

Hakon spoke to Gisele, conveying Olgood's concern. Gisele nodded and smiled at Olgood. They held each other's gaze for a long time.

Since the initial parade around the village, not much had been required of Master Nerian. Every few days he was called into the big room and presented to visitors, but he spent the rest of the time on his bed, mostly in prayer. He was not restricted from venturing outside the house but if he was noticed by children and even some adults like Torston, they would physically assault him and call out obviously insulting words which, even though he did not understand their exact meaning, were clear enough in their intention.

Olaf had taken Olgood up the river to a location where he and Ragnall were building a new ship. Olgood related that he was initially put to work cutting trees but, as the days passed and his skill was recognised, he was instead given the task of shaping and preparing the wooden planks. It was hard physical labour but Olgood was satisfied with the work and talked about the ship as the building progressed, declaring that he had learned a lot about the 'art of barbarian shipbuilding'. Olgood was as impressed by the ships of these Northmen as Fenn was about their seamanship. His shoulder continued to heal and did not cause him any discomfort.

The work required of Fenn was more varied. He was given any heavy or dirty farm work that the Northmen did not want to do, with Hakon often labouring at his side. He fed the pigs and herded the goats, sheep and cattle – this work was similar to his labours at the monastery with the exception that, although they were kept together, the animals had different owners and Fenn quickly learned he needed to be able to match animal and owner. He also cleaned out the barn, spread the cattle manure and dug it in among the crops. He built walls and fences and repaired thatching. He was shown how to plough – something he hadn't done at the monastery. He found he enjoyed it. The work reminded him of the precision needed in the scriptorium and he tried to keep his furrows straight and neat.

Fenn had not seen any of the others from the monastery since the day of their arrival so he was glad to meet Audrey by chance in the village when he was heading back from a day herding the cattle at the top of the valley. She was walking past him with her head bowed, carrying two fish threaded onto a thin rope in one hand and keeping close to the far wall of the alley. He recognised her out of the corner of his eye and reached out to stop her. Audrey recoiled with a cry and raised her free hand, her face an expression of terror.

Fenn released her arm quickly and said: 'Audrey, it's me, Fenn.'

Audrey stared at him for a moment and then her face relaxed and she drew in and let out a breath of relief.

'Oh, Fenn, it's you.' She gave a small embarrassed laugh. 'I'm sorry.' She looked up at him, eagerly. 'Have you seen...?' She stopped and seemed bewildered. 'I'm sorry,' she said again. 'I'm getting confused.'

Fenn smiled reassuringly and reached out to her again. 'Are you being treated well?'

'Well enough, I suppose, but it's lonely. There's nobody to talk to – nobody who can talk...' She trailed off and waved her hand vaguely.

'Are you staying in Birgitta's house?' Audrey nodded. 'Where is that? Maybe I can visit you.'

'It's high in the hills – a long walk.'

'I can ask where it is. I'll come to see you if I can.'

Audrey nodded again, without conviction. Fenn squeezed her hand but there was no answering pressure.

'Olgood's arm is...' began Fenn. He wanted to tell her that Olgood's arm had healed well thanks to the use of her needle but Audrey glanced over his shoulder, gave a small gasp and pulled her hand away.

She turned and continued up the alley without looking back.

Fenn stared after her and Birgitta brushed past him, casting a stern look over her shoulder as if rebuking him for delaying her thrall, but she did not stop. He watched as she caught up to Audrey and strode on by without pausing. Audrey had to quicken her pace to keep up.

In the annex, Fenn told Olgood he had met Audrey and confided: 'I'm worried about her. I'm sure she almost asked me again if I had seen her son Ames.'

Olgood shook his head sadly, but made no reply.

Fenn gave a heavy sigh of frustration. 'I'll ask Hakon where Birgitta's house is, and next time I'm herding in the valley I'll try to check on her.'

As each subsequent day passed, Fenn's expectations grew – firstly that Ragnall would return from Borg and, secondly, that he would be asked to do herding in the valley, so he could visit Audrey; but neither event occurred.

A week later, he was on the beach unloading a catch of fish into baskets when a horn announced a ship coming down the inlet. He continued working while the ship approached but paused to watch it pull alongside the pier and, just like before, push its bow lightly onto the beach. A man leaned over the rail to tie up the ship.

Ragnall jumped from the ship onto the pier followed by the other Lognavik men. Birgitta was waiting there to greet him and they embraced, Ragnall holding her with one hand, the other resting on his sword. Haldor stood in the ship and he called out loudly to Ragnall, pointing toward the village. Fenn was surprised at his tone – he seemed to be ordering Ragnall to do something. Fenn could see Ragnall was angry and people were running onto the beach, drawn by the ship arriving and by Haldor's shouts.

Ragnall drew his sword and pointed it at Haldor, shouting back at him and waving him away. He slashed at the two ropes holding the ship to the pier, causing the man tying the second rope to hurriedly jerk his hands out of the way. Birgitta called to some men and they pushed the ship off the beach. It drifted slowly away from the pier. Haldor was shouting angrily now, joined by many of the others on the ship, some shaking their fists. The men hurried to the oars and waited for Haldor's orders. Fenn could see Haldor was trying to decide whether to row to the beach and confront Ragnall. More people had now joined the crowd on the beach and the men had moved to the front, standing ready with their hands resting on their weapons.

Ragnall walked to the end of the pier, sword still drawn. He pointed to the north, held his sword above his head and bellowed forcefully at the still drifting ship. Even though he did not understand the words, the message was obvious to Fenn.

Ragnall was telling Haldor: 'Go home!'

Hakon came triumphantly into the annex that evening. He wore a large smile and strutted about the room while he delivered his news.

'I am prophet. It is as I say! Haldor talk to Yarl Harald about raid. Harald want more gold, more thralls – not give Ragnall thralls back. Ragnall not want trouble at Borg. He say yes. But in Lognavik, he say no.'

'What will happen now?' asked Fenn.

'They fight. Ragnall not obey Harald so Harald must come.'

'Ragnall doesn't seem worried.'

'Ragnall think it time for *him* to be Yarl.'

CHAPTER EIGHT

A bear encounter, and a revelation…

Weeks passed with no further action from Yarl Harald and the air became chilled with the quickening approach of winter. Ice formed in every damp place and the occasional flurry of snow whitened the ground but didn't last. They had been given cast-off woollen undershirts that Gisele had repaired where repair was needed. While these were very welcome in the cold nights; during the day even they did not provide sufficient protection from the malevolent cold thrust of the wind which seemed to gather force from the mountains and easily pierce their clothing. There was no allowance given if the day dawned with driving sleet or frigid winds; the work was expected to continue just the same. It was a constant struggle to keep warm and Hakon did not help by constantly reminding them: 'Winter not yet here.'

Fenn was digging peat for the fires on the day that Ragnall sailed for Hedeby to trade his captured thralls and gold, so he had no opportunity to say farewell to his fellow captives from the monastery. When he learned that Ragnall had departed and the purpose of his voyage, he felt a heavy sadness but he forced it aside. He could not change anything, so to dwell on it served no purpose.

Master Nerian found some slight relief from having to remain in the annex all day when Olaf decided he should help Gisele grind corn in the kitchen.

The Master was happy to help and did not understand that kitchen work was reserved for women and, for Olaf, it was a way of having the priest engaged in undignified labour.

Fenn had still had no opportunity to visit Audrey. He had been given the task of building a stone wall at one side of the pig enclosures, helped occasionally by Hakon. The wall was going to take another week or more to finish and he asked Hakon, who was still herding the cattle on some days, to check on her when he was next in the valley. Hakon had gone to Birgitta's house but Audrey had not recognised him and refused to talk to him.

Fenn was not supervised continually at the wall but at intervals a Northman – it varied as to which – would check his progress and either be satisfied or not. Fenn learned to just nod and agree with whatever they said.

Torston, in particular, gave him a bad time. The archer would insist Fenn move huge stones and then laugh at his struggle. He would tear down parts of the wall and watch them being rebuilt, looking for any misalignment. Fenn stoically did exactly what he was asked without complaint, and Torston eventually tired of the 'sport'.

With Gisele's help, Fenn fashioned some gloves for himself and Hakon from a tattered woollen blanket that Hakon had 'found', to protect their hands from the cold, sharp stones. The gloves saved the skin on their hands but that was only one of the difficulties. Apart from the physical effort, building the wall was disagreeable because of the foul smell from the pig pens. It was heavy, exhausting, unpleasant work that made Fenn even more reluctant to start each new day.

For the last week or more, Olgood had not been returning to the village at night. Instead he and Olaf were staying at the shipyard working on some part of the new ship that they wanted to be completed before winter.

On a particularly chilly day, just before sunrise, Torston had come to the annex as they were eating their morning meal of mashed oats. He ordered Hakon and Master Nerian outside.

Hakon returned a while later and came to Fenn with an anxious look on his face.

99

'Torston has christian cleaning pigs. He only do this because Olaf and Ragnall away.'

'How can you clean the pigs?' asked Fenn, concerned.

The pig enclosures and the pigs were always filthy and muddy. People disposed of food scraps and anything else they wanted to be rid of into the pens. The pigs trampled what they didn't eat into a foul-smelling, repulsive mixture that was difficult to approach, let alone work in.

Fenn was expected to resume work on the wall at sunup, so he left the annex. Walking down the entranceway he could hear the noise of people gathered outside. He shivered and wrapped his arms around himself. The scene that appeared was lit by the red and yellow glow in the sky that preceded the rising sun.

Torston was standing at the pig enclosure, casually resting against the fence. Several other townspeople were also there, looking into the enclosure. They had the appearance of an audience watching a travelling show of dancers – clapping and calling out appreciatively. Fenn couldn't see past the small crowd, so he walked around the side of the pen and found a space to look through.

Master Nerian was not cleaning the pigs – he was being forced to clean the filthy floor of the pig pen. He was kneeling in one corner of the pen and, using a hand-sized cooking ladle, was transferring the foul mess into a bucket. His arms and clothing were already covered in the filthy muck from the pen. The pigs had been moved to an adjacent pen but were curious and were pushing their snouts through the fence, snuffling and trying to catch hold of Master Nerian himself or his ladle with their teeth. Even if what he was attempting was possible, the tool was completely unsuited for the task, and Fenn realised at once that the affair had been staged by Torston to humiliate and degrade the Master. Even the pigs were actors in Torston's show.

Torston called out to Master Nerian and some people in the crowd laughed.

'He say he want to see dry earth,' explained Hakon at Fenn's side.

'We must stop this,' declared Fenn.

'How? We cannot interfere.'

Fenn thought for a moment and said: 'Can you count slowly to twenty then make a noise so everyone looks your way?'

'I… I… yes… I think.'

'Good,' said Fenn. 'Start counting now.' He moved away, circling around the pig pens.

Hakon paused in a moment of indecision, then started counting.

When he reached twenty, he shouted out as loud as he could, repeating a phrase several times.

It had the desired effect. All heads turned to him and he pointed at the sun now rising over the mountains.

Fenn arrived at the adjacent pig enclosure and crouched by the gate. When Hakon's shouts came he reached up, quietly unlatched the gate and pushed it wide. He crouched back down and, keeping to the shadows, continued along the side of enclosures to where he was building the wall. He could hear Hakon still calling out. He unwrapped his sling from his belt, felt about for a broken piece of stone, then stood, looked quickly about to ensure nobody was looking his way, whirled his sling and sent the stone into the rump of the pig nearest the gate. The pig squealed in pain and started to run, noticed the open gate and dashed for freedom. Another stone on another rump and soon all of the pigs were scattering into the pasture, squealing loudly.

There were shouts as the escaping pigs were noticed and the crowd dissipated as people set out to recapture their animals.

Fenn replaced the sling on his belt, and bent to place a stone on the wall.

He looked up after a few moments to see that Torston, his audience gone, had given up his humiliation of the Master and was wandering away muttering angrily to himself. Master Nerian got to his feet and looked around, baffled. He walked hesitantly toward the house, shaking his arms to rid himself of the bulk of the mud and filth sticking to his clothes.

A little while later, Hakon joined Fenn at the wall, and they resumed working where they had left off the previous evening.

'Thank you, Hakon. I know I put you in a difficult position.' Fenn paused. 'I'm curious. What did you shout?'

'I shout nonsense. I shout: 'Baby in the sky' and point at sun. People not understand. They think me crazy.'

Fenn smiled. 'I'll tell Master Nerian how you helped him.'

Hakon nodded, then he laughed. 'You know what is best thing?'

Fenn looked at him, puzzled. 'What?'

'They say to Torston he not close gate when he move pigs.'

Fenn laughed out loud. That pleased him and for some time afterwards the work did not seem quite so bad.

*   *   *

At mid-morning a few days later, Fenn was completing the last part of the wall. He could see the end was near but there was still a lot to do, especially without Hakon who was again herding in the valley – but he could possibly finish the wall today. He looked up at the sound of someone approaching and was surprised to see Olaf who had never before concerned himself with the building of the wall. The huge Northman motioned for Fenn to stop work and follow him. Fenn had a stone in his hand and made to place it on the wall, but Olaf indicated he should just put the stone aside and beckoned urgently again.

Fenn followed Olaf to the beach. They waited at the pier with Olaf looking impatiently about. After a while Ragnall appeared. Fenn had not heard that he had returned from his voyage south and was surprised to see him. He strode swiftly down the beach followed by Hakon. Hakon came up to Fenn and stopped, panting, beside him. When he didn't speak right away, trying first to catch his breath, Ragnall took him by the shoulder and spoke one word sternly to him, waving his hand at Fenn.

'Ragnall say you go with them. Bear has been seen.' Hakon paused for a breath. 'Will be fat for winter. Good catch. You not hunt – help with meat and skin. Ragnall, Olaf not want others to know where is bear and you not tell.'

He asked a question of Ragnall, then shrugged and said: 'I not come.'

Fenn wondered where Olgood was if not with the brothers, but he had no time to ask this of Hakon as Olaf directed his attention to a small boat that was tied at the pier. It was like the one that Kael had taken up the river. It may have been the same vessel. Olaf nudged him toward it with his hand; the brothers were in a hurry to depart.

When they reached the boat, Olaf pointed to the centre seat and Fenn climbed aboard. Lying on the floor were two thick-shafted spears with leaf-shaped iron points and in the bow lay two battle axes, their hafts wound with strips of leather, dyed red, which Fenn knew was Ragnall's colour. They were the axes that hung on the wall inside the entrance to Ragnall's house. If these were the weapons that would be used to kill the bear, Fenn was impressed. He had never seen a bear, but Master Oswald had described one once and mentioned that it was the only animal not afraid of man.

He sat on the centre seat and Olaf pushed past him to the bow. Fenn felt the stern dip as Ragnall stepped in. They immediately pushed off and with powerful strokes they left the pier. Fenn looked around but Hakon was already nowhere to be seen. He searched for a paddle, not sure if he should be rowing, but there were none in sight and it did not seem to be expected of him.

They rounded the bluff and continued up the river. In the five months since arriving in Lognavik, Fenn had never been this far upriver from the village and was interested to see that the banks were steep and heavily forested on both sides. The river was like a smaller version of the inlet, its sides just as rugged and rocky.

The river took a meandering course, so he could never see more than a few hundred yards ahead. After a while, Fenn saw they were approaching a break in the rocky bank where a large flat area had been cleared in the forest. The partially built hull of a ship under construction was visible in the centre of the clearing. As far as he could tell, this ship was even larger than the ones that had brought him to Lognavik. This was obviously where Olgood worked and Fenn was looking forward to seeing him again. It had been almost two weeks since his friend had been in the village.

To his surprise, however, they didn't approach the clearing but paddled steadily by. Fenn searched the faces of the men he could see working on the ship but Olgood was not among them. He may be working in the forest. Some men waved at them but the brothers did not pause in their rowing to reply.

When the shipyard had moved out of sight, Fenn resumed his study of the surrounding land. The brothers paddled rhythmically and tirelessly as they passed bend after tree-covered bend where the only change was in the steepness of the sides. Once again Fenn marvelled at the majesty of the tall cliffs towering over them, making them seem insignificant. They were definitely the intruders in this untamed and primitive land.

They entered a gorge where the water flowed more swiftly. The boat was steered out of the main flow of the river and directed to one side of the gorge. Even so, the extra work required to maintain their progress brought the occasional grunt of effort. Fenn thought he may be asked to relieve someone but the request didn't come. They wanted to get to their destination as quickly as possible.

Once through the gorge, the landscape changed dramatically, becoming a panorama of rolling hills on both sides with mountains visible on the skyline. The forest thinned, with the floor no longer coloured the brown of fallen leaves and bare earth – instead it was covered with the green of grass and low bushes. Fenn could see some open glades. This was more like Northumbrian forest, he thought. He scanned the mountains, looking for a break or a low ridge, but they were unrelenting, huge and formidable, enclosing the land inside an impenetrable barrier. In spite of this he continued to study the terrain, wanting to learn everything he could about this part of the country.

Reluctantly, Fenn admired the performance of these two huge men. They had scarcely slackened their pace since leaving the pier. Part of the display probably arose from competition between them – he was sure neither would want to be the first to show tiredness. Even so, the demonstration of sheer strength and endurance was impressive.

Up ahead, Fenn could see a shingle beach where a group of four people were waiting. As they drew closer, it became clear that the beach was their destination and two of the people resolved into Askari and Thorvald. Kael was standing behind Askari who was holding the hand of a small blond-haired girl. Kael and Askari were engaged in earnest conversation, with Kael seeming agitated and Askari calming him.

The ship grounded on the beach. Olaf turned and indicated that Fenn should get out. He stepped on to the beach and moved out of the way as Thorvald handed Olaf a heavy bag and a skin of water. Thorvald pulled an axe from his belt. Instead of leather, the haft of Thorvald's axe was wound with strips of metal that looked like iron. Thorvald offered the axe to Ragnall who acknowledged it but waved it away. They exchanged a few words, then Thorvald pointed upriver and used movements of his hand to indicate some location, probably the last sighting of the bear.

Olaf dug his paddle into the shingle and pushed the boat back into the river. Fenn watched Ragnall and Olaf pick up the same rhythm as they steered the boat into the flow.

The first thing that struck Fenn when he looked at Kael was that he was clean. The second was that he was not wearing his hat which revealed the surprising colour of his short hair. It was red, the colour of clouds at sunset. He looked like a different person.

Askari beckoned to him with a friendly wave. Hakon had said that Fenn would not be hunting so he reasoned he was to wait with Askari until the brothers returned, when he would presumably be picked up again to help with the skinning and butchering. Fenn had no doubt that Ragnall and Olaf would succeed in their hunt – they seemed capable of anything.

The young girl holding Askari's hand looked to be between four and seven years old. She was staring up at Fenn with wide eyes and an open mouth. He obviously passed whatever appraisal she was giving him, because she silently held out her small hand and he automatically took it in his. Askari smiled, but Kael looked suspicious. The girl, though, was satisfied that Fenn had behaved correctly and held tightly to two of his fingers. She turned her gaze to Askari saying as clearly as if she had spoken: 'Can we go now?'

Askari indicated the girl with her head and said a few words which ended in '…Agatha.'

Fenn looked down at the child, smiled, and used his other hand to touch his chest: 'Fenn.'

The girl smiled but did not try to repeat the name as Fenn expected. She impatiently shook a head of blond curls then, pulling on Fenn's fingers, she circled around Askari and started to walk up a path that led away from the beach, leaning forward to drag Askari and Fenn behind her. The medicine woman exchanged a knowing smile with Thorvald.

Agatha led the way up a long winding path which steadily climbed upwards into the foothills and twisted back on itself several times until they reached a place that looked like a dead end. Agatha dutifully let Thorvald past and he pushed aside a thicket of vines to reveal an opening into a large secluded clearing in the forest.

Ringed by tall trees and a thick forest belt, a small hut stood in an idyllic setting on the far edge of the clearing. A stream cascaded down the hill behind the hut and ended in a small waterfall which fell into a pool of water. This overflowed into a continuation of the stream, which crossed the clearing and disappeared into the forest on its way to the river. Fenn thought it likely that this pool was the spring Hakon had mentioned, that Kael considered clean enough to bathe in. He looked again at the surprising colour of Kael's hair. It was short but fine. Fenn wondered if Kael was somehow ashamed of its colour and so wore a hat in Lognavik.

A garden of herbs and vegetables stood between the pool and the hut, and a small storage building was attached to the hut on the other side. There was another building behind the hut that looked like a barn but Fenn could not see it distinctly.

On the river Fenn had felt cold and continually damp although the day was clear but here in the clearing, sheltered by the trees, it was sunny, dry and warm. He turned slowly in a circle. The forest was dense at the clearing's edge and, if he hadn't known the clearing existed, he could have walked past a few yards away and missed it.

Agatha led them up a few steps onto a landing. Askari opened the door and invited him inside.

The interior was a single room. A place for a fire had been built into a side wall, but the fire was not lit. The only pieces of furniture were beds that doubled as seats around the other walls and a solid table on one side of the fire. There were curtain dividers separating the far wall, where most of the beds were placed, into three areas – one for Askari and Thorvald, the others for Kael and perhaps Agatha. On a set of wide shelves beside the fire were many containers containing plants, leaves and sticks and various other items. Fenn could see that some containers were made of glass, with liquids and powders of different colours inside.

Askari removed her hand from Agatha's and went to the fireplace, calling to Kael who followed her. Agatha held tightly to Fenn to prevent him from also letting go. Fenn knelt beside Agatha, pointed at her and held up a fist. He released his fingers one by one, pointing alternately at the new finger then back to her, with a questioning look on his face. Agatha understood immediately, and when he released the last finger on his hand she grabbed it to show she was five years old, jumping up and down. Fenn remembered Hakon counting the years as 'summers'.

'So she has seen five summers,' he thought. He laughed and expected her to join him but Agatha just smiled broadly, nodding and holding tight to his finger. She turned her head to check on Askari and Kael.

As if that had been a silent call, Kael turned around holding a platter of cheese in his hands. He walked toward Fenn and stopped in front of him offering the platter. Fenn gallantly waved his hand indicating that Agatha should choose first. Agatha smiled, and took a deliberately long time making her choice, moving her hand over several pieces before choosing the biggest. Fenn could not help but smile. He looked at Kael to see if he also found it amusing, and found himself under silent scrutiny, just like on the night they had first met. He smiled weakly, not understanding the reason for this close study. Agatha picked another piece and offered it to Fenn which he accepted with exaggerated grace and a bow, saying '*Thokk*' – one of the words he knew despite his reluctance to learn the language. Agatha beamed at his actions and jumped a few times in delight.

So far he had only heard Askari speak. Perhaps the others had taken a vow of silence, as he knew the monks sometimes did.

Askari was lighting the fire. Agatha led Fenn to a seat beside the table. Thorvald took his axe from his belt and placed it on a hook by the door where his staff was also standing, then he disappeared out the door. Fenn studied the axe. It was the first one he had seen with an iron handle. It was obviously the work of a true craftsman being both beautiful and lethal at the same time.

Thorvald returned with an armload of wood. When the fire was well alight, Askari offered Fenn some milk to wash down the cheese. He nodded his thanks and wondered about the source of the milk and cheese as he had not seen any animals.

After a while, Thorvald went back outside and Agatha followed him. Kael was keeping his distance, never coming close – another example of his strange behaviour. When Kael and Askari were together by the fire, Fenn tried using his hands to ask them what he could do to help, but he only succeeded in making them both laugh at his antics. It was the first time he had seen Kael smile.

He looked around to see if there was any task that needed doing but the room was tidy and nothing was out of place. Maybe he could help Thorvald get more wood. At the door he heard running feet on the landing and narrowly avoided being knocked aside as Thorvald ran past him, shouting '*Bjorn! Bjorn!*'

Fenn stared horrified at the scene outside.

Agatha was sitting in the centre of the clearing, playing with daisies, holding one in each hand and smelling them alternately. Behind her, a large brown bear had pushed into the clearing from the forest. It was walking forward with a swinging motion, its great head casting about and its snout sniffing the air. Fenn could hear the explosive sounds of its snuffling and growling from where he stood.

For some reason Agatha had not noticed the bear. Why wasn't she afraid of the sounds of a wild animal behind her? He called out a warning:

'Agatha!'

As if reading his thoughts, a voice in his ear said in perfect English: 'She cannot hear; she is deaf.'

The bear raised itself on its back legs and roared, then lumbered toward the child.

Fenn acted without thinking. He leapt down the steps and ran toward Agatha, shouting at the bear. When he appeared in its vision, the bear checked its motion momentarily, before walking forward again, slower, but still advancing, its growls increasing in volume. Unused to being challenged, what may have been curiosity had now turned to anger.

Fenn reached Agatha, who looked up at him with a smile. He stepped around her, unwinding his sling, placing himself between the girl and the bear. The bear was thirty yards away, moving steadily and confidently, growling continuously and shaking its massive head, the thick fur on its neck twisting back and forth. Fenn remembered Master Oswald's words: '…the only animal not afraid of man.' He dared not take his eye off the bear and felt frantically on the ground at his feet for something to use in the sling. He found only grass and soft earth. The bear had closed to twenty yards.

A hand grasped his wrist from behind and thrust an object into his fingers. It felt like a round stone with good weight but he had no time to check. Automatically he placed it in the pouch and swung his sling. At fifteen yards the stone struck the bear on the snout just in front of the eyes, causing a howl of pain and anger to erupt from the animal. Another stone was placed in his hand. The bear stood up again, waving its huge paws, slashing the air with claws as long as knives and then it crouched, gathering itself to leap the remaining distance.

Fenn's sling whirled and he put all his effort into the throw, loosing as soon as the sling gained speed, but before he had time to aim properly. More by chance than skill, this stone hit the bear full on the end of the nose from a distance of ten yards. The blow would have killed a man, and the bear howled mightily again, swiping at its injured snout with its paws. It abruptly turned and ran for the forest, making loud whuffing sounds. Fenn watched it crash into the forest. He slowly released a breath he hadn't realised he was holding.

After several thumps of his pounding heart, he couldn't hear the bear any longer. He replaced his sling on his belt and turned to pick up Agatha. He found Kael was standing on his left with Agatha in his arms. Thorvald was also there, his iron axe raised in his hand. The old man was shaking and Fenn reached out to put a hand on his shoulder. Thorvald had obviously been scared out of his wits but had faced the bear and stood his ground. Fenn knew he would have been afraid too, if he'd had time to think. Thorvald nodded, took some deep breaths to calm himself and lowered his axe. Askari stood on the landing, her hands at her mouth, tears running down her face.

Agatha was still smiling and holding her flowers. Kael must have held her so she couldn't see the bear. He also realised it was Kael who had talked to him on the landing. For a time, they stood just looking at each other, then Fenn released his hand from Thorvald's shoulder and the old man turned and walked quickly back to the hut, with Kael following. Fenn caught up to Kael.

'Who are you?'

Kael glanced at Askari and Thorvald but they were occupied with each other. He kept walking towards the hut but turned his head to Fenn, then cast his eyes upward in exasperation and sighed.

'I will explain, when we're alone – not now.'

'But… you can speak English.' It was both a statement and a question.

'Not now,' Kael repeated.

He moved ahead of Fenn, up the steps to the landing and handed Agatha to Askari, who fussed and comforted the girl, although of the two she was the one more in need of comfort.

Fenn stood at the bottom of the steps, trying to make sense of what had happened.

'Where did he get the stones?' he asked aloud. He was talking to himself, but Kael heard.

The strange youth gave a brief smile, and mouthed: 'Later…'

He went inside the hut behind Askari and Thorvald.

Fenn watched them go, turned for a long look around the clearing, and followed.

That had been too close. He resolved never to be without stones again.

*　　*　　*

Thorvald handed Fenn a drinking horn of mead and Fenn nodded his thanks. He knew mead was only drunk on special occasions and had to agree it was an appropriate time. He had a tingling feeling in his shoulders and arms which was probably a reaction from the encounter. He wanted to sit down but they were all standing in the middle of the room and he thought it may not be polite. He was unsure of his status here. He tipped the horn up, took a long drink, felt the warm liquid flow down his throat and gave a sigh of relief as he felt the tension leave him. He wiped his mouth with the back of his hand.

Askari came and stood in front of him. Tears welled in her eyes again. She took him by both arms looking into his eyes. She spoke with a jerky voice, saying something so heartfelt she had trouble getting it out, then she hugged him tightly. Fenn could see Kael over Askari's shoulder standing with his arms folded and thought he might offer a translation, but he saw that Kael also had tears in his eyes. Kael gave a small shake of his head and looked away. Fenn put his arms around Askari and hugged her back. Only when Agatha walked across the room and hugged one each of their legs, did Askari pull away. She picked up the girl and gave her a smile and a kiss on the cheek. Agatha traced Askari's tear-stained cheek with a finger. Askari looked at Fenn again and made some sign in front of him with her free hand, then she went to a bed and sat down with Agatha on her knee.

Thorvald took her place and stood awkwardly before Fenn. He wanted to talk but knew Fenn would not understand. He struggled, then looked at Kael. Kael hesitated but came to stand beside Thorvald. Thorvald turned his face to Fenn and talked to him with an impassioned voice. When he had finished, he grasped Fenn's forearm firmly, which Fenn reciprocated.

Kael said: 'Thorvald thanks you for saving the life of his daughter Agatha, and for saving his life and...' he paused, '...and mine. He salutes you as a brave and worthy warrior. He would be proud to stand with you in battle.'

Thorvald waited for Kael to finish then formally took a step back, stood very straight and smartly crossed his right arm over his body, thumping his chest with his fist. Fenn felt Thorvald deserved respect so he repeated the salute back. Thorvald hesitated, surprised, then nodded.

Thorvald invited him to sit and refilled his drinking horn while Fenn watched Askari and Kael play with Agatha. They had a woollen animal which they hid for her to find. He was observing Kael in a rare unguarded moment. He looked different and did not display the withdrawn nature and hard exterior he previously had. He turned his attention to Agatha.

Looking at the child, Fenn had the sudden thought that she was as old as his brother Mikhael had been when he died. That connection led him to think that today somehow, through Fenn, the life that had been taken from Mikhael had been given to Agatha. He knew the idea was irrational, but it gave him an intense feeling of satisfaction and comfort.

He tilted back his head and took a long draught of mead.

*   *   *

Fenn expected Ragnall and Olaf to arrive at the hut before nightfall but at sunset there was no sign of them.

Askari prepared some *skause* and, in stark contrast to his recent meals, it was full of tender meat with the unmistakable flavour of mutton. Some mixture of herbs made the taste very rich. She broke some bread and pushed it into his hand. Fenn thanked her sincerely, dipping the bread and savouring every mouthful. Askari watched him eat, nodding when he displayed his appreciation. When he finished, without asking she filled his bowl again and watched him eat that as well.

Fenn's stomach felt tighter than it had in months and he had to graciously refuse a third offering.

It seemed the house intended to retire early. When the meal had been cleared away, the fire was left to die and Askari and Thorvald sat together in the fading firelight talking softly. Kael went to one of the other enclosures.

Agatha insisted on staying with Fenn and curled up beside him with her play animal, her tiny hand resting on his arm. Fenn lay on his back, staring at the roof and reviewed the day.

Just as his existence had been forming into a similar routine day by day, depressingly hard and dreary though it had been; this day had come to jolt him from that pattern. He knew they were all very lucky. If the bear had reached them, its huge strength, teeth and claws would have wrought terrible damage, possibly killing them all. His life could be thought of as a series of lucky and unlucky turns and, on this day especially, he wondered how much he was really in control and how much was the whim of fate.

A little while after Agatha fell asleep, Askari came and fetched her to her own bed.

He woke to a hand on his shoulder and a touch on his lips. Kael beckoned him outside, reinforcing the need for silence with a finger to his own lips.

112

Fenn followed quietly through the door. Kael walked around the corner of the hut and sat down beside the pool. In the gentle breeze the water was shivering in the moonlight. The clear night carried the breath of winter but the softness of the wind ensured that, although the air was chilled, it was not unpleasant. Fenn felt a need to carefully check the clearing before sitting beside Kael.

Kael spoke: 'What I tell you now, please do not repeat – even to Hakon or your friends.'

Fenn nodded, but when Kael did not continue, he nodded again more forcefully.

'I will keep your confidence,' he said.

'I have to trust you.' Kael looked down into the pool and trailed a hand in the water. 'If I tell you what I have so carefully hidden, I may be placing my life in your hands for the second time today.'

Fenn thought Kael was being dramatic, but there was no doubting his sincerity. He remained silent, waiting.

'You probably thought me strange, when we first met.' Kael looked at Fenn's face for confirmation of the statement. 'And probably since then, too.'

'I find everything strange,' said Fenn, spreading his hands to include his surroundings.

Kael looked at the pool again, then spoke softly and calmly.

'While you are here at this hut, there is one thing I cannot hide for long.' He breathed deeply. 'The first thing you do not know...' Kael looked at him, '...*probably* do not know...' he paused again, '...is that I am female – a girl. The second thing – which you may have already guessed – I am from the same land as you.'

Fenn could not have been more astonished. His mouth fell open and his hands dropped to his sides.

'You will not believe me if I told you about my father, so I'll leave that till later,' Kael continued. 'I was taken from a beach near to where I was staying, four years ago. They thought I was a boy and I knew if they realised I was female it would be bad, so I hid that fact.'

Kael waited to give Fenn a moment to absorb what she had said.

'Although he wasn't the one who captured me, I was eventually claimed by a huge man, Ragnall, as payment for a debt I think – I didn't speak the language then. I thought it was a stroke of luck to be given to Askari on my first night in Lognavik, but that was Ragnall's plan from the time he owned me. His mother needed a thrall.'

'Askari saw through my disguise immediately; she's very perceptive. As soon as we came to this hut, she let me know she wasn't fooled, but I think she instinctively also knew why I had disguised myself.'

'When Askari goes to Lognavik, and needs me to take her down the river. I bind myself...' she indicated her chest, '...and keep myself dirty to discourage people from getting too close, and I always wear a hat. I know the colour of my hair alone would arouse interest.'

Kael had been leaning on one arm, but now she sat up.

'My real name is Kaela. I shortened it to be more masculine. I am pleased to meet you, Fenn.' She held out her hand.

Fenn looked at it and back at her, before reaching out to accept her handshake.

He closed his mouth.

'I was surprised to see you arriving with Ragnall. If I'd known you were coming, I would have prepared for you, and we possibly wouldn't be having this conversation. Thorvald and Addo know I'm a girl, and so, recently, do Ragnall and Olaf.' Kaela laughed. 'It was a surprise to them, but they've accepted it now. They won't risk disapproval from their mother. Oh... and Birgitta knows too. But nobody else.'

Fenn said: 'Addo?'

Kaela looked blank, and then replied: 'Of course. You haven't met Addo. He took the goats and sheep up to the high valley to keep them safe when the bear was seen. He'll bring them back in a few days. Addo is a beautiful person, but...' she searched for the right phrase, '...weak in the head. Another foundling from the forest.'

When Fenn looked puzzled, Kaela explained that both Agatha and Addo, as was the custom with disabled or deformed children, had been abandoned in the forest as new-borns for the gods to decide their fate. Askari had rescued these two and raised them as her own.

114

'Agatha is Birgitta's child, and Birgitta visits when she can. The arrangement is best for everyone. When she found out that Agatha was alive – well, it's difficult to describe her reaction. A mixture of guilt and joy and overwhelming relief. She travels here over the mountains and I walk in the hills with her.'

Her expression became serious. 'Nobody must know about Agatha and Addo. If some people knew they were alive, they may say Askari interfered with the will of the gods. Ragnall and Olaf brought you with them because you cannot tell anyone.'

Fenn nodded. Hakon had said the same thing.

'But isn't Askari's action in saving the children also the will of the gods?'

Kaela shook her head. 'It's more complicated than that.' She looked at Fenn, and changed the subject.

'I'd like to ask you a question.'

Fenn nodded.

'Why did you stand against the bear? You don't know Agatha. When the bear came close, why didn't you run?'

Fenn countered with a question of his own: 'Why didn't *you*?'

'Agatha is a sister to me, I couldn't leave her.'

'But when you had her in your arms, you could have taken her away to safety.'

Kaela did not reply right away. She stared into the pool.

'I also couldn't let you face the bear alone. Perhaps with two of us and Thorvald coming we might have scared it away – I don't know, it was foolish. But you – from the start you didn't hesitate. You protected Agatha by putting yourself between her and the bear – I think you would have died trying to stop the bear from reaching her. It was the bravest thing I've ever seen and I thank you with all my heart, just as Askari did.'

Fenn snorted. 'Me?' He reached out and put his hand on her shoulder, then, remembering her revelation of a few moments ago, quickly removed it. Kaela smiled, which Fenn briefly returned but then his face became serious and he pointed at her to reinforce his words.

'You stood, completely unarmed, with a child in your arms that you were protecting from even *seeing* the bear. And you stayed when the bear was only yards away.' He paused. 'I know who showed true courage at that moment and I know who saved us all. That was the person who stood beside me and gave me two stones just when I needed them.'

'I was terrified.'

'So was I.'

They both smiled at the same time and looked away, slightly embarrassed.

'Where did you get the stones? They were perfect.'

'I gave Agatha a bucket of sand and she made a face on the top with some sticks and those stones were the eyes. From the river.'

'But how...?'

'I picked them up as I followed you from the hut. I thought I could throw them at the bear.'

'*Throw* them at the...?' Fenn laughed at the absurdity. 'That would be like throwing an arrow.'

He laughed again and Kaela laughed with him. It became infectious and they were unable to stop. Trying not to make too much noise, they continued laughing until their eyes were watery.

When Fenn had recovered, he asked: 'So there were only two.'

'Yes.'

'And if I had missed and needed another?'

She shrugged and drew her finger across her throat, and for some reason that was funny also and they laughed again.

Fenn became serious: 'What will happen now that Askari and Thorvald know I have a sling.'

'You've given them the gift of Agatha's life – a gift they can never repay. They will say nothing. You have their protection as much as they can give it. After today, they'll never do or say anything that would cause you trouble.'

Fenn contemplated this with a feeling of relief. He had been worried that he would have the sling taken from him and he would definitely prefer to keep it, for just such an occasion as today.

He had another thought. 'But what about the bear?' he asked. 'How can they tell Ragnall about the bear being here without mentioning my sling?'

'I'll talk to them. They'll work something out, I'm sure.'

Fenn was still worried but he forced himself to let it go. He had the wild thought that he was putting his fate in the hands of the Northern gods.

He searched for a change of subject and asked: 'Why didn't you tell me earlier that you spoke English?'

'Ah...' Kaela thought for a moment about her reply. 'Here, I never need to, so it's not important and – in Lognavik – I thought it best to keep silent.'

'Why?'

'It was possible the Northmen who captured me didn't know where they were. To me it looked as though they were lost. If they or other Northmen discovered that I spoke the language of a place they planned to raid, I might be taken away from Askari and forced to join the summer raids like Hakon. I thought it best not to remind anyone. I tried to learn their language and I had a good teacher.'

'I understand. That was wise.'

They sat in silence watching the pool. Kaela had slipped her feet into the water, although it must have been cold, and her movement was causing ripples on the surface. The night had cooled. Fenn could feel it in his shoulders but he wanted to learn as much as he could.

He looked at Kaela. In the moonlight, he realised how feminine she looked. Fenn prided himself on his observation and could not understand how he could have missed the signs that were now unmistakeable. She had a softness about her...

Kaela looked up and caught Fenn watching her. He looked quickly away, embarrassed, but she just snorted with amusement and smiled at him. He had thought Kael's eyes were dull and wary but Kaela's were bright and warm – and very deep.

He asked: 'Can you tell me how you were captured?'

He waited while Kaela organised her thoughts.

She told him she had been in a town called Dorncester near the coast when word had come that three ships had landed on the long beach that joins the Portland peninsula to the mainland.

'Exactly like at Lindisfarne,' thought Fenn.

The King's Reeve was in Dorncester and he decided to ride out to meet the ships. Out of curiosity, Kaela had followed the Reeve and his men. They found the people she now knew to be Northmen standing on the beach by their ships. They had rounded up some sheep and were loading them on board. There were fifty or more of the Northmen, armed with axes, swords and bows. They far outnumbered the Reeve's men.

'I knew this Reeve; he was a conceited fool named Beauduherd. He rode up and demanded the leader accompany him to pay the taxes on their trade goods. He was angry about the sheep. I could see immediately these visitors were not there for trade. As I said, it looked like they were lost and had come ashore to learn where they were and perhaps to get water and food.'

'Of course, they couldn't understand a word he was saying, but his arrogant attitude probably spoke loud enough. I don't know exactly how it started but suddenly the Reeve's men were fighting for their lives. I turned my horse and kicked him to a gallop but he had only taken a few strides when he was brought down by arrows. There were many arrows in the air – I was lucky not to be hit. I kicked free when the horse fell and ran but they caught me after a short chase. I did not let them take me easily; I fought them with everything I had.'

Kaela stopped, her face set hard, her fists clenched, remembering the fight.

'But they were too strong. They were in a wild mood and I was surprised they didn't kill me. At first I thought it was because they respected my struggle, or that I was unarmed. But I now know it was because of my red hair.'

'Why would…?'

She gave him a wry smile. 'Their god Thor has red hair.'

A moment later, she said: 'The others – Beauduherd and his men, were left dead and dying on the beach.'

Fenn's mind filled with questions – he didn't know which to ask first.

'You followed the Reeve and his men out of curiosity? Didn't they object? How did you get a horse?'

'I wanted to see these ships. It wasn't difficult to get a horse and, yes, I followed behind them at a short distance – what could they do?'

Kaela bent her head and closed her eyes, reliving another memory of the day.

'When they dragged me past my horse – he wasn't dead. He was blowing and his nostrils were all bloody. They collected their arrows from the sand and even pulled them from the horse but left him dying. It was awful. I begged the men to kill him. They ignored me.'

Fenn didn't speak, allowing her some time, but he was suddenly struck by his own memory.

'Oh my God,' he said. 'Four years ago! Master Nerian told me about these Northmen as we sat in the monastery courtyard on the day of the Lindisfarne raid. Of course – the landing at Wessex!'

Kaela regarded him. Her eyes were calm, but her voice was fierce.

'Yes, I am from Wessex, and I was taken from my land against my will.'

CHAPTER NINE

A scent of Opportunity …

Ragnall arrived at the hut in the early morning.

He had a short conversation with Thorvald and Askari on the landing. Thorvald went into the building on the side of the hut and returned with several knives. Ragnall selected four then signalled Fenn and Kaela to follow him and led the way through the vines and into the forest.

The bear lay about two miles from the hut in a small thicket of trees a hundred yards from the river. The ground about was torn and roughened with signs of a struggle. Fenn saw the two bloodied spears and one of the axes resting against a large tree. With the other axe, Olaf had completed the removal of the head and feet. He had long claw marks on his upper arm but was proud of them rather than worried, smiling when he saw they had been noticed.

The four of them pulled the bear to a grassy area and rolled it onto its back. Using one of Thorvald's knives, Ragnall started cuts on the inside legs and neck and carefully cut away the scent glands at the back of the hind legs. He demonstrated how he wanted the skin to be removed. He pointed out the places where extra care was needed – where the spears had pierced the skin and an axe cut in the neck. He watched until he was satisfied Fenn was able to do the job properly then bent to his own task.

When the skin was removed, Ragnall and Olaf spread it on the ground with the fur facing down. Fenn and Kaela scraped the bulk of the fat from the skin. Fenn thought it would be discarded but Kaela told him to gather it in one corner while Ragnall and Olaf gutted the bear and removed the heart. All of the other offal was discarded. Fenn was surprised the liver wasn't wanted but when he pointed it out, Kaela shook her head, grimacing in disgust.

The butchering was back-breaking as all the work was done either kneeling or stooped over. Ragnall worked on the massive chest, separating the ribs with his axe, while Olaf removed the back fillets and Fenn and Kaela worked on the legs. Ragnall showed them how he wanted the three large muscles from the hind legs cut out separately. As the meat was removed from the carcass, it was stacked onto the bear skin.

As they were finishing the collection of the last of the smaller cuts from the bones, Askari arrived carrying a large wooden basket fitted onto her back with leather straps. She was concerned about the deep scratches on Olaf's arm but he made light of them and waved her away. She inspected the bear carcass and the mounds of meat and fat lying on top of the skin, and then examined each of the feet and the claws. Finally, she busied herself separating the winter fat from the meat and bones and loaded this into her basket, adding some of the fat from the skin to fill it. The bear fat seemed to be highly prized and she took great care to keep it clean. Kaela explained it was melted and used for cooking and lamp oil, and Askari also used it in her medicines.

Behind her hand she whispered: 'It smells horrible when its melted, unless she puts lavender with it.'

When Ragnall was satisfied the butchering was complete, Fenn lay on the ground and Kaela sat beside him. Ragnall talked to her and waved in the direction of the river where their boat was drawn up onto the bank. She retrieved a water skin from the boat and passed it around. After taking a long drink herself, Kaela asked Ragnall a question. Ragnall smiled and called to his mother, inviting her to sit down beside Fenn and Kaela. He pointed in the direction of the hut, said something and then he turned about, pointing in the opposite direction. He beckoned to Olaf.

'They're going to show us how they killed the bear,' said Kaela, smiling.

Fenn didn't understand what was amusing her until Olaf joined Ragnall and they started to behave in a theatrical manner as if they were actors on a stage, exaggerating every movement. They walked away from the thicket

121

then turned and began to walk back along the path, looking to right and left, pointing to marks on the ground, inspecting broken grass and scuffed trees. Fenn understood they were tracking the bear. They stopped and Ragnall called out to Kaela. She rose and fetched their spears and axes. When she had delivered the weapons and returned to her seat, the brothers resumed their walk along the path. They talked animatedly with each other, displaying obvious concern.

'They're worried because the bear is heading toward the hut,' explained Kaela.

The brothers both froze in a crouching stance, staring ahead. They moved apart each heading to opposite sides of the path. The bear had appeared unexpectedly. The animal was returning down the path from its confrontation with Fenn and Kaela in the clearing.

Each brother had a spear in one hand and an axe in the other. They circled to each side of the bear. Ragnall raised his weapons above his head and shouted, distracting the bear, while Olaf ran in and made a thrust with his spear. He quickly retreated as the bear turned on him and Ragnall rushed in. He ran between the trees and stabbed his spear into what Fenn imagined was the bear's chest. Fenn saw that the brothers were using the close trees of the thicket to hamper the movement of the bear. Ragnall retreated and Olaf struck again from the other side, this time with both his spear and his axe. He clutched at his arm dropping his axe and fell to the ground, rolling away. The bear had caught him with its lethal claws. Ragnall ran to stand beside Olaf who got to his feet. Ragnall threw his axe aside and they both grasped their spears in two hands, moved apart and thrust forward in unison.

They mimed watching the great bear slowly fall and then they clapped each other on the shoulders, Olaf wincing, and completed the performance with a childish dance of victory.

Fenn and Kaela both stood up and applauded. Askari laughed aloud at their antics and went to them, drawing them into an embrace. The brothers towered over her and engulfed her in their arms but there was no mistaking their pleasure at her approval.

At the hut, Askari cleaned the wounds on Olaf's arm. She chose two clay containers from the shelves by the fire and mixed a white paste from the contents which she applied to each cut. Olaf nodded with satisfaction. He made a comment and Kaela laughed.

'He wants to be sure he has some good scars,' she told Fenn.

Thorvald handed Fenn another drinking horn of mead. Fenn thanked him and drank from it. This time its sweet honey flavour was tinged with something else, maybe ginger.

Ragnall and Olaf sat around the table with Askari and Thorvald drinking their mead, while Kaela brought Agatha to sit with Fenn on the other side of the fire. The four at the table were soon engaged in serious conversation. Fenn was anxious because this was the time when the subject of the bear being at the hut may come up.

Kaela started to talk to Fenn, but instead her attention was caught by something being said at the table. She held up her hand to stop Fenn from talking while she listened intently. Fenn held his breath, but it wasn't what he expected.

'Ragnall is saying there was a problem with Yarl Harald at the Thing in Borg,' she said. 'He is telling Askari he sent Haldor away without giving him what the Yarl wanted.'

Fenn nodded. 'Yes, I saw that. I was on the beach when they returned from Borg.'

Kaela continued: 'But he says Harald is weak – he'll wait until spring and then try to negotiate; he'll ask for less. They will give him a few small things and he'll be happy.'

Kaela smiled. 'I think Ragnall will be Yarl soon.'

Hakon had made the same prediction. It was apparent to Fenn that the struggle to rule in the land of the Northmen was just as earnest and bitter as it was in his.

Kaela continued to listen. 'Now they're talking about the last meals of the bear.'

Of all of the subjects they might have discussed, this one surprised Fenn.

'Why…?' he asked.

'If the bear has fattened itself on berries,' she explained, 'the meat will taste good. If it has been eating fish – not so good.'

Fenn shook his head in amazement. He had learned more about bears today that he would have in a lifetime at the monastery.

Without thinking about it, he asked Kaela: 'If you could go back to your homeland, would you?'

Kaela stared at him with the same face he remembered from the first night they met.

'In an instant. I *will* go back.'

'What about Agatha?'

Kaela narrowed her eyes. She reached across Agatha and took hold of Fenn's arm.

'She is my sister, and I would die for her. I'd fight for any of the people in this hut. They're good people but they are not my countrymen and not my blood. They do not live how I want to live. This is *not* my home.'

Fenn remembered the blood on Olaf's sword when he entered the church at Lindisfarne and wondered about Kaela's definition of 'good'. He dismissed the thought and nodded slowly, considering her words.

Agatha was looking from one to the other, trying to guess their mood. Kaela took her onto her knee, smiled at her and ruffled her hair.

Fenn made a decision. 'Now *I* am going to trust *you*,' he said.

Kaela looked at him intrigued, but with a little amusement. 'A shared secret?'

Fenn didn't answer directly. 'Do you know these mountains well?' he asked.

Kaela was surprised by the question. She thought a moment, then answered: 'Better than most. Birgitta likes to walk in them whenever she visits and I walk with her. She knows the mountains like old friends. She likes to tell me about them.'

'If I wanted to go south, would you know a way? A pass?'

'Well, it would be silly to go south from here, you would need to go east first, and then...' Kaela's eyes widened and she blinked. 'Are you thinking...?'

An increase of noise from the table told him the brothers had risen and were preparing to depart.

'Just be ready,' he whispered.

Kaela brought Agatha to the small beach to watch them leave, while Askari and Thorvald remained at the hut.

While the brothers checked the load, Fenn went to Agatha, picked her up and gave her a kiss on the cheek, then deposited her gently back on her feet. She clapped her hands. He looked at Kaela, nodded to her and touched her arm in farewell. As he moved away, she stepped forward and, keeping him between her and the brothers, took his sleeve, pulled his head down to her level and whispered in his ear:

'I know of *two* passes through the mountains.'

Then she kissed him on the cheek and let go of his arm, moving away up the path, swinging an arm with Agatha. Agatha was pointing at her own cheek and smiling, with Kaela smiling back at her.

Just as she entered the trees Kaela looked back and gave Fenn the same smile.

The huge head, the feet and the skin had been left at the hut, together with a large amount of meat. The rest of the bear meat and fat including the heart had been loaded onto the boat which now rode dangerously low for the return journey down the river. The current did most of the work, with Ragnall performing the steering duties just as he had on the big ship. Fenn sat with a small bucket at the ready and bailed any water that entered over the sides.

This time they did stop at the shipyard.

Stepping from the boat, Fenn noticed a round, ball-shaped stone at his feet and stooped to pick it up. He remembered his vow to never again be without stones for his sling. He tucked the stone into his tunic. Later he would transfer it to the bag he still had tucked inside his trousers. Ragnall was holding out some cuts of meat for Fenn to carry. He noticed Fenn's action and held out his other hand to see what Fenn had just hidden. Fenn brought out the stone and showed it to Ragnall, brushing his fingers over the stone to show how smooth it was. He did not think the Northmen used a sling – he certainly had not seen any, but he would learn now whether or not his sling had been mentioned in the hut. He kept his face innocent and his breathing steady and waited while Ragnall looked from him to the stone and back. Ragnall shrugged and extended his hand holding the meat cuts. Fenn tucked the stone away and accepted his load. He followed the brothers to where some men were gathered beside the hull of the ship and Ragnall and Olaf handed the men the bear meat they had selected.

Fenn waited until Ragnall was not occupied and inquired after Olgood by saying his name. Ragnall nodded. He questioned a man and then directed Fenn to an area further into the forest where an open-sided roofed shelter had been erected.

When he got close he could hear a rhythmic tapping on wood and saw that Olgood was shaping planks with a small axe. He had his back to Fenn, who approached silently then sat on his haunches a few feet behind Olgood. He picked up a small stone and tossed it over Olgood's head to land on a stack of finished planks in front of him. Olgood looked enquiringly into the sky, then at the ground to see what had fallen. Another stone was tossed a little to the left and then another to the right. Olgood let out an explosive snort and whirled, raising his axe in mock aggression.

'Fenn!' he shouted and, putting down the axe, he stepped up and embraced his friend exuberantly, knocking the wind from him. When Fenn made a small noise trying to get a breath, Olgood released his grip, grasped Fenn by the shoulders and appraised him.

'Are you well?'

Fenn started to reply:

'You nearly crushed…', but Olgood had noticed Fenn's hands and sleeves which still showed a good covering of bear blood. His face twisted into a frown.

'What have you done? What's happened?'

Fenn looked down.

'Oh this? This is bear's blood. Ragnall and Olaf killed a bear today. They're handing out some meat down by the river.'

Fenn could see that Ragnall and Olaf were obviously retelling the story about their fight with the bear to the interested group of ship builders. They would be a while. He and Olgood brought each other up to date with their happenings over the past weeks. Fenn told Olgood about his own encounter with the bear, but did not mention Kaela or Agatha. Olgood glanced down at Fenn's sling wrapped around his belt, shook his head in amazement and clapped Fenn on the shoulder.

'So… All that practice was worth it,' he said with a proud grin.

Olgood's attitude did not change when Fenn admitted the last stone was a lucky shot.

When they had exhausted their news, Fenn asked about Olgood's arm.

'As good as new,' said Olgood. He made a fist and shook his left arm vigorously.

Fenn smiled. 'Good.'

He laid his hand on Olgood's arm and said, in a serious tone:

'Olgood, do you know the big tree at the end of the barn? The one with large roots above the ground?'

'Yes, of course.'

'If anything should happen and we're not together, that's where we will meet.'

'If what should happen? What are you thinking of? Do you have a plan?'

'I'm not thinking of anything in particular, but we should be ready – and maybe I have the beginning of a plan.'

'Are you thinking of doing something in Winter?'

'I don't know yet – just keep that tree in mind.'

Olgood studied Fenn. 'Sometimes I wonder what goes on in your head.'

Fenn grinned. 'Me too.'

Olgood returned the grin. 'If anything happens…,' he made these words sound mysterious, but finished seriously, '…I'll be at the tree.'

Fenn heard Olaf's deep voice calling his name from the river.

CHAPTER TEN

A knock on the door of death and a knock on the door of life…

Fenn stood close to the fire in the big room, dripping wet and freezing cold, his body shaking with spasms of shivering and his breath coming in irregular gasps. He had just had his clothing stripped from him by Olgood who had then dried him as best he could and covered him in a large woollen blanket. Fenn's teeth were chattering uncontrollably and he felt as weak as a baby. Gisele had offered him a horn of hot mead but he couldn't hold it. Olgood helped Fenn wrap the blanket tightly, then he held him upright and turned him in front of the fire like a roast of meat.

Fenn fought against his tiredness. He thought if he went to sleep he may not wake up.

After what seemed an eternity, the heat of the fire finally reached him and for the first time in a while he thought he probably wasn't going to die that day.

He closed his eyes.

*   *   *

Birgitta had come to him while he was cutting dead branches from trees for firewood.

Eight months had passed since the day he had stepped onto the beach at Lognavik. The unrelenting and demanding physical work had broadened Fenn's shoulders, deepened his chest and strengthened his body. The scribe struck down by Olaf, whose tools had rarely extended beyond a pen or a garden hoe, had long since disappeared, replaced by a fit and capable young man able to wield an axe or scythe with skill and carry a stone or log with ease.

Audrey was with Birgitta but she remained some distance away and Fenn had no chance to talk to her. Birgitta had taken the axe from his hand and had firmly inserted it into a nearby stump.

In front of his face she had said the word: 'Hakon.'

Birgitta was almost as tall as Fenn and she was an imposing figure standing so close to him. She was calm and her eyes were unwavering, her face showing a controlled determination. He resisted an urge to step back and he pointed to the beach. As far as he knew, Hakon had been fishing on the ice that morning.

The worst of the winter was past, but the inlet was still frozen into a solid sheet for a hundred yards from the shore. Only the centre was free of ice. Apparently, Hakon was skilled at fishing through a hole in the ice, or maybe he was just lucky. In any case it was a common activity for him these days.

Birgitta took Fenn by the arm and guided him in the direction of the beach, indicating with a gentle push of her hand to his back that he should walk ahead of her.

At the beach, Fenn looked for Hakon. There were three figures fishing on the ice that he could see, but they were crouched down and Fenn peered at them trying to determine which one was Hakon. He pointed at one of the fishermen about a hundred yards from shore and close to the bluff. The ice did not extend far into the inlet at that point, probably because of the water still flowing from the river.

Fenn did not like walking on the ice. He was always unsure whether it would bear his weight and he did not like the uncertainty of his steps on the slippery surface, but Birgitta led him onto the frozen surface without hesitation. Fenn glanced back to see Audrey step gingerly onto the ice and follow them slowly, holding her arms out from her sides for balance. A few yards from the person hunched beside a small hole cut in the ice, Birgitta stopped and called out: 'Hakon!'

Hakon turned his head in surprise and stood up, holding a fine thread in his fingers. When Birgitta beckoned to him, he placed the fishing line on the ice and held it in place with a flat rock. He walked to where Birgitta was standing. She said some words to him and he nodded.

Then Birgitta turned to Fenn and talked to him.

Hakon said: 'Birgitta say she know what you do.'

Hakon looked as worried as Fenn who said nothing. He had no idea what she was referring to. He could not think what he could have done that was wrong.

'She say she thank you, she has debt to you and she will repay if she can.' Hakon's frown showed he was still mystified, but Fenn knew what she meant. She knew about Agatha and the bear.

Birgitta reached out and grasped Fenn by the forearm, just as Thorvald had done in the hut. She looked into his eyes and Fenn could see her sincerity. She was holding her lips together firmly to prevent herself from showing too much emotion. He returned the grip and nodded.

'Please tell Birgitta I would do it again,' he said to Hakon. Hakon's frown deepened but he relayed Fenn's words.

Birgitta's grip tightened on his arm. She drew a deep breath and nodded her head.

There was a scream from the shore.

Fenn looked to the beach. Where the beach met the ice, a woman was pointing urgently beyond where they were standing. She cried out again. Together they turned their heads and followed her pointing finger.

Audrey was standing on the edge, less than a foot from where the ice finished and the deep waters of the inlet began.

Instinctively, Fenn moved towards her.

'No,' said Hakon, catching his arm. 'Ice very thin there.'

Fenn ignored him. She was ten yards away, staring into the dark water in front of her. He tried to keep his voice calm and he called to her.

'Audrey, it's Fenn. Can you come back here to me? It's not safe there.'

She did not seem to have heard him. He moved closer and felt the ice shift beneath his feet. There was a sound like the crack of a small branch. He stopped moving.

'Too dangerous go closer. Ice not hold both.' Hakon said from behind him.

Fenn took another cautious step. The ice seemed firm.

Hakon realised Fenn was not going to stop. 'You must spread weight. Lie on ice.'

It was good advice. He slowly lowered himself onto one knee. There were groaning sounds under the ice.

'Audrey. Can you hear me? It's Fenn.' There was no response. He had to get her attention.

In a louder voice he said: 'Audrey, please come here. I need you.'

Audrey lifted her head and started to turn toward him.

At that moment, the ice beneath her splintered and in a heartbeat she was no longer there.

Fenn lay flat on the ice and spread his arms and legs. He could feel the intense cold through his fingers. Using his hands and feet he squirmed like a lizard towards the place where Audrey had disappeared.

He heard Hakon shout: 'No!' Someone else, probably Birgitta, was also shouting.

Fenn reached the edge of the ice. He expected to find a thin layer and was surprised when the broken edge was a few inches thick. He pushed himself off the ice and into the water.

The cold penetrated to his heart instantly. His head felt as though his skin had shrunk and formed a tightening band around his skull. He fought against his instinctive reaction to gasp with the shock of the intense cold. He opened his eyes and looked for Audrey, jerking his head in a circle and looking down at his feet kicking frantically below him. The water against his eyes was so cold he thought they would freeze to balls of ice. He had only a few moments of vision. He could feel the tug of the flow from the river against his legs and he fought against it, trying to stay on the surface. He turned in the water, looking in all directions. It was as dark as ink and he could not see more than a few yards. In an instant he knew it was hopeless – she was gone – and at the same time he realised there was no

131

way back. His clothes were too heavy; he felt himself sinking and the cold was draining his strength from him. He had just forfeited his own life.

There was a sharp tug on his scalp. He tried to look up, but strong fingers grasped his hair more firmly and his head was pulled to the surface. He coughed, choked and spluttered and tried to hold onto the edge of the ice but his hands and arms wouldn't work. The grip in his hair shifted and he felt himself being dragged by his tunic at the back of his neck.

Like a helpless kitten he was pulled over the edge of the ice on his back. He twisted his head and saw that Hakon, lying flat on the ice, was the one who held him by the neck. Behind Hakon, Birgitta was holding on to one of Hakon's feet, pulling them both away from the edge. He saw other hands appear and take hold of Hakon's other leg to help her.

Fenn coughed water and let his eyes close. He felt tired and was so cold he thought his heart could stop at any moment.

*　　*　　*

Olgood was rubbing his arms and back and chest through the blanket to help warm him. He was not being gentle – Fenn felt himself jerked back and forth like a rag doll by Olgood's vigour, and found it difficult to remain upright. Only when Fenn thought he may sustain more damage from the rubbing than from his near drowning in ice-cold water did he beg Olgood to stop.

Master Nerian fussed about him. He was carrying a bucket of hot water and whenever he was able to get past Olgood, he pressed a hot cloth onto exposed parts of Fenn's body or knelt before him and wiped his feet. When Olgood stopped, the Master looked intently into Fenn's eyes.

After a moment he nodded and announced: 'Good colour and I see life in his eyes.'

Birgitta was standing with Ragnall and Olaf and several other townspeople in a group on the other side of the fire. They were keeping a watchful eye on Fenn but were letting Olgood and Master Nerian revive him.

When he had recovered enough to speak, Fenn related to Olgood and the Master what had happened in a few sentences. When he finished, he looked at them and said:

'Did she fall accidentally or deliberately? – I don't know. She didn't seem to try to swim.'

The possibility that she had simply given up chilled him almost as much as the icy water. Olgood shook his head in sympathy. Master Nerian waved his hands about, seeking the right words.

'She is safe with God, and freed from this place – freed from her torment.'

Fenn stared at the floor. The words were no comfort and it saddened him that he would never know the answer to his question. Gisele brought him a new drinking horn of hot mead. Fenn accepted it gratefully, glad that he could now hold it steadily, thinking that he had drunk more mead recently than he would have expected after the first night when he had learned it was only for special occasions. He felt the sweet liquid warming him all the way to his stomach. Hakon handed him some dry clothes and Fenn dressed while Hakon gathered his wet tunic and leggings from the floor. He turned to go and Fenn caught him by the shoulder.

'Thank you Hakon, you saved my life,' he said.

Hakon looked at him and Fenn was surprised to see that Hakon was angry.

'What you do very foolish. You not *think*.' Hakon tapped his own head, hard. 'Woman dead when she fall in water. If you cannot reach her from ice, she is dead. You go in water – no way to get her out. You make danger for everyone.'

Fenn was a little taken aback. He swallowed and nodded, trying to find a reply.

'Yes – yes, of course you're right. But there was a chance I could save her. If I stopped to think it would have been too late.' He tightened his grip on Hakon's shoulder. 'And if you had stopped to think, I would not be here now – so I thank you. You and Birgitta.'

He looked for Birgitta, saw she was watching him and nodded an acknowledgement to her across the room. She responded with a short nod in return.

Hakon gave a sigh as his anger dissipated. He nodded and patted Fenn's arm.

'Ragnall say when you warm go small room. Gisele bring hot food.'

Fenn drew Hakon to one side.

'Now that Birgitta has helped to save me, will she consider her debt is paid?'

Hakon laughed and waved his hand in a negative gesture.

'You risk life to save something that belong to her. Whatever her debt before – now twice.'

Fenn groaned. He could not say why, but he had a feeling that having Birgitta indebted to him may be more of a problem than a benefit.

Gisele brought him some *skause* into the annex which was warm as promised and thankfully did contain some meat. She carried bowls for Olgood, Master Nerian and Hakon as well herself. Fenn thought the generosity extending to them all was probably Birgitta's doing. Olgood expressed his thanks to Fenn that his misfortune had resulted in an extra bowl of stew.

They ate slowly, savouring the stew and the moment, aware that this time of relaxation and good food would not last. When they had finished, Olgood risked the ire of the Northmen by gathering some of the empty bowls and walking with Gisele toward the big room.

Remembering the day Olgood had teased him for walking away with Yseld after he had knocked her down, Fenn called to him.

'So, you'd rather care for a pretty girl than a friend who has just escaped the clutches of death.'

Olgood grinned broadly and when Hakon told Gisele what Fenn had said, she blushed and hurried out of the room.

*   *   *

The ice melted quickly when the days became warmer and the first buds of spring appeared on the forest trees. All of Ragnall's stock animals had been housed in the barn over the winter and these were now herded out to the pastures with the arrival of the spring grass. Many animals had wintered in houses in the village alongside their owners and these were also brought out to join the herds and flocks.

Fenn had been given the job of cleaning the pig pens once the ground had thawed. He wrapped a woollen scarf around his face to help mask the stench. If he had to make a list of the most unpleasant tasks he had had to perform since his arrival in Lognavik this would be close to the top. Unlike the first attempt by Master Nerian, he used a broad iron shovel and a bucket. He deposited the filth in a large hole he had dug as directed by Ragnall, just inside the forest. When Hakon had relayed to him what Ragnall wanted him to do, they had shared a knowing glance, both remembering the day of Torston's 'show' when the pigs had escaped.

He had cleaned two of the three pens and was searching for a suitable place to dig a new hole to contain the muck from the third when, through the trees, he noticed Birgitta appear at the edge of the forest, about a hundred yards from where he stood. She didn't see him and, curious about her behaviour, Fenn kept himself concealed and followed her as she entered the forest.

On this side of the village, the tall ridge that formed one side of the valley started at the bluff by the river and ran up to the foothills at the top of the valley. As Fenn reached the top of the ridge he saw Birgitta climbing up the next ridge. She was climbing quickly and heading toward two large boulders on the crest. He stood and watched as she passed between the boulders and over the crest. He hoped she was going to Askari's hut, and if so, he now knew where the trail started.

He descended the ridge and returned to pick up his shovel.

*   *   *

Several days later, a cry in the night woke him.

He lay half asleep trying to determine if the cry was real or part of a dream. Then he smelled smoke and came fully awake. More cries sounded in the distance and there was a bellow from either Ragnall or Olaf in the big room, followed by the sound of people moving about in a hurry.

Fenn heard Hakon say distinctly: 'Yarl Harald has come.'

It was dark – a short time before dawn. Fenn blinked his eyes. There was a shout from outside the house and an answering roar like a battle cry from the big room. Thumping footsteps ran down the entranceway. The smell of smoke was stronger – something was burning close by.

Fenn threw off his blanket and called to Olgood: 'Meet at the tree.'

Olgood replied: 'Where's Gisele?'

'She gets water,' said Hakon.

'What's happening?' asked Master Nerian, confused.

'Hakon thinks Yarl Harald is attacking the village,' Fenn replied. 'Hakon, look outside. Be careful. Master, please come with me.'

'I'll find Gisele,' said Olgood, moving toward the entrance.

Fenn started to object but Olgood was already on his way.

'The tree,' he reminded Olgood. 'As soon as you can.'

Hakon followed Olgood out and Fenn went into the big room, Master Nerian shuffling behind him. It was empty. Fenn's eyes were becoming adjusted to the dim light and he was surprised to see Ragnall's pair of red axes were still hanging on the wall. He ran over and took them down, handing one to Master Nerian who drew his hands to his chest and shook his head violently. Fenn nodded and kept hold of the axes himself, pushing them into his belt.

'Put what food you can find in a sack,' he instructed the Master, who looked puzzled but moved off to do as he had been asked. Fenn followed him to the kitchen area and searched for a knife or anything else that could be used as a weapon. The smell of smoke was stronger and it caught in his throat. Master Nerian was also coughing. Fenn found a long carving knife and slipped it into his belt to join the axes. He stuffed some fruit inside his tunic. There was continuous noise and shouting from outside the house.

'That's enough,' he called to Master Nerian. 'We must go now.'

Hakon met him at the door. Flames were clearly visible from several houses in the direction of the beach and the noise of fighting came from many directions. Cries, grunts, screams and clashes of metal mixed with the crackle of burning thatch. The mountains were rimmed with the first light of dawn which combined with the flickering light of nearby flames to provide a limited visibility around the house.

'Fighting is louder – coming this way,' said Hakon.

Fenn said: 'Hakon… The Master and Olgood and I are going to escape now. There will be no better time. Are you coming with us?'

'Escape…? How…?'

'I'll explain later. Are you coming?'

Hakon looked about. The crackling noises and the dull background roar of the flames were getting louder as sparks from the burning houses spread the fire onto neighbouring thatched roofs of the closely packed buildings. A man appeared with his sword drawn and a shield on his arm. Fenn did not recognise him and could not tell if he was friend or foe. He looked at them and then ran toward the beach. More shouting and sounds of struggle were approaching from the valley end of the village.

'I come with you.'

'Good.' Fenn handed Hakon an axe and said: 'Follow me.'

He checked that Master Nerian was behind him. The Master was holding a large sack. He grinned in the light of the flames and said: 'I found some cheeses.'

Fenn nodded and walked swiftly past the pig pens towards the barn and the big tree.

From behind him he heard the Master call: 'Fenn?'

Fenn stopped and turned back to him. Hakon stopped alongside him.

'I wonder if you will ever find that beetle again and make your wonderful ink.'

Hakon looked at Fenn with a furrowed brow. Fenn shook his head and motioned them to continue toward the tree.

Olgood was not at the tree. Fenn searched the darkness which was illuminated in brief snatches by flickering light from the fires. Hakon reached him and looked back. Master Nerian was walking towards them but had fallen twenty yards behind. He was walking steadily but was not hurrying. As Fenn waved to him, urging him to run, a figure appeared behind the Master. This person Fenn *did* recognise. Torston.

Slowly Torston raised his bow. He was too far away for Fenn to see the expression on his face but he imagined it would contain pleasure and satisfaction.

'Master, behind you! Look out!' yelled Fenn.

Master Nerian stopped, not understanding. Fenn heard the arrow hit. Without a sound, Master Nerian pitched forward onto his face lying across his sack of cheeses. His head lifted once and then fell.

Fenn felt a cry of rage surge from his throat. He pulled his axe and charged at Torston, who calmly fitted another arrow to his bow. Fenn did not care at that moment if the arrow struck him before he could reach Torston. Unless it killed him instantly he knew would have the chance of one blow and that was all he wanted. Torston raised the bow, pulled the bowstring back to his cheek, held the arrow steady, and waited. Fenn could now see he was smiling. He would let Fenn get close before he loosed. That arrogance would be his downfall, thought Fenn – 'just give me one blow'.

From out of the shadows behind Torston, a pair of hands grasped his head and twisted violently. Fenn heard the crack of Torston's neck breaking. Not content with the death, the hands lifted the limp body and tossed it ten feet to land beside the pig pen.

Olgood appeared from the darkness with Gisele beside him

'Good riddance,' he said, then noticed Master Nerian. He grimaced and added, ruefully: 'I'm sorry I didn't get here earlier.'

'You did what you could,' replied Fenn, trying to calm his breathing. 'He may have killed me too, if you were a few moments later.'

He reached up to his neck and removed the leather collar. He was about to throw it into the night when he stopped and threw it instead into the mud of the pig pen.

'See if Torston has anything useful,' he said to Olgood. 'We're leaving Lognavik today and going over the mountains.'

Olgood smiled, unbuckling his own collar. Gisele watched him with wide eyes. She touched the band of leather around her neck. Fenn could imagine what she was thinking. She had been wearing the collar for so long she had forgotten it was there. He knelt by Master Nerian. The arrow was buried deep in the centre of his back. When Fenn lifted the monk to retrieve the sack, his face looked serene and untroubled.

'I thank you Master for all you have taught me,' Fenn said. 'You were a good man. Rest in peace.'

He gently removed Master Nerian's collar, stood up and flung it into the pig pen as well.

Fenn handed the sack of cheeses to Gisele and pointed at Hakon standing by the tree, guiding her in that direction with a gentle push on her arm.

He followed Olgood over to the pens. Olgood had retrieved a knife and had some of Torston's arrows in his hand.

'Should we get his bow?' he asked.

'No. My sling is better. We don't need the bow. You should have this though.'

He handed Olgood Ragnall's second axe. They set off toward the tree.

They had only gone a few yards when the sounds of heavy fighting came from close by and quickly grew louder, forcing them to stop and turn.

A number of men were being hard-pressed by a larger group and were backing slowly into the area between Ragnall's house and the pig pens to prevent themselves from being surrounded and overcome. The clash of swords and axes on shields, and metal clanging on metal, rang clearly in the dawn air, together with grunts of effort, challenging roars and cries of pain. Smoke from the burning houses was drifting about, making details of the scene alternately clear and then obscured.

The small group was fighting desperately but they were only five or six against ten or twelve – the numbers were too great. They were holding briefly but only because the confined space did not allow all of the attackers to engage. Fenn suddenly recognised Birgitta among the defenders. She parried an overhand blow with her shield, thrust underneath with her sword and was rewarded with a cry. On her backswing she struck another man's thigh, then brought her shield up again to deflect the first man's next blow.

In two swift movements, Fenn unwound his sling from his belt and pulled out the small bag of stones he'd collected. The closest attacker was twenty yards away – a perfect distance for him. His first stone struck Birgitta's opponent above his eye, a killing blow, and he dropped instantly. Birgitta hesitated, unsure of what had happened, but then her attention was diverted by another attack.

When he saw Fenn had joined the fight, Olgood cried out, tossed Torston's arrows into the darkness and charged forward towards the conflict. Fenn shouted 'No!' after him, but he was gone.

When another stone felled her new opponent, Birgitta glanced behind her and saw Fenn whirling his sling. She faced forward again and moved to help a defender who was struggling with a large man who had him backed against a wall and almost helpless. Fenn saw with a shock that the attacker was Haldor, his face creased with rage and exertion, confirmation that it was Yarl Harald who was attacking Lognavik.

He took another stone but saw that Olgood had reached the battle. He had gained a shield from somewhere but three men had broken from the main group and were advancing on him. They had obviously recognised the threat of someone his size. Fenn's stone took out the one in the centre striking him on the helmet and knocking him to the ground where he lay unmoving, stunned if not dead. The other two were now split allowing Olgood to concentrate on one at a time. He ran at the left attacker and thrust the edge of his shield into his face. The man fell heavily and Olgood spun to receive the sword of the other man on his shield, diverting it wide while he swung with his axe at the man's head.

Fenn turned his attention back to Birgitta. In the few heartbeats since he had turned away, the situation had changed for the worse. The man Haldor had originally confronted was down and Haldor was attacking Birgitta relentlessly, raining blows onto her shield, forcing her backwards with sheer strength. She would very soon be overwhelmed. Birgitta had lost her sword and was holding her shield high with both hands, but the high shield was obscuring Haldor's head, blocking Fenn's target. Haldor leaned back to deliver a final swing with all his strength and Fenn aimed his whirling sling at Haldor's knee. The stone hit just above the knee on his thigh with the force of a hammer, taking the leg from under Haldor, but it was not the crippling blow that Fenn had hoped for. Birgitta seized the opportunity and thrust at him with her shield. He raised his arm and partially blocked her strike but the force was enough to push him onto his back. He still had his sword in his hand and a string of curses issued from his mouth as he used his shield and sword arm to raise himself from the ground. Olgood was suddenly there, his foot stamping on the wrist that held Haldor's sword and his axe swinging in an arc which ended at Haldor's neck. A fountain of blood sprayed them both.

When his fingers discovered no more stones, Fenn thrust the sling into his tunic and drew the long knife from his belt. At that moment a frightening scream erupted by his ear and Hakon ran past at full speed, his axe raised and his face twisted into a wolf-like snarl. His screams were delivered with a force far out of proportion to his size; and incredibly rose in both volume and pitch as he threw himself at the men who were now opposing Olgood, slashing at the nearest, causing the man to step back quickly and stumble against a fence post. Fenn launched himself forward, following a few yards behind Hakon, hoarsely adding his voice to Hakon's cries and waving his knife in the air. He knew he would not be able to stand against a Northman clad in a chain mail shirt and carrying sword and shield, but he was prepared to do what he could and depend on his wits and agility to survive.

He slowed his pace when he saw it would not be necessary to test either.

The loss of their leader, the arrival of the giant, and now two more screaming wild men appearing out of the smoke was enough to discourage the remaining attackers who disengaged and fled. Hakon gave chase for a few steps, his cries turning into hoots of derision.

Birgitta lowered her battered shield and sank to one knee, breathing heavily.

Fenn checked that Olgood was unhurt and then took stock of the bodies lying scattered on the ground in various haphazard positions. None were moving. Olgood wiped his bloody axe on Haldor's tunic and helped Birgitta to her feet.

She searched the ground and discovered her sword half covered by Haldor's body. She contemptuously pushed him aside with her foot and pulled her sword from under him, then stepped over to inspect the man lying by the wall. He was obviously dead. There were three other defenders still alive and although they were exhausted, they gathered around Birgitta facing outwards in a protective ring. Olgood dropped his shield to the ground.

Birgitta spoke to Fenn and Olgood. Hakon translated.

'She say you have killed her enemies and saved her and these men from death on this day. If she had died without sword in hand she may not be chosen by the Valkyries to walk in the halls of Valhalla.'

Birgitta paused for breath. Fenn saw her glance at his neck. She had realised they weren't wearing a collar.

She continued as if she hadn't noticed anything.

'Law say you kill enemy so you are free men but this not for her to say. Ragnall must say. But she will stand beside you if you need her.'

'Please tell her this,' said Fenn. 'Firstly say to her 'I would stand with her again' and secondly tell her 'farewell'.' Fenn hoped he had judged this woman correctly.

When Hakon had relayed his words, Birgitta looked at Fenn in silence. He waited while she made her decision. Then she stepped up to him and clasped his forearm, speaking to him solemnly.

'She say she owe you for two lives. She not forget. She say – may all your enemies be in front of you,' said Hakon. 'It is what they say if maybe not see person again.'

Fenn nodded acknowledgement and gripped her forearm in return. Birgitta did the same to Olgood.

She scanned the area and walked over to the man Fenn had felled when Olgood had first joined the fight. Standing over him she thrust once with her sword into his throat. Without looking back, she walked steadily in the direction Haldor's men had fled. Her remaining men followed her toward the beach from where they could still hear the sounds of fighting.

Fenn watched her go. Birgitta was lit from the fires and the glow of the rising sun. Fenn thought she looked magnificent with her golden hair, striding fearlessly to the battle, just like any of the legendary heroes from the old stories.

'Shall we go?' asked Olgood. 'Or are you going to watch her all morning?'

Fenn smiled, then straightened. 'There's something I cannot leave without.'

The smoke was swirling thickly about Ragnall's house as he ran back inside emerging, coughing, a short while later, carrying an object wrapped in a linen cloth.

*   *   *

Gisele cried out when she saw Olgood was covered in blood, but Hakon assured her the blood was not his. Fenn threaded his sling back onto his belt and looked at the people gathered under the tree.

'This is our opportunity to escape,' he said. 'It will be a long time before we're missed and with the chaos and the damage to the village it will probably be days before any pursuit can be organised.'

He turned to Hakon. 'Olgood and you, Hakon, have said you'll come with me but it must also be Gisele's choice to come with us or not, so please tell her what I've just said and ask her what she wants to do.'

Hakon talked to her. When he had finished, Gisele slowly looked from Hakon to Fenn then went to stand beside Olgood. She came barely to his shoulder but Olgood put his arm around her and she leaned against him. She lifted her chin and touched her collar. Olgood removed it for her. She held it in her hand for a moment and then deliberately let it fall to the ground.

Hakon hastily tore off his collar. He dropped it then twisted his heel on it, grinding it into the dirt.

Fenn nodded. 'Good.'

He led them along the edge of the forest to the point where, a few days before, he had seen Birgitta enter on her way to Askari's hut. Just as they were about to enter the trees, Olgood put a hand on his shoulder.

'Fenn, there are others from the monastery somewhere in the village. Shouldn't we try…?'

Fenn looked at him. He had already considered that terrible question, and made the only possible decision. They had neither the time nor the ability to save everyone even if they knew where they were. He felt his emotions churning within him – anguish, concern, guilt – but he also hoped his eyes showed his determination.

Olgood nodded. He understood. They both turned to look at the burning houses, at the smoke swirling over the rooftops, and heard the shouts and cries that still echoed in the morning air.

At the top of the ridge, they paused to take their last view of Lognavik. Fenn let his gaze pass over the village where he had been enslaved for almost a year. A third of the houses were smoking ruins and many were still burning.

The sun was up and there was movement on the beach but the distance was too great for him to see whether the fighting was continuing or not.

He turned away from the village and pointed at the pair of boulders on the next ridge where Birgitta had crossed.

'That is our direction.'

CHAPTER ELEVEN

A taste of freedom…

Fenn had not moved for a long time.

From his position on the hill behind the hut, he could see a small mixed group of goats and sheep grazing in the clearing. He had carefully circled through the forest to approach from downwind and had found a place high enough on the hillside to give him a good view. He wanted to speak to Kaela alone, and he wanted to know who was in the hut before he approached her. There was no wind and the trees were quiet. A thin trail of smoke rose vertically into the sky from the side of the hut, indicating it was occupied, but he couldn't hear any talking or movement inside.

During the time he had been watching, he had seen only two people. The first was Agatha. Fenn could only see one half of the landing from his position and she had appeared when she walked to one end to pick up some pieces of wood. The other person was a stout boy a few years younger than Fenn who was standing with the animals, carrying Thorvald's staff. He was keeping the stock confined to one part of the clearing, gently caressing the heads of both the sheep and goats and talking to them as he moved among them. His voice had a soothing quality as if he were singing a lullaby. That would be Addo.

A cramp in his leg forced a change to a different position. He was struggling to move his body without making any noise when there was movement where the thicket of vines hid the entrance to the clearing.

Askari and Kaela came into view, carrying a basket between them.

145

*　　*　　*

When they had crossed the first ridge, Fenn was unsure of the distance to the hut across country. He was depending on Birgitta's trail leading him in the general direction of the hut, but he knew it would not lead directly there. The location of the hut was a carefully hidden secret so the common trails would not pass nearby. He thought he could find the hut once they reached the area past the gorge where the land was more gentle and open. As a last resort, he could follow the river until he recognised the shingle beach.

He knew how long the journey to the hut had taken by river, but that twisting course made the straight line distance difficult to estimate. Even so, the land journey, while more direct, would take much longer because of the rough mountainous terrain. There were several high ridges and deep ravines to cross, which he knew would involve exhausting climbs and precipitous descents.

He was concerned for Gisele. She was wearing the long full-length dress commonly worn by women in the village and Fenn could see it was not going to be suitable for travel in the mountains, but there was nothing they could do about that now. He mentioned his concern to Olgood who said he would take care of Gisele. He said he would carry her if it was necessary.

Fenn had two other considerations to keep in mind.

First, would they meet anyone on this trail? If the path led to the shipyard, there may be other people using it in either direction. He decided that wasn't likely. Olgood had said they always travelled to the yard by boat. Also Birgitta would not want to pass by the shipyard each time she travelled to the hut.

The person most likely to use the path was Birgitta. Once the battle was over, assuming she survived, she may decide to bring the news to Askari herself. If she did catch up with them, despite her assertions of a debt owed to Fenn, he was not certain what her reaction would be when she saw that Gisele and Kaela were involved – and also Hakon who, although he had fought briefly, hadn't killed any enemies. He shook his head. It was probably foolish of him to have announced to her that they were leaving, but she had already noticed their missing collars.

Second, when would Ragnall or Olaf arrive at the hut? Fenn was certain that one or both would come. The answer to this question depended on the answers to several others.

Was the fighting over? Who had prevailed? Ironically, for reasons he could not explain, Fenn hoped Ragnall had been victorious, although that was certainly not the best outcome for them. If Ragnall had beaten Harald, were Harald's men being pursued? There would be the aftermath of the battle to clean up, bodies to bury, the injured to care for and rebuilding to organise. All of that should surely occupy the brothers for a few days.

There was no question in Fenn's mind that whatever the outcome of the raid, he expected Ragnall and Olaf to survive.

There were several reasons why the brothers would come to Askari's hut. They would want to tell her of the raid – or maybe to warn her, if there were still any of Yarl Harald's people about. But more importantly, once Ragnall discovered that all of the thralls from his house were missing, it would not take him long to realise that Fenn would head for the hut and Kaela.

Fenn took Hakon to one side.

'How determined will Ragnall be to recapture us?' he asked. 'He has pressing issues in Lognavik. If he does not catch us before we cross the mountains, might he give up?'

Hakon shook his head. 'He never give up. It is honour and respect. He never be Yarl if he let thralls escape.'

*　　*　　*

The further they followed Birgitta's trail, the more some of Fenn's worries were lessened when it became obvious that it was not well travelled. In some rocky areas it was necessary to climb using handholds and in the crossing of streams there were no bridges or stones to step on, forcing them to wade – often thigh deep through narrow but turbulent water. True to his promise, Olgood carried Gisele through the deepest ones. Several times, the path became so faint they had to scout ahead to ensure they were still following a trail at all.

At their first resting point, Fenn had distributed the fruit he had gathered from the big room. The apples were bruised and the berries were squashed, staining his undershirt and tunic a deep purple, but it was food, and he suggested they should eat the fruit while they could. The cheeses that Master Nerian had collected would keep.

When Fenn had told the others that he was going to collect Kael, Hakon had objected. He wanted to get as far away from Lognavik as quickly as possible. Fenn explained that Kael had been taken from the same land as Olgood and himself and he would not leave without him. He said there were other reasons which he would explain later. Olgood had asked why Fenn was in so much of a hurry. He had heard Birgitta say they were now free men.

'She said we are not free until Ragnall says we are,' Fenn reminded him. 'We gave him no chance to do that. Also, that condition did not apply to Gisele and probably not to Hakon.'

Olgood nodded.

'Or Kael,' added Fenn.

*　　*　　*

Fenn had left the others some distance away once he recognised the area, and made his way to Askari's clearing alone.

Now that he had seen Kaela, he settled to wait until an opportunity arose to communicate with her. He tried to be calm but his anxiety increased with each passing moment as the scene in front of him did not change. As much as he repeated to himself that they should have days before their escape rose to the top of the list, he could not stop himself imagining that their pursuit could be being organised right now while he remained in this place doing nothing.

He could not wait indefinitely, but it was a delicate situation and a misstep now could be fatal.

He had found it physically difficult traversing the steep and uneven terrain of the hill behind the hut, but he had discovered a small hollow in the rocks on a level with the treetops which offered a good view of the clearing while allowing him to lie with reasonable comfort on his stomach. The dip in the ground concealed his body and he was able to look between a scattering of stones and some small bushes on the lip of the hollow. The hollow was not a perfect length however and he was forced to twist his legs and bend them to one side. The sun was warm and pleasant on his back and although he tried to keep still, he needed to move from time to time to keep himself alert and to ease his stiffness. From what had previously been a clear sky, some clouds appeared in his vision and he glanced anxiously upwards. A dense formation was gathering over the river in the east suggesting the possibility of rain later in the day.

He was beginning to wonder if he should be bold and approach the hut openly, when his pulse quickened as Kaela appeared on the landing and called to Addo. She moved into the clearing as Addo walked towards the hut and they met halfway. They spoke a few words. Addo gave Kaela the staff and she took his place watching the animals. Fenn could not see Agatha and hoped she had also gone inside the hut with Addo. He waited until Kaela was standing with her back to him, then rose to his knees and picked up a small pebble which he threw at her. It missed its intended target and landed on the back of a sheep in front of her. The animal shuffled forward as if it had been given a nudge, but he could not tell if Kaela had noticed. Fenn threw another which this time fell true and hit her on the shoulder. Her head came up but she did not turn around. She was still for a moment, then she raised her hand briefly in acknowledgement.

Using the staff with gentle touches, she started the animals moving in the direction of the hill. She was unhurried, just patiently nudging them toward new grazing. Fenn climbed down the hill as quietly as he could until he was crouched behind the hut. He still had not seen Thorvald and the others could appear at any moment so he was wary of revealing himself.

Kaela continued to watch the animals and was not looking at him when she said: 'Fenn, what are you doing here?'

Urgently, Fenn told Kaela about the raid on Lognavik by Yarl Harald. She gasped and said she must tell Askari immediately.

'Please... Wait a moment.'

He told her Olgood, Gisele and Hakon were waiting nearby. Her hand went to her mouth and then she did look at him, her large brown eyes wide with alarm. He nodded in answer to her silent question and said the same words to her that he had first said to Hakon outside Ragnall's house with the sounds of the raid in their ears.

'There will be no better time.'

Fenn held his breath. If, for any reason, Kaela refused to come with them, their escape would be difficult if not impossible. Only she knew the way over the mountains.

He saw that Kaela was thinking hard. She made her decision.

'I'll meet you at the high valley where Addo kept the sheep and goats. It's a small enclosed valley about five miles away – in the mountains.'

Fenn let out his breath. 'But where…?'

Kaela gave him directions in short sentences, finishing with: 'At the entrance to the valley is a large tree with a round stone beside it that's pointed on top.'

'When?'

'When I can.'

They stared at each other.

'Go!' she said, pointing to the south.

He edged behind the hut and looked back once when he entered the forest. Kaela hadn't moved. She was leaning on the staff with her head down. He paused but then walked on. He had issued the invitation – she would either come or not.

*   *   *

They found the narrow valley in the mid-afternoon. It was a long cleft in the rock, carved as if by a giant axe in the wall of the mountain forming a space fifty yards wide and about half a mile long surrounded on three sides by bare rock face. The green carpet of the valley floor showed that it readily collected enough water to provide a good area of thick pasture. The tall tree beside the round stone was the anchor for a wood and rope fence that could be drawn across the narrow valley entrance to provide an enclosure for the animals.

The wind had freshened and the sky was now overcast. In the east, a dark grey colouring now promised the rain that he had previously suspected. They would need good shelter on this, their first night spent in the open. If Addo had stayed in the valley for a few days, though, there should be a suitable place nearby. At Fenn's suggestion they spread out to look for it and Olgood soon found a small cave with an overhanging lip of rock where there was sign of a fire.

Hakon was uneasy. He stood outside the cave and wandered back and forth. He did not consider they were far enough from Lognavik to be thinking of spending the night, and wanted to use the remaining daylight to increase that distance, in spite of the threat of rain. Fenn agreed that they were still too close to the village, but without Kaela they simply did not know which direction to go.

'That not matter for now. Dangerous to stay here. Too close. We must go high in mountains. Tomorrow we get Kael. I tell you before – they catch, they kill.'

Fenn motioned for Olgood and Gisele to join them, and asked Hakon to translate for Gisele.

'Any one of us is free to do what they wish. Hakon, I know you're worried, so am I, but I said I would wait here for…' Fenn almost said 'Kaela' but caught himself in time, '…Kael and I will do that.'

Hakon's face wore a tight smile and he shook his head in exasperation. Olgood stepped up and spoke directly to Hakon.

'I've known Fenn since he was a baby,' he said. 'I will stay with him whatever he wants to do. You should too. He's young but very smart. He makes good choices. If anyone can lead us home, it is him.'

Hakon searched Olgood's face, then let out a sigh and nodded. He shook his hands to relieve his frustration.

'I know your words are true.'

He turned to Gisele and spoke to her. She nodded and looked up at Olgood.

'Gisele stay with this big one,' Hakon said.

Although they could not understand a word each other said, it was clear she had put her complete trust in Olgood.

* * *

Kaela arrived in the late afternoon just as small raindrops began to patter on the forest leaves. Fenn was waiting at the entrance to the valley having left the others to try to start a fire in the cave. She was dressed warmly, wearing her woollen hat pulled low on her head and carrying a basket strapped to her back which she removed and placed on the ground. Fenn saw she had already taken off her collar.

He could not restrain himself. While he waited, he had alternated between being absolutely certain she would come, and then realising that many things could prevent that happening. He walked up to her and hugged her, then stepped back and smiled.

'Thank you for coming.'

Kaela did not reply to his greeting. Instead she looked directly into his eyes and said, solemnly: 'I am with *you* now. Promise me you will take me home.'

Her tone took him by surprise. He started to reply, then stopped and thought.

'I make you this promise. While there's a spark of life in my body, I will strive to get us all home. And...' he paused then added, 'I shall not leave anyone behind.'

She searched his eyes then nodded, satisfied.

Fenn picked up the basket. It was heavier than he expected.

'Did you find Addo's cave?'

He nodded. 'When we get there, I think the first thing we should do is tell the others the truth about you... but...' he continued, looking at her, '...even though that hat covers your red hair, I think they may guess as soon as they see you.'

Kaela folded her arms.

'Haven't you done that already?'

'No… because…,' he faltered, '…you said to tell nobody.'

'That was then. It's different now.' She smiled at his confusion, then stepped around him and walked into the valley heading for the cave.

Fenn watched her go, as several drops of water from the wet leaves were blown into his face by the swirling wind. He looked to the sky and saw it was now dark overhead and the light of day was fading. The wind was coming in strong gusts and the full rain was only moments away. He quickly walked after Kaela. She had a knack of unsettling him by not saying what he expected. He wasn't sure whether this was a good or bad thing.

Although enough dry tinder and small sticks had been gathered, the fire had not yet been started. Olgood, Gisele and Hakon were surrounding the tinder pile with Olgood twirling a stick into a small hollow in a log where some shavings had been placed, while the other two tried to provide shelter from the wind.

When Kaela entered the cave, Olgood stopped his rubbing and they stood up. Kaela walked up to them and smiled a greeting but said nothing. She folded her arms again and waited until Fenn had joined them with the basket, indicating he should set it down on the floor. She looked at him expectantly.

Fenn put the basket down and cleared his throat.

'I told you that there were several reasons why I wanted to come here to get Kael,' he began. 'There are three things you do not know about…' he paused and replaced what he was going to say with: '…our guest,' which brought a snort of amusement from Kaela.

Fenn continued: 'The first is that she is a woman. The second is that her name is Kaela.' He did not wait for the reaction from Olgood and Hakon, but talked on over their expressions of surprise in Olgood's case, and denial by Hakon. 'The third is that she knows where we can cross the mountains and leave this place.'

Kaela spoke to Gisele telling her what Fenn had just said. Gisele just smiled and nodded, giving Fenn the impression that she already knew Kaela's secret. Olgood and Hakon were still looking at each other in surprise.

'…And she has red hair,' added Fenn, in a lighter tone, which drew a sharp look from Kaela and then a smile.

She went to where Fenn had placed the basket. Hakon's gaze followed her, his look still astonished and disbelieving. She laughed and wagged her finger at him and said something in the Northman's tongue.

She explained to Fenn: 'It's a saying the Northmen have. It would translate as – 'sometimes something is so close you cannot see it clearly'.'

Kaela placed her foot on the basket.

'Hakon could you please translate what I'm about to say for Gisele?' She waited for Hakon's acknowledgement.

'Another thing you all do not know is what is in this basket.' She paused for effect, taking on a dramatic pose like a queen about to deliver gifts to her subjects.

She turned to look at Fenn. 'Thorvald gave me a gift for you.'

Not for the first time, a simple statement from her caused several questions to form in his mind at once.

'What? How did Thorvald know you would see me? Does Askari know?'

'Of course.' Kaela smiled as if that was all the explanation that was necessary.

Their exchange was being followed intently by the others, their heads turning from one to the other. Fenn couldn't think where to begin. Finally, bewildered, he started with: 'But…'

Kaela interrupted him.

'I had to tell Askari about the raid. As I said before, she's very perceptive – she understood everything in a few heartbeats. She guessed you had come from Lognavik to tell me and, before I could tell her, she realised I would be leaving with you.'

'She didn't try to stop you?'

'No.' Kaela smiled at the thought. 'She always treated me more as a daughter than a thrall and she knew I would not stay forever. I'm sure she thinks this is best for me. I've lived with her for four years and during that time she continually amazed me. It was Askari who prepared this basket.'

She opened the basket and lifted out Thorvald's axe.

'Thorvald asked me to give this to you.'

Fenn's eyes widened. 'I cannot possibly take his axe from him. It's magnificent – a work of art.' He paused to think. 'I can leave it here. He's sure to find it in the cave.'

'He'd be extremely offended if you did – you would be rejecting his gift which would mean you were rejecting him. He'd think you didn't respect him.'

'But he loves that axe.'

'And now he's passing it on to you. He told me he thinks you are worthy of it.'

When Fenn still looked undecided, Kaela said, seriously:

'Thorvald said he would stand with you in battle. He cannot fight in this battle. He wants his axe to stand at your side in his place.'

Fenn shook his head. He would never fully understand the contrasts that were in these people. Bloodthirsty, cruel, arrogant and vengeful – yet gallant, generous, loyal and honourable at the same time. They loved war and peace equally.

Kaela handed him the axe. He ran his hand slowly down the iron-covered handle and then slipped it into his belt.

Kaela bent down to the basket again.

'Now for the clothing. A hat and gloves for everyone.'

She lifted out the woollen coverings from the basket and handed a set to each person in turn. Fenn looked with astonishment at the items she handed to him. They were well made, thick and warm. She next brought out a folded set of a tunic and trousers. These she took to Gisele, who smiled and nodded, and immediately began to change out of her dress.

When she saw Fenn's look of appreciation, Kaela said: 'The clothes belonged to Askari. When I mentioned who was with you, she told me Gisele would need new clothes.'

When Fenn shook his head again in amazement, Kaela said to him: 'I told you before there is not much Askari and Thorvald would not do for you. This basket is for you as well as for me.'

Olgood said: 'I think we have not been told all there is to be told about your previous visit to this area, young Fenn. It seems to me you did more than skin a bear.'

Fenn and Kaela shared a glance and Fenn said: 'Indeed – and I'll be sure to tell you about it sometime.'

Kaela continued her list of contents: 'There's food – goat's meat, dried bear meat and cheese and some of Askari's medicines. And two water skins and some snares.' She showed each item as she mentioned it.

'But most importantly – this!'

She held up what looked to be a small rock.

Fenn stared at the rock. It wasn't sharp so it wasn't a spearhead. How could it be important? Then he understood.

'Is that… flint?' he asked.

'Yes,' she said with a grin. She pointed to the carving knife in Fenn's belt. 'Hand me your knife.'

Gisele finished changing into the tunic and trousers which fitted her well. She had her dress and linen under-shift rolled into a ball. Kaela indicated she should put her old clothing into the basket.

'They may be useful,' she said.

Using the knife and flint stone, Kaela shaved some sparks into the tinder and blew when a glow appeared. The glow was followed by a small flame which she fed with small twigs until the fire was well alight. Just as the first strong flame appeared, there was a rushing sound outside the cave as the rain arrived in a heavy downpour.

Fenn was standing just under the lip of the cave. He moved further inside to avoid the splash of the rain and watched her at work. He knew then that, rather than him doing her a favour by inviting her to escape with them, she was doing them all a favour by joining them. She had brought items that would be essential for their survival and her knowledge of the passages through the mountains would be crucial. They had prepared poorly for their journey when they first left Lognavik and he regretted not taking more time to collect useful things from Ragnall's house, but time had been in short supply.

He closed his eyes and spent a moment in remembrance of Master Nerian, and that led him to also think of Audrey. He felt inside his tunic and touched the item wrapped in linen that he had rescued from the house.

Kaela came to stand with him. She paused for a moment, watching the fire, then said:

'You look sad.'

'Just remembering.' He realised she didn't know and added: 'Master Nerian was killed during the raid.'

'Oh…' She touched his arm. 'I'm sorry to hear that.'

They stood in silence, each with their thoughts. Kaela stared into the rain. Her eyes misted, and her head lowered.

She said quietly: 'It's a sad time.'

She looked up at him. He could see her eyes glistening in the firelight, tears now wet on her cheeks. Her face was twisted in pain.

'It was very hard to say goodbye – especially to Agatha.'

She drew her hands to her head and bent at the knees and her body shook with sobs. Fenn put his arm around her and held her into his shoulder. He looked at the fire, now blazing and spreading its warmth into the cave – and at the three people gathered around it, comparing their hats and gloves. A small band of fugitives with the whole country and its people against them. The chances of success on their journey were slim but he had more hope now than he had ever had.

He tightened his hold on the still shaking girl in his arms and bent his head to rest on hers.

CHAPTER TWELVE

Into the mountains, into the snow...

The wind and rain eased during the night but it was still a dull and overcast day that greeted them next morning. The cave had been warm and dry and in spite of the circumstances nobody had any trouble sleeping. They breakfasted on cheese and some cold goat meat from Askari that was not dried and so would not keep. Olgood added Master Nerian's sack of cheeses to the basket before he fastened it.

Kaela inspected their footwear and pronounced them unsuitable, but of course what they wore would have to suffice. She told them it was important to take care of their feet and footwear, drying both as soon as possible if they got wet.

They gathered at the mouth of the cave to discuss the plan of travel for the day. Fenn asked Kaela to translate for Gisele.

He repeated his reasoning, for Kaela's benefit, for thinking that any pursuit would hopefully not begin for a few days. He told them that Ragnall and Olaf were very good trackers as he had seen for himself when they followed the bear. He looked at Kaela who nodded her agreement.

'We must be careful not to leave an easy trail,' he urged. 'Step carefully. Disturb as little as possible.'

'We should hide places where we have fire – bury ashes,' Hakon added.

'I can walk at the back and cover our tracks where we need to,' said Olgood.

Fenn nodded and turned to Kaela. She crouched down on the dirt floor of the cave mouth and picked up a stick. She asked Hakon to take over keeping Gisele informed.

'I know places on this side of the mountains where we can stop for the night but once we cross the pass, the country will be as unknown to me as it is to you.'

Fenn's limited knowledge of the route back to Lindisfarne was based on tales from travellers to the monastery and on information from Hakon. He had told Kaela that he thought they should travel south to the coast, cross the water to the land of the Danes, then go further south through the land of the Saxons and Franks, and finally cross a second stretch of water to his homeland.

'We cannot go directly south,' she told them. Using the stick, she drew in the earth a shape like a pair of trousers with the right leg twice as long as the left.

'We are here.'

Kaela let the stick rest on a point on the outer edge of the short left leg near the middle.

'The mountain range runs all the way down this leg to the southern sea. We must first cross the range by heading east...' she carved a furrow across to where the legs joined, '...then we can go south along the coast – like this.' The stick traced a line down the inner side of the right leg. 'Anywhere along this coast we can get a boat to the land of the Danes – the further south, the better.'

Kaela pointed upriver. 'We can follow this river valley into the mountains until the river turns north. There are two passes we could take to the east. I think we should take the northernmost one. It's the easiest climb and not the pass we would be expected to use, because the southern pass leads more directly to the coast.'

'They may think we take north pass for same reasons,' said Hakon.

Kaela shrugged, and after a moment Hakon nodded. They could only make the choice they thought was best at the time. Fenn looked around and saw that the others were accepting Kaela's judgement.

Olgood said he would carry the basket but before he could lift it, Gisele indicated she would like to look inside. She selected two snares then spoke to Kaela.

Kaela and Hakon both smiled. 'Gisele says if you give her a little time in the evening, she can catch food. Rabbits, hares, birds, squirrels, fish. She says she used to do this for her family.'

Fenn looked at Olgood, silently asking if he knew of this talent. He shook his head but his admiration was apparent. Fenn drew the carving knife from his belt and offered it to Gisele. She recognised the knife and smiled her thanks. Her smile was so much like Yseld's.

Olgood shouldered the basket and Kaela and Gisele adjusted the leather straps. Fenn checked the cave site, brushing their tracks with a tree branch. He could not erase their presence here but he thought it worthwhile at least to try and conceal the number of people in their party. He asked Hakon to keep the tinder they had gathered so it could be used for future fires, then he and Hakon scattered the unburnt wood and the warm ashes of their fire in the forest, leaving a pile of previous ashes so the scene was as it appeared when they first arrived.

Fenn looked at the others. Everyone was wearing the hats and gloves Askari had provided, which made them all look alike. Each person met his eyes with confidence and stood ready to go.

Kaela led, walking east with Fenn following, then Hakon, Gisele and finally Olgood.

The walking was not difficult for the most part and they kept a good pace. They occasionally followed established paths but mostly Kaela led them across unmarked country. Olgood carefully masked the points where they left and joined the paths. There were some steep climbs when crossing ridges, but nothing that was as difficult as the terrain they encountered when they had first left the village.

It had started to rain soon after leaving the cave. It was not heavy but it was persistent and could have been annoying but, for the first time, Fenn was thankful that he had been forced to work outdoors in all weathers through the winter. He was able to easily ignore the conditions and concentrate on their progress. Hakon and Olgood would also not be troubled by the rain and he had no concern for Kaela, but he checked how Gisele was faring. He saw he need not worry. Her long hair showing beneath her hat was plastered to her neck and shoulders by the rain but she looked as though she was on an afternoon stroll and she smiled so broadly at him when she caught him watching, water coursing down her face, that he had the impression she was enjoying herself. Whenever she had the slightest difficulty, the strong arm of Olgood was there to assist her. They looked similar, both with long blond hair showing beneath their hats.

Fenn hoped it was also raining in Lognavik as it might hamper whatever efforts were being made there and further delay their pursuit while they were now steadily increasing their distance away from the village.

There were periods of brief respite but the rain continued throughout the day. It did not dampen any spirits, however – all Fenn saw were expressions of determination.

They had been used to two meals a day, morning and evening, but now Kaela suggested they eat some dried bear meat at midday, to keep up their strength. Fenn found the taste strong, almost unpleasant at first, but it became palatable after a while. They continued to walk while chewing on the meat.

In the late afternoon the wind started to rise again and Fenn asked Kaela the distance to a place where they could stop overnight. She moved to where she could see through the forest cover and pointed to a group of trees that were visible high in the foothills of the mountain ahead.

Gisele passed Hakon and talked to Kaela, who nodded and showed her the distant trees. Gisele then stepped from the path and in a few moments was lost from view in the forest.

'Will she be able to catch anything in this rain?' asked Fenn. He hoped that, having made the offer, she didn't feel she had to try to get food no matter what the conditions.

Nobody replied. It seemed they were all thinking the same thing.

After a while Kaela answered with: 'We'll see.'

She moved off along the path and one by one they followed.

Kaela seemed to recognise a particular place. She turned off the path and pushed into the forest, climbing through the undergrowth towards the trees she had pointed out. She told Olgood to cover their tracks where they left the path.

The small copse of a dozen trees was nestled tight against the vertical cliff of a mountain spur which was an anomaly among the still steep but elsewhere evenly sloping foothills. The cliff face displayed a mixture of bushes and bare rock and continued to rise upwards for hundreds of feet before levelling and joining the base of the mountain. The spur appeared like a giant fist jutting out from the mountain's cloak. The copse of trees at its base occupied a small area of relatively flat land amidst the otherwise steep slopes of the foothills. It was a good location to spend the night but they wouldn't be able to light a fire there because it would be visible for miles.

Once they reached the group of trees, Fenn looked back in the direction they had come and could see that they had climbed above the forest. The shrubbery at this height had thinned, forming a smaller and sparser ground covering, and the air was distinctly colder. Snow lying in small clumps was visible higher up the slope. He hunched his shoulders and stared into the distance, looking for movement, but could see no sign of other people. Olgood came to stand beside him. He too stared over the forest.

Fenn said: 'She seemed very confident.' Olgood nodded but he continued to scan the trees with a worried look on his face.

They turned when Kaela called Fenn's name. She beckoned to them and then disappeared around the side of the rocky spur. Fenn followed her with Olgood close behind and discovered, when he rounded the edge of the cliff, that the flat area extended around the cliff-face and on this side there was an overhang which provided reasonable shelter from both rain and wind. Hakon had already gone out to search for dry wood. A fire built against the rock wall here would be invisible to anyone travelling in the direction they had come.

He welcomed the prospect of heat and the ability to dry himself in front of a warm fire.

*   *   *

Gisele appeared out of the dusk, carrying two large hares, one in each hand, already skinned and gutted. She was greeted with cries of appreciation and surprise. While Kaela took the hares, Olgood ushered Gisele to a place beside the fire, then disappeared into the growing darkness himself, returning with some branches which he fashioned with his knife into two forked stands and a spit for each hare. When she was warmed and somewhat drier, Gisele insisted on taking over the roasting of the hares. She moved some of the burning wood from the centre to the edges of the fire and waited for the flames to reduce to glowing embers so the heat was low and even and intense. She called to Kaela and talked to her while she turned the spit. The smell of the cooking made Fenn's mouth drool. It had been a long time since he'd smelt anything as good. Kaela put her arm around Gisele and hugged her, then stood up and spoke to everyone.

'Gisele wants you to know that she buried the remains of these hares and left no mark of her hunt. She says it feels good to be free and to hunt again and she wants to thank you for allowing her to come with you.'

Hakon crouched beside Gisele and placed his hand on her back, talking to her. He turned around, grinning broadly.

'Thor has sent us this goddess – his wife Sif – to hunt and cook for us. He smiles on our journey.'

Gisele look at him inquiringly and he repeated his words to her. Her mouth formed a circle of astonishment then broke into one of her beautiful smiles and she playfully pushed him away.

Kaela laughed and explained: 'Sif is the goddess of the harvest and she provides in times of need.' She walked up to Gisele and lifted her hat to reveal Gisele's long wheat-blond hair.

'It is said Sif had beautiful hair, so maybe she *has* visited us tonight to make sure we do not go hungry.'

'Please tell Gisele I agree with you, Hakon,' said Fenn. 'Only a goddess could have caught two fat hares in the rain and we're very lucky to have her with us. And I also agree with Gisele too…,' he stretched his back and spread his arms, '…it *does* feel good to be free.'

There was a grunt of agreement from Olgood who was sitting with his back against the rock, a contented smile of satisfaction on his face.

As Gisele continued to turn the hares over the glowing embers, Kaela came to stand with Fenn.

'Tomorrow we'll follow the river north a little way then climb up into the mountains to cross the north pass. It's only early spring so there will be plenty of snow at the top and we must be well over the pass and find shelter before nightfall. So far, I've avoided the main paths to lessen the risk of meeting anyone but we may meet others in the pass.'

'I'll ask Hakon if he can walk ahead in the pass, so we can be warned.'

'No. I will lead,' said Kaela, firmly.

Fenn looked at her and smiled. 'Of course. As you wish.'

He thought a moment and then asked: 'What will we find on the other side?'

She shrugged. 'I've been to the top of the pass with Birgitta but all I could see from there were more mountains.'

Kaela sat down against the rock wall. Fenn joined her, extending his hands to receive the warmth of the fire, and they waited impatiently for Gisele to announce that the hares were ready to eat.

*   *   *

As Kaela had foretold – when they stood at the summit of the pass, flanked by towering mountains on both sides, all they could see in front were more mountain ranges.

She remarked that the view was very different from the previous time she had been there. There was an unseasonably heavy covering of snow. The thick snow obliterated all signs of the path ahead but also allayed their fears of being surprised by other travellers – any movement against the white of the snow would be easily noticed. Indeed, thought Fenn, only desperate people such as themselves would be attempting to cross the mountains in these conditions. Thankfully, the rain that had accompanied them all morning had ceased when they reached the snow line.

There was a short discussion about whether they should wait for the snow to melt a little, but Hakon said that could take days. Fenn said they had no choice and could not afford to wait.

Kaela led them down a narrow ridge. She said that if they kept to the ridges, the snow cover would be thinner and provide easier going. After the first mile, however, their progress was so tiring that Fenn had to admit to himself that had they been travelling through the pass for any purpose other than escape, he would have turned back. He was concerned about the deep tracks they were leaving in the snow but Hakon assured him that one good snowfall would erase them.

A graceful curving valley dropped away on each side of the ridge. It looked beautiful but was filled with snow of an unknown and therefore possibly treacherous depth. Even on the ridge, with each step they sank into the snow to the level of their knees, and their thin footwear gave such poor protection that Fenn's feet at first ached and then grew numb from the cold. Hakon, being the smallest, was finding the going especially difficult.

Fenn knew that severe cold could cause injury and he was concerned that if they walked in the snow for too long, their feet could be seriously harmed. Nobody had complained but he was aware they would all be suffering in a similar manner.

From mid-afternoon, Fenn had been searching the terrain for a suitable place to spend the night. As more time passed without success, the need became more urgent and he called a halt beside the remains of an ancient fir tree still clinging tenaciously to the rocky ridge. Beneath the tree there was a small patch of ground that was free of snow.

Everyone stamped their feet to shake the snow from their clothing and warm their legs.

'It looks as though we need to at least cross the ridge ahead before we're out of the mountains, and that may not be the last one.' He looked at Kaela for confirmation and received a nod. 'We can't continue to walk through the snow for much longer or we'll damage our feet. We need to get to shelter and start a fire. Does anyone have a suggestion?'

As if to emphasise the urgency, a light pattering of snow started to fall.

They all gazed about, searching the mountains for an indication of a cave or group of trees – any place that would provide shelter. In every direction lay a bleak landscape of snow and rock, dotted with a few isolated fir trees.

165

'I hear of cave made in snow,' said Hakon, 'But I not know how.'

Fenn nodded. It was something to try as a last resort.

Olgood moved around the tree to the far side. He stared for a moment then said:

'Fenn, what's that?'

The twisted roots of the old fir were exposed on that side and the ground was much steeper, falling away almost vertically at first but easing in steepness as the descent into the valley continued. As Fenn moved to join him, Olgood did not take his eye from the object that had caught his attention and pointed at three trees surrounding a dark square shape on the far side of the valley a few hundred feet below where they were standing. The trees and the shadow of the parallel ridge revealed the shape only as an indistinct dark form against the white snow. Was it just a rock or something more?

Fenn stared hard until he felt his eyes stinging from lack of blinking. He was aware that Kaela was at his shoulder.

They peered through the veil of wafting snowflakes.

'I think that's a hut,' said Fenn.

'Yes,' agreed Kaela. 'But how do we get there?'

*   *   *

Hakon said they would need snow shoes to cross the valley, and explained to Fenn and Olgood how they worked. Olgood thought he could make some, but one look at the hard and brittle dead wood of the fir tree showed that it could provide nothing suitable and the next tree was as far away as their destination. Fenn recognised that they should have prepared for the snow much earlier but it was too late for regrets, they could only move on. Before they started, Olgood reached up and tore a straight branch from the fir which he shaped with his axe into a staff.

It was too steep to cross the valley directly from that point, so they continued down the ridge until Fenn decided it was safe enough. Olgood led the way into the valley with Fenn, now carrying the basket, behind him. Kaela and Gisele followed with Hakon in the rear.

Olgood used the staff to test the snow ahead for firmness, then, lifting his knees high, he took a few steps forward, compacting the snow and forming a trench which made it easier for those following. The snow was deeper than on the ridge, reaching their thighs. Progress was excruciatingly slow as they moved forward one laborious foot at a time. When Olgood tired he stepped aside. Fenn accepted the staff, passed the basket back and took over the lead. He found he was tired after only a few steps but forced himself on until he could not lift his legs. Kaela then took over and they rotated the lead among the five of them.

With his height and strength, it was Olgood who made the best headway by far. Hakon insisted he take his turn but he was unable to move more than a few yards at a time, which was due entirely to his size – he was waist deep in the snow – rather than from lack of effort.

In the valley, the firmness of the snow was uneven – sometimes it compacted readily and steady progress was made. Often, however, an area contained soft snow and, despite testing ahead with the staff, the person in the lead would fall into a hole up to their chest and would need to be hauled back to firmer ground, the struggle always leaving everyone exhausted. It was then necessary to find a detour around the soft snow, resulting in long delays before their forward progress was resumed.

Fenn had planned a route across the valley to the hut which took advantage of two rocky outcrops that pierced the covering of snow. These two points were not at the same level which meant they would need to descend to the second outcrop and climb from there to the hut. Fenn thought their best chance of reaching the hut by nightfall was to use the rocks both as waypoints to guide them across the valley and as places where they could safely rest free from the enveloping snow.

It took much longer than Fenn had anticipated to reach the first group of rocks. From their starting point, the distance had not seemed far, but he had not expected their progress across the valley to be so agonisingly slow.

Each person finally stepped with relief onto the first firm rocky area and sat down heavily, breathing hard. Fenn looked anxiously about. The sky was grey and snow was still falling, the combination lessening his visibility significantly. He was relieved to see, however, now they were closer, that their destination could be clearly confirmed as a hut.

Their exertions were keeping them warm, except for their feet, but the hard work sapped their energy. There was obviously a limit to how long they could keep going. He checked the location of the second group of rocks and took the lead towards them. Although the second group were downhill from the first, this was not as much of a benefit as Fenn thought it might be. Only a slight advantage was gained by heading obliquely downhill, the work required to push through the snow was unchanged. They would spend a long time battling forward only to look up and seem to be no closer to the rocks. They could only lower their heads and concentrate on the next step.

After having had the feeling that he could almost reach out and touch the rocks for some time, Fenn was in the lead when he finally broke free of the snow and fell forward onto his hands on the rocky promontory.

Resting at the second waypoint, it was obvious that Gisele was no longer able to make much progress on her turn at lead. Being unused to physical work she was tiring quickly, and so it was agreed that she and Hakon would remain at the rear for the climb up to the hut and they would take turns carrying the basket. Like Hakon, she had tried until she was physically unable to move, but it cost them more time and effort to keep changing the lead than they gained in distance.

From here, they could see the hut clearly. It looked abandoned and not in good repair – part of the roof had collapsed – but it offered them a much better chance of survival than spending the night in open terrain surrounded by snow.

Looking back across the valley, Fenn could no longer see their starting point – the fir tree on the ridge – through the fading light and the falling snow. He checked the distance they still had to go to reach the hut and knew they wouldn't make it before the light faded completely. He wondered briefly if he had made the right decisions, firstly to continue into the pass, and secondly to cross the valley to try and reach the hut without snow shoes. Had he only put their lives in more danger? But, as usual, he reasoned that those decisions, right or wrong, could not be changed now.

*   *   *

When darkness came, they linked themselves by holding the belt of the person in front. At each change of lead, Fenn called out their names to check they were still together.

The bulk of the progress was still being forged by Olgood. At his turn in the lead he was making more distance than Fenn and Kaela combined. But his massive effort was taking its toll.

Olgood was in the lead but was only moving a few steps and then resting for long periods before taking another two or three steps. Fenn tapped him on the shoulder to take over the lead, but Olgood shook his head stubbornly and roared his frustration into the night, crashing upward into the snow and making ten quick yards before he fell to his knees, his chest heaving, unable to continue. Olgood was finding it hard to accept that his great strength was failing him. Fenn stepped past him, picked up the fallen staff and, using it to balance himself, pushed forward into the snow. He automatically called out the names and received replies from everyone and a grunt from Olgood.

It had stopped snowing and the parting clouds now revealed the hut in brief moments of moonlight reflected off the snow. It was only fifty yards away but every yard was uphill and the distance could have been a mile for the effort it would require to get there. The cold was intense even without any wind and Fenn could no longer feel most of his body. He counted twenty steps before he could go no further. He felt Kaela move past him and called out the names again. Olgood didn't answer. Fenn called his name once more, but the night returned only silence.

Standing beside Fenn, Hakon said: 'I go back,' but just then a call sounded from down the hill behind them.

'Gisele say she find Olgood,' said Hakon. 'He look like dead.'

Hakon was carrying the basket, so Fenn said to him: 'Wait here.' He stumbled back down the trench they had carved through the snow, with Kaela following, and called to Gisele. She replied from the darkness.

Olgood was lying full length in the snow. Gisele had obviously just turned him on his back – his tunic was covered in frosted snow as if he had fallen face first in the trench. Fenn bent to put his ear close to Olgood's mouth.

'He's still breathing.'

'What can we do? We can't carry him,' said Kaela.

'No,' agreed Fenn. It was by no means certain anyone would reach the hut, and nobody had the strength to carry Olgood. Any attempt to carry or drag him would lessen everyone's chances.

Fenn drew back his hand and slapped Olgood hard on the cheek. The only reaction was a gasp from Gisele.

Fenn slapped Olgood again and shouted his name.

Olgood's eyes blinked open and he stared up at Fenn who put his arm under his shoulders and with a grunt of effort, raised him to a sitting position.

'You big ox,' said Fenn, in a mildly scolding tone. 'What happened to you?'

Olgood looked around and Fenn saw recognition appear in his eyes.

Gisele gave a cry of relief and bent to help Olgood to his feet while Fenn put his shoulder under Olgood's other arm and struggled to raise him, his legs burning with the effort. Olgood stumbled upright and gained his balance. Kaela handed him the staff and he leaned heavily on it.

'How far?' he asked with a slurred voice.

'Only twenty yards,' replied Fenn. 'We're almost there.'

With one arm across Fenn's shoulders and using the staff in his other hand, Olgood was helped to stagger uphill. When they reached the place where Fenn had left Hakon, he was not waiting there as expected. Instead a ragged hole had been dug in the snow. Then, in the gloom, he saw Hakon inside the hole, the basket still strapped to his back. He had removed his gloves and was digging with his bare hands, flinging the snow to each side. He had advanced the trail another ten yards. Fenn and Kaela were close enough to be able to see each other's face in the moonlight. Fenn could see his sudden determination mirrored in her eyes.

Olgood was breathing in slow shallow gasps. He said: 'Go on... Get us there... Gisele can help me.' He lifted his arm from Fenn's shoulder.

He and Kaela waded through the snow to Hakon. Fenn put his hand on Hakon's shoulder and eased him away from the snow he was digging into. He could hear Hakon's teeth chattering.

In another ten yards Fenn would be able to touch the side of the hut – it was tantalisingly close. As he closed the distance foot by desperate foot, however, the snow deepened. He saw there had been a recent fall from the roof creating a hill of soft snow in front of the door. Fenn tightened his jaw and attacked the hill using his hands just as Hakon had done. Kaela appeared beside him pulling at the snow and stamping it underfoot and from her throat Fenn heard a growl like a caged animal.

Together they breached the final snow barrier and a door appeared before them.

* * *

The hut had not been used in a long while.

The floor was dirty and the walls were damp and covered with grime and the room smelled of mould and stale air. The walls and roof were solid except in one corner where the roof was sagging due to a part of the wall that that was cracked and bent but not broken. It was still weather-proof and looked as though it would certainly last one more night. The only opening was the door and the square-shaped interior was completely bare of furniture.

As each person entered and glanced around in the moonlight that shone through the open door, they breathed a sigh of relief at the large pile of wood set in a corner next to an alcove with a conical top that had been built to house a fire. A quick investigation revealed that the smoke hole was blocked. Hakon volunteered to go onto the roof and clear it but Fenn saw that he was shivering violently and said he would go himself.

Hakon stopped him at the door. 'I am lightest,' he said. 'This for me to do.'

'Are you sure?' asked Fenn. He had the thought that Hakon might think he had not been contributing.

'This mountain not get me yet,' Hakon replied, and slipped out the door, Fenn closing it behind him.

With the door closed it was black inside the hut. Now that he was no longer involved in a continual struggle through the snow, Fenn's body asserted its need for movement and warmth with bouts of involuntary shivering and he found he was breathing in gasps. Fenn and Kaela felt through the wood pile for pieces that were dry and suitable for starting the fire, while Gisele tried to warm Olgood by rubbing his skin. Fenn used Thorvald's axe to split some of the wood into smaller pieces, taking care with his numb fingers in the dark. There were some thumps from the roof and eventually a shower of snow and soot dropped into the fireplace. Fenn brushed it aside but then had to wait for Hakon to return with the tinder he carried. He resisted the urge to go outside to see if he needed help, and was relieved when the door opened and Hakon stumbled in and fell to his knees. Fenn helped him to stand, clapped him on the shoulder and said: 'Well done.'

Kaela produced her flint. Unfortunately, Hakon's tinder was damp and Kaela's movements were slow and clumsy. She had to pause each time she shivered, but Fenn knew he could do no better. It took a worryingly long time for the sparks to catch, everyone watching anxiously but without comment. Many times smoke appeared but the tiny ember quickly died. Kaela stubbornly persisted through each disappointment and there were loud murmurs of appreciation when a flame flickered and the fire was finally underway.

The damp wood was smoky and initially more smoke came into the hut than went out the smoke hole, causing them all to cough and cover their mouths and noses, but as the fire gained heat and strength, it created a draught which drew the smoke directly upwards and vented it outside.

Fenn suggested they take off their footwear and trousers, hats, gloves and anything else that was wet and put those items closest to the fire to dry and warm them. He was worried about Olgood who looked listless and confused. He recalled the monastery physician, Master Egbert, saying that near-frozen hands and feet must not be heated too quickly and suggested they sit with their backs to the fire while the hut warmed.

He and Kaela helped Gisele take off Olgood's wet clothing, then Gisele retrieved her dress from the basket and also the sack that had carried Master Nerian's cheeses, and used them to dry everyone's feet and legs. She wrapped the dress around Olgood's feet. Each person found a place on the dress or sack to keep their bare feet off the floor and they huddled together as close as they could around Olgood, bodies shivering violently.

The only noises were the crackling of the fire, the involuntary shuffling of shivering limbs, and the clattering of teeth.

Nobody must sleep,' said Fenn. 'Keep each other awake until we're warm.'

Fenn remembered his recovery from the cold after his attempt to rescue Audrey. That time the cold had affected his entire body, whereas now his body and his limbs felt separated. His legs and arms were not a part of him, merely attachments to be dragged about.

He clung to Kaela and could feel a trace of warmth where they touched. He hoped she was getting as much from him. After a while he noticed that his bouts of shivering were occurring in perfect tandem with hers. He found this fact fascinating and wondered whether it was coincidence or whether one was triggering the other. He concentrated on that question for a long time until he realised that their shivering was becoming less intense. The room was warming and so were they. He reluctantly let go of Kaela and crawled to build the fire and check the clothing they had laid out to dry. The smaller items were dry and warm and the trousers were dry enough so he handed them back to their owners.

Everyone was now responsive, even Olgood, and Fenn could see a change in each person – from a single-minded focus on just staying alive and getting warmth back into their bodies, to a readiness, now, to consider the next step.

With his trousers, stockings and shoes back on as well as his hat and gloves and the hut warming noticeably, Fenn soon felt the pain of warmth returning to his hands and feet. The pain became intense and unrelenting. He tried to stand and move about and discovered that the pain lessened if he moved away from the fire, but movement was also difficult and he decided it was best to be still and endure. He could see that everyone was suffering.

He could not remember if Master Egbert had told him whether the pain was due to their flesh regaining life or a sign of permanent damage.

*   *   *

Their exhaustion and the welcome feeling of being warm had contributed to each of them getting the sleep they needed to recover from their ordeal and Fenn woke feeling refreshed. His body ached but it was a bearable ache that he knew would disappear when he was moving again.

When his eyes opened, they looked straight into Kaela's face only inches from his own. He could feel her breath on his chin. His eyes travelled along the gentle curve of her eyelashes, the slope of her nose and the rosy pinkness of her lips. Their arms and legs were so mixed he couldn't move without waking her. Past the top of Kaela's head, he could see Gisele using her knife to cut strips from her linen under-shift. She looked up and, catching his gaze, she smiled and made a soft noise in her throat. Hakon came into view and Olgood behind him.

'Awake at last,' whispered Olgood, with a big smile of his own. 'You two look so cosy.'

When Kaela woke a few moments later, they pulled themselves apart and Fenn went outside to check the day. The three sets of amused eyes that silently watched his walk to the door somehow made him feel like a naughty boy caught with his fingers covered in honey.

Olgood was searching the trees for suitable material to make snow shoes based on the design Hakon had drawn in soot on the floor and modifications suggested by Kaela. Hakon had asked if everyone could ski, as skis would make for even quicker travel. Kaela had tried skiing with Birgitta, but Gisele, Fenn and Olgood had never skied so snow shoes were preferred.

Kaela had tended to any raw skin or blisters with ointment from Askari's medicines, and now she was melting snow in front of the fire in one of the skin bags. When melted, a bag stuffed full of snow only yielded a surprisingly small amount of water, which Kaela diligently poured into the other bag and then patiently repeated the process. Fenn and Hakon had collected wood to replenish the amount they had used. There was a discussion about whether they should add more wood to the stack beside the fire. Hakon did not want to do anything that may aid Ragnall, but Fenn said they would be dead if someone hadn't left wood for them and he would like to do the same for any other traveller in a similar situation. Hakon had reluctantly agreed.

Fenn was not worried that, by mid-morning, they were still at the hut. He did not expect their pursuers would appear any time soon as trackers could only move slowly, looking for signs – but there were two other reasons that they could not leave yet. Firstly, apart from their tender feet, their leg muscles were also sore from the unnatural action they had been forced to use in their prolonged walk through the snow and they needed rest. Secondly, and more importantly, Olgood and Hakon needed time to make a pair of snow shoes for each person.

Fenn planned to leave as soon as the shoes were ready. He hoped to be out of the snow before nightfall. In the meantime, just in case, he kept a constant watch on the part of the pass that he could see from the hut.

Using green wood from the living firs, Olgood selected thin branches that he could readily form into the base of each snow shoe by twisting them into a shape like a teardrop and tying the ends together. With Hakon's help he wove smaller branches into a mat which was attached to the teardrop with the cloth strips Gisele had cut from her shift. One of the branches in the middle of the weave was raised as a hoop for a foot to slip into and their normal shoe would be tied to this hoop.

Hakon demonstrated how to walk with snow shoes and they all practised on the first pair. When Olgood gave Fenn his own pair, they worked perfectly. He walked across the snow using the shuffling motion Hakon had shown him, moving with such ease that it took him only a few moments to walk down to their second waypoint, shaking his head ruefully when he arrived as he recalled the time and effort the same distance had cost them last night. He checked his own tracks which were so light that they would quickly disappear in the wind and snow.

Fenn stood beside the rocks and looked across the valley. It had snowed during the night and the deep trenches they had created were gone. He could see evidence of their crossing but it was faint and he suspected it was visible only because he knew where to look. He scanned the land slowly, taking his time, until he was sure that the five of them were the only living things in sight. He marvelled at the view laid out before him. The mountain scene was both peaceful and breathtakingly beautiful under the clear sunny sky and seemed to be welcoming their onward travel showing no hint that during the preceding night the same awesome mountains had nearly snatched their lives away with blind indifference. He carefully turned around without tangling his snow shoes and climbed back to the hut.

Gisele came out of the door and sat beside Kaela to tie on her snow shoes. She whispered something in Kaela's ear and they both laughed. When Hakon emerged a few moments later he was also smiling and looked pleased with himself. Fenn shuffled over to help Olgood shoulder the basket and looked at Kaela.

'What's so funny?' he asked her.

'Hakon left a rude message to Ragnall on the floor,' she replied. She whispered in his ear.

Fenn couldn't help but chuckle.

'So...' he said to Hakon, '...no need to cover our tracks inside the hut then. But if he sees that message he will be angry.'

'If he catch us...' said Hakon, '...whether he angry or not, he still kill us.'

CHAPTER THIRTEEN

Hope dared and Hope dashed...

Under different circumstances, the journey out of the mountains would have been pleasant. It was a beautiful day and the sun blazed so brightly off the snow that they were forced to narrow their eyes to slits and use their hands as shades in order to see.

With the snow shoes they moved easily on top of the snow and as they became more confident with their new mode of travelling, Fenn pushed the pace to get off the snow as quickly as possible.

Yesterday, from the old fir tree, it had seemed their way was blocked by a series of mountain ranges, but now they could see that the valley they were following curved like a river of snow among the mountains, effectively becoming a pathway around and between the jumble of ridges.

Their descent became so steep in places that they had to zig-zag across the valley, stepping downhill sideways in their shoes. Hakon remarked that these almost vertical slopes would be fun to ski. When someone fell over or tumbled down the hill there was laughter and a sense of enjoyment in helping them to their feet that was in stark contrast to their exhausting experience in the soft snow on the previous day.

The steep twisting descent continued to wend a path between high ridges until well into the afternoon. Moving diagonally from side to side often resulted in long periods in shadow, accompanied by a noticeable drop in temperature – a sharp reminder of how cold they had been just the previous day, so Fenn was relieved to finally walk out of the shadow and into sunlight at a point where the valley straightened. He stopped and waited for the others to catch up. For the first time since they had stood at the top of the pass, there were no mountains in front of them and Fenn could see for miles. The valley continued to descend sharply for some distance yet, but the gradient then eased to become rolling snow-covered hills that eventually levelled onto a large plateau several miles wide, which seemed to extend all the way to the horizon.

With the end of their mountain crossing in sight, they traversed the final slope and started across the hills in good spirits. The snow had developed a thin crust which held their snow shoes well but the snow itself was still knee-deep as Fenn discovered when he took a foot out of his snow shoe and tested the hardened snow. In the shoes, however, they could move even more rapidly over the crusty top and Hakon demonstrated a stride that was half walking, half running but comfortable for everyone, allowing them to make fast progress.

When they reached the start of the plateau, Fenn called for a short rest and Kaela distributed some cheese and meat while they drank from the water skins. The water was cold and refreshing.

They knew they were over the mountains and soon to be out of the snow when tufts of grass appeared, breaking the expanse of white with patches of green and brown. Although the ground was more uneven than it had appeared from the initial vantage point high in the valley, it was relatively easy walking under the cloudless sky, and they crossed the wide plateau without difficulty using the same ground-eating stride.

'We'll rest again at the top of that hill.'

Up ahead, it could now be seen that the plateau terminated in a small rise which confronted them like an ocean wave about to break on the shore. Fenn asked Kaela to check the way ahead from the top and followed her footsteps in the thinning snow, climbing sideways up the steepest part, and concentrating on pushing his snow shoes firmly into the snow to avoid slipping backwards. Nearing the top, he glanced up to see that Kaela was waiting at the crest. She was staring ahead and did not turn as he approached. She had removed her snow shoes. Fenn followed her gaze and took in the spectacular view that appeared before him. As the others joined him, he bent to remove his own pair.

The view that had been hidden behind the hill was much more familiar than the white wilderness of recent days. A green luxuriant forest stretched before them as far as the eye could see. Where they now stood on the crest of the hill, the snow was abruptly gone, replaced by a mixture of bare earth, grass, loose stones and large boulders extending down the hill until the forest trees began. Automatically, Fenn searched the ground and gathered some stones suitable for his sling.

When they had all removed their snow shoes, they sat for a moment in the warm sun. Fenn was enjoying the unusual experience of having warm feet, but stood up reluctantly when he thought they had waited long enough. He looked back at the plateau they had crossed and beyond that to the hills and the valley. He narrowed his eyes and then stiffened and dropped to one knee.

'Everyone lie down,' he said. 'I can see movement at the top of the valley.' He lowered himself to his stomach.

He counted six black dots moving fast across the valley at the point where they had first stopped to look over the hills and plateau below.

'They have skis,' said Hakon beside him. 'They catch up quick.'

The sun was nearing the mountain tops and Fenn tried to estimate how long it would be before it lowered behind the peaks. He checked with Hakon who agreed that their pursuers – who else could they be? – would not be able to cross both the hills and the plateau before nightfall, even on skis, so they would not catch up today.

Fenn allowed himself a small satisfaction to know the figures he had seen would be spending the night in the snow. For now, though, the group needed to get into the forest quickly and use the daylight they had available to find a suitable place for themselves to spend the night.

They gathered their snow shoes to hide in the forest.

Fenn paused at the edge of a large open space. A stream ran through the centre of a clear grassy valley two or three hundred yards wide, bordered on both sides by the forested hills they had been travelling through since leaving the mountain plateau. The forest so far had contained little undergrowth to impede their progress which was mostly downhill, and they had covered the ground at an easy loping run. The valley and the stream should lead to the coast. They would be more exposed in the open ground of the valley floor but they would be able to move even quicker than they would through the forest. A hundred yards from his viewpoint, a solitary stone as tall as a man stood starkly in the centre of an otherwise featureless flat area as if it were a sentinel set there to survey or guard the valley beyond.

They needed to refill their water skins so Fenn led the way into the meadow heading for the stream. Kaela touched his shoulder and with an inclination of her head suggested that he follow her, turning toward the large stone. Curious, Fenn followed and after a moment the others also changed direction toward the stone.

On the side of the stone that faced down the valley, a large vertical rectangle had been deeply carved and that border was filled with a series of markings laid out in four columns, worn by time but still legible. Fenn knew these were runes but they were meaningless to him.

Kaela stood before the stone and with her hands tracing the runes, said:

'Aesir and – his brother – Hengst – defeated – the Jutes – at this place – Yarl Winnid – was killed.'

Fenn wasn't sure which fact attracted his interest more – that Kaela could read the runes or that they were standing on the site of an ancient battle that had been important enough to carry this large stone up the valley and carve the message upon it. He looked about, trying to understand why a battle would be fought here – it seemed such an unlikely isolated place, miles from any villages.

He imagined the clash of two armies and the men struggling, swinging their swords and axes; the ringing of metal, the thud of arrows and weapons striking flesh and bone and war cries mixed with the screams of the dying. He remembered the fight outside Ragnall's house and he expanded that a hundredfold in his mind – imagining the ground smeared with blood and the river running red. He could almost hear echoes of the conflict surrounding him from the distant past.

Now there was no sign of the bodies and the abandoned weapons and arrows that must have littered the meadow. How many lives had been ended here? How many lives had been saved because this fight had been fought?

Only the stone remained, conveying its timeless reminder of an event that had happened long ago on the spot where he now stood.

*   *   *

'Yes,' agreed Fenn, surveying the place Kaela had chosen. 'This is good.'

He turned to talk to Gisele but she had already disappeared into the trees.

The tall bank beside the river would conceal a fire as long as it did not smoke. There was plenty of dry wood on the river bank and also, for his own use, better-shaped river-rounded stones to replace the ones he had gathered from the hilltop. Olgood had arranged two large stones, one on each side of the fire, and he was shaping a branch to serve as a spit for whatever Gisele could catch. He did not seem to doubt that she would return with something.

While they waited, they sat in a sombre mood around the fire.

The sighting had confirmed that they were being pursued and dashed any hopes that the brothers might not follow this far, corroborating Hakon's opinion. Their trudge through the snow and the speed of their pursuers using skis had brought the two parties closer together far quicker than he had anticipated. He had expected that the need to track them would slow the brothers down. They must have either made their choice of which pass to use and headed directly there or sent people to both. The efforts they had made to mask their tracks on the other side of the pass seemed to have been for nothing. He wondered if the brothers had split up – one chasing while the other organised the defence and rebuild of Lognavik.

Fenn estimated that they were less than half a day ahead of those following them. At least the pursuers would now lose the advantage of their skis and, perhaps for the first time, would need to actually follow their tracks, so Fenn had to find a strategy to somehow lose them or lead them in the wrong direction. Now that he understood the resolve of the Northmen was greater than he had calculated, he determined that he would not underestimate them again.

His thoughts were interrupted by a form emerging out of the gloom, walking towards the fire so confidently on the stones of the riverbank that

181

for a heart-stopping instant Fenn thought it was one of their pursuers and they had been discovered.

In each hand, Gisele was holding a strand of thick grass, tied in a loop. On one loop, threaded through mouth and gill hung a large salmon. On the other reed dangled three squirrels, attached by their tails – already skinned. Fenn stared in astonishment.

When he found his voice, he said to Kaela: 'Please ask Gisele how she caught the fish – surely not with a snare?'

To Kaela's question, Gisele held the fish horizontally and stroked it on the underside then she held it still and with her other hand, snatched it away.

'But... How could she even see the fish underwater in this light?'

At this question Gisele shrugged. Kaela said: 'I think the evidence proves she *was* able to see it.'

When Gisele had cooked the hares for them two days ago, Fenn had not tasted anything so enjoyable since Askari's *skause*.

The salmon was even better.

A few moments before serving, Gisele added a sprinkling of an aromatic wild herb she had found somewhere. The meat was so tender in his mouth that at first it felt firm but it softened and seemed to melt an instant after his teeth touched it. He savoured every mouthful with the gentle scent of the herb filling his nostrils, and it seemed a pity to swallow. The squirrel meat was a delicious opposite – tangy and sharp – in complete contrast to the bland food he had been used to at the monastery and he marvelled that he had once thought that fare tasty.

When he had sucked a squirrel bone until he could get nothing more from it, he rose and went to where Gisele was sitting beside Olgood. He squatted in front of her, took her hands in his and said to Kaela: 'Can you please tell Gisele what I say.'

To Gisele he said: 'I want to thank you. To find squirrels and salmon and that herb in the darkness is a miracle. To cook them as you have tonight under a bank beside a river is another. How you do what you do I'll never know, but I do know this – if I live to a very old age, I will remember this delicious meal.'

Kaela spoke to Gisele, telling her what Fenn had said. He was surprised to see tears appear in Gisele's eyes and looked questioningly at Kaela.

'She hasn't often been thanked like that.'

Fenn leaned forward and put an arm around Gisele's shoulders, kissing her gently on her cheek. When he let her go he was rewarded with one of her dazzling smiles.

*   *   *

The dawn glow was in the sky and the sun would soon be appearing. They crouched in a circle while Fenn explained his plan, drawing with a stick in the sand of the riverbank. When he finished, he asked each person to repeat their part. Satisfied that everyone understood, he stood up and scuffed out his drawing.

'It's unfortunate we need to split up, but we must – to save time. We must prepare this site and also lay a false trail.'

Olgood, Gisele and Hakon walked into the river and set off downstream, keeping to the shallows.

The absence of clouds promised a clear sunny day which was disappointing because Fenn would have preferred rain to obscure their tracks. The wind was fresh, however, with strength enough to blow leaves about which should be helpful to some extent.

Fenn and Kaela cleared the area. They buried the remnants of their fire and the animal bones and Kaela suggested using water from the river to smooth the earth. When they had removed all traces of their overnight stay, Fenn took out the wrapped package he had been carrying inside his tunic and said to Kaela: 'Before we leave, I'd like to show you this.'

He removed the linen wrapping to reveal the cover of the Lindisfarne Gospels that Olaf had taken from him in the monastery church – the item he had retrieved from Ragnall's house on the day he had left Lognavik. Kaela saw a leather book cover, overlaid with silver edging and divided into sections by gold and silver borders, with one side that was ragged and torn but it was otherwise in perfect condition. Each bordered section featured a large gemstone set into the centre.

Her hand went to her mouth as she drew in a breath.

'What is that? It looks very valuable. Where did you get it?'

In a few sentences, Fenn told her how his attempt to save the Lindisfarne Gospels had been thwarted by Olaf's actions in the church. He then related his rescue of the stolen treasure from Ragnall's house when he decided to escape. He repeated his vow to bring the torn cover safely home to be reunited with the Book of Gospels.

'I think it will be safer in the basket when we cross the river,' he said.

'May I hold it?'

Kaela examined the cover, running her fingers over the encrusted jewels.

'The workmanship is magnificent. Do you know who made this?'

'Master Oswald told me it was made by an anchorite named Billfrith.'

'An anchorite?'

'A hermit. He lived in a cave but he was an excellent metal crafter and jeweller.'

'Obviously.'

Kaela turned the cover in her hands to allow her to view it from different perspectives.

'This is certainly the best work of this type I've ever seen. I'm happy you're taking this back where it belongs.'

Kaela spoke as if she was comparing the cover with other works of art that she had experienced. Fenn thought how little he knew of her life before she had been captured. However, that was a discussion for later. Kaela handed Fenn the cover which he rewrapped tightly in the linen and placed inside the cheese sack for further protection before stowing the bundle back in the basket.

He lifted the basket onto his shoulders and Kaela adjusted the straps so that it rode as high as possible. They brushed their footprints with small branches while walking backwards into the river. Standing in the river, the branches were tossed into the fast water in the middle to be washed downstream and then they threw more water onto the ground. Fenn surveyed their work and thought that, to him, it looked like any other piece of riverbank with no indication that five people had spent the night there. However, other trained eyes may see it differently.

Kaela turned and stared across the water. 'So now we must cross this river.'

He looked at her. Her brow was creased and she seemed apprehensive.

'Yes,' he replied, thinking she was worried about the pursuit. 'And you're right, we should be going.'

The river, swollen by spring rain, was about fifty yards wide but only twenty yards in the centre was swift-flowing deep water, the remainder consisting of slower-moving shallows and swirling eddies. It was difficult going as they had to feel their way across, step by step, negotiating boulders and varying depths of water, and holding their footing as the current strengthened. The water was icy and anything wet was attacked by the biting wind, but it was not as cold as their night in the snow so it was tolerable.

As they approached the faster flowing water, Kaela seemed nervous and walked forward reluctantly. Fenn frowned at her.

'What is it? Shall we cross further down?'

She answered so quietly he could not hear her above the rushing water.

He bent his ear to her mouth.

'That water is very deep and fast.'

Fenn regarded her with mock astonishment, realising her problem.

'You can't swim?'

'Not very well.'

'What does 'not very well' mean?'

'It means… It means I can't swim. I don't like deep water.'

Fenn assessed what she was saying.

'We'll be crossing many rivers.'

She nodded with a resigned look in her eyes.

He smiled at her. 'So we need to do this together.' He took her hand. 'You hold here…' he placed her hand on his belt, '…and I'll hold onto *your* belt. I'll hold you up. With your other hand, just push the water behind you like this. And don't worry – I won't let you go.'

Fenn took the upstream side. When the water reached his waist, he looked at Kaela to see if she was ready. She nodded and they stepped into the current letting it carry them while swimming with one hand each towards the far side. Now Fenn felt the cold of the water intensely and he was reminded of his dive into the frozen inlet. He tightened his grip on Kaela's belt, kicked his legs and struck out strongly with his free arm.

He found the basket floated well and kept him high in the water. By the time he felt rocks beneath his feet again they had been swept a hundred yards downstream. He found solid footing and strained to hold Kaela who was still in the current. She was wide-eyed but calm, pushing at the water with her free arm. Fenn took a step and pulled her with him then stumbled and the water took them both another twenty yards before he was able to stand again and haul Kaela out of the centre flow. When she could also reach the riverbed they moved into shallower water. They didn't exit the river, but started to walk back upstream in the water keeping a few feet out from the bank.

They came abreast of the site of their overnight stay, now on the other side of the river and continued upstream. Fenn had told the others he would continue walking in the water at least a mile before leaving the river, hopefully where the ground was rocky and they would not leave tracks, if such a place could be found. The river bed was extremely uneven and the walking was tiring with a high risk of injury to their feet and ankles. Fenn found that he needed to lean forward to balance the weight of the basket, which didn't help his steadiness.

They came to a rocky bank that was accessible but they were not far enough from the campsite so they pushed on. After Fenn estimated they had covered a mile he looked for a suitable place to leave the river. After another half-mile, the sound of rushing water was loud from around a bend up ahead and he feared rapids or a waterfall, so he was relieved when an area of rock appeared on the riverbank just before the bend and they were able to step from the river onto a smooth rocky shelf.

While Kaela checked the contents of the basket, Fenn walked on so he could see around the bend.

He returned in a few moments, smiling. 'This is perfect,' he said.

They found a place inside a thicket of grasses where they could see but not be easily seen. The basket was hidden behind a bush and he and Kaela settled there to wait as the chill in the air lessened with the sun's slow rise into the sky.

'Where did you learn to read the runes?'

Fenn had been listening to the river and the occasional buzzing of insects for a long time. He could feel the sun warm on his shoulders and the top of his head and was tempted to close his eyes. Kaela had disturbed his lethargy when she shifted her position to ease the strain of remaining seated for so long.

She didn't answer immediately. Fenn wondered if she had heard him.

'From a man.'

Fenn waited, but when she didn't continue, he asked: 'What man?'

'A teacher.'

Fenn laughed. She was being deliberately frustrating.

'When? Where? What else did he teach you?'

She smiled, then sighed.

'I learned the runes from the man who also taught me Latin, Greek and Frankish. But that…' she held up a hand, '…is all I want to say.'

If she had said 'the man who taught her to speak to animals', Fenn could not have been more surprised. He thought for a moment she was joking, but she looked serious. Every scribe at Lindisfarne was familiar with Latin. Most of the texts were written in that language including the great Lindisfarne Gospels, and he did not think many people outside of the church would have such knowledge. But Greek and Frankish?

He waited for her to elaborate.

She shook her head. 'Fenn, please. Don't ask me any more than that. I have my reasons. I'll tell you more when we are safe in our homeland.'

'You can speak Frankish?'

'Yes, but there are many dialects.'

Fenn looked at her. He reviewed what he knew about the girl in front of him. Apart from the fact that she came from Wessex, he knew little of her history. Did he need to know more?

'Show me how to write 'Fenn' in the runes.'

Kaela laughed and reached for the water skin to wet her finger, then used it to draw on the smooth rock surface.

Fenn studied the letters, tracing them with his finger. 'Now, write 'Kaela'.'

She did so, and he watched as the sun slowly erased their names.

A noise drew his gaze to the river as someone came into view and stepped onto the rocks fifty feet away from where he and Kaela were concealed.

Fenn was relieved to see Olgood followed by Gisele and Hakon.

'About a mile downstream, we found a grassy bank leading to a big rocky mound,' related Olgood.

'We swam across and climbed out there. We all walked up to the base of the mound and then Hakon and Gisele walked backwards in their own footsteps into the river and came out onto the bank again as if five people had left the river. Our tracks were faint on the grass but I'm sure they'll be noticed by Ragnall.'

'We climbed the mound and found a hard rock top there just as we hoped. It will take a long time to search that place to discover where we left the rocky area. We descended again and carefully walked backwards in our footsteps into the river.'

'If they find we trick them on rock, they not know if we then go back up or more down river,' added Hakon.

The three of them looked so pleased with themselves, Fenn had to smile.

'We looked hard at the place we spent the night as we passed and couldn't see anything. You did a good job,' said Olgood.

'Hopefully not too good,' replied Fenn. 'We want it to look like we tried to cover our tracks. It would be suspicious if we didn't.'

He bent to pick up the basket but Olgood took it from him.

Fenn thanked him with a nod, then said: 'Follow me, I have something to show you.'

He led them around the bend where he had walked earlier. The sound of rushing water grew louder and they were confronted with a wide waterfall fifty feet high. Fenn had to shout to be heard above the roar.

'They cannot be certain that we came this way, but even if they somehow get to this point, I would not climb that if I didn't have to.'

He pointed at the waterfall. On their side of the river, the edge of the waterfall looked to be a sheer rock face but closer examination showed cracks and irregularities that might make it climbable.

'What do you think?' he asked, his question directed to them all. 'Can we do it?'

Kaela led the way to see if the cliff could be climbed. Twice she reached a position where she could not progress any further and had to retrace her steps. She was surprisingly agile, climbing both upward and downward without effort. On the third attempt, with the others calling encouragement and suggestions from below, she reached the top and pulled herself over the edge.

Now that a successful route had been found, they were confident they could climb the cliff.

Hakon followed. There were several parts of the climb he found difficult but he persisted and at each obstacle he made adjustments and found a way around. Kaela helped him over the top and he gave a dance of joy. Gisele climbed next. Fenn had noted that Gisele was sure-footed on rough ground and she showed the same confidence with the climb. She had watched Kaela carefully and placed her hands and feet in exactly the same places.

Olgood made sure the basket was tight and began to climb without hesitation. What he lacked in dexterity he made up for with reach and strength. When his fingers locked onto a hold, they looked so solid that Fenn thought that maybe he could have ridden on Olgood's back.

Fenn took a last look about to make sure they had not left any sign of their presence. The rock was wet from the river water that had dripped from their clothing but that would soon dry in the wind and sun. He went back to the bend and checked downstream for any movement and was pleased to see that it all looked normal.

Returning to the waterfall he started up the rock face.

He was nearing the top with ten feet to go when a rock that everyone else had used to pull themselves up onto a small ledge, felt loose in his hand. His right leg reached the ledge and he frantically grabbed for another hold as the rock came loose and tumbled down to crash onto the rocky shelf below. His new handhold was thankfully secure, but the sudden lunge had broken the grip of his other hand and his left foot was also dangling in space. He tried to twist his body to get another purchase with either his free hand or his foot, but couldn't find anything to take his weight and instantly felt the strain in his arm and his bent right leg that were the only points where he was attached to the cliff. His foot slipped fractionally on the ledge – it would not hold him much longer. He knew he would not survive a fall from this height.

Olgood's voice called urgently from above: 'Reach for the strap!'

He looked up to see that Olgood had lowered the basket and one strap was hanging two feet above his head. Fenn didn't hesitate. He put all his strength into his one arm and leg and thrust himself upward, reaching with his free hand for the strap – at the same time he felt his right leg slip off the ledge.

His hand closed over the strap and he swung out from the cliff held only by Askari's basket straps and Olgood's strength. He managed to get his other hand onto the strap and held tight as the basket was dragged upwards. At the top he was able to put his toe into a crack and push himself over the edge where he lay for a few moments to catch his breath. Kaela knelt and grasped him by each shoulder with a concerned look on her face which only eased when he gave her a reassuring smile.

He sat up to see Olgood looking at him with a satisfied expression.

'Not today,' said Olgood and he reached out to help Fenn to his feet. Fenn understood Olgood was acknowledging how closely he had cheated death.

'Not today,' agreed Fenn. 'Thanks to you.'

'Kaela emptied the basket and handed it to me before I could even think what to do. And I would have joined you at the bottom if these two hadn't held my feet.'

Fenn reached out to each one and conveyed his thanks with a touch.

He walked to the edge and looked down at the rock and other debris that had fallen from the cliff.

'We cannot leave that there,' he said. 'I need to go back down.'

Kaela stepped forward and pointed to herself. 'No, it should be me.'

From the corner of his eye Fenn saw Olgood look at Kaela and then nod. Gisele looked at Olgood and then Kaela and finally Fenn. She nodded her agreement. Hakon made it unanimous. It was obvious from what they had observed, that Kaela was the best choice.

She lay on the clifftop looking over the face with Olgood holding her legs, and planned the route she would take. Olgood then held her hands as she eased herself over the edge, feeling with her feet. Once she had started, she moved smoothly and steadily, pausing occasionally to feel for a hold. She took it slowly until she was below the place where the rock had fallen and, from that point, she reached the bottom without any problems.

Fenn paced back and forth at the top of the cliff while, below him, Kaela threw the rock and smaller stones into the river and brushed away the dirt, moss and grass that had been torn from the cliff with the rock. She looked up and they signalled that it was good.

She scanned the cliff and started her return climb.

Kaela reached for a small protrusion she had used on her way down. This time, just like Fenn's rock, it came away in her hand. The cliff face was obviously much less secure than it looked. Like Fenn, she was left with only two points of contact on the cliff. There were cries of alarm from above when they saw the rock give way.

Kaela had no time to look down. She immediately jammed her foot back to where the toe-hold it had just left should be. Her toes slid into a crack and held there. Somehow she had had the presence of mind not to let go of the piece of rock in her hand. This rock was smaller than Fenn's but would still unmistakably announce their presence if it fell onto the rock shelf below. So far, luckily, nothing else had been dislodged.

Olgood already had the basket over the edge but Kaela was lower than Fenn had been and couldn't reach it yet.

Kaela looked up at the faces peering anxiously down at her. She called out.

'I'm safe. I'm going to throw the rock up to you.'

'Can you put it inside your tunic?' called Fenn.

'Maybe, maybe not,' said Kaela. 'It's too risky.'

Olgood stayed where he was with the basket hanging over the cliff in case it was needed. Fenn and Gisele lay on either side of Olgood so they both had a chance to catch Kaela's rock. Hakon set himself to hold on to anyone in danger of falling.

Fenn called to her when they were ready.

Kaela extended her arm, slowly lowered it then flung the rock upwards.

Fenn could see they wouldn't be able to reach it.

'Hold me!' he shouted.

He felt someone's weight on his legs and he pushed himself out over the cliff, reaching at full extension. He caught the rock at the apex of its flight with the tips of his fingers, felt it slip and took a second hold, then, bending at the waist, he let his upper body fall forward against the cliff cushioning himself with his other arm. Hands held his legs and pulled him backwards.

Fenn raised himself to his knees, called out to tell Kaela they had caught the rock, and tossed it into the river. He turned back to join the others following Kaela's climb.

Now that she was wary of the rocks in that area, Kaela carefully examined and tested each hold before trusting it and made sure she did not loosen anything else. Cautiously, moving only one limb at a time, she made her way slowly but surely upward. Seeing that Kaela should make it unaided to the top, Olgood set the basket on the ground next to its emptied pile of contents and made ready to help her over the edge. When she was finally safe, Fenn enveloped her in a huge hug while the others crowded around to offer their congratulations.

They rested for a short time to allow everyone to recover, then Kaela repacked the basket. Fenn picked up the sack containing the book cover and unfolded the wrapping. He could see that it had not been affected by the hasty emptying of the basket.

He gathered the others and related to them what he had already told Kaela about this valuable and important treasure and his vow to take it home. He explained how the cover had been ripped from the book by Olaf in front of his eyes. Olgood had never seen the Book of Gospels at the monastery and he was as amazed as Hakon and Gisele were at the jewel-encrusted, gold and silver lined book cover.

When Fenn handed the cover to Gisele to examine, she didn't want to touch it and held her hands out of the way while she looked closely at the gemstones, moving her head from side to side to catch the light from the jewels at different angles.

Hakon remarked it was heavier than he expected. 'This was part of book?' he asked.

Fenn smiled and nodded. 'A magnificent book that is as beautiful as its cover.'

Olgood took the cover reverently and seemed to enjoy just holding it. He held it tenderly feeling the texture of the leather with his fingertips and took some time to study Billfrith's work with the eyes of a master tradesman before handing it back to Fenn and saying, with resolve: 'Yes, we must take this back to Lindisfarne where it belongs.'

The cover was rewrapped and placed in the basket which Olgood shouldered while Hakon and Gisele removed any marks they had made at the top of the cliff.

Fenn stood at the edge of the waterfall looking over the turbulent rushing water below and issued a silent challenge to their invisible pursuers.

'Follow *that* path if you can.'

CHAPTER FOURTEEN

Freedom: A capricious companion ...

They travelled for ten days through a land of forests, rivers and lakes, crossing valleys and ranges, avoiding any sign of habitation. The lakes caused the greatest delays as they were all of one type, long and narrow, always aligned north-south and barring their route to the east. As they reached each water barrier, it was necessary to choose whether to head north or south to get around the lake. If there was no indication of which choice was the better, Fenn always chose to head south.

They resisted the temptation to swim across the small lakes – the far side always looked so close but Fenn knew the distance was deceptive.

He had a good sense of direction which was confirmed by Hakon when he could look at the stars, and he kept them on the right heading despite their forced detours.

Each day, when they reached a suitable river, Fenn devised a variation of the evasion they had used when crossing the first river after leaving the mountains. They left false trails or carefully stepped in one set of footprints, or all scattered in different directions to reunite at a distant point. It delayed them, but it would hopefully delay their pursuers more.

For the larger rivers, they crossed where the flow was slow and Fenn could tow Kaela. When he felt the weight of his clothing and Kaela's extra drag pulling on his shoulders in the middle of a wide river, he would think of the day they arrived at Lognavik and the Northman swimming ashore with his weapons and heavy mail and use that memory to spur his determination.

When they crossed hills of any size, Fenn would stand for a while at the crest where he could see for miles and carefully search the country behind them but he saw no sign of pursuit.

*   *   *

The fishing village occupied an area of cleared forest situated on the shore of a sandy bay. From the hill where they lay, a small piece of cultivated ground was visible with some cows and goats grazing nearby but these were so few in number it was obvious that farming was not the principle occupation for the village. A peninsula closed in the bay from one side forming a natural sheltered harbour. Fenn counted six piers extending into the bay and nine vessels each of similar size were either tied alongside a pier or at anchor in the harbour. He expected other boats of the fishing fleet would be at sea.

The day was warm with a fresh breeze which ruffled the surface but the sea was otherwise calm. Fenn could smell the grass under his fingers and the scent of the pines behind him. In other times he would have liked to turn onto his back, spread his arms and enjoy the warmth of the sun on his face.

In the three days since reaching the coast and turning south along it, they had already passed inland of several villages. After guessing incorrectly regarding the brothers' actions in the mountains and seeing them catch up much quicker than anticipated, Fenn wanted to make their choice of the place to find a boat less obvious than their choice of a mountain pass.

The plan was to find a boat and sail it to the land of the Danes.

'I watched the Northmen during our voyage and I learned every day at the shipyard – I know how to sail a small boat,' Olgood told them.

Hakon said that further south there were large islands that formed a bridge between this land and the Danes with only small passages of water between them, but Fenn thought the longer they spent on land the more likely Ragnall or Olaf would catch up to them. Also it would be more difficult to cross many small passages than take one longer voyage.

195

It was decided that Hakon and Kaela would enter the village and go to the harbour to see if it were possible for a boat to be taken. Gisele would stay with Fenn and Olgood and would be able to talk with anybody who happened to discover them. If asked, they were a group of freemen farm workers heading south to look for work. It was springtime and the frequent seasonal harvests made the story plausible.

A small stream ran through the valley behind the hill. Hakon and Kaela removed their hats and dusted their clothing, then washed their hands, hair and faces. Kaela replaced her hat to cover her red hair and, their new clean appearance having received appropriate approval, they set off down the hill towards the village.

Fenn, Gisele and Olgood settled down to wait for their return.

After a while Fenn examined the contents of the basket and announced that they only had dried meat and cheese enough for one more day. They had been using the stored bear meat and cheese only as a supplement to the fresh food that Gisele brought them every evening and they had also collected berries so, up until now, their diet had been fulfilling, but the depletion of their stocks was a concern.

*   *   *

When Hakon and Kaela returned in the late afternoon, Hakon had a big smile on his face. Fenn thought they had discovered a boat they could use but Hakon's happiness was for a different reason.

'Good news. We help man when apples spill from cart – he ask us all eat with him and family tonight.'

Kaela told them that the boats at the pier had people visiting them continuously but the ones anchored in the harbour seemed unattended. All the boats were of a similar construction, wide-beamed and short. Like Ragnall's ship they were pointed at bow and stern with a steering oar at the stern and a central mast with a squared sail. She and Hakon thought it was possible one of the anchored boats could be taken but they would need to check the harbour at night to be sure they were able to do so safely.

After Hakon and Kaela had looked over the boats in the small harbour, they had returned through the market where the stall owners were packing up for the day.

Kaela related what had occurred there.

They were passing through an area where fruit was sold. There was a lot of activity as each stallholder was in the process of taking down their stall and loading their unsold produce into carts pulled by a variety of animals. Kaela was amused to see a cart that was harnessed to two dogs, but there were several donkeys and, for the larger stalls, horses.

Before them a man was loading barrels of apples onto a cart. His horse was untethered and was stepping about twisting its head to each side, nervous of a yapping dog that it could hear but not see. The man was trying to keep the horse calm as well as load the last barrels onto the cart. Kaela put her hand on Hakon's arm to stop him, apprehensive about the situation developing ahead.

A young boy was approaching carrying a bundle of long poles topped with triangular flags. The horse ceased moving its head and stared wide-eyed at the flags. Kaela called a warning just as the horse shied sideways causing the cartload of apple barrels harnessed behind it to tip onto one wheel and then overturn with a crash. Kaela and Hakon stepped back in alarm as the loaded barrels crashed to the ground, the wood splintering. A wave of apples flowed around their feet. A woman screamed. The stall owner was knocked to the ground by the falling cart and lay there stunned and unmoving. He was in immediate danger of serious injury – lying directly in the path of the cart, now on its side, with the panicked horse still attempting to pull it forward.

Hakon ran to take hold of the man's shoulders, pulling him out of the way a heartbeat before the cart was dragged over the place where he had fallen, its wheel hub screeching on the stony ground. Kaela reached for the horse and took a firm hold of its mane with one hand, holding its head with the other while talking in soothing tones to quiet it. When it was calmer but still breathing heavily, she tied the animal to a post and untangled the twisted harness while Hakon helped the man to his feet. With the help of several willing people, they righted the cart which seemed to be undamaged and took some time to collect as many of the spilled apples as possible.

The man was extremely grateful, realising Hakon had probably saved his life. He thanked them profusely, and invited them to his house for a meal. Hakon told him there were five in their group and the man happily included all of them in the invitation.

Fenn saw Kaela was not as happy as Hakon was about the invitation, and asked why.

'It is not a good idea for the five of us to be seen together. If Ragnall or Olaf come to this village they will be asking about five strangers.'

At her words, Hakon realised he may have made a mistake by mentioning their number, but Fenn said he didn't think the number was important. Groups of five would not be uncommon in the harvest season. He was quiet for a moment while he assessed the risk.

An opportunity to have a good meal was tempting but he did agree with Kaela that it would be best if they were not seen together and would have preferred that only some of them take up the invitation and maybe bring food to the others. However, Hakon had already told the man there were five. A more important problem was that he and Olgood did not speak the language. That fact could cause immediate suspicion if the man and his family had been asked to watch for five escaped thralls.

He proposed that he and Olgood could be unable to go for some reason, but when this was relayed to Gisele, she was not happy to be separated from Olgood. She felt safer with him around. Kaela thought it would be less suspicious if they all went, rather than try to fabricate a reason why two of the group were unable to accept the kind invitation. She suggested that Fenn and Olgood could reply to any questions with nods or shakes of the head as prompted by her or Hakon. It was a workable suggestion but Fenn was still uneasy. He balanced his unease with the thought that, if all went well, they should be away from this place sometime tomorrow, either by sea or land. They eventually agreed that the prospect of a wholesome home-cooked meal was worth a small risk.

There was one further discussion involving whether to hide the basket and the book cover and return for it later or to take it with them. There seemed to be equal risk with both options so they decided to take it.

The man's apple orchard was on the outskirts of the village so there was no need for them to enter the village itself which reduced the risk of being seen together.

Hakon knocked on the door which was opened by the man who introduced himself as Gudrod and bid them a warm welcome before standing aside to let them enter. He presented his wife who was a stern and dour woman. She seemed to have a permanent scowl on her face and Fenn got the impression that she was not happy to have five extra people to feed. As soon as possible, she withdrew to her cooking pots.

Her husband portrayed a much happier countenance and cordially invited them to sit on some stools set before the fire while the meal was being prepared. He poured a liquid into some wooden cups and handed one to each person. When he sipped the contents, Fenn tasted a sweet apple cider that left a tingle on his tongue. He gazed around the room.

The house was large. Like most of the houses he had visited, it consisted of a single room with a fire set in the centre but in this case more to one end than the other. At the far end of the room behind the fire Fenn could see a table and some benches. The floor was packed earth. One interesting feature was a large metal grill set into the floor between the fire and the door. Fenn wondered what could be stored in so large a hole and then thought of the answer – it was an apple cellar.

Kaela, Hakon and Gisele chatted with Gudrod and when a question was addressed to him or Olgood, Fenn kept Kaela in his vision and nodded or shook his head as she indicated. On each occasion, Kaela promptly drew Gudrod's attention back to her.

He caught several glances from Gudrod's wife while she fussed with the cooking. Her looks were distinctly unfriendly as if she'd been offended somehow. Fenn would have expected her to be grateful that her husband had been saved from injury or death and couldn't understand her attitude. It was the only disturbing aspect of an otherwise pleasant evening and it nagged at his mind.

The aroma of a meaty stew drifted from the cooking pot and Fenn felt the pangs of hunger. Their food since leaving Lognavik had been exceptional – much better than he had anticipated thanks to Gisele, but there had always been a sense of not being able to fully relax. Here in this warm house with a cup of sweet cider in his hand and the smell of cooking wafting through the room he felt that maybe he could relax for the first time in a long while.

Probably because he was not being engaged in the conversation, Fenn had drained his cider quickly. Gudrod refilled his cup and also topped up the others. After a few more sips Fenn was surprised to be feeling dizzy. In Lognavik, the ale they had been offered had been weak compared to the monastery brew. In contrast, the cider on this side of the mountains might be deceptively strong. In any case he decided to slow his consumption.

His thoughts were interrupted by a knock on the door.

Gudrod acted surprised and started to rise, but his wife called something to him and went to answer the door herself.

An older man with long pale blond hair stepped confidently into the room. He was broad-shouldered with a big girth and was dressed in a fine tunic with a fur collar extending over his shoulders and an ornate sword buckled at his waist – obviously a man of some importance.

Fenn was instantly alarmed when the wife spoke with the newcomer and pointed to the visitors sitting in front of the fire. He stood up and his hand went to his axe. The others also rose to their feet. Gudrod called to his wife, asking some question of her.

She shouted back at him and spat on the floor.

The man at the door moved passed the woman so he could get a good view of the people in the room. He left the door open.

Ragnall followed him into the room.

Behind Ragnall more men crowded through the door.

Fenn stood for a moment in disbelief then cursed and sat back down on his stool. He looked at each of the others and saw dejection in their eyes. Olgood was the exception. He had his axe in his hand and was checking each of the men as they entered, his body tensed. Hakon, who probably knew better than anyone what fate awaited them, put his hands up to his head and uttered a sound like a moan.

'Olgood, no…' Fenn said. 'It would serve no purpose. There are too many. While we live there is hope.'

Fenn stood and took Olgood by the arm, holding his grip there until he felt the big man relax with a sigh of resignation and lower his axe, slipping it back into his belt.

Ragnall nodded in satisfaction then walked up to Fenn and held out his hand. His face was both arrogant and triumphant. Fenn stood up, took Thorvald's axe and handed it to Ragnall whose eyes widened as he recognised the axe and then narrowed with anger. Before Fenn could react, Ragnall struck him with the back of his hand knocking him to the ground. As Olgood made to intervene, two men stepped up beside Ragnall, both with swords drawn.

Ragnall held out his hand to Olgood. Olgood folded his arms and stared at Ragnall. The two were of equal height and while Ragnall carried more bulk, Olgood's heavily muscled arms displayed his obvious strength. Having worked beside him at the shipyard Ragnall would be well aware of Olgood's capabilities.

Fenn pushed himself off the floor, his lip bleeding and already feeling swollen.

'Olgood, please give *me* the axe.'

Olgood looked at Fenn and smiled, pulling the axe from his belt and presenting the red handle to Fenn.

'I will gladly give my axe to you,' he said. 'I was not going to give it to *him*.'

He then turned his back on Ragnall and sat down as if he was about to continue his meal. Fenn turned to Hakon and requested his axe also which Hakon handed to him without raising his head.

He presented both axes to Ragnall who took them and passed them to the man alongside him. Thorvald's axe he placed in his own belt. He turned to Kaela and said something angrily to her. She answered with equal anger. He pulled Thorvald's axe from his belt and brandished it in front of her, his eyes blazing fiercely. He asked another question through gritted teeth.

Kaela folded her arms and answered calmly.

Ragnall reacted to her words by narrowing his eyes and stubbornly setting his jaw. He replaced the axe in his belt, took her firmly by the arm and pulled her out of the area bounded by the stools. Fenn started forward but Kaela shook her head at him.

Ragnall took a moment to calm himself then he turned to face the group by the fire. He adopted an arrogant stance, hands on hips. He was about to comment, Fenn suspected, on the ease of their capture.

He addressed Fenn, indicating that Kaela should translate.

'This is my uncle Alfarin.' Ragnall gestured at the man who had first entered the room. 'He is the Yarl of Alfheim and his kingdom extends along this whole coast to the south.'

Ragnall paused, then said with a satisfied smile:

'You were surprised to see me.'

He searched their faces for confirmation but was met with dull stares from everyone except Hakon who was still sitting with his head in his hands, taking no interest in the proceedings.

Ragnall shrugged as if it did not matter and continued:

'When we discovered you had gone, I had some men sail immediately to Alfheim where I thought you would eventually arrive, and Alfarin sent word along the coast offering a reward to report five escaped thralls. A group of two women and three men, one as big as this one, cannot hide for long. As soon as I could leave Lognavik, I sailed here myself. I arrived only this afternoon and received some good news.'

'When this good woman…,' Ragnall nodded at Gudrod's wife, '…sent a message to her Yarl that five strangers were coming to her house, it was too much of a coincidence. I knew I had caught you before you set foot through this door.'

Ragnall waited for a moment, enjoying his triumph, before continuing in a softer tone.

'Birgitta told me you saved her life when you fought with her against Yarl Harald's men. You helped defend my village and killed some of the attackers…' he looked at Olgood, '…including Haldor. I thank you for that. It would have given me pleasure to make you two…' he waved his hand between Fenn and Olgood, '…freed men. Maybe you too Hakon – I hear you fought also and you have served me well.' Hakon glanced up but then returned his head to his hands.

Ragnall continued: 'I would have given freedom…' he paused, pointing his finger at them with a face like stone, '…*if* you had not run.'

202

He took a breath and when he resumed Fenn thought he heard genuine regret in his voice.

'You have taken that choice from me. I have left Birgitta in charge of Lognavik but you have caused Olaf and me to be away from our village when we are needed there. You have chosen your own path before the gods and you must now face your fate.'

Since his wife had opened the door, Gudrod had been standing with an incredulous expression watching the scene unfolding before him. Now he stepped forward and talked forcefully to Yarl Alfarin, reinforcing his words with waving arms. Fenn could see he was asserting his rights in his own house. Gudrod was not a big man but he spoke with authority and Fenn saw some of the men give each other worried looks.

By way of answer, Alfarin drew a small leather bag tied at the top from inside his tunic. He offered this to Gudrod who stepped back and made no move to accept it. His wife, standing beside Alfarin, reached out and took the bag. This brought an exclamation of anger from Gudrod and he held out his hand to his wife expecting the bag to be returned. Instead she moved away from him, muttering to herself, and walked quickly towards the other end of the room, tucking the bag into the top of her dress. Her actions drew a burst of laughter from the assembled Northmen.

Gudrod's face reddened with anger and he shouted at the men who had invaded his house, pointing to the door and obviously asking them to leave. Ragnall looked at him but gave no reply. He deliberately turned his gaze to his uncle. Yarl Alfarin put a conciliatory arm on Gudrod's shoulder and drew him aside speaking softly but forcefully to him.

Ragnall signalled to his men and several moved forward. They searched each person and took the knives they found.

The basket had been placed against the wall and Fenn hoped it would not be noticed but one of the men drew Ragnall's attention to it. Ragnall picked up the basket and seemed to recognise it as one of Askari's. He opened it delved amongst the contents with his hand. Fenn's heart sank when he withdrew and unwrapped the sack. His exclamation of surprise told Fenn that he had not known that the gilded book cover was missing.

Yarl Alfarin was immediately interested and asked to look at the find which he turned over in his hands with obvious admiration. To Fenn's further dismay, Ragnall gave a slight bow and offered the treasure to Alfarin as a gift. The Yarl was very pleased and the two embraced, slapping each other on the back.

Ragnall walked to stand beside the metal grill set into the floor that Fenn had noticed earlier. He asked a question of Gudrod who hesitantly and with reluctance demonstrated how the grill was opened by removing a locking bar. Ragnall peered inside the hole and then lowered himself into it. He reappeared smiling and indicated the fugitives were to be placed into the apple cellar. One of the men evidently asked if their hands should be tied. Ragnall thought about it but shook his head.

* * *

'Kaela, I want to know everything they're saying up there.'

If he could learn what Ragnall's intentions were, it may help to form a plan of escape.

'They're very happy with themselves. They intend to celebrate with some of Gudrod's cider which Alfarin says is famous in the village.'

'And they will eat our stew,' said Olgood.

Fenn found the fact the Olgood was still thinking about the stew very funny and he laughed out loud. At the sound of his laughter, the conversation quietened in the room and a face appeared above the grill to check what was happening in the cellar.

Fenn stared back at the man with a blank expression.

Fenn settled his back against the wall of the cellar while Kaela kept up a commentary on the conversations above.

'I think they have separated into two groups. I can hear Ragnall and Alfarin talking and I think Gudrod and his wife are with them but the others are too far away.'

'What are they talking about?'

'Alfarin asked about Ragnall's journey by sea and Ragnall is telling him about the weather and sea conditions.'

Fenn sighed with frustration. They may have slipped by Ragnall if they had not taken up Gudrod's offer of a meal. Once again, he had underestimated the reach of the Northmen.

*   *   *

Fenn paced slowly, listening to Kaela's voice softly relaying the words she could hear. The length of the cellar allowed only five steps before he needed to reverse his direction. As he walked, he listened to her only with half of his mind, the other half searching for possibilities of escape. They had now been inside the cellar long enough for a meal to be served to the men above and he had still learned nothing about Ragnall's plans.

Kaela touched his arm.

'Alfarin has just asked about Olaf.'

She was silent for a moment, listening. She exhaled and looked at Fenn.

'It *was* Olaf who followed us over the mountains. He was due to meet Ragnall in this village, but he hasn't arrived.'

'Hopefully still trying to find our trail,' said Fenn, but he was worried that escape would only be more difficult if the brothers reunited.

Olgood sat on the earth floor with Gisele beside him, his arm around her shoulders. Both wore calm expressions of acceptance of their situation while patiently waiting to see what would develop. Hakon however, had been downcast from the moment Ragnall had entered the room and now sat apart with his head lowered.

Fenn asked Kaela to keep listening and crawled to sit beside Hakon.

'What are you thinking?' he asked.

Hakon didn't answer. Fenn touched his shoulder: 'Hakon...?'

Hakon seemed to come out of a sleep. He raised his head slowly and stared into the gloom of the cellar. Fenn repeated his question.

Hakon shook his head. He raised his hands and shrugged.

'I not see my father again,' he said, so quietly the Fenn almost didn't hear him.

Fenn realised that Hakon had given up hope and accepted that he would soon die. He tried to think of words he could say, but a hiss from Kaela diverted his attention.

'Alfarin has just asked Ragnall if he will kill us in Alfheim and that be the end of it. Ragnall replied that our punishment would be delivered in Lognavik as an example for other thralls to watch and learn.'

Kaela looked grim, but Fenn whispered encouragingly to Hakon: 'Did you hear that, Hakon? A journey back to Lognavik will give us many chances to escape.' Fenn tried to sound confident.

Hakon just grunted.

The conversation in the room became more commonplace. Kaela relayed talk of harvests and trade but she eventually stopped reporting each sentence.

'Their voices are becoming slurred. They will now all get drunk,' she said.

As the evening lengthened, the conversation got gradually louder and more boisterous and there were many bouts of raucous laughter and thumps on the floor above as men either fought or danced. It seemed that some men were trying to shout louder than others, and the noise above often made it impossible to hear themselves talk below.

The celebrations, if that's what they were, continued well into the night. Abruptly though, the shouting and thumping stopped and there was another noise from the room that sounded as if it was coming from deep inside someone's throat like the growling of a dog. The sound rose and fell in a strange rhythm.

Kaela saw Fenn's astonished expression and said: 'They are singing.'

'Singing? That noise is singing?'

Kaela snorted. 'Yes. I've heard it before.'

Fenn listened but could not distinguish anything melodic or attractive in the growling. The noise persisted, sometimes dying to silence but then it would be revived by someone and other voices would join in.

Fenn leaned back against the earth wall and tried to block his ears.

He could not see a way out of their situation. The grill could not be opened from the inside and there was no other exit from the cellar. The only items in the cellar were apples sorted into piles of different types. He entertained the ridiculous idea of using the apples in his sling to hold the men at bay, but they were the wrong size and there was not enough space and even if it were possible he did not think apples would stop anyone for long. The only hope was to see what opportunities might arise on their journey back to Lognavik.

The light that entered the cellar from the fire gradually decreased indicating that the fire was being allowed to die. The only sound from above now was the snoring of people in a deep sleep. In the cellar each person was occupied with his own thoughts. Fenn decided the best thing to do was to get some sleep so that he was fresh in the morning. He was trying to find a comfortable position when the silence was broken by a whisper from above the grill.

'It's Gudrod,' said Kaela. 'He asks us to make no noise.'

A scraping sound followed as the locking bar was drawn slowly out of the grill.

Kaela was the first out of the cellar. While the others clambered out as silently as they could, Gudrod gestured urgently at the door suggesting they should leave as quickly as possible.

Fenn looked at the scene in the room.

Ragnall, Alfarin and Gudrod's wife were sprawled across the table with the loudest snores coming from Gudrod's wife but fair competition was sounding throughout the room. The other men were lying in different poses, some on benches and some on the floor, all seemingly in a drunken stupor.

'We need to get weapons and the book,' Fenn said.

When he saw Fenn start to walk towards the fire, Gudrod held up his hand to object with alarm on his face. He dropped his hand when he saw Fenn was determined, turning to Kaela, pointing again at the door and imploring her in a whisper.

Olgood found Ragnall's two red axes lying against a wall. He handed one to Hakon, who took it eagerly, his eyes sparkling with renewed hope.

Hakon bent over one of Ragnall's men sprawled on the floor and took a knife from his belt which he tucked into his tunic. Fenn saw that Thorvald's axe was still in Ragnall's belt and knew the book cover was inside Alfarin's tunic. These would not be so easy to retrieve. He hesitated, weighing the risk, but he could not leave the cover behind.

Alfarin was seated on a stool with his upper body lying across the table, arms spread-eagled and head turned to one side. Fenn would need to somehow lift him to be able to reach inside his tunic. Olgood came to his side and without hesitation put his arms under Alfarin and lifted him to a sitting position. Olgood held Alfarin's head in such a way that Fenn knew, if he woke up, Olgood would snap his neck. He reached inside the tunic and located the wrapped bundle. As he was carefully extracting his prize, Kaela's hands appeared, deftly unbuckling Alfarin's sword.

'I can use this,' she said, and stepped back, buckling it around her own waist which was much slimmer than Alfarin's, the belt requiring a generous readjustment.

Olgood lowered Alfarin onto the table. He had not stirred in his drunken sleep.

Fenn handed Kaela the bundle containing the cover and reached to pull the axe from Ragnall's belt, deciding to follow Olgood's example and act boldly. At that moment Ragnall groaned and made as if to push himself up from the table. Fenn froze in position.

Ragnall managed to get himself onto his elbows and hung there, breathing heavily, head pointed downwards, his long blond hair covering his face. Slowly, his arms slid from under him and he collapsed back onto the table, his head hitting the table with a crack. A long snore came from his throat.

Fenn transferred the axe from Ragnall's belt to his own and was about to turn away when he saw Ragnall also wore a knife. He withdrew the knife from its sheath and held it in his hands. He looked up to see Olgood watching him. Olgood carefully did nothing to disclose his opinion of the action he knew Fenn was contemplating.

If he were to kill Ragnall now, would that help their chances or make them worse?

It only took a moment for Fenn to realise that the answer to the question was irrelevant as he was simply not capable of killing Ragnall in cold blood.

In spite of the fact that Ragnall would kill him if he could, and was in fact honour-bound to do so, Fenn admired the man. Ragnall was a person in complete command of his environment. Within the rules and traditions of his society he was a fair man – his acceptance of Kaela as well as Agatha and Addo attested to that, as did his statement that he would have set them free. Fenn had to admit neither Ragnall nor Olaf had ever been deliberately cruel to their thralls. Their lives had been harsh but that was part of the society. He knew he would have been treated much worse if he had been thrall to someone like Torston.

He raised the knife and thrust it into the table an inch from Ragnall's nose so it would be the first thing he saw when he woke up.

*   *   *

Outside the door, Fenn was eager to depart but wanted to thank Gudrod. Before he could do so, Gudrod started speaking and Kaela translated his words.

'I want you to know why I have released you,' he said, extending his arms to cover them all.

'You saved my life today and I offered you food in my house under my protection. Yarl Alfarin and his nephew dishonoured my hospitality which is very important to me. I heard what Ragnall said about you and I have now set you all free as you deserve for what you did for me. Now you know.'

'Will this be a problem for you?' Fenn asked through Kaela.

'No. I'll now drink my cider until I'm as drunk as the others and I will wake up in the morning with a sore head like everyone else to find you have mysteriously disappeared. Nobody will know how you escaped. The Yarl can threaten me as much as he wants. I'm not afraid of him. In any case I'm prepared to face whatever happens.'

'You have certainly saved our lives in return so your debt is paid in full. I wish you well. If our paths ever cross again I will be certain to treat you as you have treated us,' replied Fenn.

When Kaela had finished the translation, Gudrod held out his hand which Fenn grasped firmly.

Kaela, Olgood and Gisele added their thanks and Hakon expressed his with an embrace which seemed to both surprise and please Gudrod.

Fenn cast his eyes over his companions. He saw Olgood had the basket on his back and was happy to note that Gisele had the carving knife again in her belt. Hakon stared back at Fenn with anticipation, eager to be on his way. Alfarin's ornate sword looked out of place at Kaela's waist, but that was a consideration for later.

He turned and walked into the orchard and heard the door close behind him.

CHAPTER FIFTEEN

A second encounter with the sea...

They could not afford to waste any more time. Speed was just as important as caution. With a half-moon shining fitfully between thin clouds, there was enough pale light for Fenn to lead them to the shore. Thankfully both the beach and the harbour were deserted. Fenn took in a deep breath. The fresh smell of the salty sea air reminded him of Lindisfarne, specifically of the times he had spent sitting on the hilltop rock. It was good to be beside the sea again.

Kaela tapped his shoulder and pointed to a ship tied to one of the piers. This was obviously Ragnall's ship with its familiar tall carved bow and stern. It may have been the same one that had taken him from Lindisfarne.

'That was not here earlier today,' she said.

Fenn thought of disabling the ship somehow but there may be someone on board and even if not, the noise would be certain to bring attention. He wanted to be away from the village without delay. They ran along the beach toward the harbour, not bothering to hide their tracks in the soft sand, and chose the nearest anchored vessel. Hakon swam out to check the boat and waved to signify it had a sail and steering oar on board.

Olgood and Gisele entered the water, Olgood balancing the basket on his head while he swam sideways to the boat. Fenn took Kaela's hand and placed it on his shoulder.

'Hold on here.'

He swam on his stomach while she floated behind him. They reached the boat just behind Olgood and Hakon leaned over to take the basket and then helped them aboard.

If he had been asked later whether the water that night was cold or warm, Fenn could not have answered truthfully. He simply did not notice.

Fenn checked that everyone was aboard and said: 'Olgood, you're in charge on the boat. Hakon, you tell us the direction to sail.'

Fenn and Hakon helped Olgood attach and raise the sail. While it flapped in the breeze, Olgood demonstrated how to adjust the angle of the sail and told Fenn and Hakon that was their job, one on each side. Kaela gave a snort and said that if anyone found they could not do their job, *she* would take over.

There were two oars in the boat but no oar holes so Fenn assumed they were for paddling ashore rather than rowing. One interesting feature of the boat was a wide lip protruding along each side to make the task of pulling in a net easier. He couldn't see a net, but that was probably too valuable an item to be left on board. Apart from the wide sides, it was similar to the boats Fenn had sailed in from Lindisfarne, except that those boats had been squarer in the stern.

Fenn used the leather straps to attach the basket to the base of mast while Olgood pulled up the anchor.

As soon as the sail was turned to catch the wind and pulled tight as Olgood had instructed, the boat started to move through the water. Olgood settled himself beside the steering oar, Gisele next to him. The others found places to sit. Fenn picked up an oar to use if they got too close to another boat but Olgood steered deftly between them and headed for open water.

A shout came from the beach. They all looked back to see some lights moving on the shore. In the gloom it was difficult to see what was happening but their moving boat had obviously been noticed and the alarm raised. They rounded the end of the harbour peninsula and immediately the boat was buffeted by a series of short waves and they had to struggle to stay on their seats.

'Shallow water over sand bar,' called Hakon, pointing downwards.

'Will they follow?' Fenn shouted back.

Hakon looked up at the sail and then out to sea. Fenn followed his gaze. In the moonlight you could see a few hundred yards but outside of that range the sea and the sky quickly became black. The sail was dark grey in colour with a pattern of blue crossed swords woven into the centre. It would not be easy to see in the night.

'I not think follow in the night. When we cross sand bar we are too far away – they not see us.'

Gisele was clinging tightly to the side of the boat looking anxious, unsettled by the rough movement. Fenn realised this may be her first time in a boat. Olgood also noticed and he put a comforting arm around her shoulders, keeping his eyes ahead but bending his head to speak into her ear.

In a few moments, the jostling caused by the agitated waves over the bar eased, to be replaced by the longer rolling motion of deeper water. Fenn asked Kaela to take over the sail from him, endured her 'I told you so' expression and moved to sit beside Hakon.

'The land of the Danes is your land. Where is it best to go?'

'We can sail to Hedeby,' said Hakon.

He wet his finger and drew on the seat. Fenn had to bend close to see.

'This Land of Danes. Here Hedeby.' Hakon made a mark in the centre of the area he had drawn. '*Schlei* is big water from here to here.' He drew a line from the east coast to Hedeby.

'A river?'

'Bigger than river. Like Lognavik *fjord*.'

An estuary or inlet then.

'How long is *Schlei*?'

Hakon considered. 'As you say it – twenty miles.'

It seemed a long distance. Fenn thought for a moment.

'Does Ragnall know you come from Hedeby?'

Hakon shrugged. 'I not tell him. I tell only you. I am taken by other Northmen, not Ragnall, when Hedeby attacked. I am with them two summers. Then Ragnall buy me when he learn I speak English. I not know if he ask where I from, but he not ask me.'

213

Fenn nodded. Hakon desperately wanted to get to Hedeby and the quickest way there would certainly be to sail up the *Schlei*. But if Ragnall knew that Hakon had been captured in a raid on Hedeby, once again he would know exactly where they were headed. He would know the market town well. Only a few months ago he had sold some of the Lindisfarne captives in the Hedeby slave market.

Fenn laid a hand on Hakon's shoulder. 'How long will it take us to reach the *Schlei*?'

'I think three days.'

'Then we'll need to make the food in the basket last three days.'

Fenn patted Hakon's shoulder and sat down again beside Kaela. He leaned back resting his elbows on the wide lip of the side of the boat. Kaela looked at his face and put her hand under his chin to turn his head. He wondered what she was doing until he remembered his lip was split where Ragnall had struck him.

'You'll survive,' she said and leaned forward to kiss him gently beside his mouth.

Fenn started to smile but the action pulled on his cut lip. 'I will now,' he said, and leaned back again.

Should they land on the coast and make their way to Hedeby overland? That would just ensure that Ragnall arrived in Hedeby first. Fenn did not consider the option of leaving Hakon to fend for himself while the others headed further south either by land or sea. He had made a pledge to get everyone where they wanted to go. Although the pledge had been made to Kaela, Fenn considered it encompassed them all. It was all or none.

So they would race Ragnall to Hedeby. Ragnall's ship would undoubtedly be faster than their little fishing boat. Their only advantage was that they would have a good lead. Perhaps Ragnall would wait for Olaf?

Fenn leaned forward. This was something they all needed to agree upon. It was time to share his thoughts. He asked for their attention then told them why he thought they should sail to Hedeby and ended by relating his pledge to Kaela – and to them all.

The moon and stars provided enough light to see be able to see their faces although they were shadowy. He peered at each person to gauge their reaction.

Olgood shrugged and simply nodded. 'I'm with you,' he said.

Kaela looked hard at Fenn and then nodded also, as if something had been confirmed in her mind. She said nothing.

Hakon rose from his seat and stood before Fenn, holding the mast.

For a moment he didn't speak. He cleared his throat and said:

'When you call Olaf's name in courtyard, I think you brave and smart both. I see I not wrong. I thank you from heart.' Hakon bent and hugged Fenn. Fenn felt Hakon's warm tears on his cheek.

He understood that Hakon *had* been worried that they would not want to go with him to Hedeby. He struggled to place Hakon's reference to the monastery courtyard then he remembered calling to Olaf when he was about to use his sword to make Master Nerian tell where more gold was hidden.

Hakon wiped his eyes with the back of his hand. He sat down in his place and averted his gaze out to sea.

Fenn looked toward Gisele. She had yet to speak.

Gisele called for Kaela to sit beside her. Her head turned to each person one by one as she talked – with Kaela translating her words.

'I have no family. They were all killed while I watched.' She choked and held her hand up to her eyes as if to shut out the scene she was now recalling. 'My brothers, my sister Senna... two years... only...'

She stopped and Fenn could hear how hard it was for her to speak. Kaela gasped and rested a hand on Gisele's shoulder, realising what she was about to say.

'My sister,' Gisele's voice was husky with emotion, 'a baby, only two years old; my mother, father and uncle – alive one moment and then all dead on the ground. I was eight and I have been alone since then.'

She took a deep breath and said forcefully: 'Now I have a family again. I have brothers and a sister who look out for me and want me with them. I have a man...' she paused and then said a phrase which Kaela translated as 'if the gods allow'. Gisele took hold of Olgood's arm and looked up at

215

him. He met her gaze and used his other hand to tenderly push a wisp of hair from her face, his eyes wet in response to her words.

Gisele turned to Fenn. 'Wherever my family goes I go too.'

Fenn could feel his own eyes were moist. As much as he had thought his life since he was taken from Lindisfarne had been hard, he could not imagine what Gisele had endured.

He could not think of any adequate words. He went to where Gisele was sitting and hugged her and Kaela together. Olgood's arms surrounded them all. A moment later Fenn felt Hakon join in, but immediately there was too much weight in the stern and the boat twisted violently as the bow rose and then slewed to one side, throwing everyone except Olgood onto the floor.

Fenn fell onto his back and Kaela landed on top of him. She laughed and kissed him on the cheek then made to get up but he held her back. They stared at each other, faces a few inches apart and he gently pulled her down and deliberately kissed her on the mouth, feeling surprisingly little pain from the cut on his lip. His gratitude when she didn't resist was immense. Her lips were soft and he tasted the salt there. He released her and she slowly got to her feet.

Gisele had tumbled to lie in front of Olgood and she gasped in surprise and delight when he effortlessly lifted her and in one movement sat her beside him. Her mood was instantly lightened.

Fenn rose also. Hakon was watching him, the moonlight shining on his teeth revealing a huge grin on his face. Fenn playfully made as if to hit him, which made Hakon's grin even broader.

Kaela sat beside Gisele and talked softly to her.

They each retired to their thoughts. After a while, Fenn's turned to an old topic.

Three pieces of luck had aided their escape from the cellar. First, Gudrod had set them free when there seemed no way out; secondly, the harbour had been deserted when they needed it to be, and then the tide was high enough to allow them to cross the sand bar at the harbour entrance.

A Northman would say the gods were smiling on them, but such good luck could not continue forever, whether the gods smiled or not.

Fenn expected they would sail directly away from the land but Hakon, after checking the stars he could see, pointed along a line that took a shallower angle to the coast, a direction Fenn judged to be roughly south-east.

'Which stars are you following?' he asked Hakon.

'Freya's chickens.' He pointed at a bright group of stars, low in the southern sky. 'They point the way south.'

Olgood called out the sail adjustments he wanted and the small boat pointed its bow at the dark horizon across the sea. Fenn watched the land recede and be swallowed into the night and saw no sign of following boats.

They had no idea of the hazards that might be waiting in the darkness – a dangerous rock or a reef could lie dead ahead. They could only put their trust in the gods or the fates – or luck – and try to be as far across the sea as they could before Ragnall awoke – hopefully far enough out to sea so their sail could not be seen from shore.

Being on the water inevitably reminded Fenn of their voyage from Lindisfarne, but he was surprised that he did not feel seasick. The ability to move about at will, in charge of their own destiny; the need to keep his mind on his job, and the thrill of escape combined to make this experience the complete opposite of the early days aboard Ragnall's ship.

He felt exhilarated.

The movement of the boat and the sounds of the sea developed into a constant and familiar rhythm. Fenn felt his tension ease and fought a desire to relax and close his eyes, forcing himself to stay awake and keep watch.

He heard the rattle of her new sword against the wooden seat before Kaela sat beside him. She put her arms around his waist, resting her head on his shoulder.

'I'm happy now.' She sounded as excited as he was. 'The air is fresh and we're speeding over the waves. I believe we *will* get home.'

'There's a long way to go yet, and Ragnall will chase us as soon as he wakes.'

'That's what I expected you to say.'

Fenn sighed. It felt good to have Kaela so close; he could feel her warmth. He rested a hand on her knee and stared past the sail into the night, thinking of all that had happened since the moment Master Nerian rushed through the gates of the monastery calling for the Bishop. He thought of Yseld; of them lying together on the rock on the night before the raid when they had seen the red dragon in the sky, foretelling the coming of the Northmen according to the Master. If events had not unfolded as they had since that day, he would have strived to continue his budding relationship with Yseld and he would probably have been very happy. But, as he had ruefully contemplated on previous occasions, he seemed to have little control over his destiny.

He must have moved because Kaela lifted her head and asked: 'What is it?'

'Nothing... I'm just remembering how my journey to this land began.'

'Don't dwell in the past. We have a future to look forward to now.'

Fenn turned his head so he could see her. By 'we', did she mean the two of them or all five? He let it lie. He didn't think it was wise to try to clarify her meaning.

Instead, he asked: 'What did Ragnall say to you at Gudrod's house?'

She lifted her head, surprised at his question.

'Do you mean when he first talked to me?'

'Yes.'

After a moment, she said: 'He said he did not expect this of me, meaning my attempt to escape.'

'And what did you reply so angrily?'

'I told him I had been kidnapped and brought to Lognavik and that I would never wear a collar again. I was angry because he expected me to be grateful.'

'That's what I expected you to say,' said Fenn, smiling as she hit him softly on the cheek with her fist. He reacted as if she had hit his cut lip and she was immediately apologetic but then saw it was the wrong cheek and hit him again, harder, on the shoulder.

'And what did he say about the axe?'

'He said if anything has happened to Thorvald he will make sure we all die slowly. I told him that Thorvald had given the axe to you. I don't think he believed me.'

So Ragnall had not talked with Thorvald or Askari, but Olaf would surely have called at the hut on his way into the mountains. It gave Fenn no comfort to realise that Ragnall would know that Kaela had spoken the truth when he eventually met up with Olaf. He knew it would make no difference to Ragnall's resolve and he must never think that the brothers would give up their attempts to recapture their thralls, no matter how far away from Lognavik they were. He would not feel safe until they stood on the shores of the land of their birth.

He turned his attention back to Kaela.

'Had you heard of Alfarin before?'

'No. Askari and Thorvald never spoke of him. I don't think he can be related to her – he must be the brother of Ragnall's father.'

'Let's hope Ragnall has no more relatives on the other side of this sea.'

He felt Kaela nod her head against his shoulder and her arms tightened around him.

As the night wore on and their small boat continued its bumpy ride across the sea, Fenn found himself unable to rest. He returned to his earlier thought about the part luck had played in their getting this far. Maybe they had got to this point entirely by luck? He couldn't get it out of his head that such luck could not last. He thought maybe he was only a part of some larger game and that whatever choices he made mattered little. He squirmed uncomfortably in his seat, disturbing a dozing Kaela.

'What is it?'

Fenn hesitated, then said: 'I'm wondering about the choices I've made – whether they've been good ones.'

When Kaela didn't answer, he continued:

'I didn't get us out of the cellar, Gudrod did. If it was up to me we'd still be there.'

He paused. 'What if there had been people on the beach and we couldn't get to a boat. What would I have done? I don't know.'

Still no comment from Kaela. Maybe she was asleep?

'I didn't think about what we needed to cross the pass and we almost died. I've made some bad decisions.'

This time Kaela answered: 'I haven't seen any bad decisions. When something needed to be done you did it. You made decisions when you needed to make them. Now stop thinking and get some sleep. I'll keep watch for a while.'

*   *   *

His eyes opened to a tap on his shoulder and Fenn felt something being placed in his hand. He looked down to see an apple then up to see Gisele smile at him and hand an apple to Hakon, who was sitting backwards on his seat watching the horizon over their wake.

It was morning.

Fenn allowed himself a wry smile. Naturally Gisele had thought to bring some apples out of the cellar. He thanked her. She knelt at the mast, took some more apples from her tunic and placed them inside the basket. She seemed much more at home on the boat now.

'Olgood, did you sleep?'

'For a time. Gisele steered and kept watch.'

Fenn stared over the sea. There was land visible on the southern horizon but they were travelling parallel to it as far as he could determine. It was a cloudy sky with a steady breeze carrying enough strength to whip spray from the wave-tops, pushing them along at a good rate. He ran his hand through his hair. It was wet so it may have rained during the night or perhaps it was morning dew or spray.

Kaela sat beside him, relaxed, leaning back with a foot up on the seat, contentedly eating her apple.

He breathed the salt air deeply. 'Am I always the last one to wake?'

'Always,' Olgood said.

Fenn stood up and took hold of the mast. By all rights, Ragnall would just now be waking with a sore head and discovering that his captives had gone. He hoped no suspicion would fall on Gudrod.

He carefully scanned in all directions. They were alone on the sea.

The apple was cold, crisp, juicy and refreshing. It was consumed in a few moments and he tossed the core overboard. He breathed deeply again, revelling in the feeling of their solid little boat charging like a wooden horse across the surface of the sea.

'Shall I take over the sail?'

Kaela stood up at the same time as Fenn moved forward causing her to quickly step back to get out of his way. Her foot came down on a loose oar that rolled, twisting her ankle – her other foot caught the side of the boat and she was over the side. Her scream and the splash as she hit the water occurred together.

Fenn didn't hesitate. In one move he pulled Thorvald's axe from his belt and dropped it at his feet then used the seat to propel himself into a dive from the boat. Even so, Kaela was twenty yards away when he hit the water.

He arched his back to make his dive as shallow as possible, broke the surface and searched for her. He wasn't sure how long she could stay afloat. He saw splashing and put all his effort into his strokes, driving himself through the water. When he knew he was close, he stopped swimming and checked the water around him.

He couldn't see her. He remembered his futile search for Audrey.

He was about to dive when she surfaced ten feet away in a gasping flurry of waving arms. In a moment he had her by the shoulder. She grabbed at him frantically, fastening on to the first things her clutching fingers found, a clump of his hair and the neck of his tunic, promptly dragging them both underwater. He kicked and pulled with his free hand for the surface, turning her face up as soon as they reached the air.

The pain from the desperate grasp of her hand twisting his hair was intense. He forced his voice to be calm.

'I have you. You're safe. Don't struggle. Let go and lie still and let me hold you. I'll keep your head out of the water.'

She calmed at the sound of his voice and the feeling of his arm around her and released her grip on his hair. She was breathing heavily and coughing but she was controlling her panic. He moved his arm under her chin and took a good grip of her tunic at the shoulder, easing onto his back and pulling her onto his chest. She suddenly coughed violently and he raised her higher, tilting her head so she could get rid of the water, kicking hard with his legs to keep them on the surface. When her coughing eased, he used his free arm to pull them both forward so her body was floating and she was stable on her back. He twisted his head to look for the boat.

He couldn't see it, but he wasn't worried, knowing the others would be doing all they could to return and rescue them. He slowly swam in a circle so he could watch for the boat without needing to move his head.

Kaela spluttered some water from her mouth. 'I thought I was going to die,' she croaked through a raw throat.

'Not while I'm alive.'

She was silent, concentrating on breathing. Fenn continued to swim in a circle but still could not see the boat. He scanned the horizon, looking in all directions in case he had become disoriented. Wherever he looked he saw only a featureless expanse of water.

The wind had not seemed strong but it was enough to create a disturbed sea which lacked any consistent rhythm. They were constantly buffeted by small waves and their faces washed by spray. It was uncomfortable but Fenn knew it could have been much worse. He had to spit to clear his mouth and blink and shake his head to keep the salt water from his eyes but, even in these conditions, he knew he could keep them afloat for a long time. He made sure Kaela's mouth and nose were well clear of the water. He was acutely aware she had put her trust and her life in his hands.

The water didn't feel cold but he couldn't tell whether that was as a result of his recent efforts. He knew they would gradually lose the heat from their bodies the longer they were in the water.

'Can you move your arms? Push backwards, it will help.'

She did as he asked. That would help keep her warm as well as give her something to do.

'That's good,' he said. 'Not so fast but keep it up.'

He slowed his movements to conserve his energy. He had no idea how long he would need to keep going.

When he did see the boat, he thought at first he must be mistaken. He had been expecting it to be close. Instead, it was an unbelievable distance away, just a blot on the horizon – almost out of sight. It was the only object on the sea. It must be the boat.

If it was, it would be some time before it could reach them.

On the next circle, he searched for the boat again but couldn't find it where he'd last seen it. He craned his head to see above the waves but that caused Kaela to sink so he quickly lowered his head back in the water.

'They will be turned about and heading towards us. Not long now.'

Fenn concentrated on keeping his actions slow and steady, just enough to keep them floating without wasting effort. He felt a surge of admiration for Kaela. The fall into the sea would have terrified her but since he had reached her and was able give her support, although her head had been underwater often and she was continually choking and spluttering, she had remained calm and trusted him to keep her afloat.

There was a continual noise of water splashing against his ears but the main sound he could hear was his own breathing, punctuated by a puff or a spit every now and then to blow the water out of his mouth. By listening to these sounds, he recognised that he naturally tensed and his breaths quickened as time passed and he had to force himself to consciously relax and slow his breathing.

'Are you getting tired?'

'No. This is just like walking. I can do it all day.'

When he mentioned walking, the shoes on his feet felt heavy. His task would be easier if he kicked them off but they were tied at the top and he would not be able to release them and hold Kaela at the same time.

After a while she asked: 'Will they be able to see us in the water?'

'Yes, I think so.'

Although his reply was automatic, the thought worried him. They were a very small object in a very large sea, and the boat, if it *was* the boat he had seen, was a long way away. Maybe they were searching in the wrong place.

He tried to think of a way to make them more noticeable. He wouldn't be able to raise a hand to wave, but perhaps Kaela could. Apart from that they had nothing…

A thought came to him.

'Do you still have your sword?'

'Yes, I think so.' A pause. 'Yes, I do.'

'Can you take it out and hold it up? Perhaps they will see it. Do it carefully and I'll hold you steady.'

He felt Kaela reaching for the sword. It must have been caught somehow because she had some difficulty. She turned her head to look for the scabbard and a wave hit her in the face.

She coughed violently just as another wave hit and he felt her body tense on the verge of panic as she coughed again. She tried to hold her breath and her head and shoulders jerked with the effort of suppressing the urge to cough, but she determinedly kept her mouth closed until the spasm passed. She took a few quick breaths which were punctuated by small coughs. He patted her shoulder for encouragement and after a moment she relaxed and breathed normally.

'I think I've swallowed at least a pail of seawater.' She cleared her throat.

He grunted that he understood and patted her again.

'I'll need to move my belt,' she said. 'The sword is sitting behind my hip.'

'Go ahead. I'm ready.'

She kept one hand moving at her side to compensate as she pulled on her belt. Fenn felt her body twist but she kept her head still and he used his free hand to adjust for the movement.

'Got it.' She spat and blinked as a wave bounced off his shoulder and the spray landed in her face.

Kaela took a few breaths to prepare herself and eased the sword from its scabbard. She held it on her chest then slowly and carefully raised it into the air, ready to drop it down if they became unstable. Fenn found he could balance the action without much difficulty. While the sword was up he just kept them steady and didn't try to circle.

224

'Keep it up there as long as you can, then replace it and we'll try again after a while.'

To reinsert the sword into its scabbard, Kaela had to use both hands and that resulted in a dunking for them both the first time, but Kaela calmly allowed him to regain control and resume his patient circling.

Five times Kaela raised the sword high. On the fifth occasion, she gasped when she thought she had missed the scabbard, and coughed again from the water she swallowed, but she recovered without dropping the sword.

Fenn found himself losing focus. Gazing out on an unchanging scene of endless sea in all directions, with a repeated pattern of small waves as far as the eye could see, it was difficult to maintain concentration. They had already been in the water longer than he expected and for the first time he worried how long he could keep swimming. He was sure the sword increased their chances of being seen, but was it enough?

It was time to raise the sword again.

He checked the sky to see if there were any hints of a weather change and he could not prevent a cry of relief when his eyes returned to the sea and a grey sail with blue crossed swords appeared only a few hundred yards away, heading directly for them.

'They've found us,' he said, and felt Kaela nod.

Fenn suddenly felt tired, his clothes were like heavy weights dragging on his arms and legs. He twisted his head to look for the boat again and seemed to lose rhythm – his coordination faltered and they rolled from side to side. It took a strong pull with his arm to steady them both. He told himself he didn't need to watch for the boat and concentrated on the need to keep them afloat just a little longer.

A strong hand slipped under Kaela's arm and pulled her upwards.

*　*　*

'Next time you want to go swimming, let us know,' said Olgood. 'We can stop the boat first.'

Fenn and Kaela were using Gisele's dress to dry themselves. Kaela still coughed occasionally. They had stripped off their wet clothes which now hung on the sail ropes to dry in the sun. Both were shivering although Fenn still did not feel cold. Maybe it was relief.

'We lost you,' Olgood admitted. 'It didn't seem to take long to turn around – Hakon and Gisele did a good job there, but then we couldn't see you anywhere. Nothing but sea. We came back to where we thought you had fallen but found nothing. We just circled wider and wider until Gisele spotted the sun glinting on the sword.'

He put his hand on Fenn's shoulder. 'That was a relief my friend. Welcome back.'

'Not today,' said Fenn, with a grin.

'Not today,' echoed Olgood.

They waited, drifting on the water while everyone recovered. Relief, together with the knowledge of how close tragedy had been, showed on each face.

When their clothes were dry enough to put back on, Fenn and Kaela dressed as Olgood got them under way again. Hakon and Gisele attended to the sail.

Kaela came to Fenn and hugged him tightly, her head on his chest.

'Thank you for my life,' she said.

'No need,' he said and hugged her back just as tightly. Her hair smelled salty and fresh. They stood until the rocking of the boat forced them to sit before they fell overboard again.

'Can I look at the sword that saved us?'

Kaela nodded. She stood up again. The sword and scabbard were now also dry and did not seem to have been affected at all from their immersion. She drew the weapon and weighed it in her hand, standing easily and steady, in harmony now with the movement of the boat.

'It has beautiful balance,' she said, flexing her wrist, twisting the weapon in the air, handling it with obvious familiarity. 'And it's the perfect weight for me.'

She twisted her wrist and presented it to him hilt first.

'A quality sword,' she said. 'I noticed it as soon as Alfarin stepped through the door.'

Fenn noted her ease with the sword and paused before accepting it.

'Do you know how to use this?'

'I know how to use it.' Kaela's voice was confident. She took a deep breath and stretched her arms out, her ordeal in the sea now behind her, happy to be back on the boat and moving again.

It was an unusual talent for a woman to have. Fenn shook his head. She was an enigma. He was about to ask if she had learned that art from the same man who taught her Greek, but remembered she didn't want that known.

He studied the sword.

Alfarin's sword was thinner and longer than the normal Northman's blade and was definitely a weapon crafted for a noble hand.

The pommel was shaped and marked like a Northman's helmet. Tightly wound leather covered the handle so perfectly that the joins were undetectable. He folded the fingers of his right hand around the handle and found it was slightly wider in the middle giving him a solid grip. Each end of the handle was decorated with a thick band of copper and, below his hand, he saw some runes had been engraved on the downwardly curved guard. Fenn indicated these with a raised eyebrow.

'They say 'Battle Leader', or maybe 'Battle Lord',' interpreted Kaela.

'So you are the Lord of the Battle,' said Fenn addressing the sword and holding it up to admire.

'It *is* beautiful.' He ran his hand along the flat of the blade, '…and unmarked.'

He lowered the sword and handed it back. Kaela began to replace the sword in its scabbard when Olgood asked to see it.

Before handing him the sword, Kaela said: 'Fenn said you're a blacksmith?'

When Olgood nodded, she said: 'Would you know Damascus steel if you saw it?'

Olgood let out a breath of surprise and held out his hand for the sword. He passed the steering oar to Gisele and held the sword flat in both hands, examining the blade.

He made several appreciative grunts, turning the weapon over. He held the blade up to his eye and looked along it.

'I've heard of these swords. Yes, I think this is Damascus steel, the highest quality. You can see the marks of the flowing steel in the blade – that's a sign. These blades are reputed to be very tough – they don't shatter and are capable of holding an exceptionally sharp edge.'

'I've been told that a hair falling on the edge of a Damascus blade will be split,' said Kaela, with a smile, 'but I'm not so sure about that.'

Fenn had been following the conversation between them with undisguised interest.

'Olgood, how do you – a peaceful village blacksmith – know so much about swords; weapons of war?' He turned to Kaela. 'And how do you, a… a…' he was unsure how to describe her, '…a girl from Wessex, also know about swords and Damascus steel?'

Olgood answered first.

'I talk with the travellers – many metal workers visited the monastery. I'm interested in the manufacture of steel. I've made some, not like this though. Do you remember the charcoal you took from my kiln? That was used for making steel.'

Olgood paused and said thoughtfully: 'I think this steel comes from the far east, but the sword was probably made by the Muslims, maybe as a gift or at the request of Alfarin or another Northman. The pommel and curved guard are in the Northman style.'

Fenn turned to Kaela.

'I keep my ears open. I hear things, and I remember,' she said.

He was irked that she evaded his question. His eye was drawn to the belt and scabbard of fine leather edged in metal which contrasted with Kaela's travel-worn clothing.

'Hopefully that belt and scabbard will soon look as ragged as you,' he said, sounding more critical than he intended. 'Even after some time in the water, they look new and we don't want them drawing attention.'

He turned away from her puzzled and indignant look when Hakon called out: 'I see sail ahead.'

A moment's observation showed that the sail was headed directly for them from the south, a small boat about the same size, travelling in the opposite direction.

'Gisele, can you lie in the bottom out of sight, and Olgood make yourself small,' said Fenn. 'Hakon will call out to them if they get close. We are a friendly family of four out fishing. Kaela, take off that sword and put on your hat.'

The two boats closed and Fenn saw they would pass about one hundred yards apart.

'Keep this distance if you can, Olgood.'

When they got closer Fenn could see there were three men in the boat. He gave a friendly wave and Hakon and Kaela followed his lead. The boat turned towards them but Olgood kept his path. One of the men called out and Hakon answered. There was a short exchange of words but Hakon's answers seemed to satisfy the man and the boat resumed its heading. Fenn gave another wave as they pulled away from each other, which one of the men answered.

'What did he ask?'

'He ask where we from. I tell him from Aarhus which is town in north. I have been there.' Hakon paused. 'And I say we go to Freibern – we too far from Aarhus for fishing.'

Fenn smiled and nodded his appreciation. 'You thought quickly.'

He gazed after the receding boat.

'If he meets Ragnall he has no tale to tell.'

Another night at sea.

Olgood slowed their progress through the night. The cloud cover had increased, the lack of stars and moon cutting visibility dramatically. Olgood gave him some instructions and Fenn took a watch on the steering oar, an experience he enjoyed. The night was quiet, apart from the normal sounds from the sea and the boat which he was able to push into the background, allowing him to consider a thought that had been concerning him.

He'd had no reason to criticise Kaela over her appearance. Her clothing was no more ragged than anyone else's. His concern about the sword was valid but there were many better ways he could have said what he wanted to say. He looked across at her. She was asleep now; he would apologise in the morning.

He watched her sleeping form, chest slowly rising and falling, her red hair folded across her ear. He could see in his mind the pink blush on her cheeks that complemented the colour of her hair, and her deep brown eyes that seemed to hold the promise of... he wasn't sure what. In spite of the mystery surrounding her – or maybe partly because of it – he was very attracted to this woman. In fact he could not imagine his life without her. He closed his eyes and thought of Yseld. She existed in another time and place far from here and seemingly long ago. He did feel sorrow for Yseld, and for what might have been, but they had been forced apart by circumstances out of his control. His life would have certainly been different if the Northmen hadn't chosen to beach their ships on Lindisfarne that day but that was then and he was here, a thousand miles from Lindisfarne – with Kaela sleeping a few feet away.

The second morning dawned overcast and cold. Fenn worried that they might be forced ashore if the weather worsened and he kept his eye on the land looking for bays and places they could land if necessary, but the clouds broke later in the morning and took with them the possibility of a storm.

Coinciding with the improvement in the skies, the wind freshened, giving extra height to the waves. For the rest of the day their vessel scudded across the sea at a speed that often seemed to be at the boat's limit, accompanied as it was by a continuous shuddering. Worried about the strain on the mast and ropes from the bulging sail, Fenn continually checked the knots were properly tied and holding. Olgood judged that the boat could handle the conditions and was not inclined to slow their pace, keeping the sail tight to the wind.

Fenn was forced to keep tension in his legs and his wits about him to avoid being knocked off-balance. He had to concentrate on the sea ahead to anticipate when to brace for a larger wave or one out of sequence with the rest. It was tiring but also stimulating.

Land appeared on their left as well and they sailed through a wide channel which narrowed in the afternoon. Hakon said the land masses they could see on each side of the channel were actually islands but, if that were so, they must be huge. Fenn had no idea how far they were from their destination or if they were still headed in the right direction but Hakon look confident.

He tried to talk to Kaela but the opportunity didn't arise. The conditions and the boat speed kept them busy. Whenever he had a moment to spare, she didn't.

Apart from another apple from Gisele – the last ones she said – the only food they had during the day were the final pieces of Askari's dried bear meat and Master Nerian's cheese. Fenn silently thanked Askari and offered a prayer for the Master when he swallowed the last piece. Their larder was now bare.

Hakon was in the bow at dusk when he identified the entrance to the *Schlei*, warning at the same time that a small fleet of three boats was approaching from the south. Olgood spilled the wind from the sail and let the other boats turn into the *Schlei* well ahead of them. These were probably fishermen heading home with their daily catch. Hakon noted where they had entered and directed Olgood to follow their line through the narrow entrance which led immediately into a large bay. Fenn was grateful they had been able to navigate the difficult passage while there was still good light. He took a long searching look in the direction they had come, but there was no other sail in sight.

Although Hakon had compared the two, the difference between this body of water and the Lognavik inlet was stark. Here, the surrounding land was flat and forested, the complete opposite of the sheer mountainsides of Viken. Olgood eased their speed and the three sails disappeared in the distance. Night fell as they crossed the bay. There were fewer clouds now and the moonlight was sufficient if they took it slowly.

In the quiet of the night, gliding almost silently across the calm open water of the bay, he decided that no time would be better than now. Even with the decision made, he hesitated. Maybe she'd think he had taken too long to offer an apology and refuse to accept it. He crossed the boat and crouched in front of her.

'Kaela, I…'

She reached out and put her finger on his lips, stopping his words.

'No need,' she said and released her finger. She put her hand on the back of his neck and pulled his head into her.

He remembered the first time she had put her finger on his lips, in the hut the night after he had driven off the bear. Fenn closed his eyes and felt at peace enveloped in her warmth.

*   *   *

Sailing along the *Schlei* was much more difficult than Fenn had expected.

Hakon knelt in the bow looking for obstacles and guiding Olgood with arm signals. He said he had sailed down the *Schlei* many times but never in charge of the boat so he did not know the channels in detail. The waterway seemed to consist of a series of lakes connected by narrower passages which contained many twists and turns and varied in width from little more than a river to open water several hundred yards wide. In contrast to their relatively straight-line voyage so far, they were constantly needing to change direction. Their untrained and sometimes uncoordinated movements often caused the boat to slow and stall, and they would then sit unmoving in the water until they had the sail set properly and could head in the correct direction.

It was tiring work but it was good to keep busy. Several times they ran aground in narrow stretches and had to re-float themselves with the oars. But with practice came improvement and they progressed steadily inland.

They were often plagued by biting insects when they ventured too close to swampy areas, everyone suddenly slapping arms and faces, and they learned to avoid the banks where reeds and grasses showed through the water, although the proximity of swamplands on both sides of the inlet meant that the unwelcome buzzing sounds in their ears never disappeared entirely.

Fenn estimated it was the middle of the night when they saw fires on the shore ahead.

Hakon whispered: 'Hedeby.'

CHAPTER SIXTEEN

Danes: Friendly and unfriendly…

Hedeby was positioned at the end of the *Schlei* inlet where it terminated in a bay. Hakon directed Olgood to the opposite side of the bay a mile across the water from the fires. They sped across the water before a brisk wind that covered the surface in small rippling waves which were reflected in the strong moonlight. Ten feet from the shoreline, Olgood turned the boat to the wind and brought down the sail. Trees and thick bushes overhung the shore and Hakon used an oar to paddle the boat up to the water's edge. He peered about and nodded with satisfaction.

'Good. Nobody come here long time.'

He indicated they should drop the mast. The knots in the ropes holding the mast and the sail had been stretched tight and those that Fenn and Hakon could not budge they turned over to Olgood.

Hakon directed the boat straight toward a group of trees and vines where there looked to be no passage but the foliage gave way before the bow and once they were through, they entered an enclosed swampy area that, in the gloomy light, resembled a drowned forest with tree trunks growing directly out of the water. Although unseen in the dark – when touched, the water surface proved to be covered with a slimy substance that also hung from all of the low branches, indicating that even twenty miles from the sea, the inlet was tidal. There were some islands that looked solid but Hakon warned they were not to be trusted. He said there were deep holes in the swamp and the tangled growth under the water was dangerous.

233

Hakon guided the boat between the pillars of wooden trunks until the bow ran aground on a small mound beside a high bank covered in vines and bushes trailing long fern-like tendrils. By pushing the boat tight into the bank, it was able to be partially covered by the abundant vegetation and was effectively hidden.

They gathered in the centre of the boat and discussed a plan. Hakon told them his father was his only relative in Hedeby but he had some friends that he could trust in the town. When everyone had had their say, Fenn summarised.

'So we agree,' he said. 'Hakon will go to Hedeby and find his father while we wait here. He will return before morning. Gisele, no hunting tonight – this swamp is too dangerous. Hakon will take a water skin and bring food if he can. If Hakon finds his father, we will decide what to do next – if he doesn't…' He spread his hands.

'We will decide what to do next,' finished Kaela, mimicking him, then squealed as Fenn caught her by the nose.

Gisele handed Hakon a water skin.

'Do you know your way out of the swamp?' asked Fenn, knowing the answer as he asked.

'I play here when boy,' Hakon said.

He raised a hand in farewell and jumped off the bow.

Fenn lay with Kaela in his arms in the bottom of the boat.

Olgood and Gisele were settled somewhere in the stern. Fenn could hear them murmuring to each other. Gisele was learning a few words of English, but she and Olgood seemed to be able to communicate without words. Fenn had watched Gisele 'talking' to Olgood. She was a talented actress and watching her body manner and facial expression Fenn was able to easily understand what she was saying. He could not recall either of them ever asking Kaela or Hakon to translate something the other had said.

He was tired and knew he should take this opportunity to get some sleep. Once Hakon had left and they had all found somewhere comfortable to lie, a chorus of frogs resumed their evening conversations and chirping

234

insects added to the night sounds. It was a loud but somehow comforting concert as if they were accepted by the other inhabitants of the swamp.

Fenn was wondering what tomorrow would bring. Would the group of five become a group of four? He would be happy for Hakon if he found his father but realised he would be sorry to see him go. Hakon had become a resilient and dependable companion. A phrase that Thorvald had used came to mind; a phrase that evaluated the trust you put in the man beside you. Fenn would willingly stand with Hakon in battle.

Fenn decided to let tomorrow take care of itself. He moved his arm so his head could rest in the crook of his elbow, disturbing Kaela who squirmed and changed her position, turning to face him.

'Are you awake?'

He grunted.

She didn't say anything for a while, then:

'When I was under the water I knew I was going to die.'

He came fully awake and waited for her to continue. He opened his eyes to look at her.

'I was struggling but I couldn't reach the surface. I looked up and saw your legs – I had to try one more time.'

Fenn stroked her hair, feeling her pain. 'That would have been terrifying.'

She nodded. Tears welled in her eyes and flowed down her face.

They were silent for a while and then, softly, he said: 'I don't think I could have lived if you…'

Kaela kissed him hard and then laid her cheek on his, holding his head tightly.

* * *

Morning arrived before Hakon.

Light gradually filtered between the trees and they were able to look out upon the uninviting landscape surrounding them. As they expected, the water was covered in a green slime, mixed with or maybe formed from decaying leaves and other vegetation. The only bare earth visible was the small mound that Hakon had stepped onto last night. When Fenn investigated he found it was only a few paces wide – a small island in a green lake. The bank against which the boat rested was soft earth, vertical and unclimbable. There was no indication of the direction Hakon had taken.

'If Ragnall knows Hakon's home is Hedeby he will be heading here and could arrive at any moment. We'll wait a while longer but if Hakon doesn't arrive soon we must go.'

'Hedeby looked like a large town from the number of fires we saw last night, there will be more people about,' said Kaela. 'Should we split into two parties in case Ragnall does arrive and asks about us?'

Fenn considered the suggestion. 'No, I think we should keep together and take our chances with the people we meet.'

The discussion was terminated when a whistle sounded across the water. Crouching in the boat, they couldn't see anyone until Hakon appeared from behind a tree fifty yards away. He came towards them seeming to walk on top of the water. He had a large sack over his shoulder. At twenty yards he stopped by a tree trunk and felt with his foot, then turned and walked parallel to the boat to the next tree from where he headed directly to the island at the bow. At no time did the water reach higher than his ankles.

'I thought you said the water was deep,' said Fenn, thinking he would have explored if he'd known the water was that shallow. He was happy to see Hakon so he made sure his comment was delivered with a grin and would not be taken as a reproach.

'Very deep. Very dangerous if not know where to walk.' Hakon laid the sack in the boat and climbed on board.

He sat facing them, looking neither happy nor unhappy.

'My father…,' he said, '…not seen in Hedeby since three summers. Since I am taken in raid by Northmen. One friend say he is wounded, maybe dead, but others say no. But he not seen since that day.'

'Hakon, I'm sorry,' said Fenn. 'I know how much you wanted to see him again. Do you think he'll be searching for you?'

Hakon nodded. 'Gods say I must wait to see him again. My friend want me to stay, wait for him in Hedeby, but I think if Ragnall come that not good idea.'

Hakon reached over to pat Gisele's knee.

'I must trust that I meet my father again one day but, like goddess Sif say before… this my family now.'

He smiled and looked around at their faces. Fenn could see the unspoken question in his eyes: '*If you'll have me?*'

Fenn reached across and put an arm around the small man's shoulders.

'Good. We're together again.' He gestured at the sack. 'What have you brought us?'

Hakon grinned broadly: 'Bread, cheese, some turnips – and this…' Hakon reached into the sack and pulled out a plucked hen.

*   *   *

They covered the boat as best they could and left it hidden against the bank. Hakon led the way through the swamp warning them to tread exactly where he trod, and eventually they stepped out of the green slimy water onto solid ground surrounded by a large grove of trees. They headed south, the trees thinning to become open rolling country.

At the top of a hill, Fenn stopped and looked across the bay. The sky was clear and the water of the *Schlei* was deep blue and sparkling in the morning sun. Hedeby was visible as a crowded collection of houses with minimal space between but seemingly formed into ordered lines unlike the scattered buildings of Lognavik. The town was the largest Fenn had seen and was completely surrounded by a huge earthen wall. He could see a road leading to a gate in the wall along which some carts and a group of people were travelling. An uncountable number of piers extended from the town into the bay looking like teeth protruding into an open mouth. The earth walls of the town were continued into the water and became two stone barriers enclosing the harbour, each terminating in a tower with a short gap between them to allow trading ships to come and go.

Hakon saw Fenn looking and stopped beside him. Olgood, Gisele and Kaela joined them at the top.

'Towers have thick chain between,' Hakon explained, moving his hands in a curve rising at the ends to indicate the hanging chain.

'Why is the town fortified?'

'Attacks by Slavs, by Swedes, by Saxons, by Northmen. Hedeby market for trade to east…,' he pointed to the *Schlei*, '…and to west river *Treene* go to other sea.' He turned to the north. 'Trade road north and south too. Hedeby in middle.'

'So, control Hedeby and you control the trade.'

'Yes,' agreed Hakon. 'And wall protect Hedeby.' He pointed south. 'Also *Danevirke*.'

'*Danevirke*? What is that?'

'More walls. King Godfred want wall from sea to sea.'

'How can we get past the *Danevirke*?' Fenn imagined the roads going through gates in the *Danevirke* just like he had seen at the Hedeby wall, which may be difficult for them pass through.

Hakon smiled. '*Danevirke* built to stop army. My friend say wall not finished yet. I know way past *Danevirke*.'

'They like walls here,' commented Olgood.

Kaela grabbed Fenn's arm and pointed. From the hilltop they could see across the bay and down part of the *Schlei*. A ship with a distinctive dragon-headed bow was sailing along the inlet toward Hedeby.

*　　*　　*

The impressive *Danevirke* fortification had been built to the height of three men and the part they saw looked to be a formidable obstacle to an attacking force but, as Hakon had said, it was not yet a complete barrier. He led them south-east along a little-used road which took them around the end of the unfinished *Danevirke* defences.

Travel in this country was much easier than in the land of the Northmen where the numerous lakes and rivers were major obstacles. They had yet to cross a river and the only obstacles were low hills. There wasn't a mountain in sight.

The road they were following took them in the direction they wanted to go – south, skirting along the side of a forest that Hakon called Skyrvid. Their simple plan was to get as far from Hedeby as possible. Hakon had described the land south of Hedeby as the neck of a narrow peninsula, so Fenn was keen to leave the peninsula so they would have more choice of directions to travel.

Although the road did not show high usage, there was enough sign of people and animals passing to make it unnecessary to attempt to cover their tracks. The air carried the smell of fresh grass and forest trees and walking on this late spring day was easy and pleasant.

Kaela, who was leading, stopped and waited at a curve in the road for the others to catch up.

About half a mile ahead, a group of people was visible, heading in the same direction but at an unusually slow pace. From this distance it looked like a family possibly heading home from the Hedeby market. Two people were riding a cart pulled by a donkey or horse and two others were walking alongside, one of whom looked to be a small child. The walking child was obviously the reason for their slow pace. It would not take long to catch up to these travellers. Fenn commented they may be able to get some useful information from the family. When nobody disagreed, he led the way forward.

They learned the group was indeed a family – a man, his mother and his wife and child. The child was a girl and Fenn immediately noticed her resemblance to Agatha. As soon as he saw her blond curls he put his hand on Kaela's neck and bent down to her ear.

'Will you be alright?'

She nodded.

When they neared, Kaela called to the man who answered with a friendly wave and stopped his cart. He was a rotund man with a big chest and an unruly mess of long hair covering a broad face. He sat with his hands resting on his knees, holding the rope that was attached to the horse's collar. A welcoming smile showed through a full beard as they walked up to the cart.

Kaela introduced the people in her party but gave each one a different name. Fenn was surprised to hear her call him 'Anteros', but he smiled and nodded when she said it.

The man presented his wife and she smiled. He called the little girl 'Ursula'.

Kaela knelt and gave the girl a hug, closing her eyes while she did so.

Just as Fenn was about to clear his throat thinking the hug had lasted too long, Kaela rose and the man introduced the elderly woman sitting beside him on the cart as his mother. She did not acknowledge the introduction, continuing to stare into the distance. The man patted her hand which she glanced at briefly then resumed her vacant stare.

Kaela talked with the man for some time, then came to stand beside Fenn who was a few paces away.

'He says his mother is sick in the head,' she said. 'She does not know her family and she is lost behind her eyes. I've told him you're my husband...'

The man interrupted her and spoke in English: 'You speak English?'

Fenn hesitated. Was it wise to admit that he spoke the language? How did the man know? Then he realised the man had heard Kaela speaking English.

The man continued, his manner friendly: 'I speak some English. I know man from that land. Good friend, fisherman.'

Fenn made up his mind. 'Yes,' he said, 'English.'

The man laughed, a slow bass rumble. He turned to his wife and said: 'English!'

She smiled and he clapped his hands together in delight.

'Good. Good. And you *not* husband, huh?' He waved an admonishing finger at Fenn, a huge grin on his face. 'But you travel with this woman – very nice.'

Fenn put his arm around Kaela's shoulders.

'Yes,' he agreed. 'Very nice.'

The man waved a hand at Olgood. 'This man big. He *jotunn*, yes?' He laughed at his joke.

Fenn laughed with him, and Kaela whispered: 'Mythical giant.'

Fenn was anxious to prevent the man from asking questions about why they were in this land and where they were headed. He changed the subject and asked: 'Where do these two roads lead?' He pointed toward a fork in the road ahead.

Two hundred yards further down the road, the forest they had been walking alongside expanded to the east covering the land directly in front. The road curved to the left to follow the edge of the forest but a branch of the road continued straight ahead into the trees.

The man followed Fenn's pointing finger.

He put an arm out to his left: 'I tell wiiife...' he emphasised the word 'wife', drawing it out and winking at Fenn, '...this road go to Kirkense.'

He moved his arm to indicate the road entering the forest. 'That go south, through Skyrvid Forest, but not good.'

'These people are going home,' Kaela added, 'to a village called Kirkense which is a few miles south and east of here. Ursula wanted to walk – she is stubborn and so much like...'

Kaela stopped herself.

'Sigrund...' she indicated the man with her fingers, '...told me the road through Skyrvid Forest will save a day if we want to go south, but it is dangerous because outlaws live in the forest and sometimes they attack and rob travellers.'

'Forest is big,' said Sigrund. 'This road old and small. Maybe Lothar's men not see you, but best you take road to Kirkense and go around Skyrvid.'

'Who is Lothar?' asked Fenn.

Sigrund gave a snort of derision.

'Lothar the Hun he call himself. Leader of outlaws in forest. He say he is son, son, son...' Sigrund held out his hand and made descending motions as if going down steps. He paused, grinning, then continued: '...son, son, son, son, son of Atilla.'

Fenn drew in a breath, thinking. Standing behind him, Hakon said:

'I hear of Lothar. He not called 'Hun' then. I walk this Skyrvid road before – never see Lothar. Better in forest if want fire.'

Fenn knew what he meant. He was hungry. The bread and cheese had been good, but enough for one meal only and the thought of roasted fowl made his mouth water. Also, with Ragnall now in Hedeby, he didn't want to lose a day if he didn't have to.

He thanked Sigrund and his family and wished them good fortune. Kaela could not help herself giving Ursula another hug and ruffling her hair.

*   *   *

The interior of the forest was light and airy. The trees were not thickly grouped and the undergrowth was sparse. The sun pierced the tree cover in visible shafts of light and Fenn watched several multi-coloured butterflies playing in the beams of sunshine. After it entered the trees, the road was covered in a thick carpet of grass and leaves that showed little sign of recent travellers.

It was quiet. The chirp of birds could be heard but always some distance away. The wind was only sufficient to disturb the tops of the trees; at ground level the greenery around them was still. They covered ten miles at a good pace, striding along in silence, reluctant to disturb the peace of the forest. Kaela and Fenn were walking together a few paces ahead of the other three.

Fenn looked down at his feet. He could feel the soles of his shoes were wearing thin and would need to be replaced soon. Maybe they could exchange some of Gisele's rabbits for shoes at a market. Kaela's pace slowed beside him.

Up ahead was a crossroads where their road met another road heading east-west. Three men were standing in the middle of the crossroad. They were in a group, talking together. When the men saw them approaching, they moved to one side to let them pass. They were all armed with swords and Fenn shared a glance with Kaela.

Fenn nodded to the men as he was about to pass by but, instead of acknowledging his nod, the men deliberately stepped into the road and spread out, hands on swords. A rustle of feet from the forest behind indicated more men had come from the trees. Fenn looked back – three more were walking slowly forward. Like the others, they had their hands resting on their sword-hilts but had not drawn their weapons.

The man in the middle of the three ahead spoke a command.

'He's asking for our purses,' said Kaela.

Lothar's outlaws. He heard Olgood slip the basket off his shoulders.

The men had hard and wary faces; there was no uncertainty or fear in their eyes. They had done this before and would not be diverted by talk. To submit to these men would put them all in danger – especially the women.

In a calm voice, Fenn said: 'Olgood, Hakon, Gisele – can you take the three behind?'

He heard a grunted assent from Olgood and Hakon saying something, probably for Gisele's benefit.

He hoped Kaela would understand what he was about to do.

He shouted: 'Now!'

In a smooth motion he drew the axe from his belt and swung it at the man on the right, a wide swing that he hoped would threaten the middle man also and draw him away from Kaela. From the corner of his eye he saw Kaela's sword appear in her hand and her thrust at the centre man was even quicker than his.

Fenn had never killed a man. He had fought as a boy – courtyard scraps – but had never seriously hurt anyone; certainly not intentionally. His swing was not full strength. He turned his hand so the back of the axe would strike the man. His idea was to surprise the outlaws with their willingness to fight. Perhaps they would decide to break off when they realised these travellers were not easy prey.

The man he had attacked moved back and Fenn's axe missed his head by inches. The swordsman stepped back further to give himself room and drew his sword, bringing it to readiness, twisting his body so the sword faced Fenn and bending his knees to steady his stance. Fenn knew he had made a serious mistake. This was a fight to the death and his half-hearted blow had lost him the element of surprise and allowed his opponent time to prepare. He wanted to check on Kaela – and the others – but could not afford to take his eyes from the man in front of him.

With new resolve, he followed the movement of his axe by taking a pace to the left, then bent his knee and swung the axe in the reverse direction – this time with all his strength – at the man's legs. The man jumped from the path of the swing at the same time raising his sword, a grimace of triumph on his face. Fenn's head was vulnerable and he instinctively raised the axe to block the expected strike from above. Too late, he realised the sword may simply break his axe and continue down to his neck.

The sword clanged harshly against the iron-covered handle of the axe and the blow was checked as effectively as if Fenn had used a sword of his own. Fenn thanked Thorvald for standing by his side at that moment.

The man was as surprised as Fenn, his eyes widening. He had expected the strike to finish the fight and was thrown off-balance when his sword was repelled. Rather than draw his axe back, Fenn continued his overhead blocking movement, turning his wrist and thrusting at the man's head, using the axe as an extension of his arm. The top of the axe-blade caught the man in the mouth, breaking teeth and knocking his head backwards. Fenn followed his thrust, stepping forward and curving his arm around so the end of the axe handle struck the man solidly on his ear. He fell heavily to the ground and didn't move.

Fenn started moving to his left, raising his axe, ready to go to Kaela's aid even before he turned his head to look for her. His eyes passed over the middle man on the ground, blood surrounding a gash in his throat. Fenn expected to see a terrified girl, inches from death, at the mercy of the third outlaw – if she was still alive. While he had been grappling with his man, Kaela had faced two opponents.

He couldn't have been more wrong.

He watched Kaela wielding the Lord of the Battle. She was enjoying herself.

The outlaw was large with the thick and powerful body of a man used to hard labour. He was attacking with all his strength. Each of his great swings, however, was simply being diverted. Kaela was not attempting to block the blows; she merely pushed them to one side or nimbly moved out of reach, negating the man's superior strength and rendering his swings ineffective. He tried to vary his attack, pressing alternately high or low or from the side. His actions were fast and smoothly executed – the result of long familiarity with a sword, but whatever he tried she easily countered.

Fenn glanced behind him. Two outlaws lay on the ground, one obviously dead, his chest covered in blood, the other unconscious or dead. Olgood had the last man immobilized with one arm fastened around his neck, the other hand still holding his bloodied axe. The man had a wound on his head with blood flowing into his eye and down his cheek and he was holding onto his wrist which looked broken; but he was alive.

Together with Hakon and Gisele, Olgood was watching Kaela – seemingly oblivious to the man struggling in his arm.

The outlaw realised this was a contest he was not going to win and attempted to back away. Kaela followed him smoothly, step for step, now interspersing her own thrusts and swings between his to keep him in the fight. Then she moved forward more deliberately, her blade moving too fast for Fenn to follow. The man now fought totally defensively but his reactions were slowing, showing less coordination as he became desperate and he was unable to stop Alfarin's long sword from reaching him – a red slice appeared on his thigh, then a cut on his shoulder and another on his forearm.

Abruptly the man threw his sword on the ground and knelt down breathing heavily with his hands in the air, head bowed and waiting either for clemency or a fatal blow. Kaela placed the end of her sword under his chin and lifted his head.

Olgood appeared at Fenn's side. The man he held had given up struggling and now stood limp-kneed in his grasp. His breathing was a rasping sound but Olgood showed no inclination to lighten his hold on the man's neck. Gisele also came into view, carrying a sword in each hand.

Fenn looked back again to see Hakon checking the man who may have been unconscious. He was unbuckling the man's sword belt.

'Is anybody hurt?'

Olgood had to look down at his body to be sure. The man he was holding went totally limp and Olgood let him fall to the ground.

*   *   *

'Ask him if he is one of Lothar's men.'

Kaela put the question to the man kneeling before her. His face maintained its blank expression and he did not reply. Kaela's sword flicked to one side and a flow of blood appeared from the man's ear. He gave an involuntary yelp of pain and put his hand to his ear, then stared at his bloody fingers.

'Ask him again,' said Fenn.

The man mumbled a reply.

'He said Lothar will kill us all, so I think the answer is yes.'

The man said another sentence and nodded at the dead man lying beside him, the one who had been in the centre of the three facing Fenn and Kaela. Kaela drew in a breath and looked at Fenn, her brow raised.

'He says this one is Lothar's brother and Lothar will be certain to avenge his death.'

'Where is Lothar? How far away?'

The man tightened his lips. Kaela threatened his other ear. When this did not entice the man to speak, she placed the tip of her sword on the side of his nose, directly in front of his eye.

The man sucked in a quick breath and attempted to move his head back and away from the sword. Easily Kaela moved with him, the sword remaining on the man's nose, until the man was bent back at the waist as far as his spine would allow.

She said something. The man scowled and he mumbled a few quick words. He waved one hand toward the west.

'What did you say to him?' asked Fenn, amused.

'I suggested it would not be wise to move again.'

She withdrew her sword and the man fell forward onto his hands.

'He says Lothar has many camps. The current one is a half day west. These men were sent to watch this road.'

'Then we'd better be on our way as soon as we can,' said Fenn.

'Do we kill them?' asked Olgood. 'Dead men cannot describe us to Lothar.'

Hakon was strapping on one of the men's swords. He looked up and nodded his agreement. Fenn took a moment to think. Killing the outlaws made sense, but to kill in cold blood would mean they were no better than outlaws themselves.

'No. We'll take their weapons and tie them and leave them and the bodies some way into the forest. We'll let their gods decide their fate.'

Olgood and Gisele also chose a sword, and Olgood handed the one that Kaela's opponent had carried to Fenn. Fenn hesitated. He had no experience with a sword, but it could be useful. He buckled it around his waist. There were two extra swords which Olgood took out of sight and threw into the forest.

Fenn had expected to use strips from Gisele's old clothing to tie their prisoners, but once she learned what Fenn wanted to do, Gisele went into the trees and returned with some grasses which she showed Hakon how to twist together to make a strong and pliable twine.

While Kaela stood guard, Hakon and Gisele tied the hands and feet of the outlaws that were still alive. They left the feet of Kaela's opponent free, the only outlaw still conscious, so he could walk to his new place of rest himself.

Olgood and Fenn carried the body of Lothar's brother into the forest.

'I apologise for pushing you into that fight,' Fenn said, following Olgood between the trees. 'It ended well but it may have easily gone differently. We were outnumbered.'

He looked at Olgood. 'Did I do the right thing? Maybe they would have let us go when they found we had nothing of value.'

'We had weapons and we had women.'

'That's what I thought.'

'You did the right thing.'

Fenn looked around. 'This is far enough.'

They lowered the body. Fenn was holding the legs and he noticed that the soles of the outlaw's shoes were in much better condition than his own. He pulled off a shoe and one of his own and tried it on. It was a good fit and he removed the outlaw's other shoe. He would suggest they all take the opportunity to get new shoes. He and Olgood realised at the same time that none of the outlaws were likely to wear Olgood's size. Olgood grinned and shrugged.

'How did your fight go?' Fenn asked. 'Gisele...?' He was worried that his decision to fight had put Gisele in danger and Olgood might not be happy with that.

Olgood let out a laugh. 'Gisele was a whirlwind,' he said.

He recounted what had occurred behind Fenn's back.

He attacked the closest man before he had time to draw his sword and struck him in the chest with his first blow. The man fell but the axe was caught and it took a moment to free it. The other man drew his sword and would have had time to swing if Gisele had not thrown her knife. It struck a glancing blow cutting the second man above the eye. He stumbled back, his arms waving. Instead of swinging his axe again, Olgood caught the man's hand – the one holding his sword – and squeezed it until the sword dropped from his fingers. Gisele somehow found a thick branch and she hit the man behind the knees forcing him to the ground.

'After that it was easy.'

'And Hakon?'

'When I saw him, Hakon and his man were circling each other. I dragged the man I was holding forward but I wasn't needed. Gisele stepped behind the outlaw and cracked his head with the branch and hit him again as he was falling. They were not woman-like taps. She was calm and determined. She swung hard. She made the difference in the fight.'

Fenn could imagine Olgood giving the man a 'squeeze' powerful enough to break his wrist.

Before they left, Hakon put a large stone into the mouths of the three outlaws who were able to talk and made sure it would be kept in place by a grass tie placed across the mouth and knotted behind the head. He checked their bindings were secure, then patted the clothing of each of the men, searching for anything that may be useful. When he was checking Lothar's brother, he gave a cry of surprise and stood up holding a leather purse. He shook the purse and they heard the jingle of coins.

'I hear gold,' said Hakon, grinning.

He handed the purse to Fenn who opened it. Inside were coins – mostly silver but, as Hakon had predicted, the purse also contained some coins made of gold. Fenn could see a gold finger ring. He closed the purse and handed it back to Hakon.

'You not keep?' asked Hakon.

'You found it, you keep it for us,' said Fenn. 'Now – time to go.'

The man Olgood had held was now conscious, his brow furrowed with the pain of his broken wrist. Fenn addressed the two outlaws who were awake, sitting hunched with bound hands, feet and mouths, and watching with sullen eyes.

'Please tell them this,' he said to Kaela.

'Tell Lothar not to follow us.' When Kaela translated his words, one man tried to laugh but choked on the stone in his mouth. The other tried to spit on the ground. Fenn waited for the choking man to recover then drew his sword and held it to the man's throat.

'We should kill you, but I've decided to let you live, so you can give my message to Lothar.'

He moved his wrist and a bead of blood appeared on the man's neck.

'Anyone who follows – dies.'

CHAPTER SEVENTEEN

Divided we fall…

The hen tasted even better than Fenn imagined it would.

Gisele had found and crushed some nuts which she mixed with small pieces of turnip and the hen was roasted with this mixture inside, imparting a tangy, almost fruity flavour to the flesh. Fenn worried the last scrap of meat from a bone and shook his head in wonder. Over the nights when Gisele was able to hunt and cook, she had produced many meals in difficult circumstances, and these so frequently surpassed any Fenn had previously experienced at the monastery that he had exhausted his words of thanks and praise for her efforts. Instead, as he always did when he had finished, he rose and walked to where she was sitting with Olgood. He put his arm around her shoulders and kissed her cheek. Gisele replied as she always did – by treating him to her wonderful smile.

Their fire had been built inside the large stump of a dead tree that had split in half long ago leaving a ten-foot high hollowed half-trunk. They had walked some distance from the road when the light was fading from the setting sun and descended a stony bank before they found the tree. Although he did not expect the outlaws to have been discovered yet and did not think anyone would be travelling the road through the forest at night, Fenn walked back to the road after their meal was complete to see if the fire was visible. By the time he returned it was dark and he was pleased that he could only see the fire when he was abreast of it.

Gisele had learned that Kaela spoke the Frankish language which apparently was her own native language and when he stepped into the firelight, the two were sitting to one side talking softly while Olgood and Hakon sat on the other side of the fire.

When Gisele and Kaela paused in their conversation, Fenn squatted on his toes beside Gisele. He picked a stout stick from the pile of firewood and hefted it in his hand.

'I didn't expect there to be such a warrior inside you,' he teased Gisele, holding up the stick.

When Kaela translated, Gisele laughed and gave an embarrassed smile but then her face turned serious. Fenn sensed she wanted to say something and waited while she sat thinking, her eyes down. Then she drew in a breath and looked up at him. Her green eyes were intense.

Through Kaela, she said: 'In Lognavik I could only fight these people in little ways – I would sometimes take an extra apple or an egg for us. I owned nothing – not my clothes, not even my life. But I have no collar now. I belong to nobody. For the first time in a long while, I can fight for myself. Kaela has given me these clothes – they are mine.' She glanced at Kaela who nodded. 'My life is mine again. Nobody can just take what is mine anymore – including my life. Those men wanted to take something from me. I did not want them to have it. Enough has been taken.'

She paused, then mumbled another few words.

'She says she is probably not explaining herself very well,' said Kaela.

Fenn laid a hand on Gisele's. 'You explained yourself perfectly,' he said.

He sat down beside Kaela and she leaned against him. For a long time they stared into the fire.

'I've been meaning to ask you something,' he said. She looked up at him warily.

'When we met Sigrund south of the Danevirke, you said my name was Anteros. That sounds Greek – why did you choose that name?'

In the firelight, he wasn't sure, but he thought she blushed.

'It was the first name that came into my head,' she said, but something in the way she said it made him think there may be more to it.

251

Before he could pursue the matter, Gisele said something to Kaela who reached up and used a handful of his hair to pulled his head down to her level. She kissed him on the cheek and then moved across to Gisele.

Fenn stood and went to join the men, stopping to stoke the fire with the stick in his hand, and sat beside Hakon.

'How long before we're out of the forest?' he asked.

Hakon thought. 'A half day,' he said.

'Tell me what you know about Lothar.'

Hakon leaned back on his hands.

'Lothar was bad man in Hedeby when I was there – a thief. He kill man in fight and not pay *wergild*. King Godfred banish him from land of Danes but he go only to Skyrvid Forest. He had some men with him, not many, and he rob traveller but only on big road to west, never this small road.' Hakon shrugged. 'But I not here for three summers.'

Fenn knew about the *wergild* – it was also used in his land. If property is stolen or a person is injured or killed, the *wergild* price must be paid to the property owner or victim's family. For people, the amount of the *wergild* differed for nobles, freemen and slaves and also for men and women.

'Maybe he has more men now.'

Olgood asked: 'Why does the king not hunt him?'

'He try. Skyrvid is big and Lothar know it too well. If one camp found he move to another.'

Fenn grunted. He rose to his feet and stepped over to the pile of wood they had collected for the fire.

'It was bad enough having Ragnall hunting us,' he said. 'Now we may have Lothar hunting us as well.'

He placed a log on the fire.

'But not tonight.'

They were on their way at first light. It was a bright sunny day from what they could see of the sky and the morning was spent following the road as it meandered through the forest. The scenery was so pleasant that Fenn had to remind himself that they should be hurrying each time his pace slowed as he found himself enjoying the day and the picturesque surroundings.

When the thinning of trees announced the edge of the forest, Fenn stopped and surveyed the scene before him.

The road they had been following curved west and then south to skirt a swampy wetland ahead. To the east the forest continued for a short distance but through those trees he could see open land. Fenn expected the road running south from Kirkense would lie in that direction. He wanted to avoid travelling on either road if possible.

'How far do these wetlands continue?' he asked Hakon.

'To lake, one day south. This swamp get bigger.' Hakon spread his hands apart. 'Town on lake is Ruslager. One day and half.' He pointed south.

'Are there any other villages?'

Hakon extended an arm to the north-east. 'Kirkense, one day.' He moved his hand to the east. 'Closest is small market village on river – half day.' He pointed west. 'This way, nothing between here and coast. Ruslager south.'

'I think it's best if we leave the road soon and walk across the country,' Fenn said. 'And I'd like to do that at an unexpected place.'

They walked steadily for five miles along the road before he found the place he wanted. Pools of clear water surrounded by reeds and grasses appeared in the swampy land that had been on their left since leaving Skyrvid Forest. The swamp was becoming wetter as it neared the lake.

Fenn had chosen a particularly uninviting location. At this point, the pool was twenty feet wide and over a ridge of grasses another pool of a similar size was visible. The water looked deep and was surrounded by muddy edges that would show every footstep.

He stopped and smiled when he received looks of surprise at the place he had chosen to leave the road.

'Yes, I know what you're thinking. We won't be able to cross the mud without leaving tracks. But that's perfect – that's what *they* will think.'

He asked Olgood to enter the water first to test the depth. His feet sank into the mud up to his ankles and the water was at his waist in the middle of the pool. Fenn pointed to a group of willows on the far side of the swamp about half a mile away.

'We'll head for those trees. Olgood, can you find the best path through the swamp from here?'

When they were all in the water and Olgood was stepping over the grassy ridge to enter the second pool, Fenn turned and showed the others how he wanted to cover their deep footsteps by placing mud from the bottom of the pool into the holes they had made in the muddy edge. They eagerly bent to the task, filling the holes then smoothing the area and splashing water about until all marks of their entrance had been erased.

Olgood called and pointed out the route he had taken across the pools and grassy patches. He was standing beside the mouth of a stream that ran into the swamp, in an area of tall wetland grasses. Beyond the grassy area, through the grove of willows and other trees, lay a broad open meadow.

Fenn was in the lead, pushing through the tall grass when he felt a sharp pain above the top of his shoe as if he had scraped past a jagged rock. Immediately the area on his leg felt hot and he bent down to pull up his wet trouser leg and check the wound. He expected to see a narrow red scratch but when he cleared aside the thick grass around his leg, he was surprised to see no blood – just a white area with two small marks. He was about to pull the trouser leg down when Gisele, walking behind him, reached out to hold his wrist.

'*Nathra!*' she said, beckoning to Kaela.

'Gisele says you have a snake bite,' said Kaela. 'Let me see.'

Fenn lifted his leg and Kaela looked at the wound. She talked with Gisele, both nodding. Fenn's leg felt hot and painful – just like a nettle sting.

'Did you see a snake?' asked Kaela.

Fenn shook his head. 'It felt like a scratch from a sharp rock or a stick.'

'Gisele says it was a male viper – because of the two marks. It can be dangerous but because you were moving it may not have made a good strike and perhaps it injected only a little of its poison. How do you feel?'

'It doesn't feel bad. I can walk.' He tried his leg and, satisfied, continued pushing through the grass, careful now and watching where he put his feet.

Fenn stared to limp as he climbed out of the tall swampy grasses. The group of shady willows was just ahead lining the stream that fed the swamp. In the centre, a large fallen tree trunk provided a place to sit and Fenn headed for it. His leg now had a painful burning sensation around his ankle that was more pronounced each time he put his weight on it. He sat on the trunk and pulled up his trouser leg again. The area of the bite had reddened and was noticeably swollen.

Gisele felt his leg and said something to Kaela. Kaela replied and turned to Olgood.

'Can you please go with Gisele,' she said calmly. 'She needs to find some plants.'

Gisele started to walk along the stream motioning Olgood to follow her. He put down the basket beside Fenn and they set off walking quickly.

'The area around the bite is already warm – you're reacting to the poison from the snake. Gisele says she knows something to use for a poultice to draw out the poison, but the best thing to use is garlic. Askari also told me to use garlic for snake bites. You must now be still – best to sit down and not move – that will slow the spread of the poison.'

Fenn lowered himself to the ground using the trunk of the fallen tree as a back rest.

By the time Gisele and Olgood returned, Fenn's leg was hot to the touch and had developed a constant painful burning feeling. His face was white and sweaty. Kaela wet the sleeve of her tunic in the stream and used it to cool his brow.

Gisele stripped the small yellow flowers from the bundle of thin branches she had gathered and then took what remained of her shift from the basket and cut a square of linen from it. The stiff green branches looked just like those that were used to make yard brooms at the monastery. She chewed the flowers into a paste, added a little water and folded the mixture into a pouch made from the linen. She cut more strips from her old shift and used these to bind the poultice over the bite.

Gisele and Kaela held a long discussion that ended with them both coming to stand beside Fenn.

'Gisele agrees that garlic will make a much better poultice to draw out the poison,' Kaela told Fenn and Olgood. 'But she didn't find any wild garlic. It's usually found in forests but it may not be wise to go back to Skyrvid.'

She turned to Hakon. 'You said the closest village is to the east – on a river?'

'Yes,' said Hakon. 'Turborg.'

'Does it have a market where we could get garlic?'

'Yes. Big market. In morning.'

'Good. The garlic we can buy in the market will be better than wild garlic anyway. Hakon and I will go to Turborg market. We'll leave now and stay overnight somewhere and should be back tomorrow afternoon.' Kaela touched Gisele's arm. 'Keep him alive until then.'

Hakon took out the purse of coins and selected a few then handed the purse to Olgood.

'Keep this, so nobody take it from me.'

Fenn waved his hand but he found it hard to concentrate. Kaela knelt beside him.

'Leave the sword,' he managed to say. 'A woman should not... and wear your hat.'

Kaela hesitated, then unbuckled her sword.

*   *   *

Fenn woke and did not know where he was.

He was lying on a bed of ferns and leaves. His hair was wet. He felt sweaty and his mind was confused. He started to rise but his shoulder hit something and at the same time an intense pain from his leg caused him to quickly lie down again. He could not remember how he had hurt his leg, but was thankful when the pain lessened to become a sharp throbbing ache.

It was dark and it must be cloudy because he couldn't see anything. It was also cold – what had happened to the fire? He tried to move onto his side

256

to draw his legs up and get some warmth from his body but again the pain from his leg stopped him. He reached up and felt the rough texture of a fallen log beside and above him. He seemed to be lying half under the log.

'Are you awake?' Olgood's voice came from a few feet away.

'Olgood. Is that you? What's happened? The fire's gone out.'

'No fire tonight. It would be seen from the road. We'll light one in the morning. Now…' Fenn felt Olgood's hand on his shoulder, '…just lie still while Gisele changes your poultice. We didn't want to wake you earlier.'

'Poultice? My leg is painful. I don't remember…'

'You were bitten by a snake.'

'Ah…' Fenn remembered the moment the snake had bitten him, and Kaela and Hakon leaving to get something from a nearby town. He couldn't recall why they had gone.

Olgood was saying something about Kaela and Hakon. He struggled to concentrate on the words but he missed some. Olgood said the word 'return'. Had they returned? It seemed too soon. Maybe they had returned early for some reason. He couldn't make sense of it.

He relaxed and felt Gisele removing a wrapping from his ankle.

*   *   *

Daylight.

He raised his head. He was lying under a fallen log and he was alone. His leg was throbbing with pain and he eased his body away from the log and sat up to look at it, gasping at the fiery agony the movement caused. His trouser leg was folded up to his knee revealing a swollen leg with a pale pallor and he could smell a sickly sweaty odour. His shoe had been removed and several strips of linen held a small cloth patch tight to his ankle. Just below the knee a single linen strip was tied around his leg as a ligature and this was biting deep into his flesh. He reached out to touch the tie but the movement caused the pain to intensify forcing a groan from him as he leaned back on his hands. The pain didn't lessen when he stopped moving.

The tie below his knee felt like it was severing his leg in half and he knew he had to get it off. It was embedded in the swollen skin of his leg but he couldn't see where it was tied – he doubted he would be able to untie it anyway, it would need to be cut. He frantically searched for something to use before the pain overwhelmed him. His axe and a sword in a scabbard lay alongside him. A dagger or a knife would be better but the sword was the best choice. He recognised Kaela's sword. He freed it and used his hands to turn himself so he could lean his back against the fallen log. A fresh wave of pain made his whole body jolt and his head became dizzy but he persevered knowing if he stopped to recover he may not be able to start again.

Finally able to lean his back against the log, he took some deep breaths to clear his head.

Around the cloth tie his skin was a dark purple colour with red flecks as if it was already bleeding inside. He tried to lever the sword under the tie but the length of the sword made the action difficult and the slightest pressure on his tightly stretched skin was unbearable. He thought he would not remain conscious if he tried to cut the cloth by inserting the sword beneath it, and he could injure himself severely if the sword slipped.

The ligature was most accessible on the bone at the front of his leg where the flesh was thinnest. Even there, the skin was noticeably swollen almost enfolding the cloth. Fenn checked the blade and was surprised at the sharpness of the edge. He had a fleeting memory of a discussion between Kaela and Olgood about the quality of Damascus steel but he could not think why Kaela would have left her sword behind.

More deep breaths to steady his hand. He laid the sword at an angle where it would cut across the cloth but there was no way he could avoid cutting into his own skin as well. Just the weight of the sword was like a hot ember against his leg but he let it lie and sucked air between his teeth, enduring the pain, trying to outlast it.

He drew one more deep breath and held it. He may not remain conscious and he did not want to have to do this a second time, so the stroke had to be bold and decisive.

He thrust the blade forward cutting across his leg.

*   *   *

His eyes opened and he remembered immediately what he'd been trying to do. He'd fallen on his side so he pushed himself back to a sitting position. His leg was bleeding freely where the flesh had been sliced by the sword so he must have been unconscious for only a short time. A swift check showed him that the linen tie had been cut but it was still wedged into his skin. He clenched his jaw and eased the cloth free, tossing it aside as the last piece was pulled from the fold of his skin. As if it had been shocked into a brief submission, as soon as the flesh was freed the pain returned with a force that engulfed him. The fresh injury made from the sword cut was indistinguishable among the waves of pulsing pain emanating from the whole leg. The intensity caused his head to jerk back and he pushed himself hard against the log, stiffening his whole body against the onslaught. He closed his eyes tightly, his breath coming in short gasps, and waited for the agony to ease.

When it was finally tolerable and his breathing had returned to normal, he relaxed enough to open his eyes. The sword lay several feet away, tossed there by some involuntary movement after he had cut the tie around his leg. The leg was now reddened and looked healthier but it was still warm and tender to the touch. He tried to move his foot and found it was possible but the movement produced acute stabbing pains. Without movement, there was only a dull throbbing ache.

For the first time since he had woken, his was able to divert his attention away from being solely focussed on relieving the pain of his leg. He needed something to put on the sword wounds.

A water skin lay at his side, the basket sat a few feet away and next to it a pile of branches with bright yellow flowers. Another pile of cut branches lay beyond these. He grabbed at the skin as his thirst was suddenly urgent. After only one quick gulp the skin was almost empty and he stopped drinking and stared at it. He would have thought Olgood or Gisele would have filled the water container before leaving. He presumed they had gone hunting. He wiped his mouth with the back of his hand and leaned over to pull the basket to him.

Inside, he could see the sack and neatly laid on top were some linen squares and strips. He selected two squares of linen, folded them together, and pressed the pad against the wounds on both sides of the tie where the sword had cut him. Already the pain of touching his skin was more bearable and he used two strips to hold the linen pad in place, tying them as tight as he could bear. He put the remaining cut linen aside and opened the sack. It contained two cooked legs of rabbit and the carcass of a bird that looked like grouse. There were some blackberries and half a dozen tubers he couldn't identify. Someone had made sure he wouldn't starve.

Next, he checked the wrapping on his ankle. When he bent his leg to reach his ankle it was stiff as if it had not been used in some time, but the movement was thankfully not as painful as he expected. The ankle bindings were able to be untied and he did so carefully, easing the pouch away from the snake bite. The two puncture wounds were no longer inflamed but the surrounding area was still white. The skin around the bite was warm but not hot and only painful if he pressed.

The linen pouch contained a yellow paste and it took him a moment to relate the colour to the flowers on the branches lying beside the basket. He stripped the flowers from some of the branches, noting they were dry and wilted but probably still effective. The action of gathering the flowers reminded him that Gisele had chewed them and mixed them with water to make a paste for the poultice. They were bitter but he chewed them thoroughly and spat the mixture into his hand, washing his mouth with a little of the remaining water and mixing that into the chewed flowers. He folded the mixture into the linen pouch and retied the poultice to his leg.

Satisfied he had done all he could for now, he raised himself and twisted his head to look over the log. A stream bubbled over rocks ten feet away. Beyond the stream were some more willow trees and through the trees Fenn could see a swampy area. The sight of the swamp reminded him of the place where he had received the snake bite and the fact that there was a road on the other side of the swamp. He remembered Kaela and Hakon leaving to find… He still couldn't remember what they were looking for.

He lowered himself again. The camp was in the middle of the group of willows mixed with some other trees which extended into a gently rising meadow displaying patches of yellow and orange daisies. It was a few hundred yards wide and maybe half a mile long, ending at the base of a hill covered with a multi-coloured quilt of red, yellow and green trees. It was a beautiful setting and would be ideal place to enjoy a restful afternoon.

260

A few feet away from where he sat, the log was blackened and charred where the remains of a fire could be seen. The ashes looked cold but there was a good stack of firewood and a smaller stack of kindling alongside. For the first time he noticed two more swords lying under the log between him and the fire. He couldn't think why *two* swords were there. One would be the sword he had taken from the outlaws, but the other…?

He was hungry. He had no idea how long it had been since he had eaten. He wondered when Olgood and Gisele would return from their hunt, but that thought was followed immediately with another. Why would they *both* have gone when Gisele had proved herself to be very capable on her own?

From the sky and the stillness of the air he judged it to be early morning. It was cloudy and dull and rain was possible but if it came it would not be for some time yet.

It was unusual for Gisele to hunt in the morning; she preferred later in the day. Maybe they had seen some bigger game – a deer perhaps? Maybe they were looking for fresh yellow flowers. From the sack he extracted a rabbit leg and he gnawed at that while he tried to remember the events of the last day or two. He recalled everything that had happened up to the moment he had been bitten by the snake. After that his memory seemed fragmented. Kaela and Hakon had gone to the nearest town. He had woken once in the night and talked with Olgood. That was all he could remember.

Hakon had mentioned the name of the town but he couldn't recall that. A half-day's journey he had said. If that were true they should be back by now – if all had gone well. Fenn shook his head. No use in speculating and no use worrying – he would be able to discuss it with Olgood and Gisele when they returned, now that his head was clear.

He reached into the sack for a few berries to follow the rabbit leg. Some of the berries were withered and dry as if they were a few days old.

As withered as the flowers.

As dry as the water skin.

He leaned back against the log.

How long had Olgood and Gisele been gone? Was it just last night he had spoken with Olgood?

How long had he been alone?

CHAPTER EIGHTEEN

Fenn's story…

He leaned with both hands on the log, standing on one leg, and straightened his injured leg so that it touched the ground. The skin felt tight and it was uncomfortable but not much more than that, so he increased the weight. A sharp pain caused him to lift his foot, but immediately he tried again until eventually he stood with even weight on both feet. He could endure only a short while, but now he had come this far he knew it was just a matter of time.

Taking a long time between steps, he shuffled a short distance and used his axe to cut a stout branch from a tree to use as a walking staff. He checked the fire, sifting through the embers to see if it could provide any more information, but all he could tell was that it had not been lit for some time, perhaps a day. He picked up the water skin and, leaning heavily on the staff, limped to the stream to fill it. This simple task was eventually accomplished but only with such difficulty that it would have been comical in different circumstances.

Unable to kneel on his injured leg, he attempted to squat on his good leg to fill the skin, using the staff for balance. A moment of unsteadiness toppled him full-length into the stream where he wallowed like a pig in mud. He could get no wetter, so he tossed the staff onto the bank and lay on his back in the stream while he filled the skin, then twisted back and forth until he could regain the bank where he lay panting with his clothes and hair dripping wet. He was thankful there were no witnesses to his ungainly performance.

By mid-morning he was convinced that Olgood and Gisele were not absent from the camp because they'd gone hunting. There were too many indicators that he had been alone for more than a day. The return of his companions was overdue, possibly days overdue. He feared that both Kaela and Hakon, and Olgood and Gisele had separately met with some problem, or maybe the same problem, and that one or both pairs could be in serious trouble.

He wasn't sure what a one-legged man could do who did not speak the language and had no idea where his friends were, but he had made a vow on their first night of freedom that he would strive to get them home while he had – he remembered the phrase he used – a spark of life in his body. His spark had fluttered and was still at a low ebb but, with each beat of his heart, it was gathering strength.

He only hoped he was not already too late.

Should he leave a message in case someone returned? At first he rejected the idea in case Ragnall or Lothar found it and discovered where he was headed. Anything he carved in the log would be in English which would identify him immediately. In the end he found a large leaf shaped like a huge arrow head which he laid on the ground where he had slept, and used a stick to write a 'T' in the dirt at the arrow's point, to signify he had gone to Turborg. Anyone looking for a message would notice it but it may not seem significant to a casual observer.

He gave a grunt and a slow smile of satisfaction when he realised he had remembered the name of the village. It may be important to remember why Kaela and Hakon were going to Turborg, but for the moment that still eluded him.

He left the poultice in place although it probably wasn't needed anymore – time would be the main healer now – but he retied the pad covering the wound below his knee, then buckled on Kaela's sword and slipped his axe into his belt. He couldn't carry all of the swords so he left the remaining two under the log, covering them with the cut branches. Maybe they could be recovered later.

He placed the water skin in the basket and, stooping, swung the basket onto his shoulders. He looked at the area where he had lain for – he wasn't sure how many days. There was no reason for anyone to look behind the fallen log but even if they did and saw an obvious campsite, there was nothing to reveal who had stayed here.

As a final act of preparation, he checked the bag on his belt was filled with stones for his sling and picked up the staff. He left the trees and limped into the daisy-covered meadow heading south-east hopefully toward Turborg. His movement was more of a shuffle than a walk but he could feel improvement already in the weight his leg would bear.

Hakon had estimated Turborg was a half-day walk but at his speed it would probably take twice that and he would certainly not get there by nightfall. Once he had crossed the meadow, the terrain was hilly and there were no animal paths to follow. The ground was uneven and he was continually going either uphill or down. In his present state both were difficult and exhausting. Already, his leg had developed a continuous ache.

He sucked on the bones from the bird while he walked to gain some strength. Even when he tasted the flesh he still couldn't identify it.

With each step he prayed that over the next hill he would find level ground – or, even better, a road, but of course that would bring its own risks. Walking on a level surface would be much easier for him and if he came across a road it would at least confirm he was headed in the right direction. A man limping along with the aid of a staff was probably a good disguise anyway. It was unlikely that he would be given a second glance even if he met Lothar himself.

He found he needed frequent rests which slowed his progress even further. Each time he sat down to rest with a groan of relief it became harder to rise again. He knew his leg would heal faster if he rested it, but too much time had already passed and his friends may be in desperate need. That thought always spurred him back to his feet.

When the position of the lowering sun in the sky and his now painfully throbbing leg told him he should look for a place to stop for the night, he paused on a rise and leaned against a tree to scan the countryside ahead.

To his relief, he could see a road a mile away running through a wide valley. There were also two small buildings situated close to the road at a place where the valley widened. In Northumbria he would have assumed this to be a road-house but here it was more likely to be a farm, although he couldn't see any farm animals or activity of any kind around the buildings. His eyes followed the road to the end of the valley and saw smoke wafting above the trees in the far distance several miles away. That may be Turborg, or it could be someone's campfire.

The road ran down the centre of the entire valley alongside a row of trees which probably marked the course of a river although the water was not visible from where Fenn stood. Fifty yards away, between him and the buildings, was a stand of trees that would allow a closer view without exposing him to the road.

From the trees, he watched both the road and the buildings until the sun was almost set and saw no sign of movement. The buildings appeared to be abandoned, and there looked to be holes in the roof of the closest structure. The rain that had been predicted by the early morning clouds, pattered the leaves of the surrounding trees and drops splattered on his head. A swirl of wind rustled the branches to confirm that bad weather was looming. He decided to take the risk of approaching the buildings – he didn't want to spend the night in the open during a storm.

He hobbled slowly forward, angling so he would seem to be approaching along the road rather than from the open country. As he got closer he could see the buildings were in bad repair – the thatch was thin and patchy and the walls contained holes with the wood supports showing through the covering of mud and straw in many places. The first building was a barn and the other a house by first appearances. The rain was now steady but he was unable to walk faster so he concentrated on remaining alert as he studied the barn. He frequently glanced both ways down the road to make sure it was clear.

When he reached the side of the barn, the rain became heavy. Lightning flashed at the top of the valley and a peal of thunder followed moments later. The centre of the storm was close. Fenn was thankful for the shelter the barn offered. The doors facing the road were standing open and he stepped inside hoping to somehow bluff his way if he met some people or animals.

The barn was empty.

He knew he should check the house so he stepped back into the rain and crossed the few yards between the buildings. Like the barn, the house was dilapidated and the roof was in an even worse state with most of the thatch having fallen onto the floor leaving only small patches of cover. The house was obviously also empty.

The barn offered better shelter so Fenn returned there and eased the basket to the ground in a corner that was dry. He gave a sigh of relief, wiped the water from his eyes and face with his hand, shook his head to remove the rain from his hair then he stretched his arms high to relieve his cramped shoulders. The floor area of hard earth was about the same size as Ragnall's barn and the remains of animal stalls were evident along the back wall. Rain water poured in a steady stream through holes in the roof but thankfully the floor sloped toward the door and the water ran in that direction. The deep ruts cut in the earth floor by the running water indicated the barn had been in this state for a long time. The wind howled fiercely around the building and Fenn worried that the roof might suffer further damage, but the barn had probably endured many storms and what was still standing must be strong enough.

When the flashing of the lightening and deafening rolling rumble of the thunder told him the centre of the storm was overhead, he was instantly reminded of the storm on the night before the raid on Lindisfarne.

He put that thought out of his mind. He was hungry so he sat on the floor and ate two of the tubers from the sack. They were charred but they were sweet and filling. He checked the poultice and decided to leave it off. The area above the ankle was no longer white and the leg below the knee was now looking normal except for a red flush. His sword wound had dried and the linen patch was attached to his leg by the blood scab so he left that covering alone and retied the cloth.

In spite of the noise of the wind, the rhythm of the rain was soothing. He tried to assess his situation and think if there was anything he should be doing but it was hard to concentrate and soon his head lolled and he fell into an exhausted sleep curled into the corner of the barn.

* * *

A sound from outside woke him. He could hear conversation. His hand went to his axe and he crept to the door crouching just out of sight beside the opening. He could hear two men, maybe more, talking and approaching the barn. Fenn steadied himself with his hand against the door frame ready to defend himself if it became necessary. The volume of the voices increased until it seemed they were just outside the opening and about to enter the barn. Fenn could feel the tension in his legs as he held his crouch. Then the voices moved away.

He risked a glance outside and saw the backs of two men walking side-by-side on the road at least thirty feet away. They were both carrying bulky sacks on their shoulders and were still deeply engrossed in conversation in a language he didn't understand. One laughed and patted the other on the back. It had sounded like they were about to step through the opening but he could see they had probably not left the road and had never been closer than twenty feet. He relaxed and pushed himself from the door frame, grimacing as a splinter dug into his hand.

As he stood up he realised belatedly that his leg was no longer painful to stand on. It felt tight and tender but held his weight and he could move it freely. He remembered that he had walked in a crouch from the corner to the door without the aid of his staff, something he wouldn't have been capable of last night. He inspected the small hole in his palm caused by the splinter to make sure there was no sliver of wood left in the wound and licked the bead of blood that had formed, then looked at the sky and muttered under his breath at his laziness. He had overslept and wasted valuable time.

He picked up the basket and shouldered it, wondered if he still needed the staff but then took it. Like everything – it could be useful. He quickly checked the area where he had slept, eager to be on his way and try to make up for lost time. At the doorway he paused and scanned the road. It was now clear. The two men had moved out of sight behind a curve in the valley.

Standing beside the door frame his eye was caught by the area of roughened wood where the splinter had pierced him. He bent closer. Someone had made several cuts in the door frame with an axe or knife. Why would they cut the frame…?

He crouched down.

Deep marks had been cut into the flat piece of wood that formed the inside of the door frame and they were fresh, one or two days old at most.

He recognised the marks instantly.

Runes.

Lowering the basket to the ground, his heart sped up as his fingers traced the carved letters. There were several runes carved across the door frame and more carved vertically. There was no mistaking the word written horizontally – Kaela had written this word a few days ago using a wet finger on a rocky shelf beside a river, close to a cliff where he had nearly died.

The runes spelt her name: 'KAELA'.

She had been here! And she had left a message. What did the other letters mean? What was the rest of the message?

He stared at the letters carved vertically into the wood of the door frame – and didn't recognise the word. But she would have known he wouldn't know this word, so why did she carve it here? He looked closer. The vertical word started immediately beneath the 'L' of Kaela's name and consisted of four runes. Then he saw that the third rune was the same as the rune for the letter 'A' that appeared twice in her name. But there were still three runes he didn't know.

He stared at the letters as if they might spontaneously reveal their meaning. He twisted about and carefully searched the barn with his eyes. Had she left something else for him? The barn was bare and he couldn't see any other areas where the wood had been marked.

Why had Kaela written her message in runes – why not English? He thought about that for a moment. So they could only be read by him? She didn't want Hakon to read them? Who else could have seen the message? He shook his head. He must accept that she had a reason. He returned to the runes. Why had Kaela written the second word vertically? Why not write it horizontally, underneath the first? There was room enough.

Maybe the word was pointing down to the floor. Something buried there? He searched with his eyes and felt the ground with his fingers, but the earth hadn't been disturbed. He rested back on his feet. By writing these letters vertically, she certainly had invited him to think about why. If she had just written the second word below the first he probably wouldn't have… He stopped.

That must be it. She didn't want him to dismiss the second word as unknown and therefore unknowable. She wanted him to think about it.

What did he know? The word was written vertically. One of the letters was an 'A'. The word started below the 'L' in the word 'Kaela'.

In an instant, he knew what the word said.

Including the 'L' in her name the word was…

LOTHAR.

Kaela was telling him she had seen Lothar, or had an encounter with him, or… had been captured by him. She could have seen one or more of the men who had tried to rob them in Skyrvid Forest. But if that were all, there was no need to write Lothar's name in the wood. She could have just told him when she returned to their camp by the swamp. When she carved the names, the runes were the only way she could communicate and she knew she wouldn't be able to deliver the message in person. How she had the time to carve the runes he didn't know, but he was now certain she and Hakon had somehow been captured by Lothar. It was the only interpretation that made sense.

He checked outside for a clue as to what had happened, but the rain had obliterated any footprints, even his own. There were hoof marks on the road but they could have been made by anyone. He couldn't see any blood on the floor or walls of the barn so there hadn't been a fight which was surprising but also a relief. He had seen Kaela with a sword and Hakon had proved he was capable and willing to fight when necessary, so they must have been surprised or more likely, simply outnumbered.

He didn't know where Olgood and Gisele were, but he now knew where Kaela and probably Hakon were – at Lothar's camp a half day west of the place where they had fought the outlaws.

If they were still alive…

That thought brought an unwelcome realisation. Even if Kaela was alive – if Lothar knew she had killed his brother, her life expectancy could be short. He was already some days behind her – at least two he thought, maybe more. He took in a deep breath.

He turned in the direction that he expected Turborg to lie. If Olgood and Gisele were in that direction, he would be heading away from them. They could also be in trouble, but he had to act on the information Kaela had given him.

Apart from the wound below his knee, which was uncomfortable but not a problem, his leg looked and felt fully recovered. The skin around the ankle was still tender but the leg could now bear his weight without discomfort. The cuts made by his sword made his knee stiff but did not affect his walking.

To speed his travel, he would follow the road as far as Skyrvid Forest. Fenn took a hat from the basket to hide his hair. The hat did not cover his hair completely but it was effective. In this country where the predominant hair colour was blond or light brown, Fenn knew his dark black hair was almost as distinctive as Kaela's so it was worthwhile to cover as much as possible. He checked his weapons and his stones, took the last rabbit leg from the sack, shouldered the basket and, gnawing at the tangy meat on the bone, left the barn at a brisk walk, heading in the same direction as his two morning visitors.

He reached the edge of the forest in the afternoon. Two sets of people had passed, travelling in the opposite direction – the first, four men walking, all carrying buckets and long brushes and the second, three men on horseback who looked to be on official business, cantering along the road and barely giving Fenn a glance. In both encounters, Fenn nodded at the passers-by then kept his gaze averted and did not slacken his pace.

He followed the road along the edge of the forest for several miles until he thought he would be roughly level with the crossroads where they had encountered Lothar's outlaws. He had expected to meet the east-west road, assuming it reached as far as the road he was now on but, like the road they had followed to the south, it may not travel in a straight line. Of course, the roads may meet just over the next hill.

Entering the forest, he pushed forward as quickly as he could without making any undue noise, at the same time alert for sign of any other people.

His hope was that he would meet the smaller north-south road that they had used and then make his way to the crossroads and from there head west in the probable direction of Lothar's camp. He had to assume the outlaw had told the truth regarding the camp's location.

The going was not difficult and he was able to keep a good pace. At a stream, he filled his water skin and drunk directly from the flow, the water cold and refreshing. He encountered blueberry bushes and spent a few moments picking wild blueberries, staining his fingers but satisfying his stomach.

When he encountered a small glade, he had the feeling that the area was familiar. He glanced around without being able to identify anything in particular, and walked slowly forward. There was a stony bank ahead which he climbed as the feeling of familiarity grew. At the top of the bank he turned in a circle. This place was similar to their camp the night after they had fought the outlaws. Then he spotted the half tree they had used to build a fire. He descended the bank and walked to the tree. The remnants of their fire inside the blackened tree trunk were still evident. It *was* their camp. At least he now knew where he was, and that was further south than he hoped to be.

Rather than follow the road, he walked through the forest, picking his way carefully and moving as noiselessly as possible. By the time he reached the site of the fight at the crossroads it was late afternoon. He checked the place where they had dragged the outlaws and found only crushed grass. The swords Olgood had tossed into the forest had also been retrieved. Returning to the crossroads, he stood where the outlaw had knelt when he waved towards Lothar's camp in answer to Kaela's prompting. The man had indicated a direction a few degrees north of the west road.

Fenn stared into the forest and selected a tall tree to use as a guide. Kaela and Hakon were just a few miles away. He automatically added the qualification: '…if they were still alive', and followed that with: '…and Lothar has not moved camp'.

He chewed on a tuber, thinking that he must thank Gisele for them. Although he had eaten some blueberries, without the tubers he would now be hungry and would be thinking he needed food which would divert him from his purpose when he could least afford it. He checked in the sack – there were still four tubers left.

The sky he could see through the trees was overcast and he hoped for rain to mask his approach to the camp.

When night fell, he thought of abandoning the staff because he needed both hands to feel his way in the blackness of the forest, but it had become like a companion so he took a moment to thread it between the straps of the basket and his belt so it was held tightly across his back. Occasionally it caught in vines or branches but he managed to wriggle free and was only momentarily delayed. He thought of the staff as another member of his group which he could not abandon. He knew the thought was irrational but it added to his determination.

Now he would have liked the sky to clear so the moon and stars could give him a little light to see by, but the gods were not obliging and he continued forward like a blind man, waving his arms and feeling with his feet. Every few moments he would stop and listen. He expected that Lothar's camp would be sizable, maybe up to twenty men, so he expected to hear them before he saw them. He could not be certain he was still heading on the right bearing toward the camp – he could barely see his hand in front of his face – but he trusted his sense of direction.

It became a ritual. Walk twenty paces, stop and listen. Walk twenty paces…

He was heading uphill. The slope steepened and contained many large tree roots which slowed him to a crawl. His reaching hands found stinging nettles and he recoiled in pain but managed to keep silent. He shook his hand. His stinging fingers reminded him of the feeling of the snake bite. He searched the ground for the dock leaves he knew would be growing nearby. He was stung again but continued feeling along the surface of the earth. He found the dock and pulled some leaves which he crushed in his hand and rubbed on his protesting skin. The relief was instant and he took a moment to recover, holding his tender hands in front of him as if in prayer.

He heard a dog bark.

Circling carefully around the nettle bushes, he crept to the top of the hill on his stomach. At the top he could not see anything but there was the unmistakable smell of smoke. Because of the dog he must keep the wind on his face. He crawled forward, descending from the ridge. A flicker in the trees. He moved his head to the side. Again, a small flicker of firelight. He could hear a stream nearby. Then he froze at the sound of a woman's laughter, stifled, then repeated and a man called out, the sounds carrying easily on the cool night air. That was not Kaela's laugh, nor Gisele's. Lothar's camp must contain other women.

He moved another foot, then two. He covered fifty yards in this slow and deliberate manner toward the firelight and the sound of voices, stopping to listen every few feet. He did not want to be surprised by any patrolling guards or someone entering the forest to relieve themselves. A foul smell came from up ahead. He was close to the camp refuse pits. He headed toward the smell thinking it would help to mask his scent from the dog.

He found himself behind a tree at one end of an oval clearing at least a hundred yards long. The stench from the pits was intense, rotting food mixed with human waste. Silently, he slipped the basket from his shoulders and laid the staff on the ground. He took the hat from his head and slipped it into the basket. His dark hair would serve him better in the night. He stood up using the tree to conceal himself and carefully peered around the trunk. His eyes narrowed at the sight before him.

A large fire was set at the far end of the clearing and in the firelight some crude huts were visible, pieced together from a mixture of fallen wood and cut tree branches and roofed with a dark substance – earth or maybe turf. There were perhaps a dozen huts built around the top edge of the clearing forming a semi-circle around the fire. Sitting close to the fire were a group of people – maybe ten or more. Fenn could hear snatches of conversation when somebody spoke loudly. A woman's laugh sounded again and one of the figures stood up and ran towards a hut with a second person following close behind.

But it wasn't the huts or the people that had he had first noticed when he had looked around the tree. He focussed on the construction of a different type at this end of the clearing that had first caught his eye.

Thirty feet from where he stood, a circular waist-high fence of wooden stakes five yards across surrounded a tall pole in the centre. Tied to the centre pole with her hands behind her back was a naked woman. She was facing away from him but he knew it was Kaela. Her hair glowed in the faint firelight. He stared at her hoping for some little movement to tell him she was alive.

There were two more buildings larger than the others standing at the clearing's edge, one on each side of the circular fence. Between each of the buildings and the fence was a gap of thirty feet.

A low growl sounded from beside Kaela, inside the fence, answered immediately by another. At the growl her head moved and it took all of his will to stifle a cry of utter relief.

He forced his mind to concentrate on the problem. At least two dogs were inside the fence with Kaela. At that moment a man detached himself from the shadows of one of the large huts. Fenn pressed himself against the tree but the man did not look in his direction. He walked lazily over to the fence and uttered some angry words at the dogs and then spat noisily on the ground before returning to the hut. Now that Fenn knew he was there, his vague outline was visible as he sat on the ground and leaned his back against the hut wall. Fenn peered at the other hut carefully to see if that was also guarded. He saw that the second hut was open-ended and, from a faint aroma that he caught on the wind, he thought he knew the purpose of that hut. A plan was forming in his head.

He waited until the man seemed settled then eased himself away from the tree, picked up his staff from the ground and worked his way through the forest towards the hut the man was leaning against, testing each footstep before he committed his weight.

The back of the hut was two or three feet from the edge of the forest trees, so Fenn stepped out of the forest where the hut would shield him from the firelight and moved to the corner. He slowly eased his head around the hut. The man had his head lowered with his chin on his chest, breathing heavily. Fenn took two steps and struck the sleeping man with the end of his staff hard just above his eye. The man toppled sideways without a sound. An enquiring 'wuff' sounded behind the fence. Fenn stood still and waited but the dog was only curious and not alarmed.

Fenn had a 'way' with animals. For reasons he did not understand himself, the animals around the monastery had never viewed him as a threat and even wild animals did not seem to be afraid. He was not surprised when his rabbit kits accepted that he would not hurt them and did not run away.

He was not afraid of the dogs and expected them to not be afraid of him. If there were no other alternative he would have risked entering the enclosure with the dogs, but if there was help at hand he would take it.

He returned the man to his sitting position so that he might seem to be sleeping if someone looked his way. It took all his will not to rush to Kaela and cut her free then escape into the forest, but he didn't know where Hakon was and, in spite of his belief the dogs would not attack him, he couldn't be certain they would not make enough noise to rouse the camp. He had an idea that would remove the threat of the dogs and to be impatient now might be fatal.

He withdrew from the hut and made his way back to the trees and moved carefully through the forest to the opposite hut. Away from the refuse pit his sense of smell soon confirmed his suspicion that this building was a food store. He could smell the high tang of hung venison.

Inside the store his nose directed him to some cuts of venison hung in a line along the wall. His searching fingers also touched the feathers of birds and smaller items but he selected two large slabs of meat, silently thanking the outlaw who had butchered the animal before hanging the kill. He couldn't carry the venison as well as the staff so he reluctantly leaned the staff against the hut wall. Using Kaela's sword to slice the leather straps used to hang the meat, he carried the two pieces outside.

One thing Fenn did know about his relationship with animals was that confidence was a key element. He walked directly to the fence. As he neared the enclosure he took note of the three inhabitants. One was Kaela. Now he could see she was tied to the pole at her wrists and ankles with her arms drawn behind the pole and then tied also at her elbows. It was a position that would have quickly become painful and she had probably been tied there for days.

The other two occupants were dogs and they were huge. Each was tethered by a thick rope to a smaller stake, one on each side of the central pole. They rose as he reached the fence but their instinct to challenge him was overcome by the scent of the meat he carried. Even so, one peeled back his teeth with the start of a snarl that was stifled when a large piece of venison landed at his feet. The other dog crouched and gave a low growl but his head tilted and then his attention was entirely concentrated on the meat Fenn held out to him. The dogs must have been hungry because they tore into their unexpected feast without the customary sniffing inspection.

Fenn made sure to keep Kaela between himself and the fire and vaulted the fence, just as a sob came from Kaela. He reached around and threaded his hand into her hair as he pressed the side of his face against hers from behind the pole.

'I said I wouldn't leave you,' he whispered.

He felt her tears. She made a small sound in her throat. 'I knew you would come... Somehow...' her voice choked. 'It was impossible – how could you find us? You may have been dead, but... I just knew you'd come.'

Fenn pulled his sword to cut her binds but she whispered urgently: 'No!'

He paused.

'Hakon is in that hut.' She nodded to the hut where the man was sitting. 'Free him first. If someone looks this way they won't raise an alarm if they still see me. But there's a man guarding...'

Fenn interrupted. 'I know about the guard.'

He hesitated. He felt a wave of relief that Hakon was also here and from the way she had spoken, still alive, but he did not want to leave her in this state a moment longer. At the same time he knew what she said made sense. He crossed back over the fence, keeping Kaela between him and the fire but before he could move to the hut, she caught his attention with a low whistle. He peered over her shoulder in the direction she was looking.

He saw a group of men, silhouetted by the light of the fire, walking directly toward him. Their faces were in shadow but two of them were huge men he would recognise anywhere.

Ragnall and Olaf.

CHAPTER NINETEEN

Four days ago… Olgood's story …

Kaela left her sword with Fenn and she and Hakon departed for Turborg market.

Olgood took note of the direction Hakon was headed then turned back to make sure Fenn was comfortable. He didn't look good. His face was sweaty, he had his eyes closed and his breathing was fast and shallow. Gisele had rolled Fenn's trouser leg up and Olgood could see the white patch of the poultice on his ankle where he had been bitten. Through mime she told him she thought Fenn needed to eat and keep drinking water. Kaela had taken one water skin so Olgood picked up the other to fill in the stream while Gisele took two snares and headed into the meadow. He watched her walk away and continued to watch until she disappeared from view.

One thing that he could do for Fenn was to make him a comfortable place to lie, so after filling the water skin he took his knife, crossed the stream and cut several long fern fronds from beneath the trees. When he returned he lifted Fenn's head to give him some water and then laid the ferns in a circular shape beside the log leaving the centre clear. He built one side of the bed tight under the log so Fenn would have some shelter if it rained. He filled the hole with a mound of dead leaves, put more fronds on top, and carried Fenn to the bed. Every movement of his foot seemed to be painful.

Olgood then busied himself preparing a fire where it would be concealed by the log from the swamp and the road. As long as it didn't produce smoke they could light it during the day but it wouldn't be wise to do so at night. He collected a large supply of dry wood and was using his axe to cut smaller pieces to start the fire when Gisele came into view across the meadow carrying two rabbits. When she was close he saw she also had a handful of wild strawberries.

She excitedly mimed to him that she had seen some ground birds that were good for eating and she would hunt them tomorrow. She checked Fenn who was sleeping and agreed they should cook the rabbits before the sun set. The fire was built and allowed to die down. While the rabbits were slow-cooking over the embers, they ate the strawberries which were small but sweet and juicy, and saved a few for Fenn.

Fenn was woken to give him some more water and also some rabbit to eat. He accepted the food readily and appeared hungry but seemed to quickly tire and actually only ate a few mouthfuls. He enjoyed the strawberries but lay back immediately after eating them. Gisele indicated it was best to let him sleep.

Olgood and Gisele ate a meal of rabbit and watercress which was delicious. She told him she wanted to look in the swamp tomorrow for something else they could eat, something they would need to dig up, but he couldn't quite understand what it was.

He wished he could do more for Fenn. Hopefully Kaela and Hakon would be back with the garlic tomorrow around midday or in the afternoon. Gisele changed the poultice while Olgood extinguished the fire and they sat against the log as the sun drifted below the horizon with Gisele's head resting on Olgood's chest. He breathed deeply and looked down at her. The smell of her was intoxicating and he knew that at that moment even with his friend lying injured beside him and facing a cold night in a land far from his own – he was very happy.

Fenn had a restless night, his head tossing back and forth and murmuring in his sleep. Gisele changed the poultice twice during the night and again in the morning but Fenn didn't wake. His leg was swollen and pale and some red marks were extending from his ankle towards his knee. Gisele seemed to think he was still strong but the snake poison was definitely affecting him.

From midday Olgood was expecting Kaela and Hakon to appear at any time. He would be grateful when they could apply a stronger poultice that should stop the spread of the poison.

Gisele took him into the swamp and pointed out some plants with big leaves that were shaped like huge arrow heads. She chose ones that were yellowed and dying and showed Olgood how to gently pull up the plants to get at the tubers in the roots. These were large and spherical and looked like an onion. Gisele told him they were very good eating. They kept a careful watch on the road but they saw no travellers and no bands of searching outlaws. Hopefully the men they had tied had not been found yet.

Back at the log, Gisele rekindled a small fire and placed the tubers in the ashes.

Fenn had some moments of clarity and ate and drank heartily around midday. He was confused about the time that had passed and thought Kaela and Hakon had just left. Olgood tried to explain that they should be in fact returning now, but he could see that Fenn was still confused and thought it best not to try and press the point.

When Fenn saw the red marks on his leg he told Olgood that if the marks reached his knee then a strip of cloth should be tied tightly around his leg to stop the poison progressing higher.

Fenn slept for most of the afternoon. He woke once and they had another short discussion about Kaela and Hakon, but Fenn was still confused about the time.

Gisele wanted to catch some of the birds she had seen. If Kaela and Hakon arrived they may be hungry so Olgood said she should go, and again he enjoyed watching her crossing the meadow. While she was gone he collected some more of the arrow head tubers from the swamp. He was wary of snakes and used a stick to beat at the grass ahead of him to announce his presence.

By the time Gisele returned, carrying a large long-necked bird with brightly coloured feathers that Olgood had not seen before, it was late afternoon and Olgood was worried something may have happened to the others. They would have hurried and should have been well back by now assuming Hakon's estimate of the distance was accurate.

Gisele was more worried about Fenn. She changed his poultice and made him drink. She had some wild onions tucked in her belt which she laid beside the fire then she showed Olgood how she wanted the bird plucked and prepared. She filled it with the wild onions and some of the chopped tubers while she let the fire die until it was a pit of glowing embers. The bird was wrapped in a large green leaf that had a slight odour of lemon and packed in a thick layer of mud from the swamp then placed in the fire and covered with embers.

When it was cooked, the bird was deliciously tender from being steamed inside its mud covering – the meat was moist and flavoured from the lemony leaves. Fenn expressed his appreciation but only ate a little. Gisele placed the tubers that Olgood had collected into the smouldering fire.

It was too late to start for Turborg that day but Olgood decided that if Kaela and Hakon did not return during the night, he would go looking for them tomorrow. He tried to tell this to Gisele. She seemed to understand but was worried that he could not speak the language. Olgood thought he would just have to take his chances, Fenn couldn't be left alone and Gisele was the best one to stay with him.

While it was still light Gisele left to get some more provisions for Olgood's journey. This time she took the snares. Olgood protested he didn't need food, he could last a day without it, but she was insistent. It was dark when she returned to the camp. She had a rabbit and a small brown fowl. These she hung in the tree branches and came to lie with him, cuddling in close.

It rained during the night. Olgood covered Fenn by leaning leafy branches against the log, while he and Giselle sat where the foliage from the trees was thickest. When the rain stopped, he removed the soaked branches over Fenn. They had provided some protection but the dripping from the leaves was now a nuisance.

Fenn woke, said he was cold and asked why there was no fire. He seemed lucid so Olgood explained that they couldn't light a fire at night and took the opportunity to explain that Kaela and Hakon hadn't returned so he or Gisele would look for them in the morning. Gisele changed Fenn's poultice. His leg was obviously still very painful but he was asleep before she had finished.

*   *   *

'You must both go.'

Fenn leaned with his back against the log and regarded Olgood and Gisele standing before him.

'We can't wait until I can travel with you. Gisele shouldn't go without your protection Olgood and you don't speak the language – how can you learn what has happened to them if you can't ask questions?'

'Someone needs to stay to look after you,' protested Olgood.

'I feel better. I've enough food for a day or two and water. In fact you can take the water skin – I should be able to get to the stream if I need to. I'll release this tie...' he pointed to the linen strip that Olgood had tied below his knee, '...as Master Egbert told me, once in a while to let the leg breathe and I'll change the poultice too. I'll manage.'

Olgood looked doubtful.

'You've had moments like this before,' he said, 'where you can speak normally and the next moment you're confused and sleepy. And you can't walk – I doubt if you can crawl either.'

'I feel better. I don't feel sleepy any more. We need to find out what's happened and both of you going is the best way to do that. By the time you return I'll be up and walking for sure.'

Olgood hesitated. He was sure the leg was causing Fenn more pain than he was showing, but what he said made sense.

Fenn said: 'The sooner you start, the sooner you'll be back.'

Gisele left Olgood to tend to the cooking of the rabbit and the small fowl that she had caught the previous day while she ran into the meadow returning a short time later with her hands full of blackberries. She insisted on leaving Fenn the full water skin.

She pointed to the berries and mimed eating them with one hand while spurning the other food.

281

'She's saying you should eat the berries first because they won't keep,' said Olgood.

Fenn protested he had more food than he needed and they should take some. Gisele shook her head and put the food into the sack which she placed in the basket and then laid some cut pieces of linen on the sack so Fenn could easily find them if he needed to change the poultice or the tie.

When she finished, she pointed to his knee and then his ankle, waving her finger at him. Be sure to change these. Fenn nodded.

Olgood laid Fenn's axe and Kaela's sword where Fenn could easily reach them and then he foraged in the basket for a moment before returning to Fenn's side. Gisele unbuckled her sword and tucked it under the log together with the sword Fenn had worn.

'We'll try to be back before nightfall,' Olgood said.

He looked back at Fenn from the far edge of the meadow. Fenn waved and Olgood returned the wave before he entered the trees.

The last thing he saw was Fenn drinking from the water skin.

They descended into a valley where there was a road heading in what was hopefully the right direction and Olgood and Gisele followed it south-east. The road ran beside a river which was encouraging – Olgood remembered Hakon saying Turborg was on a river. They passed an abandoned farmhouse and barn.

Two men appeared around a bend in the road, walking towards them. Olgood was at first hesitant and wanted to avoid contact but Gisele talked with them and confirmed that the road did lead to Turborg.

Just after midday they were happy to see a small village come into view. On the outskirts of the village, however, they were greeted by a less welcome sight. A gallows had been erected by the side of the road and hanging from the crosspiece was a human body, still raggedly clothed with bones showing through decaying flesh. The head was being picked at by two large crows that flapped squawking into the air when they were disturbed, leaving the eyeless skull to stare down the road as a macabre warning to visitors.

This must be Turborg.

Leaving the gruesome welcome sign to the attention of the hovering crows, they entered the village. In the centre of a group of buildings on the bank of the river they found the market but most of the sellers had packed and gone. The area was littered with discarded and spoiled fruit and vegetables as well as smelly offcuts of animal meat that were covered in flies. Gisele approached some people loading barrels onto a cart and one of them pointed to a nearby building that looked to be an inn. From Gisele's mimes, Olgood understood that the man who sold herbs including garlic at the market was likely to be in the inn.

Olgood noticed that people were staring at him. He assumed it was because of his height and maybe the fact that he was armed with both a sword and an axe. He agreed when Gisele suggested that he wait outside while she went into the inn to find the garlic seller and ask him if he had seen Kaela and Hakon. If Olgood was distinctive in the square he would be more so inside the inn.

He sat on a stool against the wall of the inn and gazed around the market square. A group of small children passing by stopped and looked at him. One called out something, but Olgood ignored him and continued to look over the square. The boy called again, something the others found funny because they all laughed then ran off.

A scream sounded from inside the inn.

Olgood recognised Gisele's voice. He stood up and slammed the inn door open. He was not used to being armed – his first instinct was to depend on his strength rather than his sword or axe so he drew neither as he burst inside.

Gisele was being held on a table by a heavy-set man with a red bloated face who was laughing and leering at Gisele with bulbous eyes. He had one had on her neck and the other was pulling at her clothing. Gisele was struggling and kicking but from her position she was unable to put any force into her blows and he ignored them. Several other men were gathered around the table, calling encouragement to Gisele's attacker.

Olgood silently took hold of the nearest onlooker and tossed him aside. The man went careering into a table and a set of stools by the door and the sound of breaking wood caught the attention of the others in the inn.

Olgood shouldered his way into the group and reached the man holding Gisele. He didn't want to just drag the man away because that might cause him to tighten his grip on Gisele's throat. Instead, without breaking stride, he kicked the man hard in the side of the knee. The man had turned his head at the sound of the first man crashing into the table, so he was looking at Olgood but could do nothing to stop the kick. He howled in pain as his knee bent beyond its limits, taking his hand from Gisele's neck in a feeble attempt to stop Olgood, and continued to howl as Olgood lifted him bodily in the air and threw him into the group surrounding the table, knocking three from their feet into a scrambling heap on the floor.

He picked up Gisele, turned for the door and would have left if a hand hadn't grabbed his shoulder from behind. He gently lowered Gisele to her feet as someone broke a stool across his back. Olgood turned, snatched the remnants of the stool from the man's hand and pushed it into his face, feeling his nose break.

Another man was advancing with a broken piece of wood in his hand, his face twisted in anger. Olgood swatted the piece of wood aside, seized the man by his tunic with two hands and used him to push back two others who were trying to get into the fight. He continued pushing until the men fell over some furniture smashing a table and collapsing onto the floor, adding to the stack of men already there. He ensured the man on top stayed down with a back-handed blow that snapped his head to the side. The man went limp. The red-faced man who had held Gisele now had several men on top of him. He was crying out in pain and clutching his knee, trying to protect it from flailing arms and legs.

Olgood turned back to the door. Two men blocked his way but he could see they were unsure whether to become involved or not. Gisele hit one of the men in the side of the head and at the unexpected blow he backed away holding his ear. The other stood his ground. Olgood stepped forward, brushed past the man's attempt to stop him, took hold of his head and banged it down on a table. Gisele cried a warning and he instinctively ducked as a thrown stool passed over his head and hit the door with a splintering crash. He twisted in his crouch and saw a man leaping at him, a knife raised high in the air. Olgood straightened and caught the man's upraised hand. He bent the hand back to force him to drop the knife and there was the soft crack of a breaking finger. The man yelped in pain and Olgood pushed him aside, the knife clattering to the floor. Olgood kicked it away with a flick of his foot. Two men were rising from the pile of bodies but Olgood cracked their heads together and they fell again and lay dazed.

Several men were now on the floor, either groaning or lying still, and the others wanted no more of the big stranger. Olgood placed a hand around Gisele's waist and headed for the door.

Before they reached it, the door opened. Three men stepped inside with swords drawn. A fourth followed wearing finer clothing and was obviously in charge – an official of some sort. Olgood stepped aside to let them pass thinking they must have come for the man who had attacked Gisele, so he was surprised when they levelled their swords at him and motioned him outside. Gisele spoke urgently to them but she was ignored, the official bowing to her and requesting she also accompany them outside. Before he left the inn, his gaze took in the broken furniture and the men sprawled about the room. He gave a disdainful sniff and closed the door behind him.

Outside the inn, Olgood was requested to surrender his weapons. He hesitated but the three men still had their swords out and were alert. He unbuckled his sword and handed over his axe. His knife was hidden inside his tunic and he made no move to surrender that.

The official handed Olgood's weapons to another man and politely indicated they should head towards the far side of the square. Once there, they continued up a narrow alleyway, the men following behind Olgood and Gisele, and then turned in the direction of the river. They descended some steps on the riverbank leading to a stone pier. The official approached a door set into the earthen bank of the river and opened it with a key that hung from his belt. He bowed slightly holding out his hand for Olgood and Gisele to enter a room that looked like a cellar or storage-room. There were several other similar doors visible along the length of the stone pier. The room had been dug deep into the river bank and had a packed earth floor and earthen walls. Facing the river, the front wall was two feet thick rising to the height of Olgood's chest, then stout wooden poles had been set into the centre of the wall and attached to the roof, forming a window which overlooked the river.

The man closed the door behind them and locked it. One man stayed behind to guard the door while the official and the other two mounted the steps and disappeared.

Olgood tested the poles but they were sturdy and close together – he would need to break two or three to provide enough space to climb through. He held Gisele close hoping to give her some comfort, but he felt her shrug and look up at him with a smile and a tilt of the head that seemed to say: 'Here we are – captured again.'

Gisele indicated she would like to look at his back where he had been hit with a stool. Olgood stripped off his tunic taking care to hide his knife in the side of his trousers and turned his back to the light of the window. Gisele checked that no bones were broken – her touch was gentle but Olgood could feel his back was tender in parts. She smiled and nodded to him – he would heal.

They leaned against the earthen wall in the bare room and waited. Olgood wasn't worried about the outcome of their temporary imprisonment. He assumed they were being kept here because he had injured some people and destroyed some property. He didn't regret his actions in the inn – he would do exactly the same again to save Gisele. He thought it ironic that the coins they had taken from the outlaws may now be needed to pay his *wergild*. He was more worried that while they were delayed in this damp room they were not looking for Kaela and Hakon.

Gisele attempted to talk to the guard but he didn't answer her.

They alternately sat and paced about the room as the light faded outside the window and they realised they would be spending the night in this bleak damp prison.

* * *

Olgood was woken by a kiss on his lips. He opened his eyes and saw the smiling face of Gisele inches from his own. She could have been in a palace rather than a prison for all the worry she displayed. She actually looked happy, her eyes sparkling as she looked at him and it instantly lightened his own mood. He reached up and hugged her to him, his eyes closing with the pleasure of it. He held her a long time until she protested and he realised her back was bent awkwardly. He was instantly sorry but she laughed and helped him to his feet. His body felt stiff and cold and he stretched his muscles. His bruised back was sore but it didn't restrict his movement.

The same guard was still outside the door looking as though he had spent a cold, miserable and sleepless night on the pier. He again made it obvious he was not going to talk to Gisele, probably acting under orders.

The window faced east to the rising sun and they were able to measure the passage of time by the moving shadows of the poles on the dirt floor. As the morning wore on, darkening cloud banks scudded briskly across the sky bringing the promise of a storm. Olgood regarded the river through the window poles. At this point it was a hundred yards wide with a steady flow passing the pier. Although no boats were tied to the pier, it seemed to be well used with some barrels stacked by the edge and baskets of vegetables and a pile of cut logs waiting to be collected. The water looked deep. Suspended silt stained it a dirty brown colour and Olgood thought it may be carrying extra volume as a result of the approaching storm. He was wondering whether they would be spending the day in this room when the sound of feet on the stone steps announced the return of the official, followed this time by five men.

He paraded impatiently up and down the pier while the nervous guard struggled to unlock the door and then bowed with an exaggerated flourish, beckoning them outside. As they exited the storeroom, the waiting men did not bother to draw their swords but stood at a respectful distance.

Olgood and Gisele were ushered to the bottom of the steps and held there until they heard the sound of horses' hooves clattering on the stony area at the top of the steps. A pair of horses came into view pulling a cart on which a rusted iron cage had been fastened. The cage was small. Olgood could see that once inside the cage he would barely have room to move. He glanced at Gisele. She was already looking at him with a raised eyebrow. She realised as he did that if they entered that cage they would be in a much worse position than they were right now. Whatever he wanted to do, she was ready. He squeezed her arm and she gave a slight nod.

The official pointed up the steps and barked a command.

Three men led the way up the steps. As the third man passed in front of him, he made sure that Olgood saw that his red-handled axe was hanging from the man's belt. The man tapped the axe, laughing in Olgood's face and looking back with a sneer as he started up the steps. Olgood followed him, drawing Gisele close to him. The three other men came behind Gisele with the pompous official at the end of the line.

When the official was on the first step, Olgood moved.

He grabbed the tunic of the man in front at the back of the neck and hauled him backwards, at the same time pulling the axe from the man's belt. He twisted his hold, turning in a half-circle, dragging the man down the steps and keeping him off balance. Gisele ducked behind Olgood's back as he turned and kicked at the man following her, connecting solidly with his stomach. He bent forward with a grunt and swayed a pace to the left bringing him into the path of Olgood's man. They collided, with a further push from Olgood sending them both sprawling into the men below. Like falling logs each man knocked the next down the steps, their bodies crashing heavily onto the stone pier amid cries of surprise and pain.

The man in front had his sword out. Olgood leapt two steps, ducked under the sword and swung the back of his axe against the man's legs. He pushed him aside as he fell and reached out to stop the last man drawing his sword. The man strained for an instant against Olgood's grip but could not move it. He drew back his other hand to strike but Olgood's elbow caught him in the throat before he could deliver the blow. The man started to collapse and Olgood helped him on his way by hurling him off the steps and into the river ten feet below. He hit the water with a huge splash and disappeared below the surface. Olgood stamped on the injured leg of the man he had hit with the axe to keep him down and Gisele kicked the sword away from his hand.

The men at the bottom of the steps were getting to their feet. The official was obviously hurt, having been pinned underneath the other men. He was writhing in pain and clutching his ankle. The men on the pier drew their swords but hesitated. Olgood was now armed and with his formidable size they instinctively waited for a command. Their hesitation gave Olgood a moment to think. He looked at the horses wondering if they could be used to escape, but the wide-eyed driver caught the look and whipped at his horses in a panic. The startled horses broke into a gallop.

A call from below drew Olgood's attention back. Realising the official was too focussed on his injury to give any commands, the man who had carried Olgood's axe was waving the other two forward, leading them towards the steps, wary but determined.

Olgood pushed the axe into his belt and took Gisele by the arm. She realised instantly what he was about to do. Together they leapt off the steps and into the river.

When they surfaced, they had already been swept along the pier, past the group of men and their fallen commander. The end of the pier opposite the steps terminated in an abrupt drop into the river and Olgood saw that none of them was eager to follow their captives into the water. The official was sitting up and waving one arm, calling out some orders but his men just stood and watched in frustration as Olgood and Gisele drifted away from them. The far bank looked a long way away and for the moment Olgood was content to be swept past the village towards the sea. Apart from one fisherman on the side of the river who stared incredulously as they floated by, the people he could clearly see in the village didn't notice the extra debris in the river.

The man Olgood had thrown off the steps was nowhere to be seen. Olgood cast his eyes about. He had tried not to cause serious harm to anyone and hoped the man had not drowned.

Ahead the river curved around a steep rocky cliff. The flow became faster on the far side against the face of the cliff but on their side there was a stony bank where the water shallowed. Olgood pointed and swam towards the bank.

They stepped out of the river about a mile from the village. It was possible they could still be seen from the pier but Olgood was not worried. They were fit and used to travelling fast. It was unlikely there would be an earnest pursuit over a fight in an inn and a brawl on the steps.

The day was spent circling around Turborg keeping several miles from the village. Olgood conveyed to Gisele that he thought they should return to the place they had left Fenn. It certainly wouldn't be wise to try again to find information in Turborg and they had nowhere better to go. Perhaps Kaela and Hakon had returned having only been delayed by some unusual circumstances, and he also wanted to check on Fenn. He was not convinced that Fenn was fully recovered.

Toward sunset Gisele pointed out a stand of trees that had a good view over the surrounding countryside and more importantly cover from the rain that was now even more threatening. Under the closely packed trees the grass was long and soft to lie on. Gisele wanted to hunt but Olgood held her back. They could go hungry one night. They couldn't light a fire in case they were seen and he didn't want Gisele to be out in the countryside alone. They built a comfortable bed in a small grassy clearing that was covered by a thick leafy shelter and lay down where Olgood had only to raise his head to see in all directions.

The storm broke during the night. It was preceded by a chorus of thunder claps and arrived with a wild wind lashing the trees, accompanied by torrential rain. Their canopy of leaves and branches provided adequate shelter as promised however and although some rain did penetrate it was tolerable. They were both tired and fell readily into a weary sleep.

*   *   *

A tap on the shoulder brought Olgood out of his deep slumber. He ignored the interruption and shifted his position to ease an ache in his hip. The tap became an insistent poke.

Olgood opened one eye. Two surprises greeted him. The first was that it was already light and the second was a pair of boots standing in the grass two feet from his face. He rose swiftly to his feet, reaching for his axe – his movement disturbing Gisele lying beside him. She stretched and then froze as she sensed the presence of other people. Dogs started barking nearby, a deep-throated sound. Slowly Olgood straightened, letting his hand drop away from his axe.

Three men stood before him, they were tensed and ready, swords drawn. This time they were taking no chances. Several more waited outside the trees, perhaps a dozen in all and, standing apart from them, a man on horseback was leaning forward on his horse's neck and peering into the trees, his expression one of idle curiosity. To Olgood, the man's face resembled that of a weasel with a prominent nose, beady eyes and a weak receding chin. This man was not the official they had seen before but was dressed in a similar manner and seemed to hold similar authority.

Olgood recognised the same man who had previously worn his axe was the one now holding out his hand again for the weapon. He was annoyed at himself for thinking they were far enough away from the village, and also for oversleeping. Someone was willing to spend more effort to recapture them than he had expected. Slowly, he took the axe from his belt and handed it to the man, who gave a smirk of satisfaction as he pushed it into his own belt. Gisele stood up beside Olgood.

The weasel-like man on the horse waved his hand impatiently and spoke a command. The three men in the trees stepped back carefully but kept their swords ready while the man who had taken his axe motioned for Olgood and Gisele to step out from the trees so the horseman could view them. The men outside also drew their swords and stepped back to give them room. For some reason they were being treated like dangerous animals.

A small man was struggling to control two large dogs with big drooping ears and slobbering jowls. The dogs were lunging forward at the end of leather leashes wanting to get at the quarry they had tracked from the river.

At a softly spoken command, Olgood and Gisele had their hands tied behind their backs and with a push from behind, were marched across the field towards Turborg.

They rounded a corner and saw the horse-drawn cart and cage standing outside the largest building in the square. The market was already alive; a bustling mix of people, animals, and colourful stalls, with the haggling of buyers and sellers forming a steady undercurrent of noise. There was so much activity in the square that their arrival aroused only minimal interest.

Olgood realised something he should have realised earlier when he first saw the horses with the cart and cage at the top of the pier steps. Their captors intended to transport them outside the village. They could easily walk to any location in the village so their destination must lie further afield. He thought of the man, assuming it *was* a man, swinging on the gallows on the road north. Surely brawling was not a hanging offence. He had defended Gisele, and once he was able to explain that and offer to pay the *wergild* that should have been the end of it.

Could they be taken to Kirkense? He could think of no reason other than perhaps there was a higher authority in Kirkense. But why would a higher authority be needed?

Hedeby? That was an entirely different matter. Although it had been… Olgood thought for a moment… five days since they had left Hedeby, Ragnall could still be there or, if not, it was likely he would have offered a reward for their capture. Could these people be responding to Ragnall's offer? Unfortunately, that now seemed more likely. For the first time, Olgood thought that their capture might have nothing to do with the fight in the inn or their escape from the pier.

The Weasel was helped to dismount his horse and entered the building while the other men waited outside. Some had sheathed their swords but the man with Olgood's axe kept his ready and flourished it so it would be noticed. When the Weasel returned, he was accompanied by a fat red-faced man in a black robe who inspected the prisoners closely, displaying his satisfaction with grunts and brief expressions of 'Ooh' and 'Aah'.

The two talked and their conversation became animated. The fat man was trying to argue some point but the Weasel was firmly disagreeing. At something that was said, Gisele stiffened with a quick intake of breath and looked at Olgood with alarm. She said the words 'Lothar' and 'Ragnall' and tried to tell him more about what had been said but with her hands tied behind her and her lack of English, she was effectively without a tongue. Before she could elaborate, the conversation ended with the fat man spreading his hands and shrugging. The Weasel had obviously prevailed. He indicated with a wave that the prisoners were to be placed inside the cage.

Gisele had said the names of both Lothar and Ragnall. Had that been what the argument was about? Who to deliver the captives to?

As he had expected, the roof of the cage was so low it was difficult for Olgood to enter and turn his body to sit down especially with his hands tied. Gisele squeezed herself beside him. Once she was settled, she said in English: 'We go Lothar.'

The driver locked the cage and had a foot on the step to climb up to the driver's seat when he was stopped by the Weasel who waved him away from the cart. The man protested indignantly, pointing to the horses and then himself, but his protests were ignored. The Weasel beckoned to the man carrying Olgood's axe and told him to drive the cart. The owner of the horses was obviously not required for this mission, but his horses and cart were.

The Weasel was helped onto his horse. He spoke to the new driver and seemed to be giving him directions, gesticulating with one hand and then the other. When he finished he waited for the driver to nod that he understood then turned his horse and rode away through the market. The owner of the cart and horses was pleading earnestly with the man in the black robe who was only half interested, his eyes remaining on the cage and the captives inside. The driver turned to inspect his cargo, smiling in mock apology at Olgood. He nodded to the man in the black robe and cracked his whip. The horses pulled the cart into motion and four of the men fell into step, two on each side of the cart. Olgood and Gisele shared a glance. Olgood tried to convey his regret that he had allowed them be captured again, but Gisele just smiled and leaned her head against his shoulder.

The cart crawled across the square while the market visitors flowed past them like river water around a boulder. Out of the town, the horses were held to a steady walk that allowed the men alongside to keep a comfortable pace. Olgood and Gisele were taken back along the same road that had brought them into Turborg two days ago. The last sight they saw of Turborg was the forlorn body of the hanged man swaying in the fresh breeze.

Olgood twisted his head to look to the front but the Weasel was already out of sight, riding ahead to their destination no doubt, perhaps to announce their arrival. Gisele had said they were being taken to Lothar, probably to his camp. Taken to Ragnall or to Lothar, he tried to think which was worse, but could not see any benefit in either. Their situation was fast becoming hopeless. He let his head fall to his chest and closed his eyes. He wondered if Kaela and Hakon had been captured in a similar manner.

An elbow in his ribs brought his head up. Gisele was looking at him and when their eyes met she smiled her wonderful smile. Olgood forgot his depressing thoughts and could not help but smile back.

In the late afternoon, after they had been travelling along the edge of Skyrvid Forest for several miles, the horses were pulled to a stop in the middle of the road. Olgood looked about but could not see any reason for the halt. Perhaps it was a water stop – the river was only a hundred yards away. The driver talked to one of the men but instead of heading toward the river, the man walked in the opposite direction toward the forest. He disappeared into the trees and then returned nodding his head and waving to the driver. The horses were pulled off the road and driven into the trees where Olgood could now see there was a small opening.

Their change of direction confirmed what Gisele had said – they were headed for Lothar's camp.

Olgood was surprised when the horses were stopped again after travelling only a short distance into Skyrvid Forest. The cart was taken off the road and halted in the middle of a glade where the horses were unhitched and then tethered where there was a thick carpet of grass. It would be some time before the sun went down and Olgood wondered why they were setting up camp so early. After a while he reasoned that these men probably knew they would not reach Lothar's camp before sunset and didn't want to be looking for a campsite in the dark forest, so they had accepted the first suitable place.

One of the men passed a ladle of water through the cage to allow them to drink and also put some bread in their mouths followed by some dry meat. He stood patiently while they chewed and gave them some more water to wash it down. Olgood thanked him.

His cramped position was uncomfortable and he turned his thoughts to hoping they would be released from the cage for the night.

*   *   *

Olgood was awake at sunrise. He was in pain where his shoulder pressed against the bars of the cage and his neck ached probably from being twisted while he slept, but Gisele was still asleep with her head on his chest and he didn't want to wake her by trying to adjust his position. Others were stirring in the camp and one man had already gathered the horses and was leading them toward the cart. It was only when the man started to attach the horses that Gisele woke.

By the time the group resumed their march along the road the sun was shining through the trees. The leader and driver – the man carrying Olgood's axe – hadn't hurried in getting them underway, organising the breaking of camp efficiently but pausing frequently to speak casually to the other men.

Olgood got the impression that the group had been told to follow the road but didn't know exactly how far or where their final destination was. Of course the location of Lothar's camp would be a secret. The men walking alongside the cart continually scanned the forest and the road ahead and seemed to be waiting for somebody to meet them or something to happen.

Something did.

They were walking up a rise when there was a high-pitched squeal from one of the horses and, without warning, both horses launched into a full gallop, jolting the cart forward and hurtling it along the road at breakneck speed, leaving the startled and confused guards standing in their wake.

CHAPTER TWENTY

Four days ago… Kaela's story…

Hakon led the way across the meadow and through the trees on top of the rise. They travelled at a quick pace across a few miles of rolling hills until they stood overlooking a valley. In the middle of the valley a road ran alongside a row of trees.

'Road from Kirkense to Turborg,' said Hakon.

'What are those buildings?' Kaela pointed at two isolated buildings visible in the distance, standing close to the road.

'Old farm. Nobody there many years.'

'We'll make better time when we reach the road.'

Hakon followed Kaela into the valley.

Kaela regretted the decision to leave her sword. She knew Fenn had suggested it be left behind because of its noticeable quality and because she was a woman and women did not wear swords. But she had passed as a man for a long time and could do so again if she prepared – although her hair had grown longer than she would normally have let it. Nonetheless, she should have taken the time. She would feel much safer if she had a sword. Hakon was carrying both sword and axe – she thought of suggesting that she wear the sword but decided it was probably best if he held it.

Instead she turned to him as they approached the road and said: 'If we have to fight, will you give me your sword?'

He smiled at her. 'To me this your sword. I only wear sword for you.'

They separately met two farm workers, identified by the forks slung over their shoulders, and a horse and cart laden with bales of hay coming in the other direction. In both cases they raised a hand in greeting but did not converse.

The night they spent by the river was cold without a fire, and feeling hungry did not make it easy to sleep.

They rose early, washed in the river and filled the water skin. According to Hakon, they would see Turborg from the top of the next rise.

They paused at the grisly sight of a dead body hanging from a gallows just outside of the town, Kaela briefly wondering what circumstances had led this unfortunate person to be rotting at the end of a hangman's rope, then entered Turborg just as the market was becoming busy. Kaela looked for a place selling vegetables or herbs, found just the seller she wanted on the edge of the market square and exchanged a few of Hakon's coins for a braided string of garlic bulbs. She checked the bulbs and was satisfied that the cloves were fresh and juicy.

Her nose drew her to some meat being turned over a small fire. A man cut some slices in exchange for some more coins. He said the meat was goat but to Kaela it was either an old goat or perhaps a dog – it was very chewy. In their hungry state, though, it was also satisfying. From a neighbouring seller she also purchased some apples, pears and cherries to take back to the others.

Kaela smiled when she saw Hakon look longingly at a nearby inn. He noticed her watching him and shrugged then gestured for them to make their way back through the market to the Kirkense road.

At midday, they reached the abandoned buildings, where they would leave the road and cut across the country to the willow camp. Kaela stopped outside the derelict barn and took the water skin off her shoulder to have a drink. They were about five miles from the camp and should be back there by mid-afternoon.

The group of men approaching along the road from the direction of Kirkense gave Kaela no cause for concern until they were close enough for her to see that they were armed with swords and one man also carried a bow. Even so, they walked and talked as if they were a group of friends heading for the market, although they would probably arrive in Turborg too late for that. She and Hakon stood by the barn and nodded a friendly greeting as the men walked by.

Suddenly Kaela drew in a sharp breath and turned her back on the men, taking Hakon by the arm and moving away from the barn towards the road. Hakon had the water skin up to his mouth and her unexpected tug pulled him off balance, spilling some water onto his tunic. He gave a surprised grunt as he momentarily stumbled and then caught his footing and followed her.

'Why you…?'

'Your sword,' she said, holding out her hand.

'What?'

'Give me the sword,' she insisted. 'Quickly!'

A shout came from one of the men then the sound of running feet and Kaela and Hakon found themselves surrounded. One of the men stepped forward and confirmed what Kaela already knew.

It was the man she had fought in the forest. His ear still bore the scar of her blade.

He smiled mirthlessly.

'It is fortunate for me you have no sword today,' he said in the language of the Northmen.

Kaela glanced at the hills in the direction of the willow tree camp. If she had only walked another mile before stopping for a drink…

Hakon's axe and sword were taken from him. Kaela's purchases were also taken. The pieces of fruit were shared among the men and the garlic was inspected and tossed on the ground. The man with the scarred ear, who seemed to be the leader of the group, took the water skin from Kaela's shoulder and placed it on his own. Kaela and Hakon were made to kneel while the men held a discussion which they made no effort to hide.

Two men were despatched to Turborg to complete the original purpose for their journey. They were to deliver a message to one of the town officials, a man named Malthus, that if three strangers – the number now reduced from five – came to the town, they were to be seized and delivered to Lothar. For this service, Lothar would reward him. The description to give to Malthus was to look for a blonde woman and two men – one very tall, the other with dark hair.

A man walked around the barn to check that it was secure and Kaela and Hakon were pushed towards the doors.

The outlaw with the scarred ear addressed Kaela. 'I will not kill you – Lothar wants that pleasure, but if you try to escape, I will kill him.' He pointed at Hakon with his sword.

'You will sit there where you can be seen…' he pointed to a spot just inside the barn entrance, '…and don't move. We may be here a while.'

He withdrew and spoke to the man with the bow. This man took the bow from his back and strung it then leaned against the wall of the house where he had a good view of the barn entrance. Kaela watched as the leader called to another man and spoke at length with him, both of them glancing often at the captives. When the discussion was over, the man seated himself against the barn wall a few feet away. Although he didn't look at them, he seemed attentive.

Hakon apologised for being slow to give her the sword. Kaela replied with a shrug and a dismissive wave.

In English, Hakon said: 'What we do now?'

From the corner of her eye Kaela saw the seated man's head raise a fraction. Hakon started to speak again but Kaela held up her hand to stop him.

She turned her back to the seated man and whispered: 'The man behind me is listening to us. At the crossroads Scarred-Ear heard us speaking English. This man may know English. Be careful what you say.'

Hakon nodded, then said: 'Who is Scarred-Ear?'

Kaela pointed. 'Him.'

Hakon smiled his understanding.

Still whispering she said: 'I saw you take a knife from Gudrod's house – do you still have it?'

He nodded and tapped the side of his tunic. Kaela casually shifted her position so she was further into the shadows inside the barn and out of sight of most of the outlaws. The only one who could see her directly was the archer and he was twenty feet away.

'Good. Sit in front of me and give me the knife.'

Hakon sat with his back leaning against the door frame, watching the men outside and shielding her from them. Kaela held the knife close to the end of the blade and, disguising her movements as best she could, knelt sideways and scraped a vertical groove as long as her finger into the flat piece of wood that held one of the barn doors. She gave a satisfied grunt. The wood was workable – neither too hard nor too soft.

She wanted to write two words but she couldn't carve them in English and Latin was no better. Apart from the fact that the man sitting nearby may speak English, the words she wanted to carve were names and if she used English or Latin letters they would be understood by everyone. She thought for a moment then smiled. There was an even better alternative. She cut a second mark at an angle to the first. Now, even if these men did notice the marks, they might not recognise them as a message.

For the benefit of the man seated against the wall they kept up a conversation in normal voices. Hakon warned her when anyone came too close. She would stop and lean against the wood and resume when it was safe. Her awkward position made the work laborious and difficult. After a while she found her fingers becoming tired from the effort needed to grasp the knife blade firmly and she needed to rest after each mark and flex her hands.

One of the words she knew Fenn would recognise immediately. The other he wouldn't know – but she hoped he could deduce what it said. After she had completed the first word, she paused. How could she help Fenn to know what the second word meant? He needed to think about it. The first word would get his attention, but the second contained her message. She frowned. There had to be a way of making him concentrate on this word. Then she nodded to herself and started to carve the second word.

With the frequent interruptions, it took her a long time; so long that her time-sense warned her that the men sent to Turborg must soon be returning, but at last she was satisfied and she returned the knife to Hakon.

She whispered in his ear: 'I've left a message for the others, pointing to Lothar. Scarred-Ear and his men must not see the marks.'

Hakon nodded and shifted his position so he covered what she had carved in the door frame.

Kaela also leaned back against the wall of the barn. If the others came looking for them, there was a chance that they would come this way; there was a chance that they would enter the barn; there was a chance they would notice the marks; there was a chance that Fenn would be the one to notice; there was a chance he could understand the second word…

She knew that when these chances were laid end to end, they became very small.

It was late afternoon when the men returned from Turborg and reported to Scarred-Ear. They had talked to Malthus and given him Lothar's message. From the way they spoke, Kaela got the impression they did not doubt that Lothar's request would be obeyed. She wondered what relationship Lothar the Hun had with Malthus of Turborg. It seemed the outlaw leader had a wide reach in this area.

Kaela caught a word that brought her full attention back to what the men were saying.

She looked at Hakon whose face was registering alarm. 'What did he say?'

'He said a man arrived in Turborg this morning and is offering a reward for some escaped thralls. He described us. A Northman named Ragnall.'

Scarred-Ear walked over to them, a knowing smile on his face.

'So, somebody is looking for thralls. I think we have some of what he wants. Now we must ask ourselves – do we kill you or sell you?' He watched them but when they showed no reaction, he shrugged and said: 'It doesn't matter. That's a decision for Lothar.'

Scarred-Ear gestured at Kaela and Hakon to stand up and the men readied to leave. Kaela made sure she stood in front of her carving as long as possible and left only when everyone else had moved away from the barn. She stooped to pick up the discarded garlic as she passed. If she and Hakon could escape it would be better to have the garlic than it be left here in the dirt. Fenn needed this garlic and she still planned to do all she could to get it to him. Scarred-Ear was watching her and reached out to take the braid from her but she pretended not to notice and walked by him.

'Wait,' he said. 'What are you carrying?'

Kaela turned. 'Just garlic,' she replied.

When she saw he was deciding whether to insist, she said: 'Medicine for women.'

He grunted and waved her on, giving her a rough push in the back to hurry her along.

The men formed a protective circle around Kaela and Hakon, one walking each side and two in the front and the back. The man with the bow walked a few feet behind to ensure there was no attempt to make a sudden dash for freedom.

The road reached the outskirts of Skyrvid Forest and continued to run beside the forest for several miles. It was dusk when they reached a point where Kaela could just distinguish an opening in the trees. Scarred-Ear checked the road in both directions before leading them into the forest. Once they were out of sight of the Kirkense road, he stopped and Kaela's and Hakon's hands were tied behind their backs. Kaela tried to push the braid of garlic into her tunic but the man tying her hands took it from her, sniffed at it, then threw it onto the ground. She appealed to Scarred-Ear to be allowed to keep the garlic but he turned away, disinterested. The man laughed and kicked the bunch of garlic into the undergrowth. Kaela shared a glance with Hakon, committing this spot to memory. If they were able to free themselves, they knew where to find it. A rope was tied around each of their necks and they were led forward along an old road leading into the forest.

It was dark when they reached the place Kaela recognised as the crossroads where they had fought the outlaws. Scarred-Ear and his men crossed the north-south road without pause. He saw her looking around at the area where they had crossed swords but made no comment. He and his men seemed to be at ease walking through the forest in the dark and they confidently continued along the west road.

They followed the narrow road for mile after mile with the light that filtered into the forest allowing them to see only a few feet in front. Kaela's desire for some change to the monotonous placing of one foot in front of the other along this forest trail was finally fulfilled when Scarred-Ear turned abruptly from the road and followed a smaller path as it wound its way to the top of a hill. He stopped and uttered several hoots that sounded like an owl, but no owl Kaela had ever heard. After a moment some answering hoots were heard and they moved off the hill. Kaela tried to step carefully, but the man pulling her rope didn't allow for her lack of knowledge of the path and she stumbled over tree-roots and hit her head on low branches until she learned to watch his dim form carefully and step where he stepped and duck when he ducked. She heard Hakon fall and he was cursed and roughly pulled back to his feet.

Some dogs started barking in the distance but they were quieted by shouts. From the darkness a muffled sentence, either a greeting or a challenge, was answered by Scarred-Ear. A short while later, the glow of a fire and the murmur of voices announced the presence of a camp a few moments before they entered it.

They walked through a space between some roughly-built wooden shelters and emerged into the top of a clearing shaped like a long oval. A large fire was burning nearby, surrounded by a half-circle of the wooden shelters. There seemed to be no uniform design to these structures – they were constructed from the debris of the forest floor and branches hewn from the forest trees. The turf used for the roof had grass growing on it. Beyond the fire Kaela could see the outline of some more wooden structures at the far end of the clearing. She could hear some dogs growling from that direction.

She and Hakon were led to the fire. Hakon watched closely as Scarred-Ear handed his weapons to the man with the bow who took them into a hut. There were twenty or more men – and women, Kaela noted – around the fire. Many were holding items of food and cups as if their meal had been interrupted. The voices died as each person turned to look at the newcomers. Kaela looked at their faces. Nobody was smiling. Other people appeared at the doors of some of the huts and joined in the silent appraisal. Then, one by one, their eyes moved to the largest hut at the top of the clearing.

For a long while nothing happened.

Then a man emerged from the interior. He had a large piece of meat in his hand. He stood in the doorway and then bent his head to take a bite from the meat. In the firelight, the meat juices glistened wetly around his mouth. He regarded the captives while he chewed.

He was above average height but not as tall as Olgood. He wore his dark black hair tied in a knot on the top of his head and had a long moustache that drooped below his chin. His eyes were narrow slits and seemed almost enveloped by his prominent cheeks. This must be Lothar the Hun.

He handed the meat to someone inside the hut and walked slowly toward the fire. People who were in his way moved quickly aside so he did not need to deviate from his path. Standing before Kaela he looked at Scarred-Ear and then back at her.

'Who are these people?'

'This is the woman who killed Baradin,' said Scarred-Ear. 'This man was with her. We found them on the road to Turborg.'

A sound like a soft growl came from Lothar's throat.

'You said there were five. Did the others escape?'

'No. These two were alone.'

Lothar walked around Kaela his eyes examining her from within his sunken eye sockets.

'Did you deliver my message to Malthus?'

'Of course. We told him to watch for the other three. And we learned there is someone else looking for this group – a Northman.'

Lothar threw a quick glance at Scarred-Ear as he considered the information. 'That is very interesting,' he said slowly. 'I would like to talk with this Northman.'

He continued nodding thoughtfully and turned back to Kaela, staring down at her.

'So... you are the she-bitch who murdered my brother.' He looked her up and down. 'How could you do that?' he sneered. 'You are no more than a girl.'

'This is the one,' affirmed Scarred-Ear.

'I didn't murder him; he attacked us,' said Kaela.

304

Lothar struck her in the face with his fist. She fell to the ground, so close to the fire that she had to roll away to avoid being burned. Her hat fell off and there were several gasps as her red hair was revealed.

'You will not speak until I tell you to speak,' said Lothar fiercely.

Hakon knelt beside her but could not help her with his hands still tied.

Lothar motioned to some men to help her back to her feet. When she was standing, Scarred-Ear took the rope from her neck and then reached across and removed the rope from Hakon's neck also.

Lothar stared at him, suddenly angry. 'You think this puts you closer to my side, Gunther? You would like to take the place of Baradin, perhaps?'

'No...,' protested Scarred-Ear, 'I...'

Lothar interrupted him, moving forward so they were face to face.

'I do not forget you allowed him to be killed,' he said coldly, 'and allowed yourself to be tied up by a group of farmers and women.' He sniffed, disdainfully. 'Hartmut says this small girl defeated the great Gunther with a sword.'

Gunther hesitated, looking sharply at one of the men in the crowd, receiving a satisfied smile in return. Kaela noted the man's forearm was wrapped in cloth and he had a fresh scar above his eye. She recognised the man Olgood had held by the neck.

'She had luck on her side,' Gunther said dismissively.

Lothar took a step back.

'Is that so?' he said slowly. 'Maybe I don't need to think of a way for her to die. Maybe I will let the gods decide if she is to die under your blade.' He paused, a slow smile spreading across his face. 'Or you under hers.'

'But if I kill her, her death would be too quick. Don't you want her to suffer – to feel the pain of the loss of a brother; of *our* loss? Feed her to the dogs.'

Lothar said: 'Hartmut!'

The bandaged man stepped forward.

'Cut them free and bring her... no, bring them *both* with me.'

Hartmut drew his sword with difficulty and awkwardly started to cut the bonds on Kaela's wrists with his left hand. Another man took the sword from him with a grunt of impatience and finished the job. Kaela massaged her wrists and flexed her fingers. Hakon was also freed and he looked at Kaela. Do we do anything? Kaela shook her head.

Lothar walked away from the fire toward the centre of the clearing. The people who had been sitting around the fire discarded their food and hurried to find a place to watch whatever Lothar had in mind.

'You too, Gunther,' Lothar called over his shoulder.

He walked twenty paces then stopped.

'Bring me the little one.'

A man took a rough hold of Hakon by the neck of his tunic and marched him to Lothar. Lothar took over the hold on Hakon's tunic. He pulled a long-bladed knife from his belt and held it at Hakon's neck. Hakon looked directly at Kaela and, out of Lothar's sight, he patted his tunic where she knew he had his knife. She gave a slight nod.

'Now, Hartmut, give her your sword.'

Hartmut approached Kaela watching her carefully and thrust his sword into the ground in front of her, making sure he withdrew quickly out of range. Kaela took the sword and held it out moving it back and forth to test the balance. Then she stood with the sword at her side and waited. This sword was bigger and heavier than Alfarin's sword. The grip was too big for her hand.

'Gunther, she is yours to kill. Take as long as you like.'

Gunther walked slowly forward. He moved warily.

Many of the spectators were looking puzzled, probably aware of Gunther's skill with a sword and imagining a brief contest which was not the death they would expect Lothar to choose for the killer of his brother. Gunther took a step, then another. Kaela did not move and did not raise her sword. Gunther feinted a blow but withdrew it quickly. Kaela had not flinched.

Gunther let out a bellow and thrust straight at her with all his weight behind it. Kaela lifted her sword, holding it with two hands. She stepped to the side and parried his blow, guiding his sword past her shoulder, the blade only inches from her. Gunther's momentum brought him close and she hit him on his chin with her sword hilt then moved away. It was not a heavy blow but it brought a gasp from the crowd, as if she had scored the first wound. Gunther recovered from his thrust and swung his sword back at her but she wasn't there.

The conversation died as every eye was fixed on the two people now circling each other in the clearing – the broad-shouldered man with the big arms; respected swordsman, victor of many fights, killer of many men, and the slim red-haired girl who had somehow avoided his first attack.

Kaela stopped circling when her back was to the fire and waited. Gunther did not want to attack facing the fire so he moved to the side but Kaela moved with him, keeping herself between him and the fire. He stopped when another few steps would have taken him into the forest, realising to continue would be ridiculous.

He charged again, swinging heavy blows from both sides. Kaela backed away, diverting his swings, ducking beneath them – the clanging of swords echoing among the trees. Kaela could see that Gunther had won many of his fights by sheer strength and that was his main tactic. He knew he was far stronger than this small girl and he should eventually overwhelm her.

She did not want to play with him as she had on the forest road. Alfarin's sword was perfect in her hands and she had been confident she could deal with anything he had to offer. The sword she now held was heavier and not comfortable – she needed to swing it with two hands which was not a familiar feel for her. If the fight was extended, she may tire and she could not afford a mistake.

He came forward again swinging from the side with all his strength, stepping toward her as he swung to make it more difficult for her to avoid the blow. Kaela had previously ducked under similar strikes or moved back and he expected the same. She did duck but instead of moving away she closed and before he could halt the momentum of his swing, she thrust upwards with the tip of her sword at his forearm as the sword passed by, slicing deep near the elbow. She continued her forward movement, ducking under his arm, rolling past him onto her shoulder and coming to her feet again behind him.

With a roar of pain Gunther used all the power of his arm and shoulder to arc his sword in a huge backswing quick enough to catch most opponents before they could recover, turning to face Kaela at the same time. Kaela leaned back and the sword tip just missed her neck. She felt the wind of the sword move her hair and her face was pattered with blood from his wounded arm. As Gunther's sword passed by she struck it as hard as she could with her own, pushing it further away. His arm swung wider than he had intended, exposing his whole body to her.

She could have delivered a fatal thrust then and he knew it. He brought his other arm in close in a futile attempt to protect himself from her sword. Instead of the expected killing strike, she stepped up to him and rested her sword under his chin. The fire was now at his back and she was hidden from the crowd.

'Drop the sword and live, continue to fight and die,' she said, loud enough for only him to hear. 'Perhaps your arm is too damaged to hold your sword.'

Gunther hesitated. He would know from their previous encounter that attempting to move away would not be successful. Kaela pushed upwards an inch with her sword, forcing him to lift his chin. He started to bring his sword arm back. When she tensed he stopped the movement and made his decision, sagging his shoulder, his weapon falling to the ground. Kaela withdrew her sword and stepped back. Gunther clutched at his arm.

Kaela knew it would have been very difficult for her if he had just used the strength of his sword arm to pull her in and crush her to him. In that position he could possibly have prevented her from moving her sword.

'He cannot continue,' she said loudly.

'So kill him,' called Lothar.

Gunther fixed his eyes on hers. For the second time she had him at her mercy.

'If you want him dead, *you* kill him,' Kaela shouted back. To Gunther, she said: 'If I was you I would run. You have a twenty yard start.'

This time Gunther did not hesitate. He snatched his sword from the ground and in a few strides was into the trees and gone from view.

Lothar shouted a command and several men dashed across the clearing and followed Gunther into the trees. Kaela watched them with a smile. She would not like to meet Gunther in the dark forest even if he was wounded and she was sure that the men who had just raced after him would only need a moment's reflection to come to the same conclusion.

She looked across at Lothar. He still had his knife at Hakon's neck. Hakon was standing ready despite the threat. She knew what he was thinking. She had a sword; some men had left the camp and run into the forest, they may never get a better chance. If she wanted him to, he would try for his knife.

She checked Lothar closely. He was not distracted. He was waiting for her to try something. Several other men were also now watching her. She gripped the sword tightly. With a sword in her hands and as close as she was to the forest, she knew she had a good chance of escape – but Hakon would certainly die.

In English she called: 'Hakon, we cannot win this one.'

She dropped her sword.

Lothar smiled but he also looked relieved. He realised the situation had for a moment been out of his control and she could have escaped.

'Get the sword. Tie her.'

He didn't relax the knife against Hakon's neck until his orders had been carried out then he roughly pushed Hakon aside. Hakon's hands were bound again but this time in front of him, while Lothar walked across the clearing to stand in front of Kaela.

'So Hartmut told the truth – you can handle a sword,' he said. 'A pity – I could have used someone like you.'

When Kaela did not reply, he continued: 'And nobody died. The gods have given me no clear answer as usual.' He regarded Kaela thoughtfully. 'I ought to kill you for letting Gunther go – but how many times can you die? If I can't kill you more than once, I can at least ensure your death is a long one.'

Lothar stroked his long moustache, and added with a thin smile: 'I think Gunther has done me one last service by suggesting I feed you to the dogs.'

He turned to address the people gathered around.

'The dogs get no more to eat. We'll wait until they are hungry enough to feast on this fresh meat.'

He signalled that Kaela and Hakon were to be brought along and headed toward the far end of the clearing, the end opposite the fire. Between the two huts at this end of the clearing, some waist-high stakes were set into the ground forming a circle, at the centre of which stood a tall pole. On each side of the pole, close to the fence stakes, were two smaller poles and tied to each of these by a short rope was a huge hairy brute of a dog. The dogs came to their feet when Lothar approached, standing with their hackles raised and menacing snarls sounding low in their throats. The dog's heads were at the level of Kaela's waist.

'Look my beauties – this will be your next meal.' He waved his hand over their heads and laughed when they snapped at it. He may have had affection for the dogs but they seemed to have none for him.

'Put them in there,' he said to the men holding Kaela and Hakon, pointing at one of the huts. 'You two guard them. Tomorrow we'll set a table for my beauties – tonight, I've been too long away from my own meal.' Lothar laughed again.

Before she entered the hut, Kaela saw the men who had followed Gunther into the forest returning without any sign of Gunther. As she expected they had only stayed long enough for it to be accepted that they had made an effort. Lothar wasn't happy and he pulled one of the men aside.

'In the morning take three men. Find Gunther and kill him.'

The man replied but to Kaela it was obvious he did not relish the task. She was pushed inside the hut. The guards ordered Kaela and Hakon to sit at each end of the hut about ten feet apart and they sat themselves between the two captives and also between them and the door.

Kaela lay down immediately. 'I suggest we get some rest,' she said in English. 'Let's see what tomorrow brings.'

Kaela lay in the darkness and thought of Fenn. His life may depend on her getting the garlic to him, and the garlic was now lying on the forest floor many miles away. Hakon was right – she was unlikely to have a sword in her hand again. Had she forfeited Fenn's life to save Hakon? She fell asleep wondering what Fenn would have done.

When they woke they did not speak, each contemplating their fate, until Hakon broke the silence.

'Lothar will kill you,' Hakon said, in English. 'We must take next opportunity and fight.' He paused. 'Maybe we die but better die fighting and die here than be sold back to Ragnall.'

'We're overdue back at the willow tree camp,' said Kaela. 'The others will be looking for us by now. We just need to stay alive as long as possible.'

'How they know where we are? Fenn is hurt. Olgood not leave him – unless he is…'

'He is *not* dead!' she said so loudly that both guards looked up. More quietly she said: 'I left a message.'

'Nobody read message,' said Hakon firmly. 'Why anyone look in old barn for message?'

Kaela was silent. She knew he was right about that too.

Kaela and Hakon lay in the hut all morning waiting for Lothar to attend to them. As time passed Kaela wondered if he was deliberately letting them wait or if he was just lazy. Her question remained unanswered until, sometime after midday, Lothar arrived and they were dragged from the hut. Hakon was held to one side and Kaela was taken to stand by the small circular fence.

Lothar appraised her.

'We hear the Northmen who are looking for you have offered a reward. They can have the little one…' he waved contemptuously at Hakon, '…for what he will fetch, but not you. Not the she-bitch – killer of my brother.'

'But even you I will let live a little longer if you tell me where to find the others of your group. Tell me this and you will live another day.'

Kaela looked at him as if he hadn't spoken.

Lothar waited, but he could see she was not going to say anything.

'Very well…'

Hakon spoke: 'Our leader is dead,' he said. 'He died of a snake bite two days ago. We decided to split up. The others have gone to Ruslager.'

Lothar grinned. 'Good. I have sent men to Ruslager. If they are there we will find them.'

He turned to Kaela.

'In the meantime… tie her to the pole.'

'But you said she would live another day,' protested Hakon.

'And she probably will. I don't think the dogs are hungry enough yet.'

Inside the fenced enclosure, the pole was worn smooth as if from rubbing and stained dark in places. This was obviously not the first time it had been used. Lothar caught her glance and smiled. Two men took Kaela and lifted her over the fence. The dogs growled but moved out of the way. Kaela's hands were tied behind the pole and she was also tied at the ankles so one foot was on either side of the pole. The men were about to leave her when Lothar jumped over the fence.

'No,' he said. 'This one is special. Tie her here as well.' He roughly pulled her elbows together behind the pole forcing her shoulders back. Lothar held her while one of the men tied her elbows.

'There,' said Lothar when he had finished. 'Trussed just like a pig.'

The men stepped out of the circle. The dogs came to sniff at Kaela. They growled but they were only curious.

The tie at her elbows stretched her shoulders and upper arms painfully, and the binds at her ankles meant she had to stand more on her toes than her feet. It was uncomfortable and painful and Kaela knew it would only get worse. For the moment, she did not let her discomfort show on her face. In fact it was Hakon who looked the more pained.

Lothar checked each of her ties and then turned abruptly and strode away towards the other end of the camp. Several people waited for a while watching Kaela with interest but she gave them no satisfaction of seeming to be worried, and one by one they followed Lothar. The men holding Hakon looked at each other. They had received no specific instructions and did not appear inclined to ask for them. They reached some agreement and took Hakon back to the hut and pushed him inside. One seated himself outside where he could keep an eye on Kaela as well, and the other wandered back to the fire.

The night was cold but Kaela gave it no mind as she concentrated on relieving each new pain as it appeared. The ache in her shoulders was constant but she found she could relieve other aches temporarily by standing as much as she could alternately on one foot and then the other. The act of relieving one pain would soon produce another, and the need for continual activity was exhausting. She tried relaxing and letting her weight be held by the ropes and this did provide an unexpected temporary reprieve until the pain of the pressure of the ropes became too much. She tried to push the pain out of her mind and endure for one more heartbeat.

*   *   *

She was woken by a splash of water in the face. Whether she had slept or fallen unconscious she didn't know; she thought the pain would keep her awake all night but, on opening her eyes, the pain returned re-doubled in every part of her body and this time she couldn't keep it from her face.

Lothar was standing there. He grunted with satisfaction.

'Untie her.'

Kaela collapsed when her hands and elbows were freed. She tried to stand but her feet would not bear her weight and she was lifted out of the circle like a child and taken to the hut

Once again she and Hakon were separated but this time only one man was left to guard them. Hakon asked the guard if someone could tend to Kaela but he was ignored. He asked Kaela how she was, but it was some time before she could reply.

'I'll live.'

'Why did he free you?' asked Hakon.

'Probably so I can think about the pain starting again,' she replied, with a croak in her voice.

They were given a small amount of food, some turnips and berries and pieces of fatty meat, and some water in a wooden bowl.

*   *   *

Lothar appeared in the hut in the late afternoon.

313

'I have received a message from my cousin,' he said in a gloating tone. 'He tells me two others of your group are being tracked by dogs – the tall man and a woman. We will have them soon.'

He laughed at their expressions then signalled to the guard.

'Bring her out and tie her again, just like before. I think she needs another day or two of seasoning but maybe my beauties are already hungry enough to try a nibble.'

The day had turned cold and windy, the trees moving restlessly with their branches rustling. Kaela shivered as the guard brought her outside.

When she was tied to the pole all her aches seemed to return as if they had memories of where they had been before. She tried to prepare herself for the ordeal of another night tied to the pole but she found it difficult to find anything positive to concentrate on.

Lothar had said Olgood and Gisele were being tracked by dogs. Why? It didn't make sense. Why would they leave Fenn? Was he...? She couldn't complete that thought. Maybe Fenn was the man. He was tall. Then where was Olgood? She was becoming confused.

Her thoughts were interrupted by a shout from nearby. She looked up.

'The little man is gone!' The call came from inside the hut.

Kaela stared. The guard emerged looking around in astonishment.

'Find him!' roared Lothar. 'All of you! Go!'

Men ran in several directions. It seemed nobody had noticed Hakon leaving the hut.

Kaela couldn't help herself – she laughed out loud with joy. She would certainly have counselled Hakon not to try to escape but the fact that he had, lifted her spirits enormously.

'Run Hakon!' she called in English at the top of her voice, her pain forgotten. 'Run like the wind!'

She was still smiling when the first spots of rain hit her face.

At the onset of the rain, the guard stationed himself just inside the hut where he was sheltered but could still watch her. The thunder seemed to be directly overhead. It crashed so loudly around the clearing, beating at the forest with its noise, that it physically hurt her ears. The rainwater matted her hair, coursing down her face, and soaking her clothes so they clung to her body. The wind buffeted her head, whipping her hair in many directions as it swirled through the clearing and among the trees. The dogs curled against the side of the enclosure, their heads and tails tucked into their bodies.

Kaela was happy in the storm, using it as a distraction from her predicament. She opened her mouth and let the water flow down her throat. Several times she cried into the wind: 'Run, Hakon, run!' – stopping only when she realised she was sounding hysterical.

The pain in her arms and shoulders became severe. As the ropes became wet they tightened. The effort of holding herself upright was causing the pads of her feet to become intensely painful. Finally she felt overwhelmed and no effort of will or anything she did could ease the pain. She sagged against the ropes.

$$*\quad*\quad*$$

Again she was woken with water thrown in her face. She had been released from the pole already and was lying on the ground in front of the hut. This time she was sure she had been revived from unconsciousness rather than sleep. Every muscle was aching and stiff and the pain from where she had been tied was as intense as if the ropes were still there. It felt as though her skin had been torn away. She couldn't move her head to see if that were true. Kaela didn't think she could move at all.

Lothar was standing there watching her.

When he saw she was alert, he said: 'I thought you had tried to cheat me by dying on the pole.' He crouched down in front of her.

'You can look forward to a repeat performance tonight,' he added with a thin smile. 'Now, you can recover so we can start again fresh. I would not like the pain to become your friend.'

Kaela was carried into the hut. She glanced around and was pleased to see that Hakon was not inside.

There was food and water in bowls set on the floor. Kaela found the strength to crawl to the bowls and satisfy her hunger and thirst, after which she fell into an exhausted sleep.

She woke several times through the day and each time was glad to see that she was still alone. Moving any of her limbs was painful but she was happy that, although her skin was chaffed raw where she had been bound, the damage was not as bad as she had feared. She sat against the wall of the hut trying not to play Lothar's game and think of the torment that awaited her when night fell.

The man sitting outside the door stood up and was watching something in the camp. She moved so she could see out of the door and her heart sank as she saw Lothar approaching. He was earlier than she expected. Lothar came directly into the hut with a beaming smile. He was followed by a man Kaela had not seen before. A small man with a large nose and small eyes, he wore fine clothing and knee-high boots. Kaela switched her gaze back to Lothar. She knew no benefit to her could come from his good humour. She prepared herself for bad news, hoping that it did not involve Hakon.

She was not disappointed when he announced: 'This is my cousin, Malthus. He tells me you will soon be joined by more of your friends. The big man and the other woman have been caged and will be here tomorrow morning.'

Kaela knew Lothar would be watching her reaction so she clenched her teeth and made sure she kept her face calm. He became instantly angry. He raised his hand to strike her, but stopped himself with an obvious effort.

'So that does not worry you,' he said. 'Maybe *this* will. A man you apparently know well – a Northman named Ragnall – will be arriving tonight to buy his thralls back. But not you, my pretty… *You* I will never sell.'

She raised her eyes to his to see if he could possibly be trying to goad her again. His deep eyes were as hard as flint.

To divert her thoughts, Kaela looked at Malthus. He and Lothar could not be more different. If they were cousins, the only family resemblance she could see was that they both had very small eyes. Every other feature of

316

face and build were opposites. Malthus was watching her closely, almost eagerly. Kaela was puzzled until she realised that the two men had one other thing in common. Like his cousin, Malthus wanted to see fear in her eyes.

The noise of some commotion outside filtered into the hut. Lothar strode to the door and turned to look at her with a wide smile.

'The day gets better,' he said triumphantly.

He beckoned to someone and stood back to allow two men to enter the hut with a struggling Hakon between them. His face was cut and bruised and his arms were bloodied by scratches. He was thrown on the floor but he was on his feet instantly and he stood poised as if to make another run, his eyes wild.

Lothar blocked the door and stood with his legs apart.

'I have a buyer for you little man, so you are worth gold to me.' He lowered his voice. 'But if you run again I will kill you in the blink of an eye.'

At the mention of a buyer, Hakon slowly relaxed and he looked at Kaela. She hesitated and then nodded.

'Ragnall,' she said quietly.

Hakon shook his head in disbelief. He sank to his haunches.

'That's better,' said Lothar. He looked at Kaela. 'I'll be back for you later. This time I think my beauties will be ready to taste what I put on their plate.'

To one of the men he said: 'Tie them both. Make sure *he* cannot walk.'

Lothar left the hut and when the man had tied their hands behind their backs and Hakon's feet, he too left. The guard came inside the hut and indicated they should sit at each end as before.

When Lothar was out of sight Kaela allowed her head to drop. She did not see how their situation could become any worse.

In English, Kaela told Hakon that Lothar had said Olgood and Gisele had been captured and they would be in the camp tomorrow morning. Hakon groaned at this news. Kaela remembered that Lothar had said they had been 'caged' which she could only think meant they had been confined in a cage like animals.

317

'And Fenn?' Hakon asked quietly.

'He didn't mention Fenn – so that at least is good news.'

They sat in silence for a while until Kaela asked: 'How did you free your hands? What happened in the forest?'

Hakon drew in a long breath. 'Nobody was watching so I run. I crawl into ditch covered in brambles and wait until men ran past me. I rub ropes on rock – hurt hands a little.' He turned so she could see his hands which showed many scratches from the thorns and some long abrasions from the rock.

'Then I hide in tree all night. At first light I came down but I go only small way when man step onto path in front of me.'

Hakon looked up at Kaela.

'It is Scarred-Ear.'

'Gun…' Kaela caught herself before she could say his name. 'Scarred-Ear? Are you sure?'

'Yes. He run at me with sword. I can go nowhere. I hope I can dodge when he strike, but he push me aside and attack man just behind me – I not know he there. Scarred-Ear kill him one blow to head.'

Kaela sat back in astonishment.

'Was the man behind you about to attack you?'

'Why he want to attack me? I think he want to take me back to Lothar, not kill me – but Scarred-Ear kill him anyway.'

'Why would he help you?' she asked.

Hakon shrugged. 'Maybe he just want to kill that man. He is outlaw. Outlaws are bad men.'

'What happened then?'

'Scarred-Ear say more men coming. He wave for me to follow him, but I not trust him. I think this maybe trick. Maybe *he* take me to Lothar. I climb tree instead. Men come and find dead man under tree.' He paused. 'I am quiet, but one man look up.' Hakon shrugged again.

Kaela smiled at him.

'That was bad luck, but I'm glad you're safe,' she said. 'Your escape helped me get through the night.' She stopped and breathed deeply as she thought of the night to come.

Hakon understood what she was thinking. 'You are strong as any man. Strong here,' he pointed to his head. 'If anyone can survive, you can.'

She nodded her thanks.

At dusk, Lothar arrived and Kaela was taken outside.

'Strip her,' ordered Lothar.

Kaela stood still and did not resist as some women came forward and pulled her tunic over her head and then removed her trousers, shoes and undergarments. If Lothar expected embarrassment he was disappointed. Kaela stood with exactly the same expression and stance as if she had been clothed.

'Tie her to the pole. Elbows too.'

The dogs had been two days without food. They were more belligerent than before, growling fiercely and crouching low when the men carrying Kaela approached. Each man was reluctant to be the first to step over the fence.

'Are you hungry, my beauties?' asked Lothar as if talking to children. He motioned to two other men to pull the dogs back by the ropes attached to their necks. As soon as the dogs were safely held, Kaela was tied to the pole. When her elbows were pulled back to be tied she could not prevent a cry of pain.

The dogs strained at their ropes, snarling at the men tying Kaela. They finished and moved quickly to the fence.

'Free the dogs.'

The dogs bounded forward at the last man who just cleared the fence in time and were brought up short by their ropes. Lothar laughed at the man's annoyance at the dogs being let go before he was safe. The dogs walked around Kaela sniffing at her and growling, but she had been in their enclosure for two nights now and was familiar to them. Once they had inspected her they turned their attention back to the people outside the stakes.

Lothar was obviously disappointed.

'Maybe tonight, maybe not,' he muttered. He looked down to where the ropes were already biting into Kaela's flesh. 'But tonight I think you are sure to leak a little blood.' He chuckled with pleasure.

He glanced up at the sky where the first stars were appearing. 'It will be warm enough. I wouldn't want you to freeze to death. I'll check later to see if they've started their feast. Maybe I'll need to stir them up with a stick like stirring a broth.'

He laughed at his joke and walked away followed by most of the others.

One woman stayed behind. She went to the man who would be standing guard for the night, passing him an animal skin similar to the ones used for carrying water. He drank from it eagerly and wiped his lips. When she made to take it back he moved it out of her reach. She tried again but he waved her away and sat down leaning on the side of the hut.

*   *   *

All of her strategies for relieving the pain were failing. Her feet were too sore to bear her weight. The small protection that her clothes had provided against the ropes was now gone and the coarse twine rubbed directly on her exposed and tormented skin. Nothing she could do gave her a moment's relief. Her breath came in sobs of pain. She could feel herself being overwhelmed, drifting in and out of consciousness – always brought back by a different pain that cut into her with more intensity than the others. Through her haze she heard the dogs sniffing around her feet, drawn by the blood where the ropes had rubbed her ankles raw. She felt a rough tongue lick at the rope around her ankles. She let her head fall onto her chest hoping to hasten the next short relief of unconsciousness.

She heard a noise as if something had been dropped on the ground and the dogs growled but she couldn't raise the energy to open her eyes. There was a sound of movement from behind her. She drew in a breath and almost choked.

A hand brushed through her hair and a voice whispered: 'I said I wouldn't leave you' in her ear. She felt his skin press against her cheek. Her relief was like a physical wind rushing through her. She could not believe Fenn was here, even though she had hoped for it with all her heart. All her pain disappeared and she felt as if she were floating.

She heard him draw a sword to cut her free, but she stopped him, saying that Hakon was in the hut, urging him to free him first. She felt him hesitate then step back. She thought about the dogs – why weren't they attacking Fenn? Then her attention was caught by movement in front of the fire.

She could not believe what she saw.

Some men were walking toward her. Lothar was leading and behind him were two huge Northmen she knew very well.

She gave a low whistle to warn Fenn.

*   *   *

Lothar stepped forward and waved an arm as if presenting Kaela to the visitors.

'Why is she tied like this?' asked Ragnall, an edge to his voice.

'She killed my brother and she will die here,' answered Lothar. 'As I told you, she is not for sale.'

'I'll pay a good price for her. Whatever you ask,' said Ragnall.

'She is *not* for sale,' repeated Lothar. 'The other one is in that hut.'

He noticed the guard was still asleep and waved to one of his men.

'Wake him up. What's the matter with him?'

The man walked over to the guard.

'He's drunk,' he said, holding up the skin. 'He stinks of ale.'

Lothar barely held in his anger. 'I will deal with him later,' he hissed.

His head jerked forward as he suddenly noticed that the dogs were eating meat. He roared out a curse, walking around the circle of the fence, his hands clenched into fists. Ragnall and Olaf looked at each other.

Lothar stared in disbelief. 'Who did this?' he bellowed, looking about as if he expected the guilty man to step forward. 'If I find who gave them meat, I'll have his head!'

'Shall I take away the meat?' asked a man.

Lothar stared at him incredulously and laughed in his face. 'I'd like to see you try.'

He cursed again. 'It'll take another three days to get them hungry again.'

Ragnall said: 'She belongs to me. You can double her price.'

Lothar spat on the ground and raised a finger in front of Ragnall. 'She's mine now. She will *never* be for sale.'

The two stared at each other and then Lothar turned away from Ragnall and leaned on the fence. He didn't see Ragnall narrow his eyes and share another glance with Olaf.

Lothar took a long look at Kaela. 'I'll think of another way for her to die.' He seemed lost in thought, his face fierce.

Ragnall said loudly: 'I'd like to check Hakon.'

Lothar slapped the fence in frustration and turned back. 'The little man? Over here.'

He led the way to the hut. The three of them went inside while two others lifted the guard and dragged him towards the fire. Another man took his place.

Kaela heard Ragnall say: 'Can you speak, Hakon?'

She couldn't hear Hakon's reply. The pain was returning. She gasped in agony and a moan came from her throat.

Ragnall and Olaf came out of the hut followed by Lothar.

'You said the others will be here tomorrow?' asked Ragnall.

'Yes. They are on their way. That's four of the five you wanted, but one...' Lothar reminded, waving a finger at Kaela, '...is not for sale.'

'So you say. And the fifth man, you haven't heard of him?'

'The little man said he was dead from a snake bite. He also said the big man went to Ruslager but he was captured in Turborg, so he may be lying.'

'In Turborg?' said Olaf. 'We have been there.'

'A nice town,' said Lothar, now a pleasant host. 'My cousin Malthus lives there – you met him when you arrived in my camp.'

He extended his arms toward the fire and started walking toward it.

322

'Come and eat with us – a drink perhaps and we can discuss the price for your three thralls, but I warn you…' Lothar held up his hand, his voice fading as he moved away, '…I hear the big man caused some trouble. I want to see him before I decide on *his* price.'

Kaela held her head up long enough to see Ragnall take a long look back at her over his shoulder.

She let her head fall, the pain threatening to take her over. It was no longer specific. It radiated from every part of her body. She could feel her limbs shaking involuntarily. She drew in a deep breath and, despite her agony, smiled.

Now that Fenn was here, she knew she could endure.

CHAPTER TWENTY-ONE

United we stand…

The night was cloudy and dark but the light from the fire extended down the length of the clearing to the forest where Fenn, watching from the trees, held his axe tightly in his hand. He would not let them harm her further no matter what the consequences. He felt the tension in his arms while the man he suspected was Lothar shouted and gesticulated in front of Kaela. Fenn couldn't understand what he was saying but he was obviously angry.

Abruptly the outlaw led Ragnall and Olaf into Hakon's hut and Fenn realised with a jolt they could be about to take Hakon away with them now. If that happened, the situation would change very much for the worse. With Hakon close by, in the hut, he had a chance. If he was taken by Ragnall and Olaf, his rescue might become impossible. He waited anxiously with his eyes fixed on the entrance to the hut and breathed with relief when Ragnall and Olaf emerged without Hakon. They talked with Lothar briefly and they all walked back to the fire leaving only one guard.

Fenn had left his staff in the food store and it would take too long to retrieve it, so he couldn't dispose of this guard in the same manner as the previous one. He could see Kaela was suffering. He needed to act quickly.

It took a while to get to a position where he had enough room but was also concealed from the fire and the guard. He unthreaded his sling and fitted a stone. The sling made a satisfying whirling sound as he built up the speed and released the stone then he held his breath while the missile sped unerringly to its target. He heard a thump and a soft clatter.

Fenn walked swiftly to the hut. He checked that the guard was still breathing and slipped inside.

'Hakon, it's me Fenn,' he whispered.

He heard a cough and some rustling in a corner.

'Fenn?' Hakon's voice was hoarse, disbelieving.

Fenn knelt beside him and reached for his bound hands.

'Yes, it's me. Can you walk?'

'I can walk.' Hakon could now see him. 'I have knife in tunic,' he said.

'You have a knife?' Fenn was surprised. 'Didn't they search you?'

'No. Not know why. Maybe not care. Maybe Lothar think we already searched.'

Fenn checked Hakon's tunic, found the knife and cut the ropes on his hands and feet.

Hakon said: 'Fenn… Ragnall and Olaf are in camp.'

'I know. I've seen them.' Fenn cuffed him on the shoulder. 'But we will cheat them again.'

Hakon grunted and massaged his wrists. 'Kaela…? Is she…?'

'She wanted me to free you first.'

'Go to her,' Hakon said. 'I get her clothes and I get other things.'

'I'll meet you outside. If we get separated – do you know where the refuse pits are?'

'Yes.'

'We'll meet behind the refuse pits,' Fenn said and ran to the door.

The dogs didn't even spare him a glance as he jumped the fence, the sound of crunching bones covering any noise he made. Kaela made no sound as, using Hakon's knife, he cut the rope tying her ankles to the pole; but he had to hold her up or she would have fallen. With one hand holding her, the ropes around her elbows and wrists were cut. Kaela collapsed in his arms with a groan. He picked her up and crossed to the fence where he lowered her over the stakes. He expected Hakon to be there but he was nowhere to be seen. He had to let her fall the last foot onto the ground before he could step over the fence.

A sudden chorus of shouting from the other end of the camp froze him in place, but a burst of laughter followed and someone howled like a wolf. It sounded like the camp and its visitors were having a celebration.

Fenn saw a pile of clothing lying outside the hut door.

He searched again for Hakon. Had he gone straight to the pits?

Fenn tightened his jaw in frustration. He couldn't wait for him here. At any moment someone might decide to check on the captives or the man Fenn had hit could wake up. When he picked Kaela up she felt limp in his arms and he worried that she might be unconscious. He awkwardly picked up the pile of clothing and carried both into the forest beside the refuse pits. He stepped carefully to the tree where he had left the basket. He would be able to watch the camp and the pits from there.

He reached the tree and was relieved when Kaela stirred and asked him to put her down. He dropped the bundle of clothes and lowered her gently to the ground. She reached for her clothes. There was just enough light from the fire filtering through the trees to be able to see a few feet in front and Fenn helped her dress, glancing up every few moments to look for Hakon. Because she was unable to stay upright without his help, the dressing was awkward and slow. When she finally had her tunic on, Fenn handed her the sword. She smiled and asked him to help her stand. She leaned back against the tree trunk to fasten the belt buckle.

'Thank you for bringing the Lord of the Battle to me.' Her voice was weak.

He put his arms around her. He could feel she was frail and unsteady from her ordeal but she clung to him fiercely, her head pressed into his chest. He held her and felt her short and pained breathing and didn't want to let her go, but finally he eased her down so she could rest beneath the tree. Kaela drew her feet up to check her ankles where the ropes had carved bloody rings, making sure her shoes would not rub against the wounds.

They waited with increasing impatience. The sooner they could get far away from this place, the better. Fenn was reminded of the time he waited behind Askari's hut for Kaela to appear, and had the same feeling of frustration that precious time was being wasted.

There was nothing he could do but wait. Or was there?

'Wait here, I won't be a moment. If Hakon arrives, keep him here.'

He picked up the basket and moved into the forest heading for the food store. Inside, he used his axe to cut down pieces of venison which he packed into the basket. He was going to add a fowl but it had not been plucked and would take up too much room. On an impulse, he felt for and found the staff he had left behind earlier; he would feel better if he didn't leave it behind. He shouldered the basket and left the store, glancing around the corner of the building. The festivities were continuing at the fire which had been built up so the flames were taller than a man. Between the bursts of noise from the people crowded around the fire, Fenn could hear music from a wooden flute.

He returned to Kaela. Hakon was still missing. He set the basket on the ground. Kaela looked questioningly at it but Fenn just smiled and said: 'You'll see.'

He recalled that Hakon had said he would get 'other things', but couldn't think what he had meant. If he didn't arrive soon, Fenn would go and look for him.

Just as Fenn thought he could wait no longer, Hakon appeared beside the hut and Fenn stepped around the tree to catch his attention. Hakon hurried across the clearing with Fenn motioning to him to walk not run in case the movement could be seen from the fire.

'Where have you been?' Fenn asked. He should have been annoyed but he was more relieved.

'I get my axe,' Hakon said proudly, 'but is more difficult than I think.' He held up the red-handled axe. Fenn stared at him, appalled at the risk Hakon had taken to retrieve the axe. It must be very important to him.

'I want my sword but is underneath. If I move it, it make noise. I leave it there.' Fenn had to smile at his audacity.

Hakon reached over to Fenn and put an arm around his shoulders.

'Thank you for come. You save my life again.'

Fenn returned his greeting but was impatient now to leave. He handed Hakon his knife.

'We must go,' he said and looked at Kaela. 'Can you walk? If not, Hakon can carry the basket and I'll carry you.'

'I could walk away from this place with two broken legs,' said Kaela firmly.

She rose unsteadily to her feet and winced at some sudden pain, but waved him on when he reached to help her. He headed up the ridge with Kaela limping behind him and smiled into the darkness when she took hold of his belt to help her up to the top of the ridge. He waited at the top for Hakon to catch up and in a moment of quiet he thought he heard some movement further along the ridge, but he listened and it wasn't repeated.

He found he could use the staff to give him warning of the ground ahead and thereby make much faster progress through the forest than when he had been creeping towards the camp. He wasn't as worried about making noise now that they were leaving the camp and moving further away with every step.

*   *   *

'If Olgood and Gisele are being brought to the camp it will be along this road,' said Kaela. She had recovered quickly during the night, but she looked fatigued and Fenn could see she was not yet at full strength.

The sun had barely risen and the early morning light filled the spaces between the trees with a haze. A carpet of stillness covered the forest floor in these moments before the day came awake. It was so quiet, with the day creatures still to rise and the night creatures gone to rest, that the smallest sound seemed magnified.

They had walked through the forest during the night to reach the road and followed the road to the crossroads. Fenn had checked her when it was light enough. The ropes had cut into her wrists and elbows, but it was the damage at her ankles that concerned him the most. Kaela said her wounds were not hindering her.

Fenn stared along the eastern road. 'We need a place where we can watch the road. Somewhere where we can see what's coming. We must know how they're travelling and how many guards there are.'

Hakon pointed. 'That tree. At the top I see to next ridge.'

'Can you climb it?'

Hakon smiled and ran to the tree.

To Kaela Fenn said: 'Wait here. You need as much rest as you can get. Is there anything inside the basket that can help you? The blister ointment?' She nodded. 'Good,' he said. 'Call if you see any sign of pursuit from Lothar or Ragnall.'

Kaela settled herself behind a tree where she had a good view in all directions. Fenn rested his staff against the tree and set the basket down beside her. She opened it and gave a grunt of surprise when she discovered the meat stacked inside. She searched in the bottom of the basket for Askari's medicines. Fenn gently touched her shoulder. He didn't want to leave her – Lothar could arrive at any time – but he had no choice.

He ran down the eastern road looking for a place where they may be able to ambush the people bringing Olgood and Gisele to Lothar's camp. He needed somewhere that offered concealment but also where there was room to use his sling. They were only three so he was hoping for no more than six opponents. Of these he could hope to disable two or three from long range. He had to also hope there were no bowmen. His hope list was getting too long, but he knew there would be no better chance to rescue Olgood and Gisele.

He found a perfect spot a half mile from the crossroads at the top of a small hill. Anybody coming along the road would not see Fenn until they reached the top. He imagined Olgood and Gisele walking up the rise surrounded by six men. There was a grassy area where he could stand with a clear view through the trees of the road while Hakon and Kaela could wait beside the road and also be hidden. If he could take out three of the men, they had a chance.

Satisfied, he headed back to the crossroads. He reached Kaela at the same time as a whistle sounded from Hakon's tree. In a few moments he came running from the forest.

'I see two horses pull cart. Four men and driver. I think Olgood and Gisele on cart – not see them but look like cart has cage on top.'

'Horses?' said Fenn thoughtfully. 'Are the men walking or riding?'

'One drive. Four walk.'

Fenn formed a new plan.

'Are you recovered enough to stop the horses if they're running towards you?' he asked Kaela.

Kaela hesitated. 'That depends.' She wanted to ask some questions but saw he needed a decision. 'But... yes, with Hakon's help I think I can.'

'Good,' said Fenn. 'If all goes well, the horses and cart will soon be running down this road, hopefully without a driver.'

They looked at each other and nodded.

Fenn left them discussing what each would do to stop the runaway horses and ran along the road towards the place he had chosen for the ambush.

*   *   *

The horses slowed at the bottom of the rise, and Fenn could see that Hakon's count was accurate. Two men walked on each side of the cart. Fenn crossed one 'hope' off his list – there were less than six men. None carried a bow, and he mentally crossed that 'hope' off the list also. He smiled to himself. Now the list was manageable. It took only a moment to unwrap his sling and take two stones from his bag. One he placed in the sling, letting it hang from his hand. The second stone he held ready in his other hand, his fingers absentmindedly rubbing the smooth surface.

The horses walked steadily up the rise. Fenn checked that his footing was stable with no tree-roots nearby then turned his full attention to the approaching horses. He had ensured there were clear channels through the trees and he rehearsed in his mind the order of his shots. Number one would be sent down the first channel. At their current pace, the horses will have walked two or three steps before the stone hit and two or three more before the sling was whirling again. They should then be framed in the second channel of trees for the second shot. He needed to aim slightly in front of his targets to allow for their movement. Each of the gaps between the trees was only a few feet wide so his accuracy would be tested, but he was not worried on that score – he knew his stones would fly true. No time for second guessing now, anyway – he was committed.

He set the sling swaying when the horses were only moments away from the first target area and started it swinging around his head when their heads came into view.

The first stone whistled between the trees and Fenn was already loading the second when it struck the driver on the head knocking him sideways. Fenn expected him to fall from the cart but some reflex action caused him to hold on as he fell. His body was half in and half out of the cart when the second stone struck the meaty thigh of the near horse. The animal let out a pained squeal and leapt forward startling its companion and in a heartbeat the cart was racing along the road out of control, carrying two passengers clinging tightly to the bars of the cage and the stunned driver who somehow had still not fallen.

The men stopped in alarm and looked about to see if they were under attack and by what, but Fenn was no longer in the grassy area. He was already running through the forest towards the crossroads at full speed.

When he reached his destination he was breathing hard and a hundred yards away down the west road he could see the horses and the cart carrying Olgood and Gisele inside a cage. Kaela and Hakon had them stopped but were struggling to get them turned. The shouts of the men behind him came to his ears. They were out of sight but would be here before long. If he ran to meet Kaela and Hakon he would just be drawing the men to them. Until the horses were under control it would be difficult to fight as well as hold them, and he didn't want to risk losing Olgood and Gisele now.

He turned to face the oncoming men.

They were spaced out on the road but they would reach him well before Kaela could possibly get the horses back to the crossroads. He still held his sling and in a moment it was spinning above his head. The stone flew when the first man was only ten yards away and he collapsed as if he had fallen asleep on the spot. There was no time for a second shot as the second man jumped over the first and flung himself forward. Fenn dropped the sling and reached for his axe. He parried the man's blow which was weakened from his lengthy run, swayed to his left and swung the axe at the back of the man's head as his momentum carried him past. The axe connected and the man fell.

The remaining two men had slowed and now spread out on the crossroads. Fenn could hear the sound of the horses blowing and stamping behind him but they did not seem to be closer. He would need to hold these two men until Kaela and Hakon arrived. He saw the men glance over his shoulder at the horses. They knew they had to move fast. They separated further and came at Fenn from two directions, swords held high. Fenn backed away, but they rushed forward together. Fenn raised his axe, turning alternately from one to the other but could not defend in two directions at once – he would have to choose one. The sound of the horses was closer and he also heard running footsteps, probably Hakon, but they would both arrive too late.

A man stepped from the forest to stand beside Fenn.

For a moment Fenn thought the man he had hit had revived and that now he had three to contend with. He took an involuntary step to the side, but he saw at a glance this was someone new. The man was big, as tall as Fenn, with a large chest and thick arms. With a shock of recognition Fenn knew it was the outlaw that Kaela had fought about ten feet from where they now stood. He was watching the other men and Fenn sensed that he was here to help and meant him no harm.

The man said something to Fenn but he did not understand the words. He looked back to their two opponents who had halted with the appearance of the stranger out of the trees. They looked at each other uncertainly. Fenn's ears told him the horses were only moments away, and so were the running feet, and because of their hesitation the men knew their opportunity was gone. They both turned and ran back down the eastern road.

Fenn looked back to see Hakon running hard ahead of the cart which was now approaching at speed. Fenn was concerned that Kaela would be unable to halt the horses, but she was standing on the cart holding the ropes with one hand and the whip with the other, perfectly balanced and in full control. She looked glorious, her red hair swirling in the wind. The horses slowed and stopped a few feet away and Hakon reached Fenn breathing heavily. He indicated the fleeing men, willing to chase if Fenn wanted. Fenn glanced at the men now disappearing from sight among the forest foliage and shook his head. It was unnecessary and they couldn't afford the time. Best if they were away from here as soon as possible.

Fenn turned to the outlaw. He said 'Thokk' and held out his hand, which the man, after a moment's hesitation, grasped, and then winced as if in pain. Fenn saw his arm at the elbow was bloodstained. Kaela jumped down from the cart and held the horses, stroking the neck of the nearest one and calming it and Fenn saw the reason why she had stood while driving. The driver was still lying across the seat.

Kaela said something to the big man. Fenn was surprised by her tone. He was sure this was the man she had fought but she seemed friendly toward him.

'Can you please thank this man for his help,' he asked her, 'and then tell me why you didn't throw *this* one off the cart.' Fenn stooped to retrieve his sling while she replied.

'Olgood asked us not to,' said Kaela.

'Good to see you too,' called Olgood from the cage, a trace of good-natured sarcasm in this voice. 'I want my axe and the driver has it. I also want to get out of this cage.'

Fenn pulled the axe from the driver's belt and hauled him onto the ground. He searched the man looking for a key but found nothing. He checked the lock on the cage.

'Hakon, can you cut their bonds.' To Olgood and Gisele he said: 'Welcome back, but you'll need to stay there a while. It will take something heavy to break the lock.'

Kaela said something more to the big man and seemed astonished at his reply. She was about to continue the conversation when Fenn interrupted her.

'Wait. Let's talk later. We need to leave. We'll travel faster if we take the cart.' He indicated the big man. 'Ask him what he's going to do now.'

'His name is Gunther.'

'Tell Gunther we're going south. Is he coming with us?'

She put Fenn's question to him.

He uttered a reply, sheathed his own sword and bent to pick up the sword of the fallen driver. He inserted it into the lock of the cage and, with a powerful two-handed twist, pulled the lock apart. Gunther helped Gisele then Olgood out of the cage and used the sword to slice through the ropes tying the cage to the cart. With Olgood's help the cage was lifted off the cart and thrown to the ground. Gunther tossed the sword aside and took a seat on the back of the cart.

Fenn and Kaela shared a glance; Fenn raising his eyebrows at Gunther's demonstration of ability and strength.

He checked the road and the forest. After the burst of recent activity, it now looked peaceful and quiet. How long would it stay that way? After he had freed Kaela and Hakon and they had left the camp, he had no way of knowing when their absence had been noticed. They had heard no pursuit during the night but he had to assume that by now Lothar, and probably Ragnall and Olaf as well, were looking for them.

'Everybody onto the cart,' he called.

Fenn dragged the man he had felled with the sling to the side of the road to join the other two and then passed the basket and his staff up to Olgood. Olgood frowned when he took the basket. 'This is heavier than before – what do you have in here?'

'A surprise,' said Fenn, smiling.

Olgood placed the basket and staff behind the driver's seat then took Hakon's arm to help him up. Hakon rose from the ground as if he'd decided to fly, uttering a cry of surprise.

Fenn said to Kaela: 'Drive south and don't tarry. I've a feeling Lothar is close. I want to get out of this forest and I don't care if I never see it again.'

'He said he'll come with us; he has nowhere else to go,' said Kaela belatedly, nodding at Gunther.

Fenn climbed on board and sat on the side of the cart next to the big man. He reached out to clasp Olgood by the shoulder and at the same time squeezed Gisele's hand. He had to bite down on the emotions threatening to surface now that they were reunited at last. He would have liked to give them a more personal greeting and saw his thoughts mirrored in their eyes, but he knew that must wait.

Kaela flicked the whip and turned the horses onto the south road. Fenn imagined their hooves treading over the top of the footprints they had left behind the last time they had travelled along this road. Several eventful days had passed and they were once again starting out from the crossroads.

There was a whistling sound followed by the impact of an arrow as it embedded itself deep into the trunk of a tree three feet from Fenn's shoulder.

Kaela needed no urging. With a sharp crack of the whip and a loud 'Haa!' the horses leapt forward, the cart rocking wildly as they struggled to find their rhythm.

'Hold tight!' she cried.

Through the trees, Fenn saw movement on the western road, men were running forward and more were in the forest. He could only watch as two more arrows rose lazily into the air and sped towards the cart.

CHAPTER TWENTY-TWO

An extra sword…

It was Kaela's quick reaction that saved them. The arrows thudded into the ground where the cart had been only a moment before, so close that Fenn reflexively drew up his knees to get his legs out of the way. His gaze quickly returned to the sky but there were no more arrows as every stride of the horses increased the distance between the men now gathering at the crossroads and the rapidly moving cart. Hakon let out a shout of triumph and patted Kaela on the back. He thrust an obscene gesture towards the men and called out a string of words in the Northmen's language.

When they were out of sight, Kaela slowed the horses to a canter and Fenn was able to relax his grip on the cart.

'Does Lothar have horses?' he asked. 'Hakon – can you ask Gunther?'

Gunther shook his head at Hakon's question, but Kaela said: 'Lothar's cousin Malthus arrived on a horse, so they have one.'

'One horse,' said Fenn thoughtfully.

Olgood said: 'Malthus? Did he look like a weasel?'

Kaela turned to him and smiled. 'Yes. Tiny eyes and a big nose.'

'I know him,' said Olgood.

'Do you know the colour of the horse?'

Kaela said: 'No,' but Olgood said: 'The Weasel's horse was black.'

Fenn said: 'We can outdistance men who are on foot but if I was Lothar, I'd send a man on that horse to follow us.'

As they approached the place where they had previously left the road and crossed the swamp to the willow grove, they discussed whether it was worthwhile retrieving the swords that had been left at the camp, Kaela explaining the discussion to both Gisele and Gunther. When Gunther understood they were swords taken from the first fight at the crossroads, he spoke urgently to Kaela.

'He says one of those swords may be his. He said he will fetch the swords if you want him to, and he'll do it quickly.'

'He take swords and run, sell them in market,' said Hakon in English.

'I don't think so,' said Kaela. 'In any case, Gunther doesn't know where they are. One of us must go.'

Fenn looked at Gunther who was calmly waiting for the decision, his eyes flicking to each person that spoke.

'It'll take time to get the swords, which we can ill afford. Do we all agree it's worthwhile?' Fenn asked.

'I don't think we need the swords but better to have them than not,' said Olgood.

Gisele seemed surprised to be asked her opinion. She glanced at Gunther, then nodded also.

'Hakon?'

'You all agree. You not need me.'

'If you don't agree we'll leave the swords where they lie,' said Fenn.

Hakon looked at Fenn in surprise.

'This affects all of us. We are all together,' said Fenn.

Hakon studied Fenn. He stared at the ground passing beneath the cart and blew out his breath. He nodded.

Fenn touched Hakon on the shoulder.

'When we stop, can you watch the road?'

Kaela had covered the wounds on her arms and ankles with a white paste which had hardened to form a protective cover so Fenn did not want her to enter the swamp water.

Olgood volunteered to fetch the swords. He crossed the two pools and made his way carefully through the grass, moving slowly and checking where he placed his feet. It took only a few moments to reach the log and find the hidden swords which he held aloft in triumph. Olgood retraced his steps across the swamp and handed the swords to an eagerly waiting Gunther. From Gunther's reaction one *was* his sword – he quickly unbuckled the one he was wearing and replaced it.

Hakon and Olgood did not want to wear an extra sword, preferring their axes, and neither did Fenn or Gisele, so Gunther's old sword and the second sword from under the log were laid on the floor of the cart.

Fenn looked at Olgood and said: 'We can sell these swords to replace the coins we lost.'

Olgood frowned at him. 'Lost? But we still have the purse, don't we?'

'Do you still have it? I was sure it would be taken from you.'

'No, I left it with *you*.' Olgood pulled the basket toward him and opened it. His eyes widened and he grinned broadly when he saw the contents. He felt for a moment in the bottom and brought out one of the woollen hats from which he withdrew the purse of coins.

Fenn smiled, hefting the purse in his hand. 'So it was there all this time. I didn't know I was carrying it.'

Gunther noticed the coin purse and recognised it. He said something to Kaela, who shook her head and waved her hands in denial.

Fenn was intrigued. 'What did he say?'

Kaela put her hands on her hips, reluctant to answer him. Fenn continued to look at her, until she rolled her eyes and said: 'He said the ring in that purse belonged to a Saxon lady, a noble. He thinks I should wear it.'

'And I agree with him, but I think it's best to keep it in the purse for now.'

He paused and then added with a mischievous grin: 'It's a little too fine for a dirty peasant to be wearing.'

He waited for her reaction and was rewarded by a quick intake of breath and flaring eyes but she realised immediately he was teasing and she reached out to pinch his arm with a smile. She was fast but he was waiting for such a move and stepped away keeping himself just out of her reach.

He laughed in triumph, then said more seriously: 'I'll place it on your finger when we step onto our own shores.'

When the cart was moving again, Gunther took out his sword and examined it, running his hand down the blade. On an impulse, through Kaela, Fenn asked Gunther what was special about his sword. In reply Gunther turned the sword over and handed it to Fenn. Fenn accepted the weapon and inspected it. With the weapon in his hand, he remembered that after the fight at the crossroads, it was he who had taken Gunther's sword and worn it but he had never removed it from its scabbard. He held the sword by the handle. He was no swordsman but it felt well balanced. He handed it back to Gunther.

Gunther didn't accept the sword. Instead he picked up the other sword from the floor of the cart. For a moment, Fenn thought he wanted to stage a fight of some sort, but Gunther presented the other sword for comparison. Gunther held his old sword by the handle and Fenn saw that his hand did not properly fit. Then he noticed how big Gunther's hands were. They were massive and meaty – half as large again as Fenn's although the two men were the same height. Now that he could make the comparison, Fenn also saw that Gunther's sword was larger and the handle longer than the other sword. He nodded his understanding and handed Gunther his weapon.

*   *   *

Fenn stood concealed behind a group of bushes at the top of a hill from where he had a good view of the long half-mile stretch of straight road they had just travelled. Gisele and Hakon waited with the horses by the side of the road twenty yards away over the hill. Beside Fenn, Olgood, Kaela and Gunther also gazed down the road.

'If men on foot appear, we'll simply get back on the cart and ride on,' said Fenn, Kaela relaying his words to Gunther. 'If a lone horseman comes on a black horse, whether it is Malthus or not, we must assume he's from Lothar and stop him and take his horse.'

'And if many horsemen come?' asked Kaela.

'That's a chance we have to take. We'll decide whether to fight or run. This is a good place to make a stand.' He glanced around again. 'Olgood you stay here with me, Kaela and Gunther on the other side of the road. Kaela, the horse is your responsibility.'

'I'll stand back there,' Fenn pointed to where two large trees stood with room behind them to swing his sling. 'I'll try to take the man off his horse but if I miss you three must drag him down.'

When Kaela translated for Gunther, he asked her a question.

'Gunther asks: How will you take the man off his horse?'

Fenn unwrapped his sling from his belt. Gunther's eyes widened and he gave Kaela a look of disbelief but he said nothing.

'I saw you hit a bear twice on the nose with that,' said Kaela. 'You said the last was a lucky shot. It'll take a very lucky shot to hit a man riding fast and sitting low on the horse.'

'A lucky shot or a good shot,' said Olgood. He laid his hand on Fenn's shoulder. 'I've seen his sling at work many times, and this man is very good. Even his bad shots are good.'

Kaela smiled. She stepped forward and kissed Fenn lightly on the lips. 'If Olgood vouches for you, we have nothing to worry about.'

She beckoned to Gunther and they crossed the road.

'We may have a while to wait,' called Fenn, 'but don't make yourselves too comfortable.'

Kaela turned as she was walking away and pointed at Fenn – the gesture saying: '…that applies to you too'.

Fenn sorted his stones, found the one he wanted and returned the others to his bag. The stone he had selected was shaped like a slightly flattened bird's egg narrowed at each end. He knew from experience this shape of stone flew truest. He stretched the muscles in his back and legs and was just settling in to wait when a horseman appeared at the far end of the road, riding fast. Fenn placed the stone in the sling. This was much sooner than he had expected. If they had not stopped to wait for him, at the speed he was riding the horseman would have caught up with them a few miles down the road.

There was no way he could be certain this man was riding the horse from Lothar's camp. If he had been riding at a leisurely pace Fenn's doubt may have been greater but the man was in a hurry, not riding at full speed but maintaining a steady gallop – and his horse was black. It was still possible he was an innocent man going about his normal business but the coincidence was too great and so was the risk of letting him pass.

Fenn had a clear view between the trees but he was satisfied he would not be seen by the rider. As the horse came closer, he saw that the man was riding low, as Kaela had predicted, and his head would be obscured by the horse until he was very close at which time he would be passing at high speed. Fenn estimated the point where he would have a clear shot at the man's head and, at the speed he was travelling, where he would need to aim.

He started the sling turning.

It whirled faster until it seemed to match exactly the rhythm of the pounding hoof-beats of the galloping horse. Fenn took a breath and held it. His fingers and the muscles of his arm became part of the sling as it rotated above his head. His eyes flicked to the point where he would release then back to the horseman, keeping his release point in his peripheral vision, tracking the horse and rider, his mind calculating continuously.

When all the pieces coincided he lifted his finger and freed the stone which sped between the trees and he knew the cast was good. From the corner of his eye he saw Olgood and two other figures moving onto the road. He was concentrating on the stone. Time slowed and he watched the stone spin lazily along its destined path to the place where it would converge with its target.

Fenn's focus was such that he saw precisely where the stone hit the man behind his ear, and was then diverted upwards by the impact.

The man crumpled as if his bones had been removed and slipped from the side of the horse, hitting the road with a thump and rolling over several times. With Olgood's help, Kaela caught and held the horse and they managed to bring it to a halt twenty yards down the road where it stood breathing heavily. Gunther bent over the still frame of the rider. He stood up and shook his head. He called to Kaela.

'His neck is broken, either by the stone or by the fall,' she said, walking the horse back toward Fenn.

'We need to hide him,' said Fenn. Kaela talked to Gunther who pulled the man onto his shoulder. Olgood lifted the man's head.

'The Weasel,' he said. 'Malthus.'

'So now we have each killed a relative of Lothar the Hun, and he is not the forgiving type,' observed Kaela drily.

Gunther carried the body into the trees. The others waited and he returned a few moments later. He looked at Fenn and said a sentence to Kaela.

'He says he has not seen a shot like that before. Not even the best archer he has known could make that shot – through the trees. He thinks the gods must favour you.' Kaela paused. 'I agree with him.'

Olgood smiled.

'Luck was with me,' said Fenn. 'He only had to lean forward at the wrong time…'

'Perhaps a small piece of luck, but only a small piece,' said Olgood.

Kaela drew the horse closer. 'I'll ride the horse. Hakon can drive the cart.'

Fenn nodded and walked toward the cart while Kaela mounted, feeling a mixture of emotions. He was pleased they had stopped the horseman and removed the threat he posed. He was relieved it was the horse from the camp but he was also saddened that whoever this man was and whatever he had done, Fenn's action had resulted in his death.

*   *   *

'He is outlaw. We should not trust.'

Hakon had come to talk with Fenn who was leaning his back against a tree while Kaela was watering the horses on the edge of the Ruslager lake.

According to Hakon the town of Ruslager was located at the end of the lake about ten miles away.

Olgood and Gisele were sitting a few yards away absorbed in their own company and Gunther was nearby, carefully sharpening his sword on a stone.

'Did you know him before?' asked Fenn.

'No. I not know him. But he is outlaw. Bad man.'

'He may have saved my life at the crossroads.'

Hakon shook his head in frustration.

'Yes. Maybe he try to help me too.'

'What? How?'

'A long story. I tell you another day. But he may do these things so we help him escape from Lothar. He may be dangerous man. We thank him and then he should go.'

Fenn sighed. 'We should find out more about the man. I'll ask Kaela to talk to him when she's finished.'

'I talk to him. I tell him to go.'

Fenn put a hand on his shoulder. 'I understand what you're saying, and maybe we will part ways, but Gunther deserves credit for helping us when we needed it.' He thought for a moment. 'He also said something to Kaela earlier that surprised her and I want to ask her about that.'

Kaela was now allowing the horses to graze and Fenn walked up to her. He expected Hakon to follow, but when he turned back, Hakon was staring over the lake. He crept up behind Kaela and put his arm around her waist then leaned down and kissed her neck. She turned her head to him and raised her hand to caress his cheek.

'Walk over to the trees with me,' he said, drawing her away from the horses who seemed contented with the rich grass beside the lake. They sat beside an oak that was large enough for them both to lean back against. Kaela looked at him expectantly.

'Firstly, how are your wounds?'

Kaela touched the hard ring of paste on one of her ankles, now darkened by a covering of dust. 'When this falls off, it will be healed underneath.'

'They aren't painful?'

She smiled ruefully. 'Compared with the pain when they were being made, I barely notice them.'

He looked at her.

'Tell me what happened to you,' he said softly.

Kaela drew in a deep breath and let it out slowly.

Starting at the time she and Hakon left the meadow, she related her story including the capture at the barn and the second fight with Gunther. She made little of the time she had been tied to the pole but Fenn had seen enough of that to be able to imagine her ordeal. He drew her to him and held her tightly, relieving some of his own pain with the embrace.

'That explains Gunther's appearance at the crossroads,' he said. He looked into her eyes. 'He said something to you at that time that surprised you.'

'It was nothing important,' said Kaela.

Fenn took her by the shoulders, his eyebrows raised. He could see she didn't want to elaborate, but he gave her shoulders a gentle but insistent shake.

Kaela sighed. 'He said his sword was mine.'

'His sword was yours? What did he mean? Why would he say that?'

'I asked him later, after he had regained his own sword. He said that I had spared his life twice.' Kaela stopped but Fenn could see there was more.

'And...' he prompted.

'He said his life was mine and he would fight for me. When I told him I didn't want that, he just shrugged as if it was his destiny whether I wanted it or not.'

Fenn sat back. 'He's a useful man to have on your side,' he said. 'But Hakon raised a good point. Why was Gunther with Lothar's band of outlaws? We need to know that and now is a good time to ask.'

Fenn stood up, but turned back to Kaela and asked: 'Anything more?' She hesitated long enough for him to know there was.

'Gunther calls me 'Lady'.'

'Do you know why?'

'Probably because of the sword I wear and that I know how to use it. He doesn't know it's not mine.'

'I've seen you use it,' said Fenn seriously. 'That sword belongs to you.'

Fenn walked back to the others with Kaela following. He called to Hakon and beckoned him over.

They sat in a circle. Through Kaela, Fenn spoke to Gunther.

'We need to know why you were with Lothar. Are you an outlaw?'

Gunther looked at each of them, his face worried.

Kaela said something to him and explained: 'I told Gunther you would be fair.'

Gunther took a breath and answered. Kaela translated.

'I killed a man in a fight over a woman. I didn't know the man – or the woman. He hit the woman in the street and she fell in front of me. I picked her up and he tried to hit me. He drew his sword and I had no choice. He was angry – out of control. If I hadn't killed him he would have killed me.'

Gunther shook his head, not liking the memory. Fenn motioned for him to continue.

'I'm a farmer. I had some land – it was good land but small. They took my farm for *wergild* but the man was important and the farm wasn't enough. They said I must serve his family as a thrall for ten years. I escaped into Skyrvid and found Lothar – or, rather, he found me. He heard of my fight and he wanted me to fight again and again. That man Lothar – he isn't right in the head.' Gunther tapped his forehead. 'He used me to punish and kill anyone he doesn't like. If I don't fight it is my life that is cut short. I fought the men and I killed them.' He paused. 'He said if I ran he would hunt me. Why would I run? I had nowhere to go.'

He stopped and Fenn thought he had finished, but after a moment he said: 'Then I met...' Gunther kept talking but Kaela stopped the translation. Hakon looked at her. 'You want I talk for you?'

Kaela shook her head. 'He said – then I met the Lady. She killed Baradin and could have killed me...' Kaela paused again.

Hakon added: 'He say – with sword that moved faster than snake.'

Kaela smiled grimly and caught up with the translation.

'I was ready for death at that moment. I didn't want to continue down the path my life had taken.'

Gunther let his eyes drop to the ground then he raised them and looked at Fenn while he spoke.

'I wasn't sorry to see Baradin killed. Good riddance, I say – he was as bad as his brother. But Lothar blamed me for Baradin's death. He knows I didn't like Baradin and thinks I didn't protect him – I *let* him get killed. Lothar was looking for a way to kill me and thought he had found it when he captured the Lady.'

He glanced at Kaela who said something to him in his language. She looked at Fenn: 'I told him my name is Kaela and he can call me that.'

Gunther continued, this time addressing his words to Kaela: 'I had to fight you. I think you understand. It would have been cowardly to run without fighting. I fought you with all my strength. I'm sorry for that, but Lothar would have known if I didn't, and he would have had an excuse to kill us both.' He shrugged his broad shoulders. 'But your sword is better than mine and I have never said that to anyone before. I took the opportunity you gave me to run into the forest so I could return and free you, and your small friend.' He waved at Hakon.

'I was watching when this man – Hakon – escaped, I knew they would hunt him. He hid in a tree and was safe there, but he came out of the tree at the wrong time, just as one of Lothar's men was approaching.'

He regarded Hakon. 'You didn't see him behind you. You should be dead but I was able to stop the man before he completed the blow that would have taken your head.'

Hakon was staring at Gunther with an open mouth.

Gunther turned his attention back to Fenn.

'I was going to free the Lady…' Kaela shook her head but continued. '…during the night and I was watching when you arrived and set her free. I was ready to help you if you needed it.'

'Now I think I have another chance, another life. The Lady has given me a chance. I have sworn my sword to her. My sword is hers until my debt is paid. Where she goes – where *you* go, I will go too.'

Gunther sat back when Kaela had finished and Fenn looked around.

'Does anyone want to say anything?'

Kaela stood up. 'Hakon, will you translate what I say?' When Hakon agreed, she said: 'I will say this.' She pointed at Gunther. 'You will *not* call me 'Lady' again. If you agree to that, I will absolve you of your vow and tell you that you are a free man to do as you will and your sword is your own.' She waited then said: 'You saved Hakon in the forest and I saw you stand with Fenn at the crossroads and that repays any debt you may have to me. But Fenn is our leader and it is his decision whether you stay with us.'

She turned to Fenn. 'I'm willing to give Gunther a chance. I say let him stay if he wants to stay.'

Fenn looked at Olgood, who said: 'I agree. By his account, the man has had foul luck and a bad judgement. His life has been out of his control. Everyone should have a second chance. I'll stand with him.'

Hakon got to his feet and said: 'I not sure before if man nearly kill me in forest. I believe what Gunther say is true and I thank him for my life. I say he free to do what he want.'

Kaela spoke to Gisele and translated her reply.

As usual, Gisele thought for a moment before speaking. She spoke to Fenn. 'You gave *me* another chance when my life was twisted in a way I didn't like. You freed me from a hopeless situation. I don't know this man but it would be wrong for me not to want the same for him.'

Fenn turned to Gunther and glanced at Kaela to translate.

'I agree. As Kaela said, from this moment you are a free man and your sword is your own. If you want to travel with us you are welcome to stay as long as you want but you should know we are headed to our homeland which is across the western sea.'

Gunther held out his huge hand to Fenn and Fenn grasped it firmly. Gunther then did the same to each of the others, keeping Kaela till last.

When he held Kaela's hand he bowed and said a few sentences to her before he let her hand go.

Kaela stood with her hands on her hips as Gunther stepped back. He pulled up his sleeve to reveal a bloody cloth wrapped around his elbow.

Kaela shook her head in resignation and said to Fenn: 'He said the one thing he would not give up in Lothar's camp was his honour, even though he was forced to kill. He thanks you for inviting him to travel with us, but his vow was to himself and only he can decide when his debt is paid. He said that time is not yet. His sword is still mine.'

Fenn nodded slowly. 'What happened to his arm? Did he say?'

'I did that with a sword. He said he treats it as a reminder.'

Kaela turned from Fenn and looked at Gunther with narrowed eyes.

'And he still called me 'Lady'.'

CHAPTER TWENTY-THREE

A troubled road south…

'Gisele wants to know if you liked the arrowhead tubers.'

Kaela and Gisele had come up behind Fenn who was filling the water skin in a fast-flowing stream. Wafted by the breeze, he could smell the smoke from the fire as it filtered among the trees of their camp, carrying with it the aroma of roasting venison. Nobody had eaten all day and the anticipation was mouth-watering.

Fenn was happy to have the chance to thank Gisele. 'Very much,' he answered. 'In a roundabout way they helped to save us all.' Fenn told her, through Kaela, how the tubers had allowed him to continue his search without needing to stop for food.

Gisele was pleased. 'I was lucky to find some ready to eat. They're only edible for a very short time.'

Fenn stood up. 'Speaking of food, the venison also smells ready to eat to me.'

'A few moments more,' said Kaela. 'Olgood is under strict instructions on how the meat must be cooked.'

'I can wait a few moments more,' said Fenn. 'I'm sure the venison will taste the better for it. While we're eating I want to hear what happened to Olgood and Gisele.'

Ruslager was many miles behind them. They had turned from the road and followed a small track into the hills, stopping when they were a mile beyond the road in a sheltered and watered valley.

At Fenn's suggestion they had split into three groups before entering Ruslager. Kaela said that Lothar had sent men to Ruslager looking for the group that killed Baradin, so their descriptions may be in the town.

Kaela left her sword in the cart and rode the black horse. Olgood, Gisele and Hakon drove the cart, with Olgood sitting on the back to disguise his height. Fenn and Gunther followed some distance behind on foot.

They had all passed through the town without incident. Kaela decided to buy vegetables and a small iron cooking pot at a market. When they joined up she reported she had heard that there was fighting to the south.

'The Northern Saxons have risen up against Charles the Great and his Franks. A man told me if we were travelling in that direction it would be best to avoid the area south of Hammaburg. He suggested once we cross the Albia river we should head to the coast.'

Fenn looked at Hakon. 'Hammaburg?'

'Big town on river Albia. Good market. My father sell spices there. Maybe two or three days.'

'Can we go around the town?'

'Must cross Albia somewhere. It is big river. Not sure. Never try to go around.'

When they stopped to rest and water the horses, Fenn asked to see Gunther's wound. He carefully unwound the cloth and cleaned the dried blood from the area. The cut was deep but had not caused serious damage. There was a weak scar that had not yet hardened. Fenn covered it with some fresh linen from the basket and remarked with dry humour that they should try to avoid further injury or they would run out of linen. He looked up at a snort from Kaela but her head was turned and he couldn't see her expression.

They kept the fire small enough to sit around in a circle. As they devoured the thick juicy venison steaks that had been slow roasted over the fire and picked the vegetables Kaela had bought from the cooking pot, Kaela and then Olgood told their stories starting from the time they left the willow camp with sometimes Kaela and sometimes Hakon translating for Gisele and Gunther.

Then it was Fenn's turn. When he started his story by saying how he had woken disoriented – not knowing how much time had passed and with his leg painfully swollen and constricted by the ligature, there were cries of surprise and concern. Everyone started to speak at once with Olgood overriding the others.

'But you were well when we left you, and had been for some time. You *insisted* both Gisele and I must go and search for these two.' He indicated Kaela and Hakon.

Fenn gave him a reassuring wave. 'I believe you but I don't remember that. It must have been only a temporary respite. Thankfully, I've had no more memory lapses since.'

He continued by describing his desperate cutting of the band of linen around his leg. Kaela's face became pained and she insisted on inspecting his cuts. He pulled up his trouser leg and removed the cloth covering and found the wounds had healed well. Kaela wanted to say more about him cutting into his leg to release the tie but found it hard to decide whether his action was stupid or brave and whether she should be angry or proud.

He looked at Kaela as he related how a splinter in his hand had led him to find her message in the barn. He reached out to hold her by the shoulder and tried to convey the huge relief the message brought him – it had changed his quest from impossible to possible.

He smiled as he added: '…once I understood it.' He paused and looked around the group. From their sober expressions, he could see that everyone shared his appreciation of how important that moment had been in bringing them all back together.

He described his journey to Lothar's camp and the rescue of Kaela and Hakon. When Fenn told of filling the basket with venison and finished his story at the crossroads in Skyrvid Forest, Gunther made a comment that made Kaela laugh and she translated it for the others.

'I can tell you this,' said Gunther, 'Lothar's venison has never tasted better.'

The cart proved to have a second use when it provided good shelter during a period of rain squalls as night fell. Fenn settled his back comfortably against a wheel and held Kaela close feeling her breathing slow as she drifted into sleep, her head resting on his chest.

Fenn slept soundly for the first time in many days and woke refreshed in the morning.

He could see Kaela at the stream, Olgood and Gisele transferring some handfuls of berries or nuts into the basket, and Hakon and Gunther sitting on a log in conversation. Fenn stretched and crawled out from under the cart. Everyone seemed to be relaxed and he sensed a reluctance to return to the road as they all relished the feeling of freedom from their recent torments and the lack of immediate danger. The valley was calm and the early morning sun was warm on Fenn's face. He closed his eyes and felt that warmth on his eyelids. When he opened his eyes again the scene had not changed.

Kaela rose from the stream where she had been washing the cooking pot and seeing that Fenn was awake, walked up the slight rise toward him. As she passed Olgood and Gisele, she bent to place the pot into the basket.

'I don't think it will take Lothar long to buy, borrow or steal some horses,' she said casually, when she reached Fenn's side. 'He may be riding this way as we speak.'

This broke the bubble of contentedness that had settled over the small valley. Fenn got immediately to his feet and with renewed energy they packed the cart and headed back to the road.

*   *   *

The number of people passing in the opposite direction increased throughout the day and Fenn noticed their weapons were drawing uneasy glances. He suggested that they should put their swords and axes into the cart but Kaela was not going to be without her sword again and reminded him they were heading toward a place where fighting had been reported.

Kaela stopped a family and asked where they had come from. A man and woman were leading the group which consisted of two couples, one older, and three girls ranging in age from a young woman to a child of around six years. The man was pushing a small wheeled cart laden with clothing, bedding and farm tools. Kaela talked with the man for some time with Gunther also asking questions. While Gunther was talking, Kaela reported that these people were farmers from south of Hammaburg and were moving away from the advancing Frankish army. Apparently, the Saxons had attacked the Franks at a town called Verden but had been beaten in the battle and were now being pushed back to the north. As they advanced, unruly bands of Franks were roaming the countryside on the far side of the river, stealing anything of value and taking food and livestock. The man said he'd heard whole families including children had been slaughtered if there was resistance, with the women raped before they were killed. He'd also heard some farmers were burning their crops and killing their cattle to deny them to the Franks. He said it was the fourth time his family had fled north in the last ten years. Many people were stopping in Hammaburg where there was a walled castle but the man thought the castle would be attacked. He did not think it was safe there and was taking his family further north. He advised Kaela to turn around and wait two or three weeks before trying to travel south.

Fenn watched the family walking away and thought of the hundreds of people whose lives were uprooted on such a regular basis and the innate strength that allowed them to overcome the devastation and rebuild their lives again and again. Forces beyond their control surged around them – they simply moved out of the way and when the conflict had passed they returned and tried to continue as they had before.

When they reached a fork in the road, Hakon pointed to the left road saying that was the road to Hammaburg, adding that he did not know where the other road led as he had never taken it. He agreed it was possible the right-hand road may take them around the town. It was better than the alternative, so Hakon turned the horses onto the right fork.

The next day the road branched at a major river and continued both eastwards and westwards along the river bank. Hakon said this was the Albia. They stood on a high bank and looked over the river. They seemed to be a long way from the coast but even at this point the river looked to be almost a mile wide. After a discussion, it was decided that if they went west it was unlikely they would be able to cross the river with the horses.

They reluctantly turned eastward, knowing they would be heading toward Hammaburg and followed the northern bank of the Albia for many miles. As each step of the horses took them east and not south, Fenn considered leaving the animals and the cart and swimming the river as they had done in the land of the Northmen, then continuing on foot – but the horses had proven to be such a boost to the speed of their travel he was reluctant to part with them. Hakon said there was a bridge at Hammaburg where they could cross with the horses and there may be another bridge before the town.

All day they travelled along the river bank. The Albia showed no sign of narrowing and Fenn realised that it would probably still be wide enough at Hammaburg to allow sea-going trading vessels to reach the town.

Fenn moved to sit close to Hakon who was driving the cart.

'What is Hammaburg like? How big is the town?'

'Same size as Ruslager but there is a castle there – outside of the town. Town is on river but not good place – many swamps around town.' He thought then added: 'I know *Herzog* Widukind, Saxon leader, stay there, but maybe Franks push him out. Widukind related to Danes, married to Geva, daughter of Danish king – I see him in Hedeby before.'

'*Herzog?* What is that? A king?'

'Not king. A…' Hakon struggled for the word.

Kaela was riding alongside the cart. '*Herzog* is a war leader – like a Duke,' she said.

Fenn smiled at her and then asked: 'How far to the Hammaburg bridge?'

'Not sure if we reach today – maybe tomorrow,' replied Hakon.

Fenn looked at the sky. It was a clear day with no sign of bad weather on the horizon.

'We don't want to get involved in any fighting and we don't want to stumble onto anything in the night. We'll find a place to camp so we reach the bridge in daylight tomorrow.'

*   *   *

The last of the venison that Fenn had taken from Lothar's food-store had been eaten the previous night so Hakon and Olgood decided they would hunt for the meal that evening. Gisele rolled her eyes but smiled when they insisted. Hakon performed what he said was an old hunting dance with such enthusiasm that he had everyone laughing. Fenn put an arm around Kaela's shoulders and held her close as Hakon crouched and mimed a fowl of some sort trying to escape with frantically flapping wings. Kaela laughed freely at Hakon's antics and slipped her arm around Fenn's waist, leaning her weight against him. Fenn marvelled at her laughter – it was uninhibited and sounded like pure music to his ears. It had been a long time since he had felt this contented.

Hakon finally lay exhausted and defeated on the ground and the small crowd applauded. Olgood gave him a good-natured kick to get him to his feet. He took two snares and they set off into the hills. When they were out of sight, Gisele revealed with a secretive smile another snare she had been hiding in her hand. Kaela encouraged her with a pat on the back and she strolled into the trees in the opposite direction. Gunther was looking puzzled so Kaela explained Gisele's extraordinary hunting abilities. He remained sceptical but was prepared to wait and see.

Kaela tended to the horses while Gunther and Fenn gathered wood. Fenn checked Gunther's wound and was about to discard the old covering and replace it when Kaela took the stained linen from him then walked to the stream and washed it while he completed rebinding the wound.

She offered the wet linen to him with an exaggerated flourish, deliberately flicking some water onto his tunic and, adopting a superior tone, she said: 'Look and learn some simple facts my ignorant boy – we *will* have linen enough if we just learn to wash…'

But she was unable to continue because his hand had swiftly covered her mouth. With his other arm he lifted her from her feet and carried her to the stream. She squirmed and squealed behind his hand but he held her easily with her arms pinned and she was unable to get free. He waded into the stream and stopped at the edge of a deep pool.

'Would you like to repeat that comment?'

Slowly he lifted his hand from her mouth.

She remained quiet and still until his hand was completely removed then she quickly said:

'Of course, I wouldn't expect a poor uneducated man-child to know…'

He let her fall.

In the instant her arm was free Kaela caught hold of his sleeve for purchase and hooked a foot behind his knee pulling sharply with her leg. She twisted her body, dragging his arm in the same direction as the knee that no longer supported him. Together they tumbled into the pool, each becoming fully submerged in a flurry of splashes and a tangle of limbs.

Kaela was up first, standing waist deep in the stream, water cascading from every part. She gave a whoop of triumph which turned to a cry of concern as Fenn remained face down in the pool. Kaela bent and turned him, lifting his face free of the water, her eyes and hands searching for a head wound, putting her face close to his to see if he was breathing. Fenn's arms locked around her neck and he kissed her as they fell once again into the pool and under the water.

Gunther was watching in puzzled amusement when they emerged smiling and dripping from the stream.

Gisele returned first. She displayed two plump wildfowl but allowed only brief admiration before she hid them behind a tree. Kaela glanced meaningfully at Gunther, with an 'I told you so' expression and he nodded his acknowledgement. When she had re-joined them, Gisele talked to Kaela who said: 'Gisele saw the fresh tracks of a boar but she would need to dig a pit to capture it.'

Fenn nodded, licking his lips. 'It would be nice to have but we can't spare the time.'

Olgood and Hakon arrived back at dusk, empty-handed.

Hakon rushed ahead and said: 'We get some rats in snare but Olgood not want to bring back. I say better than nothing but he rather go hungry.'

Gisele had to turn away to hide her smile.

Kaela was not so bashful. 'No matter,' she said as she walked to the trees. 'These two fowl wandered into the camp and offered themselves to us.'

Hakon stared at the birds open-mouthed and Olgood stood for a moment trying to decide if he should be angry for being made the fool. Then he gave a growl and enveloped Gisele in a hug, tousling her hair. She laughed with delight.

Fenn slapped him on the shoulder and said: 'You'll do better next time. I hear the rats are *huge* south of the Albia.' He easily ducked beneath Olgood's swinging arm.

Hakon stared at them and shook his head in bewilderment.

*   *   *

Fenn thought it worthwhile to keep a watch during the night and assigned the first period to himself. He rested against a tree, feeling the gentle movement of Kaela's breathing beside him. The air was cool and fresh and in the absence of any wind the only noises were occasional animal sounds and the regular 'hoo hoo' of an owl. There was enough light from the moon peering through thin veils of clouds for him to be able to see the sleeping forms of the others and as far as the perimeter of the campsite, and it was warm enough to not require that the fire be kept burning.

He thought of the man's advice on the road. Were they recklessly moving toward danger by continuing along the road to Hammaburg? Maybe it *would* be better to hide somewhere and wait for the conflict to die or move elsewhere. But that could take weeks, even months, and he considered Lothar and Ragnall more likely to become a danger if they did not continue to press on to the south.

An animal cried out close by. It was an unusual sound as if the animal was in some distress and Fenn listened for it to be repeated. After the forest had remained quiet for a while, Fenn turned his thoughts to his pursuers. He had been surprised before with the tenacity of the Northmen and he suspected Lothar would also not give up easily. He concluded, as he had before, that the main objective must be to put distance between them, reaffirming that he wouldn't be completely happy until he was back in Northumbria. He closed his eyes, suddenly weary, but jerked them open when the tiny cry sounded again.

Careful not to disturb Kaela, he sat upright and concentrated his hearing in the direction of the cry. Something was unusual about that noise. It sounded almost...

He was certain he had heard the cry of a human baby. He got to his feet. Nobody else had been disturbed. He stepped over Olgood's sprawled legs and walked softly through the trees towards the sound. He had good visibility but there were many shadows. Feeling somewhat foolish, he took his axe from his belt and held it ready. He paused when he reached the approximate location of the sounds and stood still, listening.

He heard breathing.

A shadow beside him moved and resolved into a small child crawling to get further behind a tree. Another shape came from behind the tree to stand between Fenn and the child. It was a woman. She held her hands out in front of her as if to push him away. He saw she was gasping with fear but determined to protect the child if she could. The same cry he had heard before came again, but it came from the other side of the tree. The woman cast an anxious glance toward the sound, started towards it then stopped. Another form, smaller than the woman, stepped forward and stood beside her with his fists raised. The boy looked to be about ten years old.

Fenn pushed his axe into his belt then spread his arms wide. He waited a moment then stepped back and dropped to a crouch still holding his arms out.

The woman realised she was not about to be attacked. She choked back her sobs and ran to the baby hidden behind the tree. The boy looked at the woman wondering what to do. He took her place in front of the small child. He kept his hands up, watching Fenn. Fenn eased himself from his crouch and sat on the ground, folding his arms over his knees.

The woman reappeared holding a bundle that emitted soft gurgling sounds. She stepped away from the tree and called to her children. The boy helped the other child, who Fenn could now see was a girl, get to her feet and together the children ran to the woman who gathered them to her and turned to walk away.

Fenn said softly: 'Wait...'

She stopped and three faces stared back at him. Fenn beckoned to them indicating the way back to the campsite at the same time miming eating some food. The woman hesitated and the moonlight reflected on her glistening eyes and the stream of tears on her face. She slowly shook her head and took a step back and was about to turn away again when her eyes widened with alarm at something behind Fenn.

Some calm whispered words in Kaela's voice came from over his shoulder and Fenn turned to see her repeat his invitation for the woman to come to their camp. Slowly, so as not to alarm the woman further, he stood up and took a few steps in that direction, again miming the eating of food.

The boy looked up at the woman. He took hold of her dress and gave it a gentle tug then took a step toward Fenn. At that moment the baby gave another cry. The women automatically hushed it and then she allowed her son to pull her forward.

Kaela walked to meet them. When she could see Kaela clearly and confirm that she was female, the woman put her free hand to her mouth, stifling a cry of relief. She stumbled and would have fallen had Kaela not taken hold of her shoulders. The boy supported his mother on the other side and the small girl took hold of her dress from behind.

Fenn led the way to the camp.

The woman's name was Mathilde.

The camp had been woken by Kaela when she had found Fenn gone and saw him disappearing into the trees. They were watchful but not worried as, apart from the baby's cry, there had been no unusual sounds to alarm them. Gisele saw Fenn and Kaela returning and added wood to the fire coaxing it to life. With wide fear-filled eyes, the woman allowed Kaela to sit her beside the fire. The two children clung to their mother but were now more interested than afraid.

The new family devoured the small amount of fowl that had been saved for the morning meal as if they had not eaten for a week. Even as she ate, the woman did not relax, her eyes continually flicking from one person to another as if waiting for the moment when her unexpected good fortune would end.

After giving her time to finish the food, Kaela introduced the people around the fire. Mathilde responded and they learned her son was called Bruno, her daughter was Gabby and the baby had not yet been named.

Gisele sat beside her and reached out for the baby. Mathilde shook her head but Gisele gently persisted and Mathilde reluctantly released the bundle in her arms. When she saw how Gisele was with the baby, and how the baby responded to Gisele, she visibly relaxed. Tears welled in her eyes again but they were tears of relief and not tears of fear. She held her children tightly and talked reassuringly to them then she said some words to Kaela and spread her hand to cover them all. Fenn understood she was thanking them for the food.

Kaela talked to Mathilde. After each exchange she repeated the conversation for the benefit of Fenn and Olgood and also at times to help Hakon and Gunther. Kaela said Mathilde spoke a dialect that was a mixture of Frankish and Saxon that she and Gisele seemed to readily understand, but Hakon and Gunther sometimes struggled.

'This is Mathilde. She and her husband, Heinrich, were fleeing with their children to Hammaburg when they met a band of Franks...'

CHAPTER TWENTY-FOUR

Heinrich and Mathilde…

Heinrich carried Gabby in his arms and stepped up onto and then over the tree trunk that had fallen across the trail. He deposited Gabby on the ground and helped Bruno across.

Bruno started to run ahead but Heinrich called him back.

'We need to be careful, Bruno, there may be bad men in the forest.'

'Shall I take Gabby?'

'No, I'll carry her.'

He took the baby from Mathilde then used his other hand to steady his wife as she climbed onto the tree trunk and then lowered herself down. Heinrich gave her the baby, picked up the little girl and together they walked quickly along the forest trail following their son.

The path skirted along the edge of the forest beside a large meadow. A log hut with an adjoining barn had been built at the top of the gently sloping meadow which was large enough to hold a small herd of cows. On the far side of the meadow was an area of swampy land – part of the series of swamps that surrounded Hammaburg providing some protection but also making access to the town difficult.

Heinrich had taken his family out of the town of Gremwald where he was *Vogt* – Kaela translated this as 'Reeve' or town leader. He had ordered the people of Gremwald to evacuate their families to Hammaburg when Widukind's retreating Saxons streamed through the town. Heinrich talked to some of them to find out what was happening and learned that a battle had been fought; the Saxons were retreating and the Franks were advancing behind them.

After organising the evacuation, he then searched the small town to make sure everyone had left. He spent some time dissuading some of Widukind's men, who were intent on looting, from taking what little the townspeople owned but once that was done Heinrich felt he could wait no longer. The number of Saxons passing by dwindled to a trickle – mainly the injured hobbling as best they could. Heinrich thought the Franks might not be far behind and he and Mathilde were the last family to leave Gremwald.

He didn't want to be caught in the crush of people trying to cross the Albia at the Hammaburg Bridge so he had taken his family east and crossed the Albia a few miles upstream during the night using a ford where the river widened into several small channels. Once on the northern side, they had to head even further north to avoid the swamps and then swing west in order to enter Hammaburg via the northern road. They had walked all night and everyone was weary.

Heinrich kept the family in the trees while he watched the meadow for movement. It was strange that there were no cows to be seen but the old man who lived in the hut may have taken them elsewhere for safety. The path continued through the forest and Heinrich would normally have followed that, but a thin plume of white smoke rising from the hut indicated it was still occupied. Heinrich had met the old man who grazed this meadow and talked with him about cows and milk. He was stubborn and independent and Heinrich was not surprised he was still here – but he needed to leave for the safety of Hammaburg now. He did not expect any Franks to be on the northern side of the Albia yet, but Charles the Great was a respected leader in time of war and had often won battles by doing the unexpected. Maybe he would want to surround the town.

'Stay here,' he said to Mathilde. 'I'll check the hut. I'll try to persuade the old man to come with us to Hammaburg.'

Cautiously, Heinrich approached the hut. When he was twenty yards from the door he called out but received no reply. He called again from outside the door. He waited a few moments then opened the door.

He was outside again in an instant, sword in hand, turning in a circle and looking around the meadow in all directions. He ran to Mathilde.

'The old man is dead,' he said, 'skewered to his table by a pitchfork. The Franks must be on this side of the river. There's water boiling on the fire so whoever did this is close by.'

'But he had nothing but his cows. Why would anyone...?' Mathilde stopped her speculation. 'Should we go back east?'

'The Franks can't be across the river in any force yet, but maybe they do intend to attack Hammaburg from both directions. This will be the work of a band of looters looking for anything they can carry.' He didn't say it, but Mathilde knew he was thinking '...and for women.'

'How do you know they were Franks?' asked Mathilde.

Heinrich thought for a moment. 'I don't. But it doesn't make sense for Saxons to harm the old man; certainly nobody from around here would – and if Franks *did* do this, they have probably come from the east and more may be following – they must have crossed the ford ahead of us. We need to get to the castle. Widukind will be waiting for us there.'

He put his hand on Mathilde's shoulder.

'I'm sorry. I've put us in danger by coming this way. We should have gone to the bridge.'

Mathilde covered his hand with hers. 'It may have been worse there. Let's just get to Hammaburg.'

Heinrich picked up little Gabby and they hurried behind the hut and re-joined the forest trail.

With his sword in one hand and carrying Gabby with the other, Heinrich led them towards the northern road. At every bend of the trail, he put Gabby down and scouted a little way ahead and listened before beckoning the family to him.

The baby became very restless and started crying. Mathilde said he needed to be fed and hopefully then he would sleep. Heinrich and Bruno waited on the path while Mathilde took Gabby and found a place to sit and feed the baby. The baby gurgled blissfully during the feed and Mathilde thought how blessed his ignorance was. Thankfully, he then fell asleep.

Their need to move cautiously made for slow progress and they reached the northern road at mid-afternoon. There was nobody visible on the road and they started walking toward Hammaburg continually looking behind as well as ahead.

On top of a hill they did see another group of people ahead. Heinrich counted eight people – men, women and children – hurrying in the same direction for the protection of the castle and the town.

'We'll try to catch up with those people. We'll be safer in a bigger group,' said Heinrich.

He took Gabby and with Mathilde carrying the baby, they ran down the hill toward the people who were half a mile ahead.

Heinrich called out and just as a person turned to look behind, a band of men ran from the trees and surrounded the group. Heinrich took hold of Bruno's arm and turned him towards the forest, shouting: 'Run! As fast as you can. Hide in the forest!'

He herded his family off the road and into the forest. Mathilde was immediately hampered by the need to hold the baby and could only fight her way through the thick undergrowth with one hand. Heinrich was similarly impeded with Gabby. As they entered the trees a shout from behind told them they had been seen. Mathilde turned to see three men detach from the people surrounding the group and run up the hill towards them. A woman screamed and there was more shouting. Mathilde stopped, searching for the best way to go – there was no path and the thick bushes looked impassable. Heinrich's hand rested on her back and urged her to push into the forest.

Bruno helped his mother through a vine thicket and from the time it took for her to struggle free she knew the men would soon be upon them. Heinrich emerged from the vines and set Gabby down.

'You three run on. This is a good place to make a stand. I'll hold them here as long as I can and give you time to get away.'

'But there are *three* of them,' Mathilde cried.

'If we run on they'll catch us all. It's the only way to keep you safe. The vines will make it difficult for them. Head west and I'll catch up. If you get to the western road, wait for me there.'

He raised his hand against further objections from both Mathilde and Bruno.

'Please. You must go *now*.'

He held Mathilde's arms and gave her a brief kiss then gently pushed her away. 'Keep heading west – I'll find you.' He gave Bruno a parting squeeze on the shoulder and stepped back.

Mathilde took Gabby's hand.

'I can fight with you,' called Bruno.

'Not today. You have no sword. Another day, when you have a sword, you can fight. Today you must take care of your mother and our family.'

Heinrich turned away, drew his sword and faced the noise of the men crashing through the forest.

Mathilde nodded for Bruno to lead the way. They pushed through some spiky bushes and crawled under a low branch. When she heard the clash of swords from close behind, she paused but only for a moment. She checked each of her children and moved determinedly forward.

Mathilde scrambled through bushes with thorns that seemed to reach out and tear at her clothes and skin, with Gabby holding onto her dress and being pulled along behind her. She thrust aside sticky vines that left her hands covered in a substance that glued her fingers together. Branches whipped and scratched at her face and caught in her hair. Roots tripped her feet and bruised her knees when she fell. She held her baby close, shifting the bundle from one arm to the other, protecting the delicate face from the branches and the tangling vines. Gabby followed stolidly behind, her face and hands scratched and dirty but she didn't complain and each time Mathilde looked back she saw a tiny face with a mouth set hard, determined to keep up and not be a burden. Bruno was beside her, in front, behind her, helping her or helping Gabby, clearing a path, holding back branches. She pushed past and through and over until she could move no more. She sank to her knees between the raised roots of a tall tree, gasping for breath.

When her breathing slowed enough for her to be able to listen, she heard only forest sounds.

'Is Papa coming? Are we waiting for him here?' asked Gabby. Bruno looked at his mother. He had wanted to ask the same question, but being almost a man, he didn't think he should.

'No, we can't stop yet. We must go on until nightfall.' She didn't mention that they must keep going in case Heinrich hadn't been able to stop the Franks. 'Tomorrow we should get to the western road. We'll wait for Papa there.'

'I'm hungry,' said Gabby in a tone that also said she was tired.

'I know. I'm hungry too.' She realised the family had not eaten anything since the previous day. 'We'll look for mushrooms.'

They had rested long enough. Around the tree the undergrowth was not so dense. Mathilde stood up and took Gabby's hand.

'Be brave. Not much further.'

When it was too dark to see the way ahead they stopped and huddled beside a tree. The baby cried.

*   *   *

When Mathilde had finished her tale, Olgood asked: 'What is this fight about? Even I know that Saxony has been a province of the Franks for years. Is Widukind trying to take back the land?'

When Kaela put his question, Mathilde gave a short mirthless laugh.

'No. He has tried that before and failed. But now the Franks need men to help them fight the Avar Khanate in the East. They are taking by force one man in five for their army. They only spared my Heinrich because he was *Vogt*. They're robbing us of our best men to throw against the Avars. Widukind says they take too many. When he learned that the Franks had moved a large part of their army to the eastern border to protect it against the Avars, the Frisians joined Widukind's Saxons and they attacked the Frankish castle at Verden.'

'I know Verden,' said Hakon. 'Why attack there?'

'Because that was the place, ten years ago, where Charles massacred four and a half thousand Saxons who had surrendered to him. But now… it seems… those bastard Franks have beaten us again.'

'Four and a half *thousand*,' exclaimed Olgood. 'In God's name… Why?'

'So they wouldn't rise against him again.'

Olgood sat back and shook his head.

'Widukind's men were retreating through my village,' continued Mathilde. 'Many were unhappy and wanted to stand and fight. They told Heinrich it was just a setback.' She paused and drew in a breath. 'Widukind will make a stand at Hammaburg because the castle can be defended and also he will want to prevent the defeat becoming a rout.'

While Mathilde and Kaela were speaking, Fenn considered the options. Their choices were becoming very limited. If they continued towards Hammaburg then attempted to cross the Albia and head south they would be entering an area of conflict, with armed and desperate men roaming the countryside. They could go back to the north – away from the battle – but that would make it easier for Lothar and Ragnall to catch up to them. If they stayed where they were, they risked being engulfed by both threats.

East or West? If they went west to the coast, the river Albia formed an impassable barrier, especially for the horses. As he had previously thought, heading west restricted their choices. They may find a boat to cross the river but it wouldn't be wise to depend on that.

To the East? Mathilde had just described a thick forest that was difficult to pass through even on foot. The only route east was by road – and that road led to Hammaburg.

Fenn's considerations were interrupted when Mathilde spoke directly to him.

'Thank you for your kindness,' translated Kaela, 'and I have no right to ask, but, I beg you, can you please take me to Hammaburg? I can get help there to find Heinrich. I fear he may be hurt or…' Mathilde glanced at her children and couldn't finish.

Fenn looked around the circle.

'We'll leave at first light.'

After Mathilde had settled Bruno and Gabby into a comfortable sleeping position and the baby was also asleep, the three women sat at the fire talking. Mathilde was asking most of the questions with both Kaela and Gisele replying at length. Hakon offered to keep a watch and Fenn rested against a tree watching the fire and listening to the murmur of conversation.

He was roused from sleep when Kaela leaned against him. Through half-opened eyes he saw Mathilde kneeling down to lie beside her children.

'Have you been talking all this time?' he whispered.

'Mathilde was interested in the story of our journey. She's a very astute woman.'

'Oh, is she? You may not have much in common then.'

He grunted as her sharp elbow poked into his ribs.

*   *   *

The day was overcast and dull and the air seemed oppressive. The wind came in heavy gusts that bent the forest trees so the branches were continuously in movement. Swirling winds twisted large patches of grasses alongside the road pushing them flat for a time before allowing them to stand again, then moving elsewhere, rippling and churning the river water in its path. Dust from the road irritated their eyes and made them water, leaving wet streaks on their dirty cheeks, and caused the horses to shake their heads and snort.

Kaela rode ahead on the horse she had decided to name Midnight. She kept to the middle of the road and her hand was always by her sword. For easy access, Fenn carried his sling tucked into his belt rather than looped around it. He had filled his sling bag with stones from the stream bed and, with Fenn's guidance, Bruno had gladly gathered more – these now forming a small pile behind the seat of the cart.

Hakon drove and Fenn sat beside him. Gisele and Mathilde, with the children between them, sat behind the seat with Olgood and Gunther at the back of the cart keeping watch to the side and behind them. A man with his head wrapped in a blood-soaked cloth also sat on the edge of the cart. Behind the cart walked six more men. All of them including the injured man were armed with swords.

A group of four had joined first, hailing the cart from the forest and asking if they could accompany them to Hammaburg for mutual protection. Fenn had invited them to walk behind the cart. Shortly after, the road had left the forest behind – which pleased him because it made an attack from concealment less likely – and had straightened to become a raised causeway with the river on one side and peat swamp on the left. Three more men emerged from behind reeds in the swamp with the same request, two of them supporting the third who had the head wound.

These seven were Widukind's men. Once they had crossed the bridge, they had been unsure, in the chaos of the retreat, whether they were supposed to defend the town or bypass it. Once they had reached the forest and had a chance to think, they had turned back, realising that Hammaburg castle was the best place to defend and the only place that offered any safety if Franks were already in the area. Both groups had encountered bands of Franks but were able to avoid them in the forest.

Mathilde asked the men if they had seen Heinrich. One addressed her very respectfully shaking his head to say nobody had seen him. Fenn couldn't tell whether she had described Heinrich or if she had expected these men to know him.

Fenn planned to take Mathilde and the children into the town, provide what help they could in locating Heinrich, then cross the bridge as soon as possible and avoid the coming conflict by immediately heading to the coast along the far bank of the Albia. Once at the coast, they could either look for a boat to cross the sea or head south.

He called a halt when the town came into view and received a confirming nod from Hakon. This was Hammaburg. Fenn could see some men were stationed at the town gate. Kaela came trotting back as Fenn surveyed the countryside.

'How can we be sure that the town is not already in the hands of the Franks?' he asked, half to himself.

'I can ride to the gates and ask,' said Kaela.

Fenn smiled and then saw she was serious. His first reaction was to oppose the idea. It was risky and he was reluctant for Kaela to take the chance. Seeing his hesitation, Olgood reminded him: 'It needs to be done. She can do it.'

'Be careful and only get as close as you need to. We'll wait here.' To Olgood he said: 'Keep a watch behind.'

Kaela wheeled the horse and eased it into a canter.

Fenn watched as she rode towards the gate, slowing to a walk and stopping within hailing distance. He found he was holding his breath only when the exchange went on for longer than he could hold it. In the next few moments she would either spin around and gallop away, possibly pursued by other horsemen, possibly dodging an arrow or two – or relax and wave.

He fingered his sling.

She waved.

CHAPTER TWENTY-FIVE

The seventh tower...

From the western town gate the road proceeded through the town and into open countryside. The castle stood to the north and east of the town with forest-covered hills visible further north and some grazing and cultivated land between the castle and the river.

Following Mathilde's directions, Hakon drove the cart to the main gate in the outer wall of the castle. There was a short conversation with some men at the gate and the thick wooden door was lowered revealing a stone tunnel leading to a courtyard. Inside the tunnel, a trench had been dug and this was covered by a short wooden bridge that could be raised to seal an inner opening. Men were working in the trench underneath the bridge, widening the hole and inserting sharpened stakes into the floor. Mounds of loose earth were piled on each side of the trench. Once across the bridge, the inner gate opened onto the large courtyard which continued around both sides of the castle where shelters had been erected to house the people from the town who had taken refuge behind the castle walls.

A young boy came forward to take the horses to the stables. Olgood put the basket on his shoulders and he and Gunther each picked up one of the extra swords. Gunther slipped his onto his belt but Olgood kept the other in his hand. Bruno did not want to leave the pile of stones he had collected for Fenn on the cart, so Mathilde talked to a man standing beside the castle doors who ran off and returned a moment later with a small sack which Bruno was able to fill before the cart was led away. The same man then

371

led them into the castle, across an entrance hall that ran the length of the front of the castle and into the great hall, asking them to wait there. Maybe because of the baby, he directed all of his attention to Mathilde, addressing his remarks to her and bowing to her as he left, closing the door behind him. Six of the seven men were still with them; the injured man having been taken to the infirmary.

Fenn glanced at Olgood. Was this another trap? Could Ragnall have possibly beaten them here? He saw that Olgood was alert.

After a moment, Fenn forced himself to relax. Everyone they had encountered since entering the town gate seemed friendly and he had no reason to suspect otherwise.

Brightly coloured woven tapestries hung from the walls reminding Fenn of the main hall of the St. Cuthbert's Monastery church at Lindisfarne. Like the church, the roof was very high with huge arched supports bulging from the walls. At the far end of the room, on a raised platform, a long table was surrounded by chairs. In the centre of the table sat a chair much larger than the rest with a leather padded backrest and leather covered arms.

They stood in the centre of the room studying their surroundings. Hakon walked to a wall to inspect a tapestry, fingering the cloth. Mathilde took her children up to the table and sat them on chairs, Bruno still clutching his precious bag of stones, then sat on one herself and attended to the baby. She seemed less awed by the room than the others and, also because the man seemed to know her, Fenn reasoned she may well have been here before.

He turned to Kaela. 'I'd like to ask Mathilde…'

He stopped as the sound of a door opening came from an alcove behind the table. Fenn tensed and rested his hand on his axe. If Ragnall walked through that door, he would not stop Olgood this time – he would join him. He did not intend to be captured again without a fight.

A man walked into the hall and held out his arms to Mathilde. Two men, fully armed, followed him into the room but stopped just inside the door and waited there. From behind Fenn there was a rustle of movement. He glanced over his shoulder and saw that the six men were standing straight.

Mathilde rose from her chair and ran to the man. They embraced, both careful of the baby. Mathilde talked rapidly with the man and they conversed for some time, so long that Fenn glanced at Kaela with raised eyebrows. What was this conversation about? Kaela waved her hand at him to say it was nothing to worry about, just as Mathilde looked at Fenn and gestured towards him several times. She was probably telling of her ordeal. The man also glanced at them and replied with some thoughtful questions. When Mathilde had answered these, she turned toward Fenn and Kaela and beckoned them forward. They walked towards the table, followed by Olgood and Gisele with Hakon and Gunther in the rear. The six men remained where they were.

As they approached, Mathilde turned suddenly to the man and asked him an urgent question – Fenn heard her say the word 'Heinrich' – and on the man's reply, she cried out but whether in joy or anguish he couldn't tell.

Kaela answered his question with a smile. 'Heinrich is alive,' she said. 'Injured, but he will live. He has a sword wound in his side. He's in the infirmary.'

Mathilde was obviously anxious to see her husband but the man calmed her, drawing her forward to meet Fenn and Kaela.

'He said: All in good time. Introductions first,' said Kaela.

Mathilde looked at Kaela who nodded and translated.

'This is Widukind, Duke of Saxony. Widukind, these are the people who saved me and the children when we were lost in the forest. They offered us, complete strangers, their last food and the comfort of their camp, without knowing who we were.'

She introduced Widukind to each of them. Widukind nodded as she said each name. When she finally introduced Fenn, the man stepped forward and held out his hand which Fenn clasped. Widukind was older than he expected. His hair was greying and his face was deeply lined but he was still a stocky and powerful man. He spoke to Fenn.

'Matti is like a daughter to me. I thank you for bringing her and the children safely to the castle,' Kaela translated.

Mathilde said something else to Kaela who explained: 'Heinrich grew up with Widukind's son, Wichbert. They are brothers in all but blood.'

Several things fell into place for Fenn. The deference many of the men had shown and her familiarity with Widukind's plans and with the castle made sense if Mathilde was almost part of his family.

Widukind spoke. 'Matti says you two work as a team.' He indicated Fenn and Kaela. 'She says you are good together, and Kaela can be your voice.'

Fenn's eyes met Kaela's.

'I will reward you for helping Matti when I can, but for now I will ask something else of you.' He looked at Fenn. 'My daughter speaks highly of you, and I know she is a good judge. Can you lead men?'

Fenn was about to say no reward was necessary but he paused in surprise at the question. Kaela said something to Widukind. She talked for a while and when Fenn inquired with a look as to what she had said, she shrugged: 'I said 'yes'.'

Widukind said a few words and Kaela smiled. She hesitated then translated: 'He said: So you *are* Fenn's voice – even when he doesn't speak.'

Widukind regarded Kaela, his eyes lingering for a moment on her red hair before appraising Olgood and Gisele and then Gunther and Hakon.

'You have unusual companions. Are these two as strong as they look?'

Kaela answered in the affirmative.

Widukind indicated they should sit at the long table. He eased himself into the big chair. Mathilde took her son and daughter from the table and sat them by the wall. She handed the sleeping baby to Bruno and then returned. Olgood put the basket on the floor beside his chair and laid the sword he was carrying beside it.

When they were seated, Widukind spoke, with Kaela translating his words so both Fenn and Olgood could hear.

'Please excuse me if I dispense with the normal pleasantries – we are pressed for time. My scouts tell me the Franks have gathered in some strength north of the town and will probably attack tomorrow. I'm not surprised they are assembling in the north; there's more room to manoeuvre and they won't be constricted by the river at their backs. They still have men scattered in the forest, but Marchant, their leader, is an impetuous young fool and he probably thinks he will earn the gratitude of Charles if he can take Hammaburg before Charles arrives.'

Widukind stopped and bellowed out an order. One of the men hastily left the hall. Widukind waited patiently until the man returned bearing a tray with wooden cups and a jug. Following close behind him, two more men entered. They had obviously been hurrying; both were breathing quickly. While the man with the tray was placing it on the table, the other two walked to Widukind and one bent to whisper in his ear.

When he had finished, Widukind indicated the two men.

'My brother Bruno, and this man is my son Wichbert.'

Fenn wondered if he had misheard the name of Widukind's brother but then realised that Mathilde's son had probably been named after him. Bruno was a darker version of Widukind, of similar stature but a little taller. His hair was still black so he was probably also younger. Wichbert looked about the same age as Olgood. In contrast to Widukind and Bruno who were dressed in clothes that did not distinguish them from any of their men, Wichbert was smartly dressed. He wore a black tunic with raised gold stitching along the seams, cut to draw in at the waist. His belt held a sword on one side and also a spiked mace on the other. He wore shiny black leather boots to just below his knee.

Widukind introduced the others at the table, and had no trouble remembering their names. Widukind indicated Bruno and Wichbert should join them at the table. Wichbert took the jug and placed cups before each person, filling them from the jug. Fenn watched as deep red wine flowed into the cups. He didn't feel like drinking wine – he had only sampled it a few times in his life – but thought it would be impolite to refuse. He took a sip. Widukind took a long draught from his cup and sighed with satisfaction.

'We are watching Marchant. Bruno has just told me that Marchant's forces in the north are now moving closer. It is too late for them to do anything today, but it confirms they will probably attack tomorrow.'

He spoke directly to Fenn.

'As a result of the recent conflict, several of my commanders are wounded or dead – some of my most able men. Leadership and bravery unfortunately are close companions and these men led their assaults from the front.'

He leaned forward.

'Now the tables are turned. This time *we* are behind walls and they must come to us. The wall around the town was built for the purpose of commerce and is not defendable, but the castle walls are strongly constructed and form an excellent barrier. The outer wall of this castle has six sides and, including the tower over the main gate, there are seven towers, one at each corner. With myself, Bruno and Wichbert, I have only three others I would trust to lead. I want you to take charge of the seventh tower and part of the south wall.'

At these words, Wichbert stood and spoke forcefully to his father.

Widukind turned to him and replied calmly but firmly.

He turned back.

'Wichbert questions the wisdom of entrusting the defence of part of our wall to a young stranger. I've told him that Matti vouches for you – she seems to have learned a lot about you and your journey here – and from what she has told me, you've proved very resourceful.'

He paused and thought for a moment, then said: 'I have a group of Danish mercenaries; twenty archers and thirty swordsmen. We have no time to assimilate them so they would better kept together and led by an outsider. I requested assistance from Gudrod some time ago. He has sent other men but this group arrived yesterday. I was wondering where to place them and that problem is now solved. I must keep some men in reserve but I can also give you the six you brought with you – and your friends of course.'

Fenn spread his hands. 'I don't know anything about defending a castle.'

'You don't need to know much. It's very simple – you must stop the enemy from coming over the walls. It's more important that you can lead, and that men will follow you. I expect the main attack will come from the north – we must prepare of course but you may not have much to do on the southern wall.'

He paused to assess Fenn's reaction.

Fenn met his gaze and after a moment Widukind continued: 'The situation is this: Marchant has no siege machines – he cannot batter down the walls so he must come over them. Our moat is only partly dug and is ineffective, so they could tunnel under the walls but Marchant has no time for that. He will want to complete his task quickly.'

He waited a moment and then repeated for emphasis: 'He will try to come over the castle walls with ladders and ropes.'

'With the townspeople here as well, is there water and food enough for a siege? What about arrows? How many arrows do you have?'

Widukind sat back, a smile on his face. He patted Mathilde's shoulder. 'Look at that. Already he is thinking like a leader. I think you were right Matti.'

Mathilde whispered in his ear and Widukind nodded. She rose from the table and gave a wave and a bow. Both Bruno and Wichbert stood but Bruno eased Wichbert back to his chair with a hand on his shoulder. He helped Mathilde gather the children and they left the hall.

Widukind continued: 'We have a spring inside the walls and plenty of food in the food store below the castle. We've been preparing this castle for some time. We could survive for months but this battle won't even last days. It will not be a siege. As I say, Marchant wants a quick victory. When he attacks, we must defeat him quickly. Mind what I say – we must *defeat* him, not just drive off the attack. Only if we take Marchant out of the game do we stand a chance when Charles arrives. We can't stand against both forces but we can stand against one of them at a time. The fact that Marchant is already moving, just a short time before darkness, tells me he will not wait for Charles. How I love the impetuosity of youth.'

Fenn sat forward. 'So, King Charles is on his way here with another force. How long before he arrives?'

'Several days. Five if he pushes the pace, more likely six.'

Fenn considered the information. 'How many men do you have? And how many are against you?'

Widukind said softly: 'Do you mean – against *us?*'

Fenn paused. He looked at Olgood and beside him Gunther and Hakon. They looked back without expression, awaiting his decision. Even Gisele looked at him calmly her hands folded on the table, seemingly unconcerned with the talk of imminent attacks, fighting, and death; waiting to accept whatever he should decide. Kaela was sitting on his other side. He turned his head. Kaela regarded him with her deep brown eyes, her tanned face framed by her fiery red hair. He studied her. She had never looked more beautiful. As he felt himself swallowed by her eyes he realised he could not walk away from this fight.

'Yes,' said Fenn, 'I mean against *us.*'

Widukind nodded.

'Inside the castle walls I have five hundred fighting men. This includes fifty-five men from the town who are able to hold a sword. Some are arriving every day, but many of these are not in good shape. My infirmary is already overcrowded. There are also about three hundred women and children.'

Fenn was about to remark on the disparity between the numbers of men and women from the town but he remembered that the Franks would have taken some for the eastern war and some would also have already joined Widukind's forces.

Instead he asked: 'How many will be opposing us?'

'Marchant has about a thousand, drawn from the castle at Verden and other places. Charles will come from further south with about the same number. Five hundred can hold this castle against a thousand as long as each man does what he must.'

He turned to Wichbert.

'How many arrows do we have?'

'Twenty thousand,' said Wichbert. 'Enough for one hundred per archer with some to spare.'

Fenn raised his eyebrows. 'Do you have any slingers?'

'Slingers? No. The Franks have slingers but we have none.'

'Well, now you have one,' said Fenn. He thought for a moment. 'How do you intend to defeat Marchant?'

'I have a plan but it depends on how the battle proceeds. We can talk about that later.'

He stood up.

'For now, I understand you're hungry. Wichbert will show you where you can get some food. When you've eaten, he will take you to your post and introduce you to your men. If you have any more questions you can ask him. I have several matters to attend to. There will be a meeting of my commanders at sunset. I'll call for you...' he paused and added, '...for you *both*... then.'

He extended his hand again which Fenn took. Widukind called out to the six who were still standing at the other end of the room and the men walked forward to join Fenn.

*   *   *

Kaela wanted to make sure Midnight and the other horses had been properly cared for before eating, so once they had been shown to the kitchens and the adjacent eating hall and Wichbert had instructed the group of women in the kitchen to provide some food, she left with Wichbert for the stables.

There were tables arranged along the walls of the eating hall. The six men chose a table and sat down. Fenn wasn't sure whether they should have asked his permission. It didn't seem worth making an issue of it.

He sat beside Gunther and Hakon.

'Hakon, please repeat what I say to Gunther and Gisele.' He waited until he had their attention. 'This applies to all of you, but especially to you Gunther.' He paused. 'I have committed to stay here and do what I can to help these people. But you are free to do as you wish. You may think this is not your fight, and I would accept that. You would be free to leave.'

Gunther didn't reply. When nobody else did, Olgood said: 'You've said it yourself. We're in this together and we will go back home together. We will leave nobody behind.'

Fenn nodded his head in acknowledgement. 'I know, but this is different. There will be a battle. People get hurt in battles. People get killed. I can't commit you all to that.'

'Why do *you* want to stay?' asked Olgood.

Fenn thought. 'I can't walk away and leave people I know in danger – even people I've just met.'

'So you see, it's simple,' Olgood said, as if explaining a puzzle. He ticked off his fingers. '*You* didn't walk away from us when we were captured by Lothar. I can't walk away from *you*. Kaela certainly won't. Hakon and Gisele won't walk away from *us*.'

379

When Hakon had finished the translation, Gisele nodded forcefully and Gunther spoke a few words.

'He say his sword belong to the Lady,' said Hakon.

The food was wholesome and very welcome. Fenn was worried his stomach might become permanently distended because he seemed to stretch it so often lately. Instead of the twice daily meagre meals he had been used to, he seemed to eat once a day or less and each time he had been unsure when he would eat next, so he had filled his stomach until he couldn't fit in another mouthful.

The women brought platters of cold meat, cheese and bread with bowls of hot thick vegetable soup to the table. If Widukind's prediction was correct, tomorrow would be a very busy day so once again Fenn thought he should eat heartily.

Kaela returned and reported that the horses were settled in the stables but the cart was to be used as part of a barricade that was being built just inside the main gate. She sat beside Fenn.

'The stables are full of horses, there was hardly room for ours, but one of the boys said he will take special care of Midnight.'

At that moment, a cook came into the room to enquire if the food was satisfactory. Her question did not need translation and there was a general chorus of agreement. Kaela muttered she hadn't had a chance to taste it yet and was mildly annoyed when Fenn stopped her arm midway to her mouth.

'Can you ask the cook how many empty flour sacks she has?'

'Why on earth would you want empty sacks?' Kaela protested, trying to extricate her arm and the cheese she held in her hand from Fenn's grip. Fenn released her.

'Please...' he said.

Kaela sighed, delayed her mouthful and asked the question.

'She says about ten in the kitchen, probably the same number in the food store below – and she also asks the same question I did. Why?'

'I'm not sure yet – it's just an idea. Ask her if I can have them and tell her I'll gladly fetch the ones in the store if she shows me where they are.'

The cook frowned at the strange request but shrugged her shoulders and beckoned him to follow her into the kitchen.

Fenn returned in a short while with the sacks folded under his arm. His hands were white from the flour and as he placed the sacks on the floor and sat down, he reached out threatening to dust Kaela's hair with flour. She warned him with a raised finger and he laughed and clapped his hands together to remove the dusting.

The six men who had been assigned to him were also enjoying the food as if it was much better fare than they had had in recent days. Fenn waited until Kaela had eaten her fill and then asked her to come with him, walking over to table where the men were sitting. Gunther stood up and followed them. The conversation fell quiet as they approached the table.

'Tell them you are my voice.'

Kaela relayed Fenn's words. One of the men, a large man with a barrel chest and a hooked nose jutting from a rugged crag of a face, placed his hands on the table and gave a short laugh of derision then yelped as the point of her blade cut into the table, slicing a large splinter from the wood less than a half-inch from his little finger. The action was so fast that the sword was in the air before Fenn had registered that she had moved. The sound of the blade leaving the scabbard seemed to follow moments later.

Gunther moved forward to stand beside Kaela, his hands on the hilts of the two swords he now wore. The man looked in astonishment at the steel blade still resting ominously on the table. He edged his hand away.

Kaela spoke in cold and deliberate words. When she had finished, she lifted her sword and allowed the flat of the blade to make deliberate and prolonged contact with the man's arm as a reminder before she sheathed the weapon.

'I told this man and the others, that if they do not wish to lose fingers – that was the last time any of them will disrespect you.'

Fenn said: 'Ask him his name.'

The man answered quickly. He said his name was Porteus.

'Tell Porteus he is now the leader of these men. Tell him the man in the infirmary is also his man. He is responsible for the welfare of his men and for every action they take.'

Porteus looked up at Kaela in surprise.

'Look at me,' said Fenn, 'and acknowledge the order.'

Porteus turned to face Fenn, he stood up and nodded.

'No,' said Fenn. 'Like this.'

He stood straight and thumped his fist on his chest just as Thorvald had done in Askari's hut a long time ago.

Porteus brought his feet together and his shoulders back. He shouted a command. His strong voice had a low resonant timbre that filled the room. The shout was so loud it hurt Fenn's ears. The other five sprang to their feet, knocking over some of the stools they had been sitting on. Porteus spoke another command. He spoke softer but his words carried easily.

Each man thumped his chest.

Wichbert returned and enquired whether they had had enough to eat and at their affirmative reply he nodded and said: 'I'll take you to your tower. Your men are assembled there.'

He led the way along the entrance hall and into the courtyard. Directly ahead was the main gate. On each side of the gate, stone steps led to the top of the castle wall. Wichbert turned and approached the first tower to the right of the gate. Some men were sitting and standing at the foot of the tower and a few rose lazily to their feet as Wichbert stopped in front of them.

He nodded to Kaela who translated as he talked. 'This is your tower,' he said to Fenn. 'The towers are numbered starting at the gate tower which is number one. That is *my* tower. This tower is the last in the ring – tower seven. You have two parts of the wall to defend – the wall to the gate on this side of the tower and the wall to the centre steps on the other side. As you see, the wall continues through the tower. These are your Danish swordsmen. Your archers are over there.' Wichbert pointed to a group of men who were talking to some of the townspeople.

Fenn thanked him. He expected Wichbert to leave but he just stepped back.

He spoke to Kaela who spoke to Porteus who spoke to his men.

Porteus and his men strode forward. They spread out in a line in front of the swordsmen, some of whom stared up at them from their still sitting positions.

Porteus' huge voice filled the courtyard. Kaela had to talk close to Fenn's ear to be heard.

'This is your commander. On your feet!' Without waiting for their response, he bellowed across the courtyard. 'Archers!'

The men were startled to their feet as much by the power of his voice as by the command. The archers scrambled to pick up their bows and formed up beside the swordsmen.

'This man is worth his weight in gold,' said Fenn quietly.

The tower was constructed as a circular column that extended twice as high as the wall and bulged out from it, allowing archers stationed at the shooting positions an unobstructed view along the outside of the wall in both directions and enabling them to shoot at anyone attempting to scale the walls. A spiral stair inside the tower gave access from the courtyard to the wall and also to the archer slots above. These allowed the archers to also cover of the top of the wall. The stairs ended at an opening to the tower roof where more archers could be stationed. From the roof, the archers had an unobstructed view in all directions on both sides of the wall.

Fenn indicated Kaela with his hand and addressed the assembled men. 'Kaela is my mouth and Porteus is my voice. Commands from them are commands from me.' He moved his hand to include Olgood and Hakon pointing to Olgood first. 'This man is my captain and Hakon will speak for him.'

Porteus voice carried Fenn's words to the men.

Fenn next indicated Gunther. 'This is Gunther. He will choose five swordsmen and he and Porteus with his five will form roving bands one on each wall, that will stop any imminent breach and go where the need is greatest.'

He faced Gunther. 'Please choose your men now.'

When Kaela had conveyed Fenn's words, Gunther cast an eye over the men. He stepped forward and quickly pointed at four men then spent a moment choosing the fifth. The chosen men moved to stand with Gunther. Several men glanced at Gunther's two swords.

'The rest of you…' Fenn paused, '…swordsmen *and* archers – will stay at your assigned position unless ordered elsewhere.'

He turned to Kaela and noticed Gisele had come to stand beside him and was waiting for his attention. He nodded to her. She spoke to Kaela who said: 'Gisele thinks she may be of use in the infirmary and she asks your permission to go there.'

Fenn was about to say she didn't need his permission, but stopped himself and drew in a breath. In the circumstances, he couldn't be half a leader, requiring obedience and respect from only some of his men – and women.

'That's a good idea, go ahead.' he said.

Gisele spoke again and mimed picking the basket up and taking it with her.

'She asks…' began Kaela.

'I think I understand her suggestion,' said Fenn with a smile.

Kaela patiently continued: '*Because*… it will be safer in the infirmary than on the wall.'

Fenn's first thought was that he wanted to keep the basket and its contents close by, but he realised she was right.

He nodded. 'Another good idea.'

Gisele touched Olgood's arm, took the basket and walked towards the castle entrance.

Fenn watched her go, then said to Kaela: 'When you went to the stables, did you see a dung pile there?'

'Yes, of course. Why?'

He smiled. 'You'll see.'

Fenn handed his flour sacks to Olgood. 'Take Hakon with you to translate. Give these to the swordsmen, one to a man, and have each man fill a sack with horse dung from the stables. If there's not enough they can use the earth dug from the trench at the main gate. Any swordsman without a sack can help the others.'

'When the sacks are full, take them outside the castle and stand in front of the walls that the seventh tower will be defending.'

Olgood saluted by thumping his fist on his chest, which took Fenn by surprise but he quickly returned the salute. Olgood took a moment to rest the extra sword he was carrying against the interior wall of the tower.

The castle wall was ten feet wide – enough for three men to stand side by side. On the outside of the wall was the stone parapet – an extension of the wall as high as a man with rectangular gaps through which the archers could shoot but still be protected.

Fenn stood with Kaela and Porteus on the wall. He leaned through one of the gaps in the parapet and studied the land in front of him. Wichbert had followed them from the courtyard and stood a short distance away. Fenn had the feeling Wichbert was not yet convinced of his capabilities and was keeping him under observation.

He watched two white doves circling the castle. These symbols of peace seemed out of place on the eve of a battle. Was it a sign? A protest against the killing to come?

There was a strip of bare land between the wall and the road. Beyond the road there was another stretch of bare grassy land where horses were grazing but as Fenn watched, men came from the castle and spread out to gather the horses and lead them toward the gate. On the far side of the grassed field was a large plot cultivated in corn. Two hundred yards further south was the river. There were some houses on the river bank and some more to the west closer to the Hammaburg bridge and adjacent to the main part of the town.

Would a good commander ask for the corn to be burned to prevent it providing concealment to the enemy? He considered the question and realised that would probably only deprive a farmer of his livelihood. Anyone concealed in the corn was no threat. The cornfield was four or five hundred yards from the tower – too far for the flight of an arrow.

He spoke to Kaela. 'I want all of the archers spread along the wall. Tell them to choose the best two among them and those two are to climb to the roof of the tower.'

Porteus received the command from Kaela and he called to the archers who started to file onto the wall from the courtyard. Fenn waited until they were in position.

'Now ask those two on top if they think they can shoot an arrow as far as the cornfield.'

An answer came from the tower top and Kaela shook her head.

Fenn grunted his satisfaction.

'Each man on the top of the tower is to shoot two arrows as far as he can towards the cornfield.'

Fenn watched as the pair of arrows flew in an arc and struck the ground fifty yards short of the corn, followed immediately by a second flight.

'Each man on the wall is to shoot two arrows as far as they can, directly out from the wall.' said Fenn.

The archers looked at each other. It seemed like a waste of good arrows. A few checked if they had understood the order, and some glanced at Wichbert who stood impassively looking on, his hands clasped behind his back.

Each one of the archers shot two arrows.

Fenn could see the arrows sticking like a band of quills into the earth forming an arc in front of the walls. He called down to Olgood and Hakon standing with the men and their filled sacks at the foot of the wall outside the castle.

'Space the flour sacks along the line where the arrows landed,' ordered Fenn. 'Put one sack where the arrows from the top of the tower landed. And I want every arrow retrieved.'

The men with the sacks walked slowly forward carrying their heavy burdens, Olgood easily holding a sack on each shoulder. Fenn walked to the tower and with Kaela and Porteus he ascended the spiral steps to the roof. Wichbert again followed a few moments behind.

Through Porteus, Fenn spoke first to the archers spread along the wall on both sides of the tower.

'You will soon see a line of white sacks on the ground ahead. That line marks the limit of your range. Do not attempt to shoot at a target beyond the markers.'

Wichbert had come forward and was watching the men place the flour sacks along the line of arrows. Fenn turned to the two archers who were on the roof. His mind was racing – what did he expect from his archers? What would he do if he were standing on the wall with his sling and a thousand men were attacking?

'Who is the better archer?'

The two men looked at each other and then one bowed and, indicating the other man, said: 'Manfredi.'

Manfredi was tall and dark-haired like Fenn. His face wore a permanent slight smile of amusement. His right arm and especially his right shoulder were noticeably larger than his left – the mark of a man who made his living pulling the string of a heavy bow. The two regarded each other, each trying to judge the merits of the man before him.

'You will lead the archers,' said Fenn. He repeated the words he had previously said to Porteus. 'You are responsible for their welfare and for every action they take. Please convey these requirements to your men. One: they will only shoot if they have a target to shoot at.'

If his archers shot arrows indiscriminately and too soon, they would waste arrows and also quickly get tired.

Fenn continued: 'Two: their targets are – in this order – first, men who are scaling the wall; second, archers; then leaders – and only if they have none of these targets – other men on the ground. Do you understand?'

The man nodded.

Fenn stepped back. 'Porteus, show this man how to salute.'

Porteus saluted and his voice roared in Manfredi's face. Fenn found himself watching to see if Manfredi's hair moved. Manfredi repeated the salute.

'Require that salute from your men,' said Fenn. 'Now, a question for you. What range advantage does being on top of this tower give you over an archer on the ground?'

Did this man know his craft?

Manfredi replied: 'The extra range is equal to the height we are above the ground. From here it would be twenty yards, from the wall, ten.'

'So,' said Fenn, 'for ten yards inside that white line, your archers on the wall can shoot their archers and they can't shoot back. Tell that to your men too.'

Manfredi saluted again and stepped back. Fenn returned the salute and Manfredi walked to his fellow archer and talked with him, both of them turning to point out and discuss features of the land visible from the tower. Fenn leaned on the tower parapet. The men had finished their collection of arrows and were walking toward the castle gate, Olgood in the lead, a head taller than most and easily visible.

What else should he be doing? He needed to assign his swordsmen and archers to their positions and work out shifts so the wall would be manned throughout the night. He would pair them up – one man on sentry duty for half the night while the other slept. And he'd talk to Olgood about finding some large stones to drop on the attackers – he'd heard about that somewhere.

Kaela realized what he was thinking. 'You'll need an archer at each gap and a swordsman to protect him, then extra swordsmen at the top of the steps to prevent the Franks getting to the courtyard if the wall is breached.'

He looked at her. He had the feeling she knew far more about castle defence than he did.

'But organising Porteus' and Gunther's bands of roving swordsmen was a good idea, as was the ring of sacks,' she said with a conciliatory smile. 'I think Wichbert thought so too.'

Fenn looked around. Wichbert had gone. Manfredi and the other archer had finished their conversation and were walking toward the steps.

From the corner of his eye, he saw the two doves reappear, flying along the line of the castle walls. Immediately afterward he noticed another movement and he focussed on a hawk circling above the doves, seeming to be lazily disinterested but as it completed each circle it kept its head pointed at the doves for a long time. Without taking his eyes from the hawk, Fenn removed his sling and felt for a stone in his bag.

Beside him, Kaela said softly: 'Fenn… is it wise to attempt a shot? That's a difficult target…'

'I don't need to hit it. If it attacks, I'll just scare it off. I don't want a hawk killing my peace doves.'

The hawk increased the size of its circle and tilted its wing to lose altitude. The action quickly turned into a dive. Fenn's sling was whirring and at the sound, Manfredi – his foot already on the second step leading from the roof – looked up. At a glance, he saw what Fenn was about to do and he pushed his companion aside so his view was not obstructed.

Fenn's eyes were glued to the hawk. The doves suddenly sensed something. They squawked and flew frantically in different directions. The hawk chose one, swerved smoothly and closed on it.

Fenn let his stone fly.

*　　*　　*

Fenn led his men into the eating hall. He had left some sentries on the wall who would eat later but the threat from the Franks at this time of day was small. It didn't make sense to attack at dusk.

Having just eaten recently he wasn't hungry himself but wanted the men to be fed. He sat at a table with Kaela, Olgood and Hakon and drank some water. Gunther and Porteus sat with the men. Fenn noticed with satisfaction that the archers and swordsmen were mixed together at the tables. He thought it was better that his men were one group rather than two separate ones.

Every few moments a man would look over to their table then return to his conversation.

Fenn looked at Kaela and saw she was smiling at him. His face took on a pained expression.

'Kaela…' he started, in an exasperated tone.

Gisele appeared at the door and caught his eye. A man stood alongside her. Fenn did not recognise him at first but then realised it was the injured man they had picked up from the peat swamp outside the town, still with the blood-soaked cloth around his head. Bringing the man with her, Gisele hurried over with her beautiful smile beaming.

She talked excitedly and Kaela said: 'Even in the infirmary they've heard about your sling shot that killed the hawk.'

Fenn sighed. 'You *know* I only…'

Kaela interrupted him. 'Did your stone hit exactly where you intended it to hit?'

'Well… yes, but…'

Kaela put her finger on his mouth. 'Stop,' she said seriously. 'The outcome could not be better. Look at your men, look at this man here – what you did has inspired them; the story has spread throughout the castle and you are *their* leader. You will only undo what you've achieved if you continue to protest. Accept it.' She paused and then added: 'If you still say it was a lucky shot, I'll say that you seem to produce far more than your share of 'lucky' shots.'

Fenn took a deep breath and nodded his acknowledgement.

Gisele gestured with her hand to the man beside her and talked to Kaela.

'This man wants to join his friends. He says he can fight.'

Fenn looked at him. The man stood steadily but he was sweating and his face was slightly flushed. In other circumstances he would have insisted that the man needed rest, but he could see the man also needed to be able to do his part. He lifted his cup in acknowledgement and pointed to Porteus. The man nodded his thanks and then hesitated. Fenn realised he was unsure as to whether he should salute. He waved his hand indicating it wasn't necessary, dismissing him.

Gisele spoke again and Kaela said: 'Gisele also came to tell you that Heinrich would like to meet you.'

Fenn put down his cup and stood up.

Mathilde's son Bruno appeared at the entrance carrying a heavy leather bag. He looked around the room, saw Fenn and walked up to him, silently handing him the bag.

Fenn raised his eyebrows but accepted the bag and peered inside. His mouth opened in astonishment; he reached inside and pulled out a flattened oval stone. He held it up for the others to see. Scratched on the flat side of the stone were some figures. Fenn put the stone on the table and pulled out a handful of others, all similarly shaped with words or figures scratched on the side. Fenn could see the markings were not the same on each stone.

He looked up at Bruno. 'Kaela, please ask Bruno where he got these.'

Bruno replied and Kaela said: 'He says some men gathered them. They are Frankish stones that were shot at them in the recent battle. They would like them given back to the Franks – with force.'

'Some of these marks look like words. Can you tell me what they say?'

Kaela picked one up. 'This one says 'Pain', this one – she turned it over – says 'Victory'. She picked up two more. 'This one just has a thunderbolt on the side; and this one says 'Catch'.'

Fenn held up his hand. 'I get the idea. Interesting. The stones not only deliver a blow but also a message.'

Fenn did not know if Bruno would understand but he bowed to the boy and said: 'Thank you Bruno.' Then he added: 'When I add these to the stones you collected from the river, I'm sure to have enough.' Kaela spoke his words to the boy.

'And please ask Bruno to thank the men who collected these stones and tell them that I will do my best to deliver the full force of these messages back to their previous owners.'

Kaela stood beside Fenn and called for attention. In a loud voice she told the room about the stones and repeated Fenn's promise. The men responded with a loud cheer and the thudding of fists on tables.

The boy stood straight and thumped his arm on his chest. Fenn suppressed his involuntary smile. He returned the salute, then turned to Olgood.

'So, my salute is also common knowledge,' he said. He looked over to his men's table and saw their meal was almost complete.

'When the men have finished, take them back to their positions.'

Olgood made as if to stand but Fenn had had enough saluting and waved him back to his seat. Beckoning Kaela to join him, he rested his hand on Bruno's shoulder as Gisele led the way to the infirmary.

*   *   *

Widukind was concluding his meeting.

The three commanders Fenn had not met were all older men – contemporaries of Widukind Fenn imagined. They looked hardened and competent; experience drawn almost certainly from the dirt and blood and sweat of many battles.

Widukind described how the women and children from the town would be delivering arrows, food and water to the men on the walls, and some women had volunteered to help with the wounded.

Although the room had high windows, it had become dark very quickly after sunset and candles had been lit around the walls with several more on the table to provide light for the parchment that was spread out showing a drawing of Hammaburg castle. The candles lit each man's face with a flickering light which, to Fenn's momentarily distracted amusement, seemed to cast a sinister intent on the gathering. He brought his thoughts back to Widukind's words being whispered in his ear by Kaela.

Widukind touched his finger on the drawing at the main gate. 'As I have said, I expect the north walls to bear the brunt of the attack, but the weakest point of our defences is here, at the main gate on the south wall. If Marchant can get *through* the gate, he doesn't need to climb over, so I would be surprised if he neglects to pay that some attention.'

Fenn recalled Widukind telling him earlier they may not have much to do on the southern wall. Now he was saying holding the gate was a key part of the castle defence. Had Widukind deliberately minimised the importance of the southern wall to get Fenn's agreement?

Widukind let his gaze move around each of the men around the table, including Kaela who was standing at Fenn's shoulder.

'The Franks normally attack at dawn or just before, so be alert and have your men alert. There is a good moon tonight which I hope will continue till morning, so we can see them coming – but we must work with what we get.' He took a step back and said: 'You all know what to do. May the gods be with us all.'

He stopped Fenn as he was turning to leave.

'Please wait,' he said, 'I want to talk with you but I must first talk with Bruno.'

While Fenn and Kaela waited beside the table, Fenn studied the drawing of the castle. He picked up a dark stick that was lying on the table and tested it on a corner of the parchment. It produced a thin black line. He grunted in satisfaction and began to modify the drawing of the castle. He didn't hear Kaela's intake of breath.

The tunnel of the main gate was elongated with a few strokes and the two bridges that could be drawn up to become doors, were sketched in outline as if they were being seen through the tunnel walls. He changed the perspective on the facing towers, enlarging them so they were in better proportion to the walls and also added height to the parapets. He added Widukind's banner that flew from the tower over the main gate but hadn't been included in the drawing, enlarging it in order to include detail of the spread-wing eagle design.

He didn't notice that the hum of conversation between Widukind and Bruno had ceased. A small warning grunt from Kaela also went unnoticed.

The shelters built by the townspeople between the north and south courtyards appeared on the parchment and he was adding windows to the central castle tower when the silence finally registered and he looked up to find Widukind and Bruno standing beside him.

'Another of your talents, I see,' said Widukind appreciatively. He studied Fenn's changes. "Normally these drawings are destroyed, but this one I may keep.'

'I apologise,' said Fenn. 'I...'

Widukind stopped him. 'Even I can see the drawing is much improved. Thank you for adding my banner.'

Bruno gave Fenn a curious look then bowed to take his leave.

Widukind said to him: 'Call in the men from the town gates and close the castle main gate.'

He turned from the table to face Fenn.

'Wichbert was impressed with your preparations,' he said. 'I've asked the other commanders to also mark their archers' range, but I fear once the Franks realise what your markers are, they will be removed.'

'I expect they will,' replied Fenn. 'But by that time our archers will have the range in their heads.'

Widukind nodded. 'Now, you've had little time to prepare, so I wanted to ask you if there is anything I can do for you. Is there anything you need?'

Fenn shook his head. 'Thank you, no.'

Widukind bowed. 'Until tomorrow.'

Fenn started to swing his arm to his chest. He stopped himself, but Widukind gave a gruff laugh.

'I've heard about that too,' he said.

CHAPTER TWENTY-SIX

Living and dying on a castle wall…

'*Franzosen!*'

The shout came from the north wall and was repeated around the castle. Fenn peered into the darkness. Kaela had been asleep beside him but she stood up and looked through one of the slits in the tower. Nothing moved in the night. In spite of Widukind's hopes, the sky had clouded over and it was like staring into black ink. Fenn was thankful there was no wind. Wind was the enemy of the archer.

'Every man alert; archers string your bows but nobody shoot until they have a target,' said Fenn. Kaela's voice was croaky and she cleared her throat. Porteus relayed the call.

Fenn moved from the tower onto the wall and immediately Olgood's bulk loomed into view. Fenn could only see a few feet in front of him. The whole Frankish army could be standing twenty feet from the wall and they would be invisible. He stepped to the parapet, knocking his toe against a large rock.

'Do you see anything?'

'No,' said Olgood after a moment. 'But I think our ears will provide better warning.'

'Tell everyone to be quiet.' Porteus rumbling voice gave the order. The small noises along the entire southern wall ceased. Fenn smiled to himself. With Porteus relaying orders, he had the whole south wall under his command. He closed his eyes and listened for a clank of metal or the shuffling of shoes. He could only hear the faint chirping of frogs.

A long time passed without any change.

'Archers can unstring.' The archers would not want their strings to get damp in the night air. They would want to keep them curled and dry inside their tunic and against their skin.

Kaela said to him: 'You sleep. I'll wake you if there's anything.'

'Anything at all,' said Fenn.

*   *   *

Fenn woke before dawn. He stretched and leaned against the wall of the tower, trying to ease the stiffness in his muscles. To the east, a tiny streak of colour showed on the horizon. The air was still and cool. He automatically checked the stones in his sling bag for the hundredth time that night and felt with his foot for the bag of Frankish stones by the opening to the wall. Bruno's pile was in the same place on the other side of the tower.

A boy appeared carrying a bucket of water. Kaela stopped him and dipped in a cup, handing it to Fenn while the boy waited patiently. He rolled the water around in his mouth then drank some and splashed some more on his face wiping it dry with his hands then wiping his hands through his hair. It was very cold and refreshing.

He shook his head and stood at a shooting slit looking toward the river.

'Anything?'

'Not a sound; not a movement.'

Fenn took a deep breath.

'Everybody awake and at their post,' he said.

For some reason, Porteus kept his voice relatively low and only disturbed the two nearest towers. Surprised grunts of men being woken came from nearby. Should he order the bows to be strung? It may be best to wait until the sun was rising and the dew had been lifted from the ground. It was probably unnecessary anyway; the men would decide when the time was right.

Fenn walked onto the wall and looked with displeasure at the rock he had knocked his toe against in the night. He could see it better now and it was no wonder he had almost tripped on it. The rock was so large Fenn doubted he could lift it. He looked along the wall. The bottom of the parapet was lined with rocks and large stones but this rock was the largest. He hadn't noticed it before. Olgood must have collected it and the others while Fenn and Kaela were at Widukind's meeting.

There was no shouted warning.

A burning star streaked across the sky and landed in front of the main gate. Immediately there was a noise that could have been a dull roar of voices.

Fenn raised his voice. 'Only shoot when you have a target.'

He exchanged a glance with Kaela and then with Olgood and Hakon who appeared out of the gloom.

The battle had begun.

Fenn stepped onto the huge rock. He could see movement in the cornfield and was pleased when none of his archers wasted arrows shooting futilely towards it. It looked as though the Franks *were* going to attack the main gate, although in what strength he couldn't tell. He could clearly see the row of white sacks standing like beacons in the night as he had intended, but as yet there was nothing visible in front of them. He spared a glance at the horizon. Day was fast approaching.

'Wait for a target,' he called again, 'Shoot at archers and leaders first until they reach the castle.' He heard Porteus' voice boom his command along the wall.

He saw a running figure come into view in front of the sacks. The man paused and made the motion of drawing a bow although he couldn't see the bow itself. Several more figures appeared alongside him. Fenn didn't see or hear any Frankish arrows hitting the castle walls let alone coming over the parapet. They were well out of range.

They're in the twenty-yard area, thought Fenn. Has Manfredi seen that?

The slap of a bowstring on a leather wrist-guard from directly above gave him his answer. Each archer had a bucket of arrows alongside him and

Fenn imagined Manfredi reaching down for another. He couldn't see where Manfredi's arrow landed, but it must have been close because the group of men withdrew into the gloom.

The light had increased markedly in the last few moments and Fenn checked both walls. An archer was standing with a nocked arrow at each parapet gap with a swordsman beside him. Extra swordsmen were stationed by the steps to the courtyard as Kaela had suggested. Gunther stood back from the parapet with his five roving swordsmen. He looked relaxed, a sword out but held loosely in his hand. Fenn saw that he still wore his second sword.

Fenn bent his head to Kaela. 'Tell Porteus to go to his men. I'll fetch him if I need him.'

A band of Franks came out of the ever-lightening shadows running steadily for the gate. Fenn saw some of the men carried large shields which they held high over their heads as they ran. They were protecting another group who were carrying a tree trunk by its protruding branches.

'Aim for their legs,' shouted Fenn and then realised he had just sent Porteus away. He heard Hakon call out the order.

Kaela appeared beside him and said she had checked the other wall and it was quiet on the other side of the tower.

It was difficult for the archers on the wall to shoot in any direction except straight ahead – only the archers in the tower were able to shoot along the wall. Fenn's sling was even more restricted – he had to stand back from the parapet to shoot through the gaps and nobody could stand near him when his sling was whirling.

Fenn took a stone from his bag and leapt up onto the parapet, standing in the gap. He started the sling turning and after four revolutions let his stone go. The men carrying the tree trunk were a hundred yards away but he had a tangle of legs to aim at. His stone struck home and one of the men fell. Another, with an arrow in the thigh, fell beside him. A third peeled away from the others with an arrow in his hip. The tree trunk slowed but then recovered as some of the men from the protecting group filled the gaps left by the fallen.

Kaela called out 'Archers!' as an arrow clattered on the stonework below Fenn's feet. Even as he turned, Fenn's sling was in motion. The open land in front of the castle was now lit by the rim of the rising sun and men were streaming across the grassland where the horses had grazed yesterday. There were hundreds spread along the whole wall. Many were carrying ladders. If the same number were attacking the other walls of the castle, Marchant must have many more than a thousand at his command.

Fenn's stone felled an archer who had just shot an arrow and had started to run closer. Another runner scooped up his fallen arrow bag. Fenn singled out a man in a blue helmet. His stone flew but the man was further away than Fenn had calculated and the stone hit the man low in his side. He fell, but rose to his knees, holding his side. A broken rib perhaps but not a fatal blow.

'Fenn, come down! You're too exposed!'

As if to emphasize her words, several arrows clattered on the parapet stones and one thrummed through the gap beside Fenn, missing him only by inches. He jumped down onto the wall with his heart racing. That was too close. He could hear the arrows being shot from his own archers in reply. He crouched down and tried to think what he should be doing. His eyes rose to see Porteus and his men standing twenty feet away. Porteus was looking away from him but his stance was still very relaxed, waiting for the time when he had work to do. His air of relaxation was just what Fenn needed to slow his rapid breathing. He forced himself to stand up straight, thankful that Porteus hadn't seen him. The men would take no inspiration from a cowering leader.

A rhythmic thumping came from the main gate. The tree trunk ram was attacking the outer door. Wichbert was in charge of the main gate tower, tower one, and Fenn silently wished him well but could spare him no more thought.

A man cried out and reeled from the parapet with an arrow in his shoulder. A woman came running up the steps from the courtyard. One of the swordsmen helped the wounded man to his feet and started to help him to the steps but Porteus stopped him and sent him back to his post. He held the man until the woman arrived. She put the man's arm over her shoulder just as the boy who had brought them water ran up to help. With the arrow still grotesquely protruding from both sides of the archer's shoulder, step by step they slowly descended to the courtyard.

The full light of the sun now shone on the battlefield revealing still more men emerging from the corn and Fenn could also see figures among the houses by the river. Widukind had either been misinformed about the numbers of Franks under Marchant's control or he had miscalculated. From the numbers Fenn had already seen, there were at least a thousand attacking the south wall alone and they didn't seem worried about having the river at their backs. He had to hope Widukind was being more accurately informed about the current situation. He had said he didn't think they could withstand an attack by two thousand men. It looked like they would find out. It may all depend on how Widukind used his men and especially the men he had kept in reserve.

He reached for a stone and stepped back to the parapet. He targeted an archer and sent a stone into his face knocking him backwards. He found he had to stand to one side of the parapet gap in order to shoot through it. With sudden insight he recalled his father Lenglan advising him to swing his sling in a vertical circle 'like the Frankish slingers'. He could see that would be an advantage now. He could release the stone from the top of the circle to shoot down and from the bottom if he wanted to shoot upwards. But he hadn't thought back then that he would be slinging stones from a castle wall.

Another archer came into Fenn's view and Fenn's stone knocked him down. The Franks were only fifty yards away from the wall. It made for easier shooting but there were too many to stop them all. He could see more ladders appearing in his window of view. He hesitated, waiting for a prime target, but realised that, despite his own orders, his view was so restricted he may as well shoot at anything that appeared. He sent a stone at the leading man of three that were bringing a ladder forward. The man fell and dragged the ladder down with him. The end dug into the ground and the following two fell over the fallen man and into the ladder, breaking rungs and hopefully, Fenn thought, bones as well.

'Ready with your stones, Olgood. Try to break a few ladders as well as heads if you can.'

Olgood bent and with his muscles bulging, hoisted the huge stone in front of Fenn onto the parapet.

'I want to use this one first. It took three of us to get it up here and if I get tired I may not be able to lift it later,' Olgood said with a grin.

Hakon barked out an order and some of the other hurling stones were lifted onto the parapet.

Fenn shot another stone through the gap and another ladder took a tumble but this one didn't break. Olgood put his hand in front of Fenn to stop him for a moment. He leaned over the parapet and took a quick peek down the wall, withdrawing immediately.

Something brushed Fenn's arm and he looked down to see Kaela holding out the bag of Frankish stones. He smiled his thanks and dug his hand into the bag pulling out three stones just as Olgood said: 'One, two, three…' and pushed the large rock off the edge.

The sound of splintering wood and screams of pain came from below the wall.

'That rock always wanted to get back on the ground,' said Olgood and stepped back from the gap. 'I'll go and find another.'

Fenn chose one of the Frankish stones and looked for a target.

There was a loud crash from the main gate and then some high-pitched screaming to match the sounds caused by Olgood's rock.

'They've broken through the first door and found the trench – and the sharpened stakes,' said Kaela calmly.

With his sling still whirling above his head, Fenn looked at her. She was leaning against the parapet with her weight on one hip with her hands folded in front of her. She may well have been at a banquet for all the concern she was showing.

'They'll use ladders to get over the trench,' he said, 'and once they're over, they'll be protected by the tunnel and only one door to stop them.'

He spied a man who seemed to be shouting orders at the other men. Fenn's stone was aimed at his head but caught him in the throat, cutting off his shouting instantly. He collapsed writhing on the ground. Fenn wished he had asked Kaela to tell him the message on that stone.

He looked along the wall. Two men were down and being attended to by some women. Their wounds looked serious. Fenn saw the water boy kneeling with his bucket beside one of the wounded men, holding the head of the fallen man and helping him drink.

Two small girls carrying a bucket of arrows between them, their hair, dresses and bare limbs plastered to a dull brown by the dust of the courtyard, were scurrying along the wall replacing the arrows the archers had used. Their bucket emptied and they ran back to the steps for a refill. Fenn noticed their feet were bare.

'There's not enough men at the barricade,' said Kaela.

He checked the barricade in front of the gate. There were men stationed there but too few to handle the numbers of Franks now crossing the grassland, heading for the gate, seemingly heedless of the deadly shower of arrows and the men falling around them.

Fenn strode quickly through the tower and took stock of the other wall. One wounded man was sitting against the parapet, a bloody cloth around his head, but he was waving away a woman and as Fenn watched, he struggled to his feet and picked up his fallen bow. Gunther saw Fenn and waved, watching for orders, but when none came he continued to scan the wall. Fenn looked through the first parapet gap. There were not as many men attacking this wall as the other – just enough to keep the defenders busy.

The main target was the gate.

Fenn ran back through the tower. Olgood had a rock over his head and he threw it forcefully over the wall.

The top of a ladder appeared and Fenn started toward it but Porteus ran up and put an arm in his way. He grabbed the ladder and twisted it violently, then pushed it out of the gap and sent it sliding along the wall. Other swordsmen were also now active, some leaning over the parapet and thrusting with their swords, others, like Porteus, struggling with ladders.

The rhythmic thumping sounded again at the gate.

'Kaela, tell Gunther and his men to come with us. We'll reinforce the barricade.'

He called to Olgood and Hakon. 'You two as well, come with me.'

Porteus looked at him but Fenn motioned him to stay where he was.

They reached the barricade just as Wichbert and a dozen swordsmen came out of the gate tower and joined them. Wichbert was carrying a sword in one hand and his spiked mace in the other. He nodded his thanks and turned to disperse his men.

Fenn saw the two girls carrying their bucket full of arrows, dodging men running in the courtyard, scampering towards the steps leading to the wall, their small grimy faces etched with determination. The smaller girl stumbled and fell to one knee, causing several arrows to tip out of the bucket. The other girl stooped to help her pick them up, then, with each one clutching a bunch of fallen arrows in one hand and the other holding the bucket, they ran for the steps. Fenn opened his mouth to tell them to stop and take shelter but the courtyard was full of noise and by the time he asked Kaela to call to them they would be too far away to hear.

He turned to Kaela and said: 'Tell Gunther the same rules apply. Keep his men together and go where the need is greatest.'

Fenn scanned the barricade and saw a solid wooden table stacked on one side. It had been thrown haphazardly onto the barricade and had fallen with its legs protruding, causing more of a hazard to the defenders than the attackers.

'Olgood, can you get me that table. Put it here.' Fenn indicated a place that gave him a good view of the gate over the barricade.

A thought occurred to him. 'Kaela...'

She smiled and held out the bag of Frankish stones. 'Were you going to ask about these?'

The thumping of the ram sounded louder. The door was about to be breached. Olgood and Hakon retrieved the table, then each of them took the red-handled axes from their belts and stood in front of the table. Hakon leaned over and touched his axe to Olgood's, the metal blades making a clink as they met.

'For luck,' he said.

Fenn squeezed Kaela's arm and looked into her deep brown eyes for a brief moment. They were out of time.

He took the Frankish stones from her, thrusting some into the bag on his belt and dropping the rest at his feet. Kaela drew the Lord of the Battle from her scabbard, the blade making a sighing sound as it was freed as if anticipating action at last. Fenn leaped onto the table just as the wood of the inner door splintered.

It hadn't yet broken and the ram crashed into the wood again with an ominous thud. Fenn had time to steady himself, select a stone and begin his sling whirling before the door finally exploded.

Shrieking their cries and screams of war, the Franks poured through the breach.

CHAPTER TWENTY-SEVEN

Desperate defence…

The man leading the charge to the barricade was as tall as Olgood with wild streaming hair. He held a two-handed sword raised above his head and his face was twisted into a mask of hatred. Fenn's stone felled him like a tree crashing in the forest; the men close behind tripped on his body and also tumbled into the dust. In spite of that holdup, there were so many Franks rushing into the courtyard it only took a moment for them to be at the barricade. Fenn took out the first man who attempted to scramble over the top. Many of the defenders behind the barricade were armed with long spears which they used with devastating effect, inflicting terrible damage and keeping the Frankish swordsmen at bay. But they were too few. Fenn's stones knocked the Franks off the barricade as soon as they started to climb, but he needed to pause to reach for more stones allowing first one then more to scramble over and engage the defenders hand-to-hand. From the corner of his eye, he saw Gunther and his men attack a group that had broken past the defenders, forcing them back against the barricade.

The air went quiet around Fenn. The only sound he heard was the whirling of his sling like a muted banshee moaning in the wind. In a smooth continuous motion, his fingers gathered the loosened sling, his thumb pinched the ends together, a stone nestled into the pouch and it whirled again – one, two, three – the missile flying to crack a head or break a knee – whatever was exposed and in his vision. In spite of Fenn's lethal fusillade and the efforts of the men at the barricade, a swarm of fighting men spread into the courtyard, resolving into a myriad of deadly man-to-man contests, with men from both sides falling and dying. For those that didn't die immediately, the injuries were hideous and their raucous screams tore at the air.

From the corner of his eye, he saw Olgood cast a spear and Hakon was knocked backwards by some blow.

The table rocked and the noises of the battle re-entered Fenn's head. An arrow appeared in the neck of a man in front of Fenn, turning his snarl into a gurgle and knocking him sideways as his sword was being lifted. Manfredi! Fenn knew without looking.

There were bodies sprawled on the ground in front of Kaela and at that moment she was engaging three men, the Lord of the Battle flashing in the sunlight. Olgood and Hakon were back together and working as a team, Olgood chopping high, Hakon chopping low. Olgood's blows didn't just knock the man down, his opponents were tossed backwards. The men in front of him were pushing back against those behind, unwilling to come within range of his lethal swinging axe.

Fenn saw bodies piled on bodies, some moving, some not, and the screams of pain were mixed with screams of rage seeming to come from every direction, assaulting his ears.

The air around him was thick with dust. He leapt from the table, adding his own guttural shout to the din, burying his axe in the neck of one of Kaela's attackers. The man fell forward and Fenn used his foot to pull his axe free. He swung at another man coming from his right and realised that they were being surrounded. Then Gunther was at Kaela's side, his blade slashing at the second man's sword arm and nearly severing it. Kaela's sword took out the last man's throat with a spray of blood that showered them all. Another man came at Fenn, his sword slashing in a downward arc aimed at his head. Fenn stepped back smoothly and let the blade sweep past his chest, countering with a swing of his axe at the man's head. The man tilted his head back but Fenn twisted the handle of his axe and the blade sliced into the man's shoulder. He felt the jar of his axe striking bone and pulled it free. Gunther's sword stabbed into the man's chest. He kicked the man away.

Kaela shouted and pointed. 'Wichbert!'

She ducked a swinging sword and her blade bit deep into the man's neck as if it was butter. Gunther knocked him down.

Wichbert was ten feet away on his knees, blood pouring from a gash in his head. His sword had fallen from his hand and he was leaning on his mace to keep himself upright. The men around him were being overwhelmed. Olgood and Hakon had already moved. Blood was dripping from Hakon's elbow. Fenn saw his mouth shouting but couldn't hear what he was saying.

He thrust the table out of his way and ran to Wichbert. With Olgood and Hakon working to one side, and Kaela and Gunther to the other, they took on the circle of Franks who obviously recognised Wichbert and were trying urgently to get to him. Kaela – her sword moving at incredible speed – dropped men like dominos, slashing with deadly efficiency. She was not wielding her sword for show – each movement had serious intent – but the showmanship was there all the same, clearly evident in her smooth economy. If one stroke was not enough, two strokes were the most it took to take a man out of the fight. The first pushed aside his sword and before he could recover, the second delivered a fatal blow, to the head, the neck or to the torso below the ribs. It was like a lethal dance where only she knew the steps, clumsy Franks flailing in her wake. Wherever her sword touched, it trailed streaks of red. Gunther circled around her, his sword moving continuously, protecting her, using his strength with such ferocity that no man could outflank her.

The axes that Fenn, Olgood and Hakon wielded made some of the Franks wary. They were used to facing swords but the long-handled axes of the Northmen topped with a wickedly curved blade were unfamiliar and many were obviously not willing to confront them.

Within moments a space had cleared around Wichbert as, in the face of the sudden and effective reinforcement, the Frankish assault stalled.

Fenn dropped his axe into his belt and lifted Wichbert with an arm under his back. Wichbert's head was lolling on his shoulders, blood covering his face, but Fenn could hear laboured breathing rasping in his throat. He reached under Wichbert's knees, picking him up and turned toward the castle. A Frank moved to intercept him but an arrow slapped into his chest at the same time as Olgood appeared beside Fenn dragging Hakon with him. Olgood shoved the falling man aside and stayed on Fenn's flank, swinging at another Frank who backed away from him, unwilling to face the huge man.

Fenn carried Wichbert to the castle doors with Olgood and Hakon plus Kaela and Gunther walking backwards to cover him. The Franks paused in their forward motion and allowed a gap to form between them; Kaela's blade and Olgood's strength having done enough damage to inspire caution even in the heat of battle.

Fenn looked back over his shoulder and threw a glance around the courtyard. Above the noise, he heard new shouts and women screaming.

Kaela called: 'They're saying the north wall has been breached!'

There were pockets of fighting near the shelters that the townspeople had erected. Franks were still climbing the barricade but in much reduced numbers. One or two at a time. Fenn could see that some were ascending the steps to engage the swordsmen on the walls. There were also Frankish archers in the courtyard but they were thankfully being kept out of the conflict by the attention of the archers on the wall and in the towers; his men were still holding to the target priorities he had given them.

The impression that Fenn formed was that the struggle at that moment was evenly balanced because, although outnumbered, the Saxons had the advantage of height and the protection of the towers, but the fight could easily tip in the Frank's favour if they continued to bring extra numbers through the gate.

A voice with authority shouted from the tunnel and, as Fenn passed through the castle doors, several Franks who had recently crossed the barricade called encouragement to the men who were reluctant to press Fenn's group and together they began again to move determinedly forward.

'Shall we hold them here at the doors?'

Fenn thought swiftly. At the doors, only two or three men could enter at the same time. They could more easily be held there than in the wide hallway.

'Yes, hold them there. I'll get Wichbert to the infirmary and join you.'

Immediately opposite the castle doors, across the entrance hall, were the doors to the great hall where they had first met Widukind. The infirmary was the next room along the entrance hall but as Fenn reached it, a group of five or six men appeared a hundred feet away at the far end of the hall and charged forward. The Franks were already inside the castle! If they tried to hold the castle doors they would be attacked on two sides.

'Close the doors,' he called. 'We'll make our stand in the infirmary!' He felt he was being crowded into a corner.

Olgood slammed the doors shut and bolted them just as a body crashed against them. The doors were sturdy but the bolts wouldn't hold for long.

Fenn stepped inside the infirmary, leaving the other four to engage the group of Franks advancing down the hall.

At a table at the far end of the room, Mathilde and Gisele were assisting a physician who was sawing at a man's leg. They both looked up and were startled when they saw Fenn carrying Wichbert, obviously injured, but each maintained her grip holding the man on the table. Fenn searched for a place to put Wichbert but every bench was already occupied and many men already lay on the floor.

Fenn heard a warning cry from behind him. '*Fenn!*'

He twisted to face the doorway. A man had somehow bypassed the defenders and was looking about with wild eyes. He spied Fenn and then Wichbert and leaped forward with a snarl that sounded more animal than human.

Fenn crouched and let Wichbert onto the ground as gently as he could. Wichbert groaned and the iron head of the mace that was still locked in his hand landed with a dull clank on the stone floor. Fenn stood before Wichbert's body to protect him and pulled Thorvald's axe from his belt bending low as he did so to escape a wildly swinging sword. He parried the man's second strike on the iron axe-handle, immediately thrusting the head of the axe forward into the surprised man's face. It was the same move he had employed during the fight at the crossroads in Skyrvid Forest and it had the same effect. The man reeled back, blood gushing from his nose. Fenn stepped to him and swung at his head. Somehow the man evaded the blow and backed away to recover his balance. Fenn followed him but unexpectedly the Frank stiffened and arched backwards. He seemed frozen in that position for a moment then fell towards Fenn, a knife embedded in his back.

His falling body revealed Heinrich on a bench by the wall, raised on one elbow, his hand still extended. Fenn nodded in acknowledgement and turned back to the door.

Olgood and Hakon, followed by Kaela and Gunther, backed into the infirmary leaving more dead or dying bodies in the hallway. Gunther's left arm was bloody from elbow to wrist. The second sword was gone from his belt.

Fenn checked the room. The infirmary was a long room, fifty feet by twenty, with shelving containing implements and bottles along the far wall and the physician's table also at that end. Benches extended into the room along both walls, each occupied by two or more wounded men. There was no other exit. In a short while they would either walk from the room or die among these wounded. The latter seemed more likely, but the day was not yet over.

He met Mathilde's eyes as she ran forward to check Wichbert, then Gisele's who stared back at him. In her hands she held the man's severed leg, the foot still encased in a shoe. She looked down at the leg and dropped it into the corner where it fell onto a bloody pile of detached limbs. She wiped her hands on a cloth then calmly chose a large knife from the table where the man now lay thankfully unconscious, and followed Mathilde towards the front of the room. The physician had a helpless expression on his face, his hands waving uncertainly in front of him, plainly unsure what he should do. Some movement drew his attention to the man whose leg he had just removed and his hands steadied. He bent to attend to the bleeding.

Fenn looked at the injured men crowding the room. None were able to fight, although Heinrich was struggling to get off the bench, holding his hand to a bloody patch on his side. Mathilde was trying to check Wichbert's wound and also keep Heinrich lying down.

Everyone turned toward the infirmary door when a loud crash came from the hall. The castle doors had been broken open.

Gisele paused beside Wichbert. She dropped the knife and prised the mace free from his hand, raising it up and testing its weight. She gave a grim smile of satisfaction. Fenn stepped away from Wichbert and together he and Gisele joined the others. Each person moved apart to give themselves room to fight, forming a curved line in front of the wounded men, twenty feet from the door. Fenn's hand went to his belt but his sling was gone, lying somewhere in the courtyard dust.

He checked his companions.

Gisele; fierce and determined, standing beside Olgood, Wichbert's mace with its heavy head of spikes clutched tightly in her hand – both of her forearms already covered in blood. She looked every inch a true shield maiden. Woe betide anyone who tried to hurt her man. Without looking at him she reached over to touch Olgood on the arm. He responded and squeezed her hand.

Olgood; solid like a towering oak, an impassable barrier, making sure he stood slightly in front of Gisele. The blade of his axe was already as red as the handle. He breathed steadily, with every fibre of his body, his trunk-like legs, his knotted arms and shoulders, taut and ready.

Hakon; feisty, never still, shifting from foot to foot, his breath hissing through clenched teeth. Fenn could see the resolve in his eyes – he would not be captured again.

Gunther; his wounded arm forgotten, easily and confidently balanced on his feet, sword at the ready. He stood on the other side of Kaela, his vow still in place, his sword still hers, still her protector. His face was lined with streaks of dried blood from a wound in his scalp and it also bore the marks of several close encounters in the courtyard. He would continue to give much more than he received.

And Kaela. She was calmness personified and her beauty in that moment took his breath away, her face framed by her flaming hair, her dark eyes sparkling. The Lord of the Battle was drawn and held loosely at her side, but Fenn knew she was a long way from unready. He had seen the speed with which she could bring the Damascus steel blade into play and her amazing skill when that blade moved in her hand. She felt his gaze and turned her head slightly. Their eyes locked and Kaela slowly smiled.

The sound of running footsteps came from the hall. Men appeared outside the door but they didn't attempt to enter. Fenn tried to count how many were in the hall. There could be as many as twenty. He wondered if they should close on the door to restrict the entry of the Franks but that would also restrict their own ability to fight.

One man stood framed in the doorway. He gazed quickly around the room taking in the group of defenders standing before him. He raised his hand and beckoned to someone in the hall.

Another man stepped up to the door. He was a young man with wavy long black hair to his shoulders and a thick moustache. He held his chin jutting forward and his eyes half-closed, projecting disdain and arrogance. The most startling feature was a scarlet cloak draped over his shoulders. Fenn could not imagine that cloak crossing the courtyard unchallenged if Manfredi's bow was still active. Maybe he had donned the garment only when he was inside the castle.

The man peered into the room and, apparently satisfied, stepped inside. As he entered, the other men followed and formed up behind him to either side.

Mathilde whispered behind Fenn: '*Marchant!*'

Marchant spoke. He had a high boyish voice.

When he had finished, Kaela said softly: 'First he said: 'So Wichbert *is* here. Good.' Then he invited us to surrender. He says the castle is lost and he has Widukind's banner. He doesn't have Widukind yet but says that is only a matter of time now that his men are inside the walls. He says we have all fought well but there is no need for any more to die. We will all be treated as well as can be expected.'

When Kaela started to translate his words, Marchant put a gloved hand to his mouth to cover a smile. He spoke again, at first with amusement and then in a serious tone.

'He sees that there are some foreigners among us who do not speak his language. He asked who is the leader of these mercenaries.'

'*I* am,' said Fenn loudly.

Marchant held out his hand and said a few words.

'He wants you to hand him your weapon as a gesture of surrender.'

'Tell him,' said Fenn, 'that I will never surrender, and I will not allow him to harm this man…' Fenn pointed at Wichbert. 'If he wants to take my weapon, let him try. He will lose many men and *he* will not leave this room alive.'

412

Fenn thought Marchant would not be worried about losing men but he may be concerned for his own safety.

When Kaela spoke, Marchant frowned and his eyes flicked around the room to confirm his assessment of the situation. He stared at Fenn then gave a feminine giggle, drew back his head and spoke sharply.

'He called you impertinent,' said Kaela. 'He says we are but six and he is growing impatient. He said: Surrender now or die, he doesn't really care which choice you make.'

'Ask the men lying dead in the courtyard and outside this door if we are *'but six'*,' replied Fenn.

When Kaela had relayed his words, one of the men leaned over and whispered in Marchant's ear. Marchant's eyes moved quickly first to Olgood and then to Kaela. He looked her up and down, noting her sword as the man continued whispering. Fenn saw his eyes narrow as they flicked back to Gisele holding the mace in her bloody hand. For all he knew the blood on her arms had been earned in the courtyard. Fenn took the moment to glance at his companions.

Nobody had relaxed. Nobody had given up. They were all watching the Franks and they were ready. He had but to say the word and each man and woman would launch themselves forward and fight to the death even though they were outnumbered two or three to one. He was not overwhelmed by the odds, he considered each of the people beside him worth two or three. They had a chance of victory in this fight, a good chance. But there was also a good chance that not all of them would survive. Was he prepared to take that risk?

He had but to say the word.

The man was still talking to Marchant who was now regarding Fenn, the light frown still on his face. Fenn smiled back at him and tightened his grip on his axe.

Time for them both to decide.

The sound of shouting came into the room. Fenn heard the unmistakeable thrumming of horses' hooves from the courtyard. It grew louder, sounding like a stampede as if a hundred horses had broken out of the stables. Clashes of metal and a series of loud cries came from close by.

Marchant looked alarmed and indicated with a sideways jerk of his head that the man beside him should investigate.

The man pushed his way through the others standing behind Marchant just as renewed fighting erupted in the hall. Marchant's men all turned to the door and started to crowd through. Fenn tensed himself to shout a command and leap forward, to take advantage of the distraction, but hesitated as he realised the noise of the struggle was now directly outside the door. He watched Marchant's men stop then reverse their direction and re-enter the infirmary, pushed back by a wall of swords.

A group of Saxons followed them through the doorway and spread out to cover Marchant and his retinue, who backed slowly into the room. With Fenn's group, the Franks were surrounded.

Widukind stepped into the infirmary.

He bowed to Marchant with a smile on his face. Kaela moved close to Fenn so she could talk in his ear. As Olgood leaned in so he could overhear, Fenn whispered to him: 'Not today, my friend.' Olgood's large hand rested on Fenn's shoulder and he repeated: 'Not today.'

'So, my little piglet,' said Widukind, the smile never leaving his face. He was enjoying the moment immensely. 'It seems we have you penned.'

Marchant said nothing. He stared at Widukind as if he still could not believe the rapid change of fortune.

'Please…' said Widukind. He pointed to the floor, '…your swords – if you will.'

Fenn stepped forward and held out his hand for Marchant's sword. The Frankish leader's head snapped back, his face furious. He drew his sword and for a moment Fenn thought he might try to use it on him, but Marchant cast it forcefully onto the floor. It landed with a ringing clatter on the stones, followed a few moments later by a sustained rattle as the other swords were dropped.

Widukind stepped back and his men rounded up the Franks and herded them out of the infirmary.

Widukind looked towards Mathilde. 'Matti – how is he?'

414

'A head wound and a heavy knock. Not as bad as it looks. He'll recover with rest.'

Widukind drew in a breath of relief then addressed Fenn, Kaela translating as he talked.

'The day is ours, no small thanks to you and your people,' he said. 'If you hadn't held as long as you did behind the barricade, we may have lost everything.'

'Your reserve was cavalry?'

'Some of them – but we can discuss this later.' He glanced at each person. 'You all seem to be in need of attention. Let's see how much of this blood is yours and how much once belonged to someone else. When you are cleaned and refreshed, I'll meet with you in the great hall – all of you – and we'll talk.'

He turned away but then turned back.

'In case you are thinking we may have won the day but not the battle and we'll go through this again with Charles…?' He held up a finger. 'No. With Marchant in our hands we are strongly placed to bargain with Charles when he arrives. If Marchant had been killed it would have been a disaster, but alive…' He waved his hand in the air indicating a wealth of possibilities.

'Was this your plan to defeat Marchant?' asked Fenn. 'Capture him and bargain?'

Widukind smiled. 'Plans have a way of evaporating the moment a battle begins – but, yes, that was the essence.'

Still smiling, he walked over to Mathilde and Wichbert.

*   *   *

They sat at the big table in the great hall. Widukind had called again for wine and this time Fenn welcomed it.

Through Kaela, Widukind related his plan to use his reserve and fifty mounted men only when Marchant was sighted, with the hope of capturing him. That plan was discarded when the Franks broke through at the main gate and Wichbert fell. At the same time, a small group scaled the north wall and the castle was in danger of being lost. The north breach was contained by Bruno, although some Franks did enter the castle. Widukind ordered his mounted men into the courtyard to clear the Franks from the main gate, but their deployment was delayed by confusion in the overcrowded stables and the crucial moment to strike – and possibly the battle – was lost.

He looked at Fenn.

'Your spirited support of Wichbert bought the time we needed to finally get order in the stables and the horsemen into the battle. You fought the Franks almost to a standstill then and it was only your withdrawal to save Wichbert that allowed them to regain their momentum. The gods were with us shortly after that though, because seeing his men break through the castle doors enticed Marchant to enter the castle – no doubt, he thought, to claim his prize.'

'My horsemen caught the Franks completely by surprise. There was no room in the courtyard to form an effective resistance to cavalry and the fight quickly went out of them. Some pockets continued to fight but, because they were not united, each was swiftly overcome. In any case, the attack was over as soon as we had isolated Marchant.'

Widukind put his hands on the table.

'Your men of the seventh tower performed well. They kept fighting even when the enemy was on both sides of the wall. I'll make sure they're given a bonus.'

Fenn leaned forward. 'I would also ask that you reward some other people of the seventh tower. The women who looked after the wounded; the two girls who brought arrows and the boy who brought water. They continued to strive to do their work until the very end.'

Fenn told about the girls determined to make their way to the wall with their bucket full of arrows even as the Franks were bursting through the gate.

'Of course. They were good Saxons and did what was expected of them.' Widukind paused, and his face softened. 'No, you're right – those women and children did much more than that.'

Mathilde's son Bruno ran into the hall from the side door. He went to Widukind and whispered in his ear. Widukind listened then laughed, nodding his head and giving Bruno a gentle push. Bruno walked around the table with all eyes upon him. He reached Fenn, stood straight and gave Fenn's salute, at the same time bringing forward the hand he had held behind his back. Clutched in his hand was Fenn's sling.

Fenn pulled the boy into a hug. 'Thank you, Bruno. How did you find it?'

Kaela asked the question and Bruno said: 'Mama told me you had lost it so I looked for it.'

Fenn leaned back in his chair. 'Olgood left a sword resting against the wall just inside the entrance of the seventh tower,' he said. 'If your father agrees, that sword is yours Bruno.'

Kaela translated and Widukind said something to Bruno who grinned then turned around smartly and ran from the hall.

Widukind sat back in his chair, his gaze moving between them.

'First you help Matti, then you help save the castle and protect my son with your lives, rejecting Marchant's offer of surrender. How can I repay you all for your services to Saxony – and to me?'

Fenn thought for a moment. 'If you believe Charles won't continue the fight and there is no further threat from the Franks, then all we ask is our cart and horses and we will bid you farewell and be on our way.'

'Matti says you are trying to get back to your home across the western sea – is that correct?'

Fenn nodded: 'Yes.'

Widukind smiled. 'Then I can do much more than give you horses. I can give you a ship!'

Fenn stared at him.

'There's a ship due at the dock tomorrow or the next day, bringing tin and wool from Hamwic and wine from Bruggas.' He smiled and waggled a finger in the air. 'Nothing must stop our trade. If Charles does not interfere, I can ensure you are all on that ship for its return journey.'

Fenn was unable to speak. Hamwic was in Wessex, Kaela's home. There was a ship that could take them to Wessex!

*　　*　　*

Fenn stood with Kaela before Manfredi.

'I think you saved my life twice and there were probably other times I didn't see. You are a true marksman. Thank you Manfredi, I'm in your debt.'

'I put my arrows where I thought they were best used,' the archer replied with a stiff bow. He stood silently for a moment as if deciding whether to say more then looked directly at Fenn.

'You led us with honour. You all stood with us and proved yourselves on the wall and at the barricade, and that, in my eyes, repays any debt. I was proud to fight with you. If you require the service of my bow again, you need only ask.'

Fenn nodded and held out his hand.

Manfredi surprised him by clasping Fenn's forearm in the style of the Northmen. When he released the arm, he smiled and his voice became less formal.

'When I saw you kill the hawk, I knew you were a Master. Only a Master would have attempted that shot.'

Fenn was startled by Manfredi's use of the word 'Master'. He was reminded of the monks of St. Cuthbert's. He had aspired to that title when he was in the monastery.

Manfredi continued. 'You were like an avenging devil with your whirling sling,' he said. 'I've never seen better. You almost stopped them at the barricade.'

When Kaela had finished the translation, Manfredi addressed some words to her and she seemed unsure how to reply. Fenn looked at her with raised eyebrows.

'He said he was… impressed… with my sword.'

'He said more than that.'

She sighed. 'He called me a Valkyrie of the dust, choosing the men who were to die this day.' She smiled at Fenn. 'He said we make a formidable team.'

Manfredi brought his heels together and gave Fenn's salute which both Fenn and Kaela returned.

*   *   *

When Porteus saw Fenn approaching, he gathered the remaining men of the seventh tower so they were standing in a group, swordsmen and archers together. Fenn was surprised but pleased to see the man with the head wound was still with them – he would have expected him to have returned to the infirmary. All of the men bore some mark of battle, from bloodied cloths binding a wound, to bruises, cuts and scratches and streaks of blood on their exposed skin – a testament to the commitment and involvement of each man.

Porteus' voice boomed out and the men straightened their shoulders. When Fenn and Kaela stood before him, he shouted one more word and Fenn felt a ringing in his ears.

In perfect unison, Porteus and his men saluted, their fists crashing on their chests with an audible thump.

Fenn personally thanked and spoke with each of his men including nine who were in the still overcrowded infirmary.

Five swordsmen and three archers from the seventh tower had been killed or died of wounds.

Over the next two days, Fenn and Kaela visited each of the families of the fallen that were still within the castle walls. They also sought out and spent some time with their water boy and his family and they found the two sisters who had so valiantly carried arrows to the archers on the wall, with their mother. Their father was in the infirmary with a serious hand wound. He may lose some fingers but was expected to live. Fenn gave the mother a handful of coins from the basket. She protested it was too much but Fenn said it wasn't enough.

*   *   *

As Fenn and his companions left the castle gates, the two doves reappeared and flew in circles overhead as if to thank Fenn for their salvation and to bid him farewell.

Fenn watched them soar against the clear blue of the sky and realised he had something in common with the snow-white birds. Both had faced an attack and their survival had been doubtful until they had received unexpected help. Now they continued with their lives, the outcome the same as if their continued existence had never been threatened.

The doves swooped low across their path enticing them forward. To Fenn, the doves were now symbols of hope.

Kaela was sad that she was leaving Midnight; she had become attached to the horse, but Mathilde had assured her that she would take the horse back to Gremwald and take good care of Midnight personally. Kaela held Fenn's arm as she walked away from the castle with a mixture of relief and regret in her eyes.

Widukind, Mathilde with her baby, and Wichbert – his head wrapped in a tight cloth – together with a detachment of Widukind's men, accompanied them to the Hammaburg dock.

They crossed the fields and Fenn was thankful that, in the days since the battle, the bodies of the dead had been removed, but he saw many of his flour sack markers were still in place. He kicked one as he passed and Olgood called out: 'Aye! *I* filled that sack and placed it in that spot and I'd rather not have it disturbed.'

Fenn laughed out loud and Olgood joined him. Fenn slapped him on the shoulder.

'Then we'll let it lie – it served its purpose well and may be useful again sometime.'

He tapped Askari's basket.

'Was everything intact inside?'

Olgood smiled and nodded.

'And filled with more food. We have everything we need.'

He reached out to pull Gisele closer.

Widukind had sent emissaries to Charles to inform him of Marchant's capture, but they had not yet returned. The ship Widukind had expected had duly arrived the previous afternoon and had been unloaded and received its return cargo: salt, wheat, spices, silver from the Harz mountains – and also six passengers.

The ship's captain was called Tollemarche, a tall wiry man with a huge black beard who walked with a swaying gait even when on land. He surprised his passengers by speaking to them in English as well as the local dialect with the result that he said most things twice, but he didn't seem to mind. He expected his passengers to work when he asked, even though he had been paid for their passage, his black eyes boring into each person to enforce that he would not tolerate dissent.

The farewells at dockside were prolonged, with multiple embraces and several short speeches. Widukind eventually took his leave after formally shaking each person by the hand and returned to the castle accompanied by some of his men but Wichbert indicated he wanted to speak more with Fenn and Fenn had to pull on Kaela's arm to detach her from Mathilde and the baby to translate for him.

'I have you to thank for my life. I won't forget that,' Wichbert said.

'I was not alone and you would have done the same,' replied Fenn. 'It's what happens in a battle.' As he said the words, he felt foolish – he had spoken as if he had been in many battles.

Kaela smiled but Wichbert didn't notice.

'Maybe,' he said and then continued solemnly, 'but I want you to know this – you will always have a friend in Saxony.'

'And you in Northumbria,' said Fenn.

Hakon called from the ship: 'I think captain want to leave on high tide.' He stood with Gunther by his side, both with their left arms bandaged; both keen to depart.

Mathilde saw Wichbert was finished and came up to Fenn.

'Heinrich is sorry he can't be here...' she said, '...to say farewell and thank you again but I have talked with him and we are agreed.'

When Kaela finished the translation, Fenn looked at her, puzzled. Had he missed something?

'We have named our baby 'Fenn',' added Mathilde.

*   *   *

They had noticed other travellers on the western road since leaving the dock at Hammaburg and at first it was just another group of people with horses standing on the river bank, taking a break at midday from their journey.

The ship was in the main channel of the river, which at that point was close to the northern bank. The flow was steady but sluggish so some of the oars were manned to help keep the ship in the centre of the current. Both those in the ship who were not rowing and the people on the shore, idly watched each other as they drew closer.

Tollemarche's ship, like Ragnall's, had a single mast with a rectangular sail and also oars, but the oars were more spaced than on the ships of the Northmen, and seemed to be used only for steerage. The sides were high and a section of the side could be removed for loading and unloading cargo. An elevated deck had been built over a small room at the rear where the sides rose even higher, but, in contrast to the Northern ships, the bottom of the ship was flat except where the planks curved around the bow. There was also a small platform at the bow from which a bowsprit jutted upwards forming an anchor point for the mast ropes.

The day had turned from bright and sunny with small white clouds dotted across the sky, to dull and overcast with a freshening wind and the promise of heavy squalls. Tollemarche looked on the change with favour, hoping, Fenn thought, for a sustained north-easterly to blow him down the coast. According to the captain, they were only a few miles from the mouth of the Albia.

The south bank was low and marshy, and had been since Hammaburg, but the north bank, along which they had driven the cart only days before, was steeper. The group of men standing on the bank were twenty feet above the water.

Suddenly Kaela stiffened. She ducked behind the high side of the ship.

'It's *Lothar*!' she said urgently.

At that point they were only fifty yards from the bank. At her cry, Fenn, who had been leaning against the mast, focussed on the men. He counted ten men with horses. Two had bows slung over their backs. At the front, on the edge of the bank, a hand shading his eyes, peering at the ship, stood a tall man with a moustache and his hair tied on top of his head.

'It's safe to stand,' Fenn said, after a moment. 'He has archers but he would gain no benefit from shooting at us. Even from that height, we have good cover behind the ship's sides.'

'He might not agree,' said Kaela but she stood up. Gunther came to stand beside Kaela. He looked calm but Fenn could see his hand slowly clenching and unclenching on the hilt of his sword. Fenn touched the sling on his belt. If the archers made a move to string their bows, it would only take a moment to bring it into action.

Lothar continued to stare at the ship. He could see Kaela and Gunther clearly now, but he seemed to agree with Fenn. Although they could hear his bellowed cursing, and see his frustration in the fist he shook in their direction, he gave no order to his archers.

Hakon was grinning like a fox who's seen that the hound can't reach it. He stood up to the side, taunting Lothar, shouting at the top of his voice and using both hands to form a series of rude gestures.

'Send him to *Náströnd* with a Frankish stone,' urged Hakon, whirling his hand above his head.

'Náströnd?'

'Part of *Niflheim*, the mist-world – the Northmen's hell,' said Kaela, not taking her gaze from Lothar. She continued slowly, relishing the words. 'Where the corpses of the evil have their blood sucked out and are then eaten by the dragon *Nidhogg*.'

Fenn grimaced and shook his head. He knew that Lothar had hurt Kaela badly; she still bore the marks of his cruelty. Lothar had wanted her to die slowly and painfully. But, despite that knowledge, Fenn couldn't take revenge in cold blood. He thought it was possibly a weakness in his character. Perhaps, on reflection, it would have been better if Lothar *had* shot arrows at them.

Fenn looked at Olgood and Gisele, standing by the mast, both impassively watching the scene unfold. Some of the sailors were also watching, puzzled looks on their faces. They could see the two groups knew each other and also that there was animosity between them.

He glanced at Kaela. Did *she* want him to try to kill Lothar? Kaela was watching the outlaw with a blank face, her thoughts unreadable, only her slightly narrowed eyes betraying the intensity of her stare.

Hakon saw Fenn's reluctance. 'Then just hurt him little bit,' he pleaded.

Fenn laughed and put his arm around Hakon's shoulders.

'He can't touch us anymore.'

Lothar turned away from the ship and urged his men onto their horses. Hakon gazed after them with an expression that said he hoped they would not regret the missed opportunity.

Lothar and his men followed the ship for some time, trotting along the road beside the bank. The river widened with the main channel switching away from the north bank to the centre. At the same time, the bank became steeper and the road gradually took the riders further from the river until they finally disappeared from view.

Fenn leaned on the railing next to Kaela.

'Where are Ragnall and Olaf, I wonder?'

'They will probably have returned to their ship. They're sailors not horsemen.'

Fenn nodded in agreement. By now they could have been several days at sea. The question was: Which direction would they sail?

North to Lognavik – or South; to continue the chase?

CHAPTER TWENTY-EIGHT

A tavern conversation and a third sea voyage...

When Tollemarche pointed over the bow of the ship and told him that the expanse of water he could see past the edge of the land ahead was the ocean, Fenn could feel the presence of Lindisfarne. Only sea now separated him from the island. He stared across the mouth of the river and the waves beyond, westward to the horizon, imagining the monastery he called home lying somewhere in that direction.

He knew they would be sailing along the coast to Bruggas where Tollemarche would unload goods and load more on board and only then would they sail for Hamwic and Wessex, *but*, at this particular moment, the ship's bow was pointed at Northumbria – at the land he had for so long been striving to reach.

The diversion to Bruggas and Hamwic was a necessary detour. He accepted that, and he was happy to go to Wessex – for Kaela's sake. But, in due time, as sure as night follows day, he would fix his eyes north and head for Northumbria – for Lindisfarne.

What would he find there? A ruined, gutted, deserted monastery, stripped bare of its once glittering beauty, inhabited only by memories and ghosts – or a rebuilt thriving community with a new church, a working scriptorium and the start of a new library?

And the people? Who had survived? Would the same people be there?

Lenglan and Aerlene – did they often look out to sea wondering where he was? Master Egbert, the physician? Bishop Higbald?

Yseld…?

Or… would the people he used to know be scattered over the land?

*　　*　　*

There was a small settlement on the south bank at the mouth of the Albia. Tollemarche announced the town was called Ruekert and they would be anchoring there overnight. He said not to be alarmed if the ship rested on the river bed as the tide receded – they would sail again on the morning's high tide. Apparently, there was an inn of fair repute in Ruekert and the talk among the sailors centred on the evening's visit to the establishment.

Because Ruekert was located on the south bank, Fenn felt they were safe from Lothar. To reach them, Lothar would need to cross the river mouth – a mile or more of sandbars and deep-water channels – which may not be impossible but would certainly be very difficult.

The wind was strongly gusting from the north, clearing the clouds from the sky and revealing a wash of stars to light the land. Fenn's mind tried to convince him that he had nothing to worry about but, even so, his eyes scanned the dark waters of the Albia river. The surface was painted with fractured moonlight but who knew what lurked in the shadows.

When Olgood lifted the basket, Tollemarche expressed surprise.

'It will be quite safe here. Two men will remain on board and will be replaced by another two during the night.'

'Thanks,' said Fenn, 'but we're used to carrying the basket and would prefer to take it with us.' He turned his hands and lifted his shoulders, requesting indulgence.

Tollemarche shrugged and waved toward the plank of wood leading from the side of the ship to the shore.

They had accepted Tollemarche's invitation to join his crew at the inn after he had told them it was not a rowdy dirty foul-smelling alehouse such as they might expect to find by the docks, and assured them that women would be accepted. This inn catered mainly for travellers, he said, providing a place to sleep in an adjacent barn and a meal he described as 'filling', as well as ale. Although the floor was thatch, it did look as though it was changed once in a while – there was a stale aroma but it was not unpleasant.

The inn was only half-full and Tollemarche secured a table in a corner for himself and his passengers while his crew dispersed to other tables. Fenn made sure he sat with a view of the door. And he made sure that Kaela sat beside him.

Olgood placed the basket behind his stool against the wall.

There were other women in the inn but their occupation became obvious when they began displaying their wares to Tollemarche's crew. Three men decided there were activities more inviting at that moment than drinking ale; a brief discussion resulting in each being led through a door at the back of the inn. The others settled on their stools, the level of noise already rising as they anticipated the night to come.

A buxom woman, whom Tollemarche introduced as the innkeeper, asked if they wanted food or ale or both. Tollemarche replied for them all, asking for generous amounts of both. He spread his arms to Fenn: 'Widukind paid me well; we have had a good voyage to the coast and I'm in a generous mood. The food and the first ale...' he held up a finger to emphasise he was talking of the *first* ale only, '...*I* will buy.'

There was a chorus of approval. Fenn met Hakon's eyes and winked. Hakon was carrying the coins for the evening because it had been agreed that he would be the most reluctant to part with them. He would be happy that the cost of the food would not be troubling his purse.

Steaming bowls of stew arrived, accompanied by a large round loaf of crusty bread and moments later foaming mugs of ale were placed on the table. Fenn found himself automatically checking how much meat was in the stew and gave a sheepish grin when Kaela noticed his search. She told the others and each of them was amused but there was also understanding in their eyes.

A man who had been observing them and, in particular, Kaela and Gisele, stood up from his table with purpose in his eyes and made his way towards them weaving slightly in his walk. Just as he reached their table, Olgood stood up. The man looked him up and down with wide eyes and suddenly decided his interest had actually been in something on the wall behind them. He gave the wall due attention then steered himself in another direction and Olgood sat back down.

'I was hoping you'd let him come on,' said Kaela. 'I wanted to see his reaction when I showed him some steel.'

Fenn smiled. He would have liked to see that too, but he said: 'We don't want any trouble.'

'It would have been no trouble at all,' purred Kaela.

*　　*　　*

With bread and stew inside him and a second mug of ale in front of him, Fenn felt as though a stiffness that had been gripping his shoulders for some time was loosening.

'I feel we're almost home,' he said to Kaela. 'Just one more step.'

Fenn thought she would say they weren't there yet and he had his reply 'That's what I expected you to say' ready. But Kaela was silent, her hands grasping her mug but not attempting to lift it, immersed in her thoughts.

Fenn reached across and gently rubbed her shoulder.

'Your mind is elsewhere. What are you thinking about?'

She continued to stare into her mug. Then she said: 'You and me.'

Fenn felt his heart skip a beat.

'Oh…' was all he managed to say and waited for her to continue.

'When we get back home will it be different or will it be the same?'

'Do you mean between us?'

'Between us and between all of us.'

Fenn wanted to keep the others out of the discussion.

He turned her head to face him. 'Right now, I'm interested in *us*,' he said. 'You and me.'

He was surprised to see a small tear form in the corner of her eye.

428

'Fenn…' she drew a quick breath in through her nose.

This time his heart probably stopped. He knew he stopped breathing. She was going to say something important. He forced himself to wait.

She let her breath out. 'You know I haven't told you everything about myself.'

Now he breathed. He nodded slowly.

She looked into his eyes. 'You're right. We're almost home. I've decided I don't want there to be any secrets between us.'

She glanced quickly about. Gunther and Hakon were talking and Gisele and Olgood were listening to one of Tollemarche's animated stories. Nobody else was within hearing distance.

She reached her hand up and held onto his arm, to reinforce her words.

'My father… I am…' she paused and then forced the words out.

'Fenn, my father is Beorhtric, King of Wessex.'

She stared at him as if she was still surprised she had said it out loud. The next words came in a rush.

'My father loves me but he wanted a son and I was determined to *be* his son. Part of my education was at the court of Charles the Great where I was taught Frankish, Latin and Greek. A master swordsman from Lombardy taught me to use a sword. I trained with him every day for four years until he told me I was better than he was. I've been educated to rule since the time I could walk.'

She stopped for a breath, regarding him intently.

'I couldn't tell you this before. If the Northmen had known, they would have used me to make my father pay… or do… I don't know what, but it would be bad. Lothar would have been worse. Even Widukind has no love for the Franks who are my father's allies.'

'I would never have told…'

'I know. I *know* that.' She took his face in her hands. 'But if nobody knew, nobody could say anything. That's what I thought. Please…' she finished so softly he could hardly hear. 'Please… forgive me.'

His stomach was twisted into a tight knot and a vice was clamped around his chest.

Icy thoughts ran through his head. *She's trying to tell me she's too high born for me – that we could never be…*

He reached up and took hold of her wrists.

'I said I would get you to your home, and I will,' he said gently. 'I'll make sure you're returned to Beorhtric and to your mother Queen Eadburg…'

'*She is not my mother,*' Kaela hissed. 'She's a *witch* who poisons my father against his friends. He married *her* to secure his alliance with Offa of Mercia.' She breathed deeply to calm herself. 'I fear for the damage she's done to Wessex while I've been away.'

'I never knew my mother,' she continued, in a softer tone but Fenn could hear the ache in her voice and it hurt him. 'She died giving me life. The only mother I've ever known is Prudy, one of my father's household. She's not my real mother but I wish she was.'

Her eyes dropped to her mug again, as if to find solace there.

'Prudy tells me my mother was beautiful…'

Fenn tried to speak normally despite the numbness spreading inside him.

'I've no doubt of that,' he said as firmly as he could. 'Kings are only attracted to the very beautiful, and I only need look at her daughter.'

Kaela smiled her gratitude for the compliment but it was a sad smile. She had changed from confidant princess to vulnerable daughter in the space of a few moments.

She continued: 'My father won't talk about her… I think it's painful for him.' She paused in reflection, then finished: 'But at least he admits he is my father.'

Fenn had a fleeting insight into the conflict she would have felt at Hammaburg Castle. She had fought and killed Franks – Charles' men – her father's allies.

He said: 'At the castle…'

His face must have revealed his thoughts because she deduced what he was going to say. She finished his sentence.

'At the castle, I fought for *you*. And I defended myself.'

She looked up at him, startled, recalling something he had said.

'What do you mean when you said you'll *make sure* I'm *returned* to my father?'

Fenn found he couldn't speak. He had no choice but to confront his churning anxiety. He forced the words out even though each one seemed to catch in his throat.

'I'd understand… if you… didn't want me to come with you…'

She silenced him with a finger pushed hard onto his lips.

'You listen to me, Feran of Lindisfarne. I expect you to fight harder than that for me!'

'I'd die for you. You must know that.'

'I do. And I would die for you. And that is all that needs to be said.'

Fenn leaned forward and kissed her lips feeling their softness beneath his; and felt the answering pressure of her return kiss. The moment was so much the sweeter from its being born out of the utter dismay he had just experienced. He slid his mouth past her lips and pressed his cheek against hers, absorbing the healing warmth of her skin. His hand caressed the back of her neck running up into and through her hair and he closed his eyes to hold in the moistness there. He felt her hand rest gently on his face, and from that touch a radiance spread through his whole body. He knew if he lost Kaela his life would end. She was a part of him and he wasn't whole without her.

He could still feel the presence of the dread that had entered his body when the idea of losing her was a possibility. It lay at a deep level, so malignantly hard and heavy he knew it would be a long time before that horror would be forgotten.

It was some time later that he realised she had called him 'Feran'. How had she known that? He had never told her his real name, had he?

* * *

It was late when Fenn pushed away his empty mug and tapped Tollemarche on the shoulder to tell him his passengers were about to return to the ship. The captain woke with a start and pushed himself up from the table. He looked around to get his bearings then shook his head and announced he would accompany them. At the door, he waved an acknowledgement to his crew who looked as if they would be staying for some time.

On the narrow path back to the ship, Fenn walked beside Tollemarche. He needed to reach out once in a while to steady the captain, who was tending to stray from the path. Tollemarche thanked him effusively on each occasion, and on each occasion Fenn told him it was no trouble. After several repetitions, Tollemarche asked Fenn where he was raised to have such good manners.

'Do you know the Northumbrian coast?' asked Fenn.

'Of course,' said Tollemarche.

'You probably know Bebbanburgh Castle. You can see it from well out to sea. I'm from an island called Lindisfarne just north of Bebbanburgh.'

Tollemarche stopped abruptly forcing Fenn to stop also, Kaela and Gisele walking behind almost colliding with them. Tollemarche peered through the dim light at Fenn.

'Widukind said you wanted to go to Hamwic. He has paid for your passage to that town.'

Fenn nodded his agreement. He assumed Tollemarche's return voyage would be along the same route as his outward one – Hammaburg, Bruggas, Hamwic.

'You *are* headed for Hamwic are you not?' he asked.

By now Olgood, Hakon and Gunther had walked back up the path to join them.

Tollemarche's head seemed to have cleared.

'Yes, Hamwic is my home port, but the silver I carry is destined for Northumbria to be made into coins with King Aethelred's head. Some of the silver will go to Edinburgh and some to Eoforic. I'll be unloading the ore onto a barge at Berewic.'

Fenn looked at Olgood and could not stop a slow smile spreading over his face. Had Olgood heard the same words he had? Berewic was a small settlement at the mouth of the river Tweed only *six miles* north of Lindisfarne.

'Berewic?' he asked, incredulous. 'That's…'

Tollemarche nodded forcefully.

'That's…' Fenn couldn't bring himself to say it.

'That's our *home*,' finished Olgood.

*   *   *

Only when they crossed the bar at the mouth of the Albia did Fenn finally feel they had left the threat of Lothar behind. The last time they had seen him, Lothar seemed to be riding with some purpose, but Fenn could not think how he could bother them again unless he grew either wings or fins – or found a sail.

The ship approached a large island just beyond the mouth of the river. It was flat with only stunted trees and was a haven for birds of all kinds. Hundreds screeched and soared in a continually swirling cloud above the grasses and narrow beaches. Tollemarche said that at low tide the island could be accessed by foot across the muddy seabed, reminding Fenn of the Pilgrim's Way joining Northumbria to Lindisfarne, a path he crossed regularly on Saturn's Day – always at the mercy of the tide, he remembered ruefully – to collect bugs and insects. And rabbit kittens.

Those days seemed a lifetime ago.

The ship passed the island and headed out to sea, the wind south-easterly now and directly behind them, the sail stretched taut against the ropes, pushing the ship through the waves at a good speed. The ride was rougher than in the ships of the Northmen, the flat bottom seemingly more at the mercy of the ocean forces than the curved keel, but Fenn found his sea-legs were still good and the movement caused him no trouble. Gisele was unwell but only for a half-day, then, with coaching from Olgood and Hakon, she also began to enjoy the voyage. Gunther did not seem to be affected, standing stoically by the mast looking alternately back, toward the past he was leaving behind, and then ahead toward the future.

In the afternoon the wind eased and the noise around the ship was muted to the rhythmic swish of water passing underneath and the soft thumping of the waves. The relative quiet after the bustling wind was hypnotic and the hum of conversation died to whispers. A bank of clouds approached from the south and Fenn expected they would bring a return of the wind possibly from a different quarter.

One of the crew began whistling a happy tune while he back-spliced the end of a rope to prevent it from fraying. Another sailor joined and they carried the tune through several variations. Fenn was enjoying the bright melody which seemed to reflect his mood when a series of pops came simultaneously from different parts of the ship, as if someone was throwing pebbles. He searched for the source of the strange noises. A large raindrop hit the back of his hand and then another struck him on his forehead, the droplet running down his nose. More single drops hit and burst on the wooden planking and splattered the sail.

In a moment they were deluged in a heavy downpour, the rain drumming on the rear deck, plastering their hair to their heads and their clothes to their bodies. Tollemarche invited his passengers into the small cabin but – apart from the fact that they were already wet and also that they wouldn't have been able to move if they all crowded into a space built for one or two – the rain was enjoyable, freshening the air and bringing with it a feeling of euphoria and wellbeing.

The crew shook their heads at the group of young fools welcoming the rain with arms wide, swinging around the mast and ducking under the sail ropes. Fenn held Kaela's hands as she circled around him, her head tilted back with her mouth open and the rain beating at her closed eyelids, trusting him to keep her safe in the confined space. She coughed when the rainwater filled her mouth and he drew her close as she spluttered and laughed with joy.

Then they swayed slowly to a music of their own making. He held her close, water coursing down their faces and intermingling on their bodies. Fenn hummed the whistler's tune in her ear and she nestled into his neck.

'Do you remember asking me about Anteros?' she murmured.

'Yes, I remember.' It was the name she had called him when they met Sigrund and his family outside Skyrvid Forest.

'Anteros is the Greek god of a special type of love – of love that is returned.'

He wouldn't have minded if the rain never stopped and this moment continued forever.

*   *   *

Three days and nights passed while they crossed a seascape that, for the time being, tolerated their presence. Tollemarche remarked on the conditions remaining what he termed 'very acceptable' in an area he said was notorious for difficult weather. Fenn contemplated the goddess Ran being occupied elsewhere, hopefully in the North, spreading her net to entrap unwary sailors; or Thor stirring up his storms to test the seamanship of the dragon-headed ships. Wherever they were, the gods were leaving this stretch of water alone.

On their first evening at sea, after Tollemarche had told them that there was plenty of food aboard, they had feasted on the food that the castle cooks had provided – cold roast chicken and wild pork, raw vegetables and fruit. There was more than enough for a meal and the extra was shared among the crew, drawing their gratitude.

Tollemarche's dire threat that they would be expected to work during the voyage turned out to have been a product of his strange sense of humour, lacking any true intent. They spent the days in idleness, a state that *was* broken occasionally when extra hands could be used for some task. The spurts of activity were welcomed; the inactivity was difficult to get used to.

Over the previous weeks, before they had boarded this ship, every move had to be carefully considered, every direction checked, every possibility deliberated, with mistakes likely to have severe consequences.

Now they travelled without effort, seemingly without a care.

Even Tollemarche's frequent stories about pirates, strange creatures, waterspouts, monster waves, unusual people and more, were only brief interludes. Everything Tollemarche observed seemed to remind him of a different but similar occasion when something bizarre or unbelievable had occurred. Fenn found his stories fascinating but, after a while, some became so outlandish they challenged even *his* imagination.

On the morning of the fourth day at sea, the sun rose only briefly and was then obscured by a thick billowy fog that rolled in from the west, surrounding the ship in a white blanket. When he was unable to see ahead,

Tollemarche had the sail brought down and they wallowed in the swells waiting for the fog to lift.

'We should see the coast soon, if this damn stuff clears,' Tollemarche said. 'Berewic is a half day's sail away if the wind strength and direction hold.' He rolled his hand to indicate the sailing time was approximate.

Tollemarche strolled back and forth along the length of the ship clearly frustrated by the delay. His reputation would be built on his ability to deliver his goods, and excuses for late delivery would be poorly received. He could have made some way by sailing cautiously forward at a slow speed but he would be sailing blind.

The fog was fickle. It would seem to be clearing only to close in again an instant later. In one moment, they would be in clear water surrounded by banks of fog on all sides, encircled by walls of white cloud. The next, the wall would roll over them and envelop the ship. They were trapped in an ethereal zone with its own weather patterns. The wind became strangely changeable. Fenn, facing the bow, felt the wind from the front and then from the side as if it couldn't make up its mind in which direction it should blow the fog away; the frivolous indecision serving to hold them stationary on the sea.

Without any warning, they were in clear air, the sea open to the west horizon, with the fog backed into a single wall of white looming behind the stern of the ship. Tollemarche gave a grunt of satisfaction and ordered the sail to be raised. The men leapt to get the sail up and the ship underway. Slowly they moved away from the threat of the foggy fingers being able to reach out and ensnare them again. Fenn watched the fog bank behind the ship, fascinated by how ominous it looked and by how solid it seemed. He wondered if this interlude would join Tollemarche's store of stories.

For a fraction of time he saw something emerge from the mist. The carved head of a dragon, and the tall sweeping curve of a bow, a type of ship he knew well. It was there and then it was gone, swallowed again by the swirling fog.

Fenn looked around the ship. Had anyone else seen what he had just seen? No eyes met his. Nobody else was looking astern. Olgood was close by, tightening a sail rope. Keeping his eye on the receding fog Fenn crossed to him and took his arm to get his attention.

'Olgood, I saw Ragnall.'

Olgood looked at him as if he had said he had seen an angel.

'His ship,' insisted Fenn. 'In the fog. I saw it – only for a moment and then it disappeared.'

'Are you sure?' said Olgood, scanning the fog bank. Fenn also searched. The fog seemed to be dissipating, breaking up, but that could be because they were moving away from it.

Ragnall was close. Fenn had asked himself whether Ragnall would sail home or continue the chase and now he knew the answer. What drove the Northman? Was it honour, as Hakon had said, or dogged persistence, or just an unwillingness to admit defeat? Surely his thralls were not worth so much time and effort to recapture just so they could be killed? Fenn shook his head – it was beyond reason and certainly beyond his understanding.

'Yes, I'm sure,' said Fenn, in answer to Olgood's query. 'He's out there.'

CHAPTER TWENTY-NINE

An end and a beginning...

'There it is!'

Fenn followed Olgood's pointing arm and saw a smudge of land. He turned a questioning eye to Tollemarche who smiled and nodded.

'That point of land you can see, is Lindisfarne island, and ahead is the coast of Northumbria.'

The ship crawled across the water and the land seemed to grow no closer. Fenn experienced again the difficulty of judging distance at sea. Only by looking over the side and observing the water moving beneath the ship could he confirm they were indeed moving. He stared at the land until his eyes watered, hoping that something would resolve into a familiar landmark.

Tollemarche dropped anchor off the mouth of the Tweed and the ship sat in a slowly rolling swell, a half-mile from the shore. The wind was a steady breeze, enough to ruffle the sea but not enough to create waves other than those forming in the shallow water and rolling onto the sandy beaches on each side of the river mouth.

'We're too big to enter the river,' he said. 'They'll see us and send a barge.'

It was frustrating to sit on the ship. On the north side of Lindisfarne, the island was low and featureless. The beach where the Northmen had landed was on the north side. Fenn leaned forward with his chin in his hands, his elbows resting on the side of the ship. He was only a few miles from the very place where he had begun this journey to different lands, but once more time was passing with no forward progress. He felt Kaela come up beside him. She stood for a moment without speaking, probably recognising his mood.

'Fenn...' she said.

He waited for her to continue. When she didn't, he looked at her and saw she wasn't looking at him or at Lindisfarne, but over the stern of the ship. Fenn followed her gaze.

He saw nothing.

'What is it?'

'Look just to the left of the mast.'

On the horizon was a speck, a tiny dot.

The dot grew until it became a thin line. Fenn did not need any more detail to know what ship this was. Tollemarche was made aware of the approaching ship and he joined Fenn and Kaela.

'You think this is the ship you saw in the fog – the ship of the Northmen?'

When Tollemarche had learned of Fenn's previous sighting, he had been concerned that there may be a confrontation at sea. Fenn was surprised that here, with his ship lying vulnerable at anchor, Tollemarche seemed less concerned.

'It's Ragnall,' he said.

'So you know the captain? A friend of his?'

Fenn gave a dry laugh. 'We are not friends. He won't be satisfied until he captures us or kills us.'

Tollemarche frowned. He shaded his eyes to see better.

'How does he know you're on my ship?'

'I've no idea. He may be just coming to take a look, but I've learned not to underestimate him. He may know somehow.'

Kaela said: '*Lothar* knew we were on this ship but how could Ragnall know, unless...'

Fenn realised what she was about to say. If Lothar had ridden to meet Ragnall's ship on the coast, he would have told Ragnall what he had seen on the river.

'Yes, you're right,' he said. 'Lothar could have told him.' He turned to Tollemarche. 'We need to get ashore. If you can give us something that floats we can get to the beach.'

'No need. Here comes the barge.'

Two boats were being rowed out of the mouth of the Tweed river. One was longer and wider than the other but it was the second boat that caught Fenn's interest. It was full of men, about twenty, and they were armed with bows and swords.

Tollemarche grinned at him.

'Those men have been sent to guard the silver,' he said. 'They should keep your 'not friend' at bay.'

Ragnall's ship, for Fenn had no doubt who was at the steering oar, continued to enlarge until the sail could be distinguished. It closed relentlessly without slackening speed until it seemed Ragnall might be intending to ram them.

At a distance of two hundred yards, the dragon ship slowed and the sail was dropped. It was within the range of an arrow and of Fenn's sling. Fenn saw there was an animated discussion happening on the boats that were pulling alongside Tollemarche's ship. The Lindisfarne raid would be common knowledge to these men and they would know full well what the presence of Ragnall's ship could mean.

The longer boat slowed and stopped, but the boat full of guards pulled hard to close the last few yards, the men looking to attain a more stable platform on which to fight, if that became necessary. Tollemarche ordered the part of the ship's side used for cargo loading to be removed and a rope ladder to be lowered.

Ragnall's ship also seemed to contain around twenty men, probably the same men who had accompanied him to Alfheim. Fenn watched as oars were pushed through the holes in the side of the ship. They would be able to easily manoeuvre around Tollemarche's ship which was held fast by its anchor. A figure walked slowly from the stern to the bow.

Ragnall.

Fenn stared at him. He felt empty. They were only a few *yards* from the Northumbrian shore. Would this man *never* give up?'

Even Hakon was subdued, just staring at the ship with an unreadable expression.

'It's us he wants.' Fenn repeated his suggestion to Tollemarche. 'Let us use the guard's boat to go ashore. I don't think he'll follow us and he has no quarrel with you.'

Tollemarche was supervising the men from the boat coming on to his ship. He pulled the last man on board and straightened.

'I do not abandon my passengers,' he said forcefully. 'We will stand and fight with you – if it comes to that.'

Fenn glanced at him.

Tollemarche explained: 'His approach will have been seen from the shore. After the raid on St Cuthbert's, I can confidently predict the people of Berewic will have no love for the Northmen. When they see only one ship, I think we may get some more help. It would be a foolish man that would push the situation in those circumstances. Is your man foolish?'

'He's far from foolish,' said Fenn.

He looked for Olgood. Olgood had his arm around Gisele, leaning against the mast, quietly awaiting the outcome of the rolling dice. His friend had many admirable qualities, but right now Fenn admired most his calm in the face of adversity, an attitude mirrored by Gisele.

The wind had died and the sea had calmed to a glassy smoothness. Even the air was holding its breath.

There were five archers among the new men and they lined up along the side of the ship facing the head of the dragon. Using the oars, Ragnall was keeping the prow of his ship facing forward, giving the archers no target. He stood alone at the bow in full view. Fenn saw him scan the shoreline. He was wary of the reinforcements that Tollemarche expected.

Fenn moved to the side of the ship and with Kaela beside him glared at the huge Northman. He made a point of putting his arm around Kaela's shoulders, stating his claim. The three of them remained unmoving, as if under a spell. Fenn thought about presenting some further gesture of defiance but decided it was unnecessary.

Ragnall broke the spell. He disappeared from the bow and at the same time the ship's oars bit into the water. Fenn thought he was intending to ram after all, but the ship started to turn. The turn continued until Fenn could see they would not collide but they would not miss by much. There would be a moment when both ships would be almost alongside each other about twenty yards apart. It was a bold manoeuvre, considering Ragnall could have just reversed his ship away.

'Tell the archers not to shoot,' Fenn said loudly, realising a moment later the archers could understand him.

Ragnall's ship drew parallel. Fenn could see Ragnall standing in front of the mast, his hands held behind him, staring calmly across the gap. If Ragnall wasn't at the steering oar, who was? One glance was enough. Another man who could have been Ragnall's double stood there. Olaf.

Ragnall was as immobile as if carved from stone. He seemed to be waiting until the ships were at their closest point.

He brought something from behind his back. He arched his arm and with a twist of his powerful shoulders, he hurled the object across the water. While it was in the air it looked like a twirling lump of seaweed. It crashed onto the planking of Tollemarche's ship and rolled to Fenn's feet.

It was Lothar's severed head.

Fenn looked back at Ragnall and they locked eyes as the ships drew quickly apart.

He knew, with a certainty he did not understand, that he and Ragnall would meet again.

*   *   *

Fenn was sorry to take his leave of Tollemarche, a man who pursued a hard and dangerous life on the sea with humour and skill. Fenn admired him and had enjoyed his company.

On the boat to the shore, one of the guards told him that St. Cuthbert's Monastery was being rebuilt. Fenn eagerly asked him about the library, but the man knew no more than he had already said.

Fenn had requested that they be put ashore on the beach rather than taken into the town. He was the first to step from the boat onto Northumbrian sand, and he immediately held up his hand to stop Kaela from following him. From inside his tunic he brought out something which he held concealed in his hand, reaching for her with his other hand. Thinking he was going to gallantly help her ashore, she gave a slight bow and stretched out her hand for him to hold. Fenn took her hand and opened it so her fingers were extended, then he smoothly slipped the gold ring onto her middle finger.

'Welcome to the shores of home, my lady – promise delivered.'

He watched the emotions play out on her face. One, recognition of the ring. Two, he had called her 'my lady'. Three, the promise he had made outside Addo's cave in the land of the Northmen on the first night of their freedom, was finally fulfilled. She was concentrating on the ring and missed her step from the boat – later he thought this may have been deliberate – and with a shriek she fell into his arms. He collapsed backwards to sit at the water's edge and was smothered by her, his head driven back onto the damp sand. She lay on top of him making no effort to get up, her hands digging into the beach, grasping and then releasing handfuls of sand.

Only when his muffled protests about not being able to breathe became insistent, did she push herself off him to lie on her back on the sand at his side. After a moment, when his breathing had steadied, Olgood appeared in his view, Askari's basket already strapped to his back.

'We have a long walk. If we want to get to Lindisfarne in good daylight, we'd better start.'

Fenn jumped to his feet. The guards were pulling their boat away from the beach to join the barge waiting beyond the waves. He regarded his companions. Both Gunther and Hakon had discarded their bandages, exposing their wounds to the air. Everyone was healthy and eager to go.

He gave Gisele a huge hug and said: 'Welcome to your new land,' being rewarded, as he hoped he would be, by her wonderful smile. He breathed deeply as if to draw her smile in. It never ceased to brighten him.

'Thank you for bringing me to your land,' she said in English. 'I am very 'appy to be here.'

Fenn clapped his hands in astonishment and delight and caught the look of pride on Olgood's face.

He shook hands with Hakon then embraced him. 'It's been a long journey, my friend,' he said. Hakon couldn't trust himself to speak, his emotions welling behind his eyes. He nodded.

Fenn turned to Gunther as Kaela stood up, brushing the sand from her clothes.

'This is a new land, Gunther, you can start a new life here.'

Kaela talked to Gunther, relaying what Fenn had said, but adding more. She finished by taking him by the shoulders and giving him a kiss on both cheeks. Gunther unbuckled his sword. He knelt in the sand in front of her and handed his sword to her. Kaela held it flat in her hands, then she gravely handed it back to him. Gunther rose to accept it.

'I've given him back his sword and his life to do with as he wishes,' she explained. 'He has accepted my offer.'

'Good,' Fenn said, but he knew there was more and he waited with his arms folded.

Kaela rolled her eyes. 'He said now that I'm wearing your ring I can rightly be called a Lady.'

Fenn smiled, his eyes meeting Kaela's, sharing the knowledge of her birth.

'I agree.'

He reached forward to shake Gunther by the hand. 'You're very welcome to come with us of course.'

Kaela translated and Fenn was about to turn away when Gunther spoke again.

'He asked: 'Where are you going?' said Kaela.

Fenn thought for a moment. 'To Lindisfarne,' he said. 'Then to Kaela's home – Wessex.'

Fenn looked around to see if that was agreeable. Kaela was smiling broadly. He finished the circle with Olgood. He reached out to grasp his friend by both arms.

'You've been my rock every step of the way,' he said. 'I wouldn't have made it to this point without you.'

'Me neither,' replied Olgood with a twisted grin.

It took Fenn a heartbeat, but then he burst out laughing. Olgood joined him, and Fenn couldn't stop. He laughed with abandon and felt his heart fill with happiness.

He was still chuckling when he took the first steps toward Lindisfarne.

* * *

The bells of St. Cuthbert's rang mid-afternoon 'None', calling to Fenn across the Pilgrim's Way. The sound brought a lump to his throat and he swallowed hard to keep his emotions in check. He glanced at Olgood who assured him with a patient nod that Billfrith's jewelled cover was still safe in the basket.

They waited with several other people by the first stake of the Pilgrim's Way for the path to be exposed by the ebbing tide. There were a mixture of pilgrims and other travellers but nobody Fenn knew. Several worried looks were directed at the swords and axes hanging from their belts. Of the people waiting for the path to clear, they were the only ones armed.

He could wait no longer. He ignored the looks of surprise at his impatience and strode into the water. It reached to his knees but he knew that by the time he stepped onto the island a mile away it would be only ankle height. He pushed his way through the flowing sea, feeling the resistance around his legs and was reminded of the almost fateful night they had struggled through the snow to the safety of the mountain hut. The reminder was enough for him to slow his pace so he would not arrive exhausted. He could hear the others splashing behind him.

There were cows grazing outside the monastery gates which were open to the courtyard. Fenn stopped to wait for the others. His eyes turned towards the beach, following the route they had walked under the guard of the Northmen. He was glad the sun was shining – he would not have liked to be returning on a dull or rainy day. He felt Kaela's hand slip into his.

His mind was filled with images from the day of the raid.

The bodies of the monks sprawled in the courtyard. Olaf standing in the doorway of the church. Master Oswald hurrying down the church lane to talk to the 'traders'. Columns of smoke rising into the sky. His first view of his bound hands. Birgitta knocking Nameth to the ground for stepping out of line to ask about his wife.

Kaela squeezed his hand, telling him she was there.

He looked down. He was standing on the spot where Master Wilfred had been killed.

Fenn didn't know the date but, as far as he could determine, the season was late summer or early autumn – a full year plus two or three months since he had been taken on board the ships of the Northmen.

He walked through the gates.

Across the courtyard he saw Yseld.

Her back was toward him but he recognised her hair. She was talking to another woman Fenn didn't know. So many new faces. The woman looked up as Fenn came through the gates and Yseld turned to see what had caught her attention.

She saw Fenn and her hand went to her mouth.

She had changed. She was no longer a girl on the verge of becoming a woman. Her hair, which she had previously tied into a tail, now shone full in the sunlight. When she removed her hand from her mouth, it revealed her own beautiful smile; the smile that Fenn had so often seen reflected in Gisele's.

Yseld was also unmistakeably pregnant.

Fenn felt Kaela's hand withdraw from his and give him a gentle push.

Yseld ran the last few steps into his arms, tears streaming down her face.

'I thought you were gone forever,' she managed, through her sobs.

'So did I,' said Fenn, smiling, happy that she had not only survived but was thriving. He held her tightly, his head nestling into her hair.

When she had caught her breath, he regarded her at arm's length.

'You look wonderful.'

She smiled, her eyes glowing with happiness, and for a moment she was the same girl he had held on the hill when they had seen the fiery dragon in the sky.

'I have something to show you,' she said, pulling at a leather cord around her neck. A small pouch was attached to the end. She reached in and pulled out a folded piece of parchment.

Yseld held out Fenn's drawing of the rabbit kitten. The parchment had been folded and unfolded so many times the creases were barely holding the segments together.

As Fenn held the parchment, Kaela and the others joined them. Olgood recognised the drawing and patted Fenn on the shoulder to show he understood its importance, then he was distracted when he was greeted enthusiastically by some friends. Fenn introduced his companions to Yseld and she graciously welcomed each one. He hoped Yseld would recognise the special relationship he had with Kaela without him having to explain, and was not disappointed when Yseld looked back and forth between them and then greeted Kaela very warmly, stepping forward to give her a genuine hug.

The scene was disrupted when a keening wail sounded from inside the craft room. Aerlene burst from the room in full flight almost colliding with the corner of Olgood's wood store in her haste. Fenn quickly but carefully handed the drawing back to Yseld and was able to take a few steps forward before he was engulfed by Aerlene, her face, as Yseld's had been, streaming tears of relief. Aerlene held him as if he would disappear if she let him go and she shook violently with the force of her joy. When she finally drew back she checked him from head to foot for signs of damage, her hand absentmindedly brushing through his hair.

Fenn looked over her shoulder and asked: 'Where is Lenglan?'

There was a gasp from Yseld and Aerlene's face twisted in pain. Fenn gathered her again in his arms and soothed her renewed sobbing while he closed his eyes tightly and felt his own keen sorrow for the only father he had known.

A crowd had now formed and instead of new faces, Fenn saw old friends around him. They were all greeting him happily, reaching out to touch him. Aerlene wiped her tears and linked her arm in his, ready to display her son, recently returned from the dead, to the community.

*   *   *

When Aerlene paused and looked about to find someone she hadn't talked to, Fenn took the opportunity to ask her about Ames, Audrey's son.

'He was taken in by his aunt, at Bebbanburgh,' said Aerlene, her eyes asking the obvious question about Audrey's fate. When Fenn shook his head, Aerlene's face tightened with regret.

'She was a good friend,' she said sadly.

Fenn nodded, and they stood for a moment in silence.

He looked at her closely. 'And you, have you been well?'

Aerlene's reply was to hold his face in her hands and smile. She was now.

When she freed him, Fenn let his gaze roam the courtyard.

Kaela and Gunther were surrounded by children. The boys wanting to see and touch their swords, the girls wanting to touch Kaela's red hair. Olgood and Gisele were talking with a group of monastery workers, farmers and gardeners. Olgood had his arm proudly and protectively around Gisele and was trying to answer the myriad of questions being asked of him.

Hakon stood alone by the barn, where he had last checked the bonds on the captives and ordered everyone to their feet, reliving his own version of that day.

Aerlene begged her leave to organise a homecoming celebration, taking Yseld with her. Fenn wanted to avoid being besieged with questions like Olgood so he walked across the courtyard to join Hakon.

He stood quietly beside him for a moment then, recognising Hakon's mixed emotions, said: 'You allowed us to talk with the Northmen, Hakon, and you gave us information we badly needed. You were a light in the darkness. Without you we would have been without hope.'

Hakon turned to look at Fenn with tears in his eyes.

Thank you,' he said.

Fenn put a hand on Hakon's shoulder.

'Will you come with us to Wessex, or will you return to Hedeby to look for your father? Lothar is dead and Ragnall knows we're out of his reach in Northumbria. It should be safe for you to return.'

'I go back some day,' said Hakon thoughtfully. 'If my father come back to Hedeby, my friends will tell him I live.' He brightened and said: 'Gunther talk to me about farming. I know spices – if Wessex is warm maybe I grow cloves, pepper, ginger and even cinnamon trees…' he paused, thinking, '…but those need *very* warm… I need talk some more with Gunther.'

'Good,' said Fenn, pleased. He looked around the courtyard, his eyes lingering on the goat enclosure picking out the spot where he had been standing when Master Nerian ran through the gates…

'I think it's time to visit the Bishop,' he said.

Fenn led the way up the church lane. He had gathered Kaela, Olgood and Gisele and Gunther, wanting them to be together when he returned the cover of the Gospels to the Bishop. He walked through the church, noting the blackened but still solid doors, the new tapestries and the replacement chalices on the altar. He stood behind the altar and pointed at the floor.

'Olaf captured me here,' he said to Kaela.

'And now you stand here again, a free man,' she said.

He nodded. 'A free man.'

The crowd had remained in the courtyard, sensing Fenn and his companions wanted to see the Bishop alone.

Olgood took the basket from his back and opened it. He handed Fenn the cover of the Lindisfarne Gospels still wrapped in linen. Fenn held it as he had last held the complete book before Olaf had snatched it from him. This precious bundle in his hands was also now returned to the place from where it was stolen.

Bishop Higbald greeted Fenn at the entrance to the short passageway connecting his rooms with the church. He'd been expecting visitors. He stood aside and invited everyone to enter.

It was crowded in the room. The others moved aside to allow Fenn to approach and stand before the Bishop. Fenn indicated with his eyes that he wanted Kaela to stand with him. Olgood stood on his other side still holding the basket in front of him, Gisele next to him and behind them Hakon and Gunther.

Fenn started to unwrap the cover, but the bishop held up his hand.

'Excuse me,' he said, 'but first... Master Nerian...?'

'He endured with fortitude, and found great support in his prayers,' said Fenn, 'but unfortunately... he...'

Bishop Higbald held up his hand again, a sadness in his eyes.

'An esteemed and worthy colleague. May he rest in peace,' he said. He made the sign of the cross and whispered a prayer.

When he was finished he stood with his head bowed in silence. Then he said: 'For all those who suffered and died on that horrible day and since.'

He nodded to Fenn who continued to unfold the linen. The Bishop watched with a furrowed brow, as if he expected some macabre evidence of Master Nerian's demise to be revealed.

When Fenn removed the last piece of linen to expose the cover of the Lindisfarne Gospels in its bejewelled magnificence, the bishop drew a sharp intake of breath which he expelled as a long heartfelt audible moan.

Fenn presented the cover to him, the Bishop receiving it reverently. He stared at the object in his hands for a long while, breathing heavily, and then looked up.

'It caused me terrible anguish when I learned this had been ripped from the Gospels. You've returned to me – to the monastery – a treasure beyond value.'

He looked at each person in the room with profound respect, holding their eyes, the depth of his feelings evident.

'I can only imagine the trials and hardships you have all endured to return this to us,' he said. He paused to give weight to his words. 'You have my undying gratitude and the gratitude, I'm sure, of everybody at St. Cuthbert's and the whole of Northumbria.'

Bishop Higbald stepped forward with his hand extended.

'I shall personally ensure that the King is made aware of what you have done.'

*   *   *

Fenn and Bishop Higbald stood at one end of the refectory, in the midst of Aerlene's hastily organised 'celebration'.

Before them, the tables were filled with bowls of food and jugs of ale and people enjoying an unexpected but welcome break from their daily tasks. Olgood was in earnest discussion with a young lad that Fenn didn't know, but from his build he guessed that his profession was similar to Olgood's, probably the replacement blacksmith. Kaela and Gisele were surrounded by women, Yseld among them; Kaela's flame hair distinctive among the blonds and the browns, a constant stream of chatter coming from the group that had not diminished from the moment they had sat down.

Hakon and Gunther were sitting among some farmers. Gunther was asking questions and Hakon was translating for him. Gunther would be wanting to learn about farming in his new land.

Fenn asked Bishop Higbald about the library.

'Thanks to God, the library was almost entirely saved from destruction. Many of the wooden racks were destroyed but we concentrated on saving the books and manuscripts. It took some quick action, but most escaped the fire and the fury of the Northmen. We lost only twenty-two manuscripts, which we have already replaced.'

Fenn released a heartfelt sigh. The loss of the library had weighed heavily on him. To hear that his own work and the work of so many others was safe was a huge relief.

Neither spoke for a time, until the Bishop said: 'Will you stay with us?' There was hope in his voice but also resignation.

When Fenn had entered the refectory with Olgood, he had put the same question to him asking if he was going to stay at the monastery. To Fenn's relief, Olgood said sincerely: 'I've talked with Gisele. We both think the 'family' should stay together. We'll come to Wessex.'

Fenn had a cup of monastery ale in his hand and, when he had sipped it a moment ago, he had recalled all of the other ales, meads and ciders he had tasted since his forced departure from the monastery. He knew he had been right to place this ale above the other beverages. Ale brewed at home did indeed taste best.

Fenn shook his head slowly in reply to the Bishop's question.

'My heart lies elsewhere, and I have some unfinished business.'

'Master Oswald spoke very highly of your skill. We need people like you. Please know that you will always be welcome here of course, but…' the bishop paused, '…if I am any judge of men, I believe you have an important destiny.'

'Thank you, your Grace. Lindisfarne will always be my home.'

*   *   *

The morning brought with it a cloudy sky with an unusually warm wind blowing from the north, a welcome wind for travellers heading south.

Fenn looked back at the monastery gates and the small group of people standing there. Aerlene was standing at the front. He knew she would be crying but he also knew she was happy for him. Yseld stood beside Aerlene and next to Yseld, his arm around her waist, was the young blacksmith.

Fenn raised his hand in farewell and Kaela slipped her arm around *his* waist.

'At the beginning, outside Addo's cave, did you really think you could do it?' she asked.

'Do what?'

'Bring the book cover home. Bring us all home.'

Fenn looked at her.

'Yes,' he said with conviction. 'I did – because of the people who were with me. If any *one* of those people…' he cast his hand to include Olgood and Gisele, Hakon and Gunther, '…and especially *this* person…' he put his finger under her chin and lifted it, '…had *not* been with me, we would not have made it home – we would not be standing here today, on the Holy Island of Lindisfarne.'

The circle was complete.

In a few moments, when he turned his back to Lindisfarne, he would be starting a new journey. This moment, right now, was an end to part of his life.

He looked down at Kaela. She returned his look frankly and honestly; her deep brown eyes containing promises and more than a hint of mystery, both of which he was eager to explore.

It was an end and it was a beginning.

HISTORICAL NOTES

The information below was researched using literary and internet sources during the creation of this novel in the interest of historical accuracy. Where possible the data has been corroborated from more than one source and where two or more sources conflict I have used the version that seemed most likely. Many names of both people and places in the late 8th century are recorded with various spellings – I chose one.

The information is accurate to the best of my knowledge but is intended as helpful or interesting notes rather than a definitive or academic presentation of historical data. All dates are CE/AD unless stated.

The notes have been ordered according to the timeline of the novel.

Lindisfarne and St. Cuthbert's Monastery

Lindisfarne (also called Holy Island) is a tidal island off the coast of Northumbria (present-day Northumberland), in the north-east of England. It is connected to the mainland by a mile-long causeway that is only usable for several hours each day at low tide. The monastery was founded by the Irishman St. Aidan who was summoned from the island of Iona – on the western coast of Scotland – by Oswald, King of Northumbria, in the year 635 to establish a monastery in Northumbria.

When St Aidan died on August 31, 651, a young shepherd boy called Cuthbert who lived in the hills near *Mailros* (Melrose) Abbey on the river Tweed, reputedly saw a vision of St. Aidan's soul ascending to heaven at the time of Aidan's death. The vision convinced Cuthbert to take up the life of a monk and in 665 he came to Lindisfarne, where his gift of healing and ability to work miracles achieved far-reaching fame for the island. Cuthbert become Bishop of Lindisfarne in 684, the fifth successor to Bishop Aidan. The monastery was an important destination for pilgrims who crossed the tidal flats along the Pilgrims Way, a path marked by tall stakes set into the seabed. The Pilgrim's Way is still marked by stakes today.

When Cuthbert died on March 20, 687, he was buried on the island of Lindisfarne. Eleven years after his death, his body was found to be 'uncorrupted' by the astonished monks. The monks decided that Cuthbert was a saint and the monastery came to be referred to as St. Cuthbert's.

The Lindisfarne Gospels

The Lindisfarne Gospels are presumed to be the work of a monk named Eadfrith who became Bishop of Lindisfarne in 698 and died in 721. The manuscript contains the gospels of Matthew, Mark, Luke and John and was written in Latin in the period 698-715.

The pages of the Lindisfarne Gospels are richly decorated (a feature called 'illumination') and were originally encased in a fine leather binding covered with jewels and precious metals made by Billfrith the Anchorite (hermit). During the Viking raid on Lindisfarne this jewelled cover was stolen.

There is a story that some monks who managed to flee from the raid by boat, took the Lindisfarne Gospels with them (minus its cover) but they were shipwrecked. Amazingly, the Gospels were recovered when the tattered manuscript washed ashore.

The British Museum acquired the Lindisfarne Gospels in 1753 from private ownership. The original manuscript, with a replacement cover made in 1852, now resides in the British Library.

The Lindisfarne Raid

The raid on St. Cuthbert's Monastery on Lindisfarne island, on June 8, 793, was the first recorded Viking raid on English soil. The success of the raid led to a series of summer raids by the Northmen (from Norway, Sweden and Denmark), at first only for plunder and slaves (their goals later changed) because the undefended monasteries were isolated and easy targets. The monastery at Jarrow on the river Tyne was raided the following year in 794 and Iona in the Inner Hebrides was attacked three times in 795, 802 and 806.

An incursion at Portland, Wessex four years earlier in 789 was probably not a planned raid, but more likely an opportunistic landing. On this occasion, the King's Reeve (named Beauduherd), believing the men were traders, went to identify them and collect taxes and was killed.

The Lindisfarne raid was recorded in several surviving documents:

The Anglo-Saxon Chronicles

"793: In this year dire forewarnings appeared over Northumbria and terrified the wretched people: there were exceptional flashes of lightning, whirlwinds, and fiery dragons were seen flying in the air. A great famine soon followed these omens, and a little after that in the same year on the sixth day before the ides of January* the ravaging of the heathen men destroyed God's church on Holy Island (Lindisfarne) through pillage and slaughter."

*The chronicle dates the raid in January but it is generally accepted that this is an error as the Vikings did not raid in the winter. It is also unlikely that all of the events recorded as preceding the date of the Viking raid (especially the 'great famine') could have occurred in the first few days of January.

January (*Ianr*) should be June (*Iun*) which is the month of the Lindisfarne raid recorded in the Annals of Lindisfarne.

In the Roman calendar, still used in the 8th century, the date of the 'ides' depended on the number of days in the month. For March, May, July and October, the ides was the 15th. For the other months including June (and January) the ides was the 13th. Six days before the ides of June (counting the ides as the first day) refers to the 8th of June.

Simeon of Durham

A monk and a chronicler of medieval England. He lived in the 12th century but sourced his information from contemporary manuscripts.

Section 4 of *Historia Regum:* composed from lost Northumbrian Annals covering the years 732-802, records:

"They came to the church of Lindisfarne, laid everything waste with grievous pillaging, trampled the holy places with polluted feet, dug up the altars and

plundered all the treasures of the holy church. Some of the brethren they slew; some they took away with them in fetters."

<u>Alcuin of York</u>

A scholar and educator, residing at the court of Charlemagne, writing immediately after the Lindisfarne raid.

"Never before has such terror appeared in Britain as we have now suffered from a pagan race... The heathens poured out the blood of saints around the altar, and trampled on the bodies of saints in the temple of God, like dung in the streets."

The Vikings

There are many theories of how the Northmen came to be called Vikings.

- They may have originated from the province of Viken (i.e. men from Viken). In the novel, Lognavik is situated in Viken province.
- The name may derive from the same root as *vika* or 'sea mile' – the distance one shift of rowers could row. A *vikingr* (masculine form) would have been a rower on a sea journey.
- It may derive from *wic* – an Old English word referring to a settlement especially a trading settlement (as in *Hamwic*). The word *wicing* appears in the 9th century poem *Widsith*, and is usually translated as 'Viking' referring to a Scandinavian raider but may have originally had a trading connotation.

The period commonly known as the Viking Age lasted for three hundred years from 793 (the year the novel begins) to the 11th century. The era was characterised by a rapid and sustained military, economic and geographic expansion by people from the Scandinavian countries, extending from the North and Baltic Seas to the Black Sea in the east; to the Mediterranean Sea and North Africa in the south and the British Isles, Iceland and Greenland (and even North America) in the west. The expansion was facilitated by their ability as seafarers and their magnificent longships.

After the Lindisfarne raid in 793, Viking raids against coastal areas of England, Ireland and France became regular occurrences. However, from the 850's, the Vikings began to employ different tactics. Instead of

458

returning home to tend their farms in the winter, they established semi-permanent bases at the mouths of the big rivers, allowing them to attack further inland.

After 865, the Vikings' intent (specifically those from Denmark) changed to colonisation. They attacked with larger armies which eventually resulted in the Danish occupation of large areas of the British Isles and France. The area of England under control of the Danes was called the *Danelaw*, which covered northern and eastern England except (roughly) for Wessex, eastern Mercia, and Northumbria.

In France, the area in the north-west colonised by the Northmen (a name later contracted to 'Normans') was called *Normandy*.

The Viking Longship

The Viking Longship was an advancement in seafaring technical design. The ships were a significant factor in facilitating the rapid expansion of Viking influence from the North and Baltic seas to the Mediterranean and along all of the major rivers of northern Europe.

The solid keel and clinker or overlapping plank design provided the longships with the strength to survive ocean voyages, while the ship's shallow draft also allowed navigation in waters half a metre deep, so they could sail up rivers as well as land on beaches. It's light weight also enabled it to be carried over portages. Longships were double-ended, the symmetrical bow and stern allowing the ship to reverse direction without the need to turn – another advantage for beach landings.

The image of a Viking Longship is still an awesome sight today with its squared sail and high dragon-headed prow and it is not difficult to imagine the panic the sight of these magnificent and distinctive ships would have caused when the Vikings were sighted at sea.

Bebbanburgh Castle

'Bebbanburgh' was the Anglo-Saxon name for Bamburgh Castle, which lies on the coast about five miles south of Lindisfarne. Aethelfrith, king of Bernicia (in northern Northumbria) from 592 until 616, named the castle after his wife Bebba (Bebbanburgh meaning 'Bebba's Castle').

The Sling as a weapon

The sling was used by many cultures throughout the world for both hunting and warfare, from as far back as 2500BCE. A pair of slings was found in the tomb of the Egyptian pharaoh Tutankhamun (died ~1325BCE), probably to be used for hunting game in the afterlife.

A sling shot could equal and even exceed the range of an arrow. *Chris Hamson* in *'The sling in Medieval Europe'* says "a sling bullet lobbed in a high trajectory can achieve ranges in excess of 400 metres (1,300 ft)."

Many armies contained specialist slingers. The people of the Balearic Islands off the coast of Spain were considered particularly skilful. *Strabo*, a Greek historian (~63BCE-24CE), records that the islanders carried three slings of varying length (for different distances) wound around their head and bodies and that they were trained from infancy for a life as a mercenary warrior – their mothers allowing them bread only when they had struck it off a post with a sling.

The Persians, Greeks and Romans all used slings as range weapons in ancient times, as did the Franks more recently. The Greeks used 'bullets' moulded from lead and inscribed with symbols such as lightning bolts, snakes and scorpions and also words such as 'for Pompey's backside' as well as other insults like 'Ouch' or 'Catch'. Examples of inscribed Greek lead sling 'bullets' from the 4th century BCE are in the British Museum.

Use of wool for suturing wounds

From *'Suture Materials and Techniques'* by *Gregory H. Branham MD:*

> *"The use of sutures to close wounds dates back to as early as 2000BCE to the time of the Egyptians. The body cavities of the mummies were sutured closed once the internal organs were removed. Early suture materials included horse hair, silk, wool, cotton, wire and animal intestines or tendons."*

Other references suggest wool was commonly used to suture wounds in the first millennium. A Roman, *Cornelius Celsus* in his work *De Re Medicina* (~30CE), wrote that sutures should be "soft and not overly twisted, so that they may be more easy on the part". *David MacKenzie* in *The History of Sutures* suggests he could be referring to wool or linen.

Viken

A province that was situated in southeast Norway (Oslofjord and Skagerrak areas) and extended into the northern part of Sweden. The area includes the modern day Norwegian city of Oslo (established in 1314).

In the novel, the province of Viken is placed on the south-*west* coast of Norway.

Ranriki

The old name for one of the districts that made up the province of Viken. Ranriki translates as 'Ran's kingdom' and takes its name from *Ran* – goddess of the sea, and *Riki* – kingdom or empire.

Lognavik

A fictitious village located in the district of Ranriki within the province of Viken. The village of Borg is also fictitious although at least one village of that name did exist in the area.

Lognavik combines the Norse words *logn* meaning 'calm' and *vik* meaning 'bay'.

Thrall

A Thrall was the term used for a slave in Scandinavian (and also Anglo-Saxon) society. The capture and sale of thralls was a key part of the Viking economy and a major reason for their raiding. It was a non-discriminatory trade; thralls were taken from all countries even from within Scandinavia. Thralls were taken in their thousands after major battles. The Slavs of eastern Europe provided so many thralls that the term 'slave' is derived from their name.

One could become a thrall:

- by capture during a raid or after a losing a battle,
- to pay off a debt – either voluntarily or by court order, or
- by being a child of a thrall.

Thralls had no rights and their living conditions depended entirely on their owner or master. *Wergild* was not payable if a thrall was killed, but compensation would be expected as if, for example, the damage had been done to another person's pig.

The universal sign of a thrall was the slave collar around the neck, made of leather or iron.

A thrall could gain a measure of freedom in times of conflict by fighting and killing enemies, or by being specifically freed by their master (e.g. in a will), or by buying their own freedom (some were paid small amounts for their services). They then became a 'freedman', but still owed allegiance to their former master and would be expected to ask permission, for example, to marry or change residence. If a freedman had no descendants, his former master would inherit his land and property. It took at least two *generations* for freedmen to lose this allegiance and become full freemen (minus the 'd') with the same rights as free-born men.

The term is still in common usage (with a slightly changed meaning) in the verb 'to enthrall' but in this sense only the imagination is captured.

Jarl

'Jarl' was a Scandinavian title (from which the English 'Earl' is derived) for a leader of one of the petty kingdoms or provinces of Norway and Sweden. 'Jarl' is written as 'Yarl' in the novel to convey the correct pronunciation.

Reeve (England), Vogt (Europe)

A Reeve (or its Germanic equivalent *Vogt*) was an administrative official appointed or elected to implement the decisions of a high noble or a court. Each level of court from town to shire appointed a reeve.

At the shire level, this official was called the shire-reeve which is the predecessor to the word *sheriff*. The King's Reeve was an enforcer of the king's laws.

Alfheim (from Old Norse – 'Land of the Elves')

A coastal 'petty kingdom' existing in the 790's between the Glomma and Gota rivers, an area that is now part of Norway and part of Sweden.

Alfarin

Alfarin was Jarl of Alfheim from ~790 until 804 – in some references he is called 'King Alfarin'.

Only in the novel is he the uncle of Ragnall and Olaf.

Dorncester

The Anglo-Saxon name for Dorchester where Kaela was located before she was captured.

Damascus steel

A type of steel used in the manufacture of swords in Damascus where a weapons industry thrived for centuries.

The 'Damascus' process was based on *Wootz* steel – a high carbon alloy steel imported from Southern India, but the actual method used to create the famed steel has been lost. 'Wootz' is thought to be derived from 'Wook', itself a corruption of *ukku,* the word for steel in several languages of Southern India.

Damascus steel blades are characterised by distinctive swirling patterns on the blade reminiscent of flowing water. Such blades were reputed to be very strong and capable of being honed to legendary sharpness.

Hedeby (German: *Haithabu*)

Hedeby was an important trading settlement near the southern end of the Jutland peninsula, now part of Schleswig-Holstein, Germany. The settlement developed as a trading centre at the head of the *Schlei* inlet, which connects to the Baltic Sea. The location was favourable because there is a short portage of less than 15 km to the Treene River which flows into the Eider River with its North Sea estuary, so goods and ships could be ported overland for an almost uninterrupted passage between the Baltic and the North Sea, thereby avoiding a dangerous (pirate-infested) and time-consuming circumnavigation of the Jutland peninsula. Hedeby was also located on the major trade route between the Frankish Empire and Scandinavia, i.e. it was a north-south as well as east-west trading hub.

Because of its strategic importance, it was attacked and changed hands many times between its founding around 770 and the time it was destroyed by Norwegian king Harald Hardrada in 1050. It was finally abandoned after an attack by a Slavic army in 1066.

Danevirke

The *Danevirke* ('Work of the Danes') was a series of fortifications consisting of trenches and mounds of earth or stones, topped by a wooden stockade. It stretched for 30km across the Jutland peninsula and, together with the barrier of the Schlei inlet, protected the trade routes (especially the portage between Hedeby and the Treene river) against raids from the south. It was not one structure but several interleaving or adjoining constructions. There's evidence that some fortifications were begun as early as 650 and these were improved and expanded many times over the next three centuries. King Godfred of the Danes reconstructed and enlarged the Danevirke in the late 8th century and further expansion continued until the middle of the 10th century. The earth mounds are still visible today.

The last military use of the Danevirke occurred in 1864 during the Second Schleswig War when the fortifications were occupied by the Danish army facing the Austro-Prussians. However, the Danes, fearing being out-flanked because the Schlei had frozen over, evacuated and retreated before battle was joined.

It has been suggested that at least some of the trench construction of the Danevirke was intended as a shipping canal to provide a passage between the Schlei inlet and the river Treene and so avoid the need to move boats and trading goods via portage.

Skyrvid Forest

A fictitious forest located south of Hedeby. The nearby towns of Kirkense, Turborg and Ruslager are also fictitious.

The name of the forest combines *Skyr* meaning 'Shire' and *vid* (or *vidr*) meaning 'wood' in Old Norse. 'Shire Wood' is also the original name of a certain forest made famous by tales of the 'outlaw' Robin Hood.

Use of Broom and Garlic for snake bites

Broom flowers were used as a poultice throughout Europe in medieval times and by the American Indians.

The Greek *Dioscorides* (40–90) recommended garlic as a remedy against snakebite (however he suggested a drink containing a mixture of garlic and wine) and against mad dog's bite (suggesting an application of garlic on the wound directly). The Greeks called garlic a 'snake grass'.

In the seventh century, the Slavic people are reported to have used garlic against lice, spider bite, snakebite and ulcers.

In the novel, Kaela and Gisele intended to use garlic as a poultice but they weren't able to apply the treatment.

Note: These remedies and especially Fenn's use of a ligature or tourniquet are *not* recommended for the treatment of snakebite.

Albia

Albia was the name at the time for the river *Elbe*, a major river in Northern Germany, being derived from the Roman name of Albis. The word *Elbe/ Albia/ Albis* simply means 'river'.

Saxon Wars

The Saxon Wars lasted more than 30 years. They began in 772, when Charlemagne (Charles the Great) first brought a Frankish army into Saxony with the intent to conquer and convert the Saxons to christianity. He destroyed the important pagan sanctuary, *Irminsul*, near Verden and, from this time, there were a series of Saxon uprisings against the Franks until 804, when the last rebellion was crushed.

In 792, the Westphalians (a province of Saxony) rose up against the Franks in response to forcible recruitment of Saxon men for the war against the Avars. The Eastphalian and Nordalbingian Saxons joined them in 793, but the insurrection was completely put down by the Franks in 794.

In the novel, the fictitious battle of Hammaburg Castle (in 794) occurs during the final part of this Saxon rebellion.

Widukind (735-807)

The name translates as 'Child of the Forest' meaning 'Wolf'. Widukind was the leader of the Saxons during a large part of the Saxon Wars with the Franks, with the title of *Herzog* or Duke. It was customary that the title of Duke was given to men who ruled only in times of war but the series of rolling rebellions against the Franks resulted in Widukind remaining the Saxon leader for decades. He married a Danish princess Geva Eysteindottir and fled to Denmark to escape retribution after several defeats. He surrendered to Charlemagne in 785, and was baptised. According to myth, Widukind rode a black horse prior to his baptism and a white horse afterwards (given to him by Charlemagne). The black and white horses of Widukind feature on the flags and coats of arms of many districts of Northern Germany. After his baptism, the records of his fate are sparse and disputed.

The Saxon uprising of 792-794 (in response to forcible recruitment by the Franks for their war against the Avars) is factual but only in the novel did Widukind come out of 'retirement' to lead the Saxons one last time.

He did have a brother named Bruno and his son Wichbert was also Duke of Saxony from 799-827.

Heinrich, Mathilde, and their children, are fictitious.

Massacre at Verden

The Massacre at Verden in what is now Lower Saxony, Germany, was a beheading of 4,500 Saxons under order of Charlemagne in October 782. The massacre is said to have occurred in a single day with the river Aller flowing red with the blood.

Widukind is reported to have persuaded a group of Saxons, who had previously submitted to Charlemagne, to rise up against the King. The rebel army annihilated a Frankish detachment at the battle of *Süntel* killing two of the three Frankish leaders (i.e. the King's envoys), four counts and twenty other nobles.

Charlemagne responded by gathering his forces and marching to Saxony, where he unleashed his massacre at Verden to demonstrate his sovereignty and the terrible punishment for treason (oath-breaking) and rebellion.

The entry for 782 in the *Royal Frankish Annals* reads:

> *"When he heard this, the Lord King Charles rushed to the place with all the Franks that he could gather on short notice and advanced to where the Aller flows into the Weser. Then all the Saxons came together again, submitted to the authority of the Lord King, and surrendered the evildoers who were chiefly responsible for this revolt to be put to death—four thousand and five hundred of them. This sentence was carried out. Widukind was not among them since he had fled to Denmark."*

Hammaburg

The early name for Hamburg.

The name derives from *Ham* (meadow) and *burg* which in medieval times could mean a walled town or a fortress or a castle – hence 'Castle in the Meadow'.

Hammaburg Castle

The castle depicted in the novel is entirely fictitious.

In the late 8th century the 'castle' represented by the 'burg' part of the name Hammaburg was a far more primitive structure, described in a contemporary reference only as 'a ring-shaped fortification'.

A castle *was* built at Hammaburg by Charlemagne in 808 to protect against Slavic incursions, but this was after the Saxon wars had ended in 804. There is evidence that the Hammaburg castle was destroyed in 845 in a Viking raid.

Hamwic

The Anglo-Saxon name for the settlement that became Southampton, deriving from *Ham* meaning meadow or field (or village, or home) and *wic* – a trading settlement.

The name 'Hamtun' is also used by chroniclers to describe the same area. Some references say Hamwic and Hamtun existed as separate settlements with Hamwic located "South of Hamtun" and this became known as

South Hamtun and eventually Southampton (spelt with only one 'h', but pronounced as if there were two).

Bruggas

The old name for the city of Bruges in the Flemish region of Belgium. The name means 'Bridges' in Old Dutch. Its tidal inlet made it an important trade centre joining the northern and southern trade routes.

Berewic

The old name for Berwick or Berwick-on-Tweed is derived from *bere* meaning 'barley' and *wic* meaning 'trading settlement'. It is only 2.5 miles from the present-day Scottish border and five miles north of Lindisfarne.

Eoforic

The old name for York, derived from *eofor* meaning wild swine or boar, and *ric* meaning rich (i.e. a land rich in wild boar). In 866, the Danish army captured the city and its name became *Jorvik*. The name is first recorded as 'York' in the 13th century.

Anteros

In Greek mythology, Anteros, the god of requited love or 'love returned', was the son of Aphrodite (goddess of love and beauty) and Ares (god of war) and the brother of Eros (god of love). He was also the avenger or punisher of those who scorn love or reject the advances of others – that is, of unrequited love – love given but not returned.

LIST OF CHARACTERS

In order of appearance

* Indicates a historical person

St Cuthbert's Monastery, Lindisfarne	
Fenn (Feran)	Apprentice scribe. Orphan. Lindisfarne captive.
Master Nerian	Monk, Maker of Inks. Lindisfarne captive.
Higbald*	Bishop of Lindisfarne, 780-803
Master Oswald	Monk, Teacher of penmanship.
Olgood	Carpenter and Blacksmith, Fenn's boyhood friend. Lindisfarne captive.
Yseld	Milkmaid, kitchen servant.
Mistress Miriam	Cook in charge of the kitchen.
Master Wilfrid	Monk, Parchment maker.
Master Egbert	Monk, Physician.
Lenglan	Stone Mason, husband of Aerlene, Father to Fenn
Mistress Aerlene	Craft worker, Lenglan's wife, Mother to Fenn
Mikhael	Baby son of Lenglan & Aerlene. Brother to Fenn
Nameth	Cook. Lindisfarne captive.
Audrey	Weaver, son Ames. Lindisfarne captive.
Ames	Son of Audrey, age 7-8
Eldric	Farmer. Lindisfarne captive.
Briony	Infirmary worker. Lindisfarne captive.

Frankish/English	
Charles the Great (Charlemagne)*	King of the Franks, b.742-d.814
Alcuin*	Monk, scholar, from York. Educator, Court of Charlemagne.
Billfrith*	Anchorite (hermit). Created metalwork/gemstone cover of Lindisfarne Gospels.
Eadfrith*	Bishop of Lindisfarne, 698-721. Scribe of Lindisfarne Gospels.
Aethelred I*	King of Northumbria, 774-779 and 790-796
Elflaed*	Daughter of Offa, married Aethelred.
Beorhtric*	King of Wessex 786-802, married Eadburg.
Eadburg*	Daughter of Offa, married Beorhtric.
Beauduherd*	King Beorhtric's Reeve. Killed Viking incursion 789
Offa*	King of Mercia 757-796. Father: Eadburg, Elflaed.
Land of the Northmen	
Olaf	Viking Raider, brother of Ragnall.
Ragnall	Viking Raider, brother of Olaf. Leader of Lognavik village. In Command of Lindisfarne raid.
Birgitta	Viking Raider from Lognavik. Mother of Agatha.
Hakon	Thrall of Ragnall. Interpreter on raid.
Torston	Viking Raider from Lognavik. Archer.
Haldor	Viking Raider from Borg.
Kael/Kaela	Thrall of Askari.
Askari	Medicine woman, partner of Thorvald. Mother of Ragnall & Olaf.
Thorvald	Viking man, partner of Askari.
Gisele	Thrall of Ragnall. Kitchenhand.
Harald	Jarl of Ranriki district. Leader of Borg village.
Agatha	Daughter of Birgitta, foundling, age 5, deaf. Raised by Askari.
Addo	Foundling. Raised by Askari.

Land of the Danes	
Godfred*	King of Danes. Died 810
Sigrund	Danish Farmer from Kirkense.
Ursula	Sigrund's daughter, resembles Agatha.
Gudrod	Apple grower, Alfheim.
Alfarin*	Jarl of Alfheim 790's-804
Lothar the Hun	Leader of outlaws in Skyrvid Forest.
Baradin	Lothar's brother.
Hartmut	One of Lothar's outlaws.
Gunther	One of Lothar's outlaws, aka 'Scarred-Ear'.
Malthus	Lothar's cousin from Turborg, aka 'Weasel'.
Land of the Saxons	
Mathilde	Wife of Heinrich, like a daughter to Widukind. Son Bruno (10), daughter Gabby (3), baby son.
Heinrich	Husband of Mathilde. Grew up with Wichbert.
Widukind*	*Herzog* (Duke) of Saxony, b.735-d.807 Brother Bruno, son Wichbert.
Bruno*	Brother of Widukind.
Wichbert*	Son of Widukind, friend of Heinrich. Duke of Saxony 799-827
Marchant	Leader of a Frankish army.
Porteus	Saxon swordsman. Loud voice.
Manfredi	Danish Mercenary. Archer.
Tollemarche	Ship's captain.
Prudy	Household servant of King Beorhtric. De Facto mother to Kaela.

ABOUT THE AUTHOR

OWEN TREVOR SMITH

I now live on the Kapiti Coast of the North Island of beautiful New Zealand but I have lived and worked in Australia, England, Germany and Switzerland.

I share my home with two dogs (Harry and Jacko) and three guitars (not named). I've travelled throughout the world for extensive periods of time and I've sailed the Atlantic from England to Brazil in my 41-foot ketch 'Adastra'.

I have written and published poems (that rhyme!) and short fiction in diverse genres (western, science fiction, war, crime, adventure, mystery), and also children's stories and plays.

Lindisfarne: Fury Of The Northmen is my first novel.

Visit www.owentrevorsmith.com

Or email me: otsmith@nowmail.co.nz